Bleak City

Marisa Taylor

This book uses New Zealand English spellings and style conventions.

First published by Taylfin Ltd, 2016

Marisa Taylor
PO Box 779
Christchurch 8140
New Zealand

Website: bleak.city

ISBN 978 0 473 36341 3 (Paperback)
ISBN 978 0 473 36342 0 (mobi eBook)

Disclaimer

This is usually the place where it says 'All individuals, organisations and events in this story are completely fictitious.' Except this story is set during the very real events of the 2010 and 2011 Canterbury earthquakes and the real situations that unfolded as a result. To tell the story and not include in it the actual organisations and people that directly contributed to the post-earthquake environment in Christchurch would be bizarre, and to create fictionalised organisations and people filling the same roles would only result in inevitable parallels and comparisons being drawn between the fictionalised players and the real counterparts.

This story, therefore, includes many actual events (although some selected events are fictional), along with some real people and organisations. All efforts have been made to ensure nothing has been attributed to people or organisations that they did not say or do. At times, fictional characters express opinions about some of the things said or done by people or organisations, and these opinions are those of the characters and should not be confused with the author's. Any organisation or individual who feels criticised by a fictional character should note that very real critics have publicly made far worse comments and expressed far more vicious opinions than those of any of these made-up people.

The key characters of the story are fictional. The things that happen to them are fictional, but at the same time are real in the sense that the things that happen to them have been drawn from actual events that have been happening all over the city to real people. To readers living outside of Christchurch, it may seem like these tribulations are unbelievable or exaggerated for effect, like explosions in a thriller movie. It may seem like this story focuses on a family unbelievably unfortunate to be at the nexus of a series of distressing events. Sadly, these situations are all too common, and pretty much any Christchurch resident could regale you with tales of the things that have happened to them or to their friends and family.

New Zealand's Place on the Pacific Rim

New Zealand is on the Pacific Ring of Fire, straddling the plate boundary between the Australian and the Pacific tectonic plates.

In the 5½ years following 4 September 2010, Christchurch and the Canterbury region experienced over 16,000 earthquakes.

4 earthquakes measured over magnitude 6.

65 exceeded magnitude 5, not counting the magnitude 6+ earthquakes.

At least 528 exceeded magnitude 4.

Christchurch and the Canterbury Plains

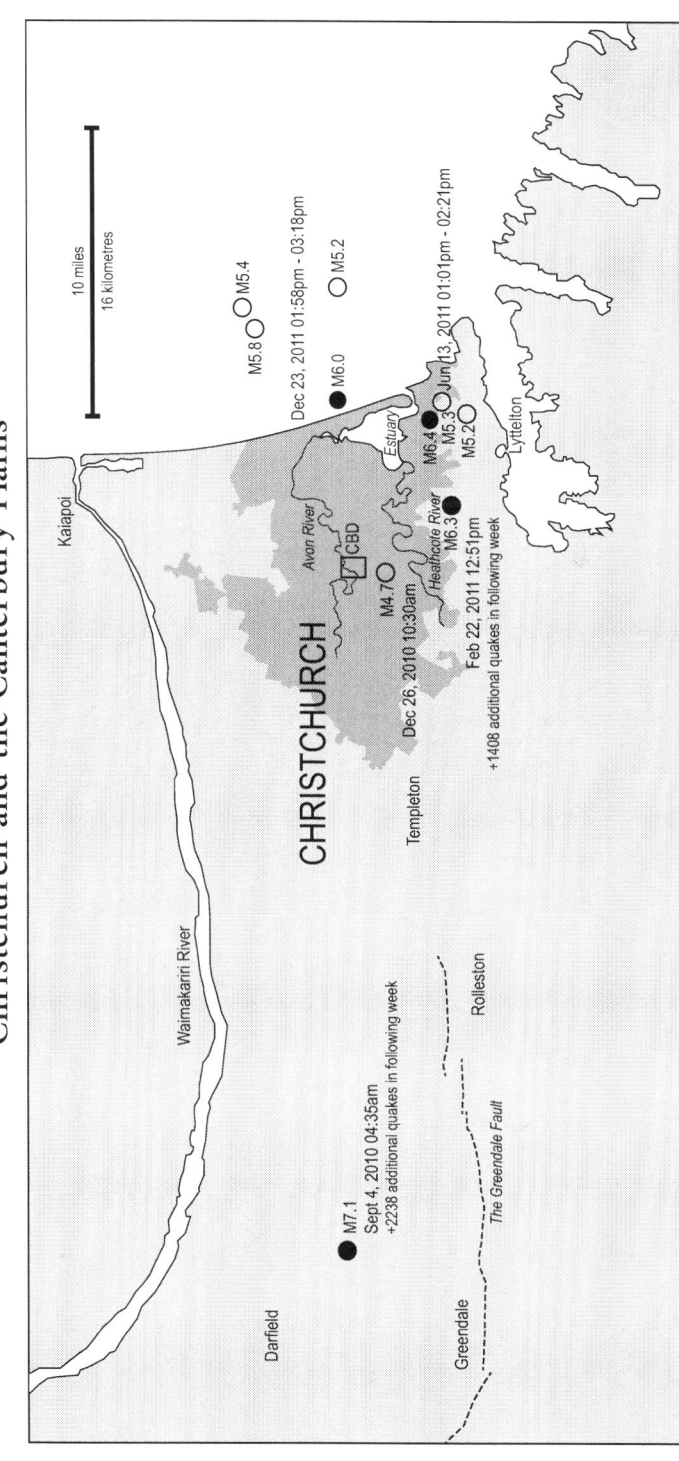

Darfield

Waimakariri River

Kaiapoi

M7.1
Sept 4, 2010 04:35am
+2238 additional quakes in following week

Greendale

The Greendale Fault

Rolleston

CHRISTCHURCH

Templeton

Avon River

CBD
M4.7
Dec 26, 2010 10:30am

Heathcote River
M6.3
Feb 22, 2011 12:51pm
+1408 additional quakes in following week

Estuary

M6.0

M6.4
M5.3
M5.2
Jun 13, 2011 01:01pm - 02:21pm

Lyttelton

M5.8
M5.4

M5.2
Dec 23, 2011 01:58pm - 03:18pm

10 miles
16 kilometres

The Shaky Isles
Author's Note

New Zealand is known throughout the world for its majestic beauty, and many dream of one day visiting that far-off place, of cruising on Milford Sound, taking a helicopter ride over one of the South Island's glaciers, whale-spotting off the Kaikoura coast, fly fishing on Lake Taupo or walking the Tongariro Crossing. What many of these aspiring visitors don't realise is that there is one common reason for this abundance of beauty: New Zealand's position on the Pacific Ring of Fire.

The islands that make up New Zealand straddle two tectonic plates, the Australian plate and the Pacific plate. In New Zealand, the two mighty plates meet in what geologists call a 'convergent plate boundary'. That is, these plates are pushing against one another, and the force of their motion produces the mountain ranges of the Southern Alps, the deep, drowned valleys of Fiordland, the rich feeding grounds of the Kaikoura Trench, the dramatic volcanoes of the central North Island and the geothermal fields of Rotorua. The city of Auckland, New Zealand's largest, lies atop the Auckland Volcanic Field, a series of fifty-something dormant volcanoes. Not extinct, dormant.

The Pacific Ring of Fire is not a complete circle, but rather a series of boundaries between different tectonic plates. Open any map viewer and select a satellite view and you can see these plate boundaries in the ocean floor. The Ring of Fire runs from just southwest of New Zealand up to the northeast, up the coast of Asia, across to Alaska, then down along the coasts of the Americas, ending just west of the bottom end of South America.

The southwestern end of the New Zealand leg of the Pacific Ring of Fire starts in the Southern Ocean, where the boundary between the two plates comes ashore in Fiordland, around Milford Sound. This is known as the Alpine Fault, and it runs up the West Coast of the South Island, under the township of Franz Josef, where, notoriously, it runs under a petrol station and the police station. The Alpine Fault continues up the island, its course marked by the spine of the ranges of the Southern Alps, its total length some 600 kilometres. In the upper South Island, the Alpine Fault starts to break up, fragmenting into a series of smaller faults known as the Marlborough Fault System. What is going on here is that the nature of the boundary between the Australian plate and the Pacific plate changes, near the top of the South Island. Whereas through the South Island the Pacific plate is riding over the top of the Australian plate, to the east of the North Island the Australian plate is on top, with the Pacific plate diving under it. Think about that. Open your first and second fingers on each hand, jam the two Vs together and then push. Your fingers are locked in the same way these plates are locked. Beneath Wellington. The nation's capital and home to some 400,000 people.

The plate boundary continues up alongside the eastern coast of the North Island, forming the Hikurangi Trench. Onshore, the pressure of the two colliding plates causes a series of faults through the central North Island that run roughly parallel to the plate boundary. The volcanoes of the central North Island result from the subduction of the Pacific plate.

The pressure is enormous, and pushes back into the South Island, resulting in a kind of twisting of the South Island from northwest to southeast, clockwise, at a rate of a few tens of millimetres a year. It doesn't seem like much, until a fault slips.

Maori told European settlers of violent earthquakes, which they attributed to the god Ruaumoko walking beneath the earth. European settlers experienced their first earthquake less than a year after arriving in Wellington. The nation's early decades were reasonably tectonically active, with two or three magnitude 6+ earthquakes every decade. There were few fatalities, though, as the country was sparsely populated and epicentres were, largely, not right under population centres.

The pattern continued into the 1920s: two or three large quakes each decade. Then in 1929 began five terrible years in New Zealand. On the 9th of March 1929, a 7.1 earthquake in the Arthur's Pass area of the Southern Alps went for four minutes, damaging buildings and triggering landslides across railway lines and roads. No one was killed. It was a different story three months later on the 17th of June, when a 7.8 quake struck in the upper South Island, about 150 kilometres north of Arthur's Pass. The worst-hit community was Murchison, where landslides engulfed houses, killing fourteen people. Seventeen people died altogether and, with homes seriously damaged and numerous aftershocks, residents camped outdoors and many left the region.

Less than two years later, a 7.8 quake struck in Hawke's Bay, in the North Island. The quake lasted for two and a half minutes, and within minutes of the earthquake, fire took hold in central Napier. Together the earthquake and the fire levelled Napier, killing at least 256 people in the region. Napier is today famous for rebuilding in the art deco style popular in the 1930s.

Then, in 1934, the North Island was hit again, by a 7.6 in the town of Pahiatua in the Wairarapa. Nearby Hawke's Bay was badly shaken once again, and shaking was felt from Auckland down as far south as Dunedin. Two people died in the Pahiatua earthquake.

In 1942, two earthquakes three months apart shook the Wairarapa region in the lower North Island, causing damage to the region's many small towns and in nearby Wellington, where a man died after a coal gas pipe ruptured. Many older buildings in Wellington city were badly damaged in the first earthquake, and it was recognised that had the earthquake occurred during a busy shopping day, many people would have been killed.

The earthquakes of the 1920s, 30s and 40s had long-lasting effects in New Zealand. The New Zealand government established committees to investigate the reasons for the building collapses in the Napier quake and the guidelines developed by these committees resulted, eventually, in the building standards used today to protect life in the event of earthquake. Then, in 1945, the Government established the Earthquake Commission. The EQC was a response to over a decade of regular, damaging tectonic activity and the disruption of the war years. Its intention was to train New Zealanders to protect themselves during natural disasters and then provide New Zealanders with the economic protections necessary to recover quickly. As of the start of the twenty-first century, EQC pays the first $100,000 of damage resulting from natural disasters, and private insurers top up coverage over that 'cap'. The result is that the New Zealand residential property market is one of the most heavily insured in the world, and New Zealand is one of the few earthquake-prone regions where residents can easily obtain earthquake insurance.

Since the 1940s, New Zealand has settled back into the pattern the early settlers experienced: big quakes every few years, but nothing so near to towns and cities to cause widespread destruction. In the years between 1943 and 2010, there were fewer than a dozen deaths from earthquakes in New Zealand. Most large earthquakes in New Zealand occur offshore or in remote areas, well away from large populations and potentially lethal buildings.

Our tale starts to unfold in 2010, a repeat, some might think, of the shaky 1930s. But this is a very different story, because the unfortunate reality is that in the modern world, a natural disaster is followed, inevitably, by a manmade one of greater scale and longer duration.

Part I: Shaky City

Fear has many eyes and can see things underground.
— *Miguel de Cervantes*

Winter

August 2010

Cold winds off the Pacific Ocean batter the city of Christchurch every winter, blowing their bitter breath across the Canterbury Plains from the east and south. During Alice's first winter away from home, these winds carried more moisture than the ground could absorb, filling gutters and leaving pools of water that persisted even on dry days. The air was always wet or damp, never dry, never warm. In her cold flat at the end of each day, Alice despaired. She would tuck down into her bed, weighed down by her duvet and two blankets. Why had she thought leaving home was a good idea? There she would be warm and dry, maybe studying in the lounge in front of the wood fire rather than spending as long as she could each day in the warmth of the university library.

Alice was eighteen, nearly nineteen, and in her first year at university, studying engineering. In high school, her maths and physics scores were excellent and her teachers had encouraged her to study engineering. It was good advice, better than she got at home. Her mother had completed a single year of a law degree, sitting her exams while pregnant with Alice, and the only real advice she offered was 'Don't get pregnant'. Her stepfather was a painter and plasterer and had done trade courses at the local polytech. University was, he said, an alien planet he knew nothing about. Alice enjoyed her courses, they were hard work, satisfying when she got it right, motivational when she didn't.

She saw her family at least once a week. She had worked with her stepfather in his painting and plastering business during weekends and school holidays since she was fourteen, and she continued to work with him on Saturdays if he had too much work on, which he often did.

On those evenings when she buried herself in her bed trying to stay warm, she told herself being away from home was a good thing, she was getting along better with her mother and was missing her little sister and brother, rather than finding them annoying.

Living with people she wasn't related to and learning about how they looked at the world made her think about her own world. That was another good thing, maybe it was helping her to grow up? Mature? Whatever it is that people do in those years when they're not really teenagers any more but they're not adults either. At first, she couldn't put her finger on what was missing, only that something was. Whatever it was, it made her restless, as though the ground under the feet of her life wasn't nearly as stable as she had grown up thinking it was.

After a couple of months away from home, Alice had decided to look up her father. It wasn't hard finding him on the whitepages website, after all, his surname was the same as hers and Moorhouse wasn't all that common. He was listed with an M, for Michelle, his second wife. She did remember that much, him remarrying while he lived in Auckland. She had seen him a couple of times while he lived there, flying up to stay with him for long weekends. He and Michelle had moved back to Christchurch and she had seen them once after that, then nothing. At first, she asked her mother when she would see him again, but after months of non-specific answers, she stopped asking.

She decided it was best to ring him one evening, but each day she would talk herself out of it, her stomach pitching with the weight of the decision. Should she just leave things as they were? Finally, though, her curiosity overwhelmed her caution and she made the call.

A woman answered and Alice could hear children in the background as the woman called for Andrew. More brothers and sisters? She wasn't ready for that. She was about to hang up, concluding that calling was a mistake, when there he was, an oddly familiar voice on the other end of the phone line.

'It's Alice,' she said.

'Alice.' It was all he said, drawn out, like he was mentally flicking through all the Alices he knew.

'Your daughter,' she said, cringing, wishing she had thought to hang up when the woman answered. Or not call at all.

'Yes, I know,' he laughed. 'I'm just surprised. I didn't think...'

'I'd like to see you,' she blurted.

'Of course,' he said. 'How about lunch one day next week? I'm in the city. If you're nearby, of course. Where are you?'

'In Christchurch,' she said. She told him she was at university, what she was studying and where she was living. And there didn't seem to be much else to say at that point, so they agreed to meet the following Tuesday at a café near his office, not too far from the Central Library.

It was an awkward meeting, and short, just long enough for each of them to study one another's features, looking for commonalities and differences. She had his hair, dark and curly, although the length and weight of hers pulled the curls out into waves. His eyes were darker than hers, as much grey as blue. Andrew was working to a deadline he had forgotten about the night she called, and he said he didn't want to cancel on her or postpone them meeting up. But it was a start, and for the next few months they settled into a pattern, meeting for lunch every second Tuesday at different places near the law firm where he worked.

Those lunchtime conversations became more comfortable, but were never deep, always skirting the topics Alice had started thinking about more and more since the night she first called Andrew's house and heard the sound of his other children in the background. Why had Andrew been so distant, missing for all those years when he had been less than ten kilometres away? Why hadn't she been reintroduced to Andrew's second wife? Why didn't she know her half-siblings? There were four, three boys and a girl, but she hadn't met them yet and Andrew never gave any indication of when she would. But they were slowly getting to know one another. After more than a decade of no contact, she told herself, of course it was going to be slow.

The last days of summer had quickly cooled into autumn, which had then faded into winter, grey days, the sky heavy with clouds that dumped their rain until the ground was sodden, and then kept going. The ground was too wet to take any more, and pools of water formed in parks and yards all over the city. Drains clogged with autumn leaves regularly backed up, flooding gutters and sometimes roads.

It was a Tuesday in August and they hadn't agreed on a place. Instead, Alice was to meet Andrew outside his office at a quarter to one. But it was getting close to one o'clock and there was still no sign of him. Alice was outside, where it was raining and a cold wind from the east made it impossible to shelter from the rain. Her layers of clothes weren't enough to keep her warm and her feet were icy, in spite of the thick socks and boots she was wearing. Alice went into the building and brushed off her raincoat as best as she could before getting into the lift.

Upstairs, the receptionist took an instant dislike to Alice, carrying out a survey of her from top to waist, which was as far as the receptionist could see over the giant stone reception desk that arced across the foyer. The woman was about a decade older than Alice, maybe as old as thirty. Her long blonde hair had been fiercely straightened and swung like a pendulum as she turned her head. She was wearing enough makeup that Alice could see it lying over her skin, lining her eyes, dusting her cheeks, making her delicate features appear older. Maybe she was closer to Alice's age than thirty, all that makeup made it hard to tell. The woman's head came to just above the edge of the desk and Alice pulled herself up to her full height. She said she was there to see Andrew.

'Can I say who's here?' the receptionist said, reaching for the phone. There was an edge of disdain in her voice, and she studied Alice the way someone might study an enemy, sizing them up, assessing their strengths and weaknesses. Alice wasn't used to be examined in that way, of seeing someone try to determine how she fit into their agenda. She decided not to play.

'Alice,' she said, ending her single word firmly, indicating there wasn't more to come.

The receptionist looked at her sharply, waiting for more, but Alice wasn't going to give her full name, that would give the game away. She simply stared back.

'Alice who?' the woman finally said, the edge in her voice sharpening up a notch. Alice couldn't understand why she was being perceived as a threat, but then realised: every second Tuesday afternoon for three months Andrew had been going out of the office for lunch. The receptionist wanted to know who his regular lunch date was. Was it normal for receptionists to be so nosy about the people they worked for? To feel so possessive of them?

'Just Alice,' Alice said, keeping her voice even and non-threatening. 'Andrew knows who I am.' She gave what she hoped was a knowing smile, and the receptionist looked down and away, uncomfortable in the presence of her apparent rival. Bizarre.

The receptionist dialled the number, said only, 'Alice is here to see you,' and Alice noticed that her voice softened, that of someone wanting to please. At this point, she wouldn't have been surprised if the woman had added 'darling' to the end of her message.

The receptionist hung up, then said, 'He'll only be a minute, you can wait over there.' She pointed towards a sofa placed to look out onto the city, over the bare branches of the trees lining the river, stretching up into the grey sky.

'Thanks,' Alice said and remained standing at the reception desk, looking down at the receptionist. She wasn't blocking anyone's way, so why not?

It was only a minute before Andrew was walking down the hallway towards her, pulling on a raincoat. She met him halfway, over the receptionist's objections, and kissed Andrew on the cheek before turning to walk alongside him out into reception. Andrew stopped at the reception desk, where the receptionist smiled up at him, demurely, like some wife-in-waiting in a Jane Austen novel. To Alice's surprise, Andrew smiled back broadly. 'I'll be back in an hour, Kate,' he said.

'Thank you, Kate,' Alice called back as she and Andrew walked away towards the lifts. Andrew gave her a funny look while they waited, but then the bell rang and the doors slid open. They said nothing inside. Alice was thinking about him flirting with the receptionist, because that was what it looked like to her. Why would he flirt back if he wasn't interested? When he talked about his second family, he seemed happy enough, well as happy as Alice's mother was with Kevin and the little kids. But who could tell? The next door neighbours seemed happy until the day the husband left to move in with some woman he had met through his job. 'I know what it's like,' Alice's mum had said to the wife. How had she known? Was Alice's dad someone who would cheat? Who had cheated?

At the building entrance, they both stopped, pulled their hoods up and zipped their raincoats, readying themselves for the outdoors. 'Where to?' Andrew said.

'Japanese,' Alice said. 'Just around the corner. The one we went to before.'

Andrew nodded. 'Sure.'

Outside they walked quickly, keeping their heads down until they reached the restaurant. There was only one occupied table, which was typical for a winter weekday in Christchurch. The weather discouraged people from coming into the city and encouraged the city's workers to stay in their warm, dry offices.

A waitress seated them at a table for two by the window and before they could ask there was a pot of tea and two cups on the table. Alice was grateful for the hot drinks, said thank you and quickly poured them both cups. She wrapped her hands around the hot cup and watched as Andrew browsed the menu. Alice had already decided, she was having the same thing she had last time they were there, but she glanced down at the menu as though there were other choices she was interested in. She wanted to observe his reaction to what she was about to say.

'She's got a thing for you,' Alice said.

Andrew looked up from the menu, then around the restaurant, confused.

'The receptionist. Kate.'

'She's like that with everyone,' Andrew said dismissively. He looked back down at the menu.

'Not with me she wasn't,' Alice said.

'Everyone male,' Andrew said. So he did see it.

'It's not exactly a great idea to flirt with someone like that,' Alice said.

'I wasn't flirting.' He folded the menu and put it aside. She had annoyed him.

The waitress interrupted them and they ordered, handing back their menus. Andrew poured more tea for each of them.

'Yes you were.'

'No I wasn't. How are your studies going? Holidays in a couple of weeks, isn't it? Lots of studying to do before exams start?' His voice was light, he definitely wanted to move on from the topic of Kate or flirting or something there he wanted to avoid. Which was probably normal for any man talking to his daughter. Maybe.

Alice took a sip of her tea. 'I'm looking forward to a break,' she said.

'Plans?'

'I'll work,' she said. 'Save up for next year.' But in her head it was niggling. She wanted to know. 'Did you cheat on Mum?'

He was sipping his tea when she asked and nearly choked on the mouthful. 'Wait, what? Is this about me flirting with the receptionist?'

'So you were flirting?'

He sighed deeply, exasperated. 'No, I wasn't. And even if I was, it was nothing. There's nothing wrong with flirting, and I wasn't flirting.'

'You haven't answered my question.'

'Where's this coming from? Did your mother tell you something?'

'No, she never says anything about the two of you.' Alice realised he had just said that there was something to say on the topic, and Andrew realised it too. He sat back in his seat, resigned.

'Yes,' he said. 'That's why we split up.'

'Who with?'

'It doesn't matter.'

'I'm sure it mattered to Mum.'

'Of course it did, but after all this time,' he said, 'it really doesn't.'

His tone was final and the look on his face set, challenging her to continue, warning her not to. It annoyed her, especially as she recognised the tactic she used on her mother when Lindsay was trying to get something through to her by repeating the same thing over and over again. Alice knew that being direct with Andrew wouldn't work, just as it never worked for her mother. She needed to try a tangential approach.

'More tea?' she asked. He was surprised that she had given up and he looked at her suspiciously. But he pushed his cup across the table. She filled it and he took it back, then sipped from it.

'The questions eleven-year-olds ask are much easier,' Andrew said.

'Well I'm not eleven,' Alice said sharply. 'You need to get used to that.'

Andrew nodded. Their meals arrived, and starting to eat gave them both the opportunity to collect their thoughts.

'Was it Michelle?' Alice asked.

'No, it wasn't Michelle,' Andrew said, without looking up from his lunch. 'It's not relevant so I'm not going to talk about it.'

She felt her face start to go red. How could he just shut her down like that? Andrew didn't seem to notice, just kept tweezing up bits of chicken with his chopsticks and directing them into his mouth. Was he unaware? Or ignoring her the way she would ignore her mother when she didn't want to 'talk things through'? Alice felt the words boiling up inside her and wanted to smack him with them.

'You guys split up and changed the direction of my life,' she said. 'I think it's relevant. Was it serious? Or was it just a fling? Why did you get to walk away from being my dad?'

'Alice,' he said, looking up at her, bewildered at her obvious anger. 'It wasn't like that.'

'Like what?'

'I wasn't trying to get away from you. I was just...'

'Immature? Confused? Blind and mistook some other woman for your wife?'

Andrew sighed, appearing to wish he was anywhere but where he was, having lunch with his daughter, who couldn't help but ask difficult questions about why he had gone missing from her life.

'It was Vicky,' he said, giving an embarrassed shrug.

'Vicky?' Alice said.

'She lived in the neighbourhood, she was going to university and nannied part-time. She would pick you up from kindy and look after you until me or your mum got home.'

'The nanny?'

'It wasn't an ongoing thing.'

'That's such a cliché,' Alice said. She could feel her anger spinning out of reach of her ability to control it. She tried to reel it back in, only to find it skipping off again. 'You're such a cliché. You're probably screwing the receptionist, too, you're such a cliché and that's what clichés do.'

'You're being unreasonable,' Andrew said. 'Calm down.'

As is so often the case when men speak that pair of words to women, the effect was the opposite of that intended. Alice stood up from the table, grabbed her handbag and raincoat and prepared to stalk out of the restaurant. But that would leave him to pay for her lunch, and she didn't want that, she didn't want anything from him, so she stopped at the till and paid for her half-eaten meal, fumbling at the eftpos machine and then fumbling again as she wrestled her way into her raincoat before fleeing out into the rain.

4:35

September 2010

Andrew had sent her a text message the evening after their last lunch together, just the words 'I'm sorry'. Alice hadn't yet replied. She wasn't sure how to or if she even wanted to. She wanted to ask what he was sorry for, cheating or not being there for a decade, but wasn't sure either answer would make a difference for her. She didn't know what she wanted from him, certainly she wanted to move on from the superficial lunchtime conversations, but she didn't want the out-of-control argument of their last lunch to be the way they dealt with each other. And, she had to admit, she was probably the one who was out of control.

University holidays started and Alice was working for Kevin. She needed to save money for her next year if she wanted to keep flatting, which she did, she was enjoying the taste of independence. She was studying for an hour before work each morning, during her lunch break and then again at night, and the rhythm of prepping, painting and cleaning up gave her the mental space to turn what she was learning over in her head, make better sense of it all. It had worked for her mid-year exams and she was feeling comfortable about the end of year ones. Not over-confident, just comfortable knowing that if she kept up her routine she would do all right. No need to panic, just keep learning and it would all be in there, waiting to be retrieved.

Alice's flatmates were all away and she was enjoying the quiet. It reminded her of the years when it had just been her and her mother, before Lindsay met Kevin. Not that Kevin's appearance in their lives had made things worse, in many ways they were better. But there was a camaraderie between mother and daughter that had changed, and Alice was never sure if that was just part of growing up or if she had actually lost something when her mother remarried.

Between work and study and getting home to see her family every few days, Alice didn't have much time left to think about what she was going to do about the situation with Andrew. She had mentioned to Lindsay that there had been an argument, but she didn't say what about and Lindsay didn't pursue it. Lindsay had always seemed reluctant to say anything about Andrew, either positive or negative, but she hadn't discouraged Alice from getting in touch with him.

Two of Alice's flatmates were back from their holidays when she arrived home from work Friday afternoon. Ben and Chloe had decided, in her absence, that they were going out for Thai food that night, which was fine by Alice. She had been busy for two weeks solid and could use a break. There was a place in the city that had good food and, more importantly, was cheap, so they walked into the city, stopping at Ben's mates' place to pick up a few more people. Alice could tell it was going to turn into a boozy night, which she wanted to avoid as she did have to work the next day. After the Thai place, she and Chloe walked home together, watched a video and crashed into their respective beds at around eleven.

Alice heard Ben stumbling around about an hour later and she got up to find him sprawled on the sofa. She heaved him upward and walked him down the hallway, dumping him across his own bed, where he would have to clean up his own mess in the morning. It was her sofa, given to her by her grandparents, and no way was he going to be spewing on it. She went back to bed and quickly fell asleep.

She knew right away what she was hearing when she woke because the bed was moving, just slightly, but she was a light sleeper, she tended to notice what was going on in the house. The sound quickly became louder, like a train coming towards the house, and she leapt out of bed. She crouched down in the corner by the doorframe and put her arms over her head as the sound of the roar surged and the house began really shaking, up and down, up and down, and Alice could see the shapes of things around the dark room being thrown up then tossed off her desk and dresser, could hear furniture slamming into walls and glass breaking elsewhere in the house, and everywhere, the thud thud thud of the house itself being shaken. She heard something falling on the roof and closed her eyes, hoping for it to end, somehow, then something smashed along the side of the house. There was the sound of more glass breaking.

The sound of the earthquake eased and the shaking stopped. Alice stood up from where she had wedged herself against the doorframe and reached up to flick the light switch and survey the damage. Nothing. The power was out. She fumbled her way to the side of her bed, where her cellphone had fallen down between the bed and bedside table. It was 4:37. She wrote a text to her mother, fumbling the phone and mistyping. It seemed like an eternity to simply say she was okay and to ask were they. The phone was showing network service, so hopefully she would hear something back quickly.

The phone had a torch function that Alice used to find some shoes. She pulled the door open and shone the torch out into the hallway. Now that the door was open, she heard Chloe crying. The house felt cold, and Alice could feel a breeze coming from the lounge. She picked her way through the doorway into the lounge, where she saw the night outside where most of the wall had been. Most of the brick wall of the lounge had fallen, both inward onto the sofa and outward onto the driveway. She heard another quake heading for the house, which started to shake again, but stopped within seconds. More bricks fell onto the driveway and plaster dust fell from the ceiling. Alice stepped back into the doorway, she felt safer there.

Alice called out to Chloe, who called back saying she was okay. 'Put shoes on,' Alice yelled. Then Chloe was beside her, sniffing, trying not to cry.

'That was so scary,' Chloe said. She was shivering and Alice put an arm around her.

'Do you think it was Wellington?' Alice said, and immediately regretted it, because Chloe began to panic and start crying again, her family was in Wellington. Alice gave her the phone to try calling them, she would call her own family afterwards. She wondered about her parents, if the quake had scared Olivia and Jack. They were only five and three, they would either be terrified or see it as a big adventure.

Someone answered Chloe's call. 'Are you okay?' she asked, her voice high-pitched and shaky. Then, 'We've felt a big quake here, we thought it was you.'

'It must be local,' Alice whispered. Chloe shook her head furiously, but the gesture meant nothing to Alice. She decided it was best to be quiet, just wait until Chloe had finished her call.

'Well I'm okay,' Chloe said. 'But the house is a mess.' They heard another quake approaching and braced themselves as the house started to shake. 'There's another one now,' she said, and her voice broke. 'No, it's stopped. I'm okay.'

Alice didn't think she was. Chloe said goodbye to whichever of her parents she had woken and said she would call them later. Chloe passed the phone back to Alice. 'There's a message,' she said.

It was from Alice's mother, who said they were all okay. Alice took a deep breath, relieved. More rumbling, then shaking.

'Ben!' Chloe said, and they moved as quickly as they could to the bedroom at the end of the hallway and banged on Ben's bedroom door. There was no answer. They opened the door and walked into the bedroom, stepping carefully. Books had slid from the desk onto the floor, landing on the shoes and clothes that were normally there. Ben was draped over the bed crossways where Alice had left him, snoring softly. Alice gave him a shove in the arm, which resulted in a mumbled grunt, but no signs of true consciousness.

'Typical,' Chloe said, and turned to leave the room. They heard the roar of another approaching quake and froze, but it didn't last long, and there was no movement from Ben.

'Let him sleep, I suppose,' Alice said, shrugging. Her phone rang. It was her mother. 'I'm fine,' she said, 'but the wall in the lounge has collapsed. I don't think we can stay here. And I don't think I'll be able to get my car down the driveway.' Her mother had been in touch with Alice's grandparents and great-grandparents and everyone was fine, but scared. Lindsay said once they got the kids settled, Kevin would pick her up. They had power at home, but from what they had heard on the radio, not many in the city did.

'Where was it?' Alice asked. She put her arm around Chloe and pulled her out of Ben's bedroom and into the hallway. Chloe was shaking again, she was probably in shock. They needed blankets.

'Darfield,' Lindsay said. Alice could hear Kevin in the background telling Olivia and Jack to stay under the table.

'Darfield?' Alice said. Darfield was a farming town on the Canterbury Plains, about forty kilometres west of the city. It was surprising because the Canterbury Plains were not an earthquake hotspot.

'What about Darfield?' Chloe said.

'I love you, Mum,' Alice said, and she started to cry. 'No, I'm okay. I'll see you soon.' She ended the call and tried to think what to do.

They couldn't do much while it was still dark and the power was off, and if she kept using her phone as a torch, it would quickly lose its charge. They decided to bundle up warm and go outside and see what was going on in the neighbourhood. Bricks from the neighbour's chimney lay scattered on their roof. Out on the street there were no signs of activity, almost as though the quake had only affected them. There was a rumble coming from the west and it became louder and louder, and they crouched down, then felt the ground under their feet rise and fall and heard the house shaking, bricks coming off the wrecked wall. It was a different experience outside, in the dark, with all the street and house lights out and only the waning moon for light. Alice couldn't decide whether it was more or less terrifying than being inside, surrounded by the sounds of the house shaking and wondering if something was going to fall on them. It seemed safer outside, but it was cold and so they went back inside. Chloe had a double bed, so Alice grabbed her duvet and they piled onto Chloe's bed to keep warm. They tried talking about nothing to drown out the sound of approaching aftershocks, but it didn't really work. Both read stories off different news websites, but the pages were loading slowly and it was the same information over and over. A 7.4 earthquake at Greendale, which neither of them had ever heard of, and lots of aftershocks. The slow network was draining their phones so they decided to turn them off, only checking every half hour or so.

Once six o'clock had passed and the news started spreading throughout the awakening country, their half-hourly check-ins had their phones constantly beeping as missed call notifications and messages came through, friends and family checking to see that they were okay. Alice was sending the same message over and over again, 'Scary, but I'm ok, luv u.' There was one from Andrew asking if she was okay, and she replied simply, 'Yes.'

It was getting light enough to get up and have a better look at the damage, and so they wrapped themselves in blankets and walked tentatively around the house. The kitchen was a mess. The oven and fridge had danced across the floor and sat at odd angles, surrounded by bricks from the collapsed wall and food ejected from the kitchen bench and pantry. The place smelled of red wine and Italian herbs.

Kevin arrived just after seven o'clock, and the sound of voices finally roused Ben, who stumbled into the hallway, bewildered.

'What've you done to the place?' he asked, rubbing his face.

'Had a bit of a party,' Alice said, while Chloe said, 'Earthquake.'

'No way,' Ben said. He seemed inclined to believe the party explanation until another aftershock rolled through, and they could hear more bricks clattering onto the driveway and something thudding on the roof.

'That chimney is dangerous,' Kevin said, looking up towards the ceiling. 'And even if it wasn't, you can't stay here with that wall the way it is. You're lucky no one was sleeping on the sofa.'

Ben went pale and slid down the wall to land sloppily on the floor.

'Get your things together,' Kevin said, 'you can all come home with me.'

At the Bowens' house, Lindsay ran out of the back door when the van pulled up the driveway. She grabbed Alice, her embrace like a clamp. 'I was so worried,' Lindsay said. 'It was only a couple of minutes before we heard from you, but it was so long and I thought...' She stopped and hugged Alice tight again.

Kevin wanted to go and check on Alice's grandparents and great-grandparents, and Ben decided he would go, too.

Inside, Olivia and Jack were under the dining table, which they had covered with a sheet. Both ran out and hugged Alice, but then scrambled back under the table at the sound of another aftershock. Olivia reached out and pulled at Alice's arm, dragging her down and under the table with them. They had pillows from the beds on the floor under the table and it was cosy under there. Alice drifted off to sleep with Olivia and Jack on either side of her, wondering if Andrew's other children, her half-brothers and half-sister, were as scared as Olivia and Jack were. Alice was scared, and she was a lot older than all her half-siblings, so they were bound to be. She hoped they were tucked up tight with their mum and dad, and she thought about how nice it would be to have all of her brothers and sisters here, under the table with her.

When she woke, it was only half an hour later, but she felt refreshed. She gently untangled herself from Olivia and Jack and left them to continue sleeping. The television was on, showing the carnage in the city, where building façades had fallen into the street, crushing cars. Lindsay and Chloe were sitting on the sofa, watching, silent. One building, a Mexican restaurant the family had been to a few times, was open to the elements. Green, white and red flags were strung across the room, its tables were still set and bricks from its Manchester and Worcester Street walls were lying all over the street, where a streetlight had bent to kiss the ground. As the morning wore on, more images were shown and more stories told. The quake had been downgraded to a 7.1, and no one had died. The shaking, someone said, had lasted forty seconds. It had been the longest forty seconds Alice had ever experienced.

In the suburbs, something called liquefaction had damaged houses, a slurry of water and soil pushed up to the surface by the force of the shaking, forming sand volcanoes where there was nothing to obstruct their passage, but where a structure was in the way, strong enough to damage foundations and rip up footpaths and driveways. There was a shot of a petrol station where the forecourt and building had been pushed up out of the ground, its entire slab sitting above the surrounding ground by half a metre.

'We haven't seen the cat,' Lindsay said softly, almost a whisper. 'They don't know.' She nodded towards the table Olivia and Jack were sleeping under.

Alice nodded. 'We'll go look for him later.'

Alice texted Andrew to tell him she was okay. She had replied to his text earlier, but now she thought maybe she should say more, that maybe she had held on to her anger for long enough. She asked about his family, and he quickly texted back saying everyone was all right. 'Glad you're ok,' he texted next. 'I love you.' She texted back saying she loved him too, and she realised that she did. It wasn't the same as she felt for her mum or for Kevin and Livvy and Jack, but it was there, and maybe over time they could be more like father and daughter than what they were now, just related strangers.

Kevin and Ben were back just before lunchtime. Alice's grandparents and great-grandparents were fine and although a lot of things had been broken, both houses had done reasonably well. Everyone was anxious from the aftershocks. Lindsay's parents said her sister's place was fine and she had power, but her brother Jason's house was in bad shape from liquefaction. Kevin wanted to go around after lunch and see what he could do to help Jason clean up. Lindsay and Kevin's own suburb didn't seem to have any liquefaction, Kevin said, although it did have a lot of broken chimneys.

While they were having lunch they heard that the university wouldn't open the following week. It was clear that the flat would be uninhabitable for some time and they would need to find another place to live. It was easy for Alice, she could stay at home if she needed to, but Ben and Chloe and the other flatmates would have to find something else.

Ben would stay another night or two and then drive home to Timaru, but Chloe had called her parents and they had booked her on a flight out of Christchurch the following day.

Kevin and Ben decided to go and help Lindsay's brother with his piles of silt. Alice helped Lindsay clean up the kitchen, then the broken things in what had been her bedroom, what would be her bedroom for a little while once again.

Later in the afternoon, Alice took Olivia and Jack for a walk around the neighbourhood. They had finally noticed the cat's absence and wanted to go and find him, in spite of Lindsay's reassurances that he would be home when he was hungry. They walked along the street and down long driveways and cul-de-sacs calling the cat's name.

There were, as Kevin had said, a lot of broken chimneys, bricks on roofs and driveways. There was one house where the chimney had fallen off the house in a big chunk and landed on top of a car parked beside the house. The car was a crumpled wreck, the front seats crushed into the tiniest of spaces. It would be impossible to retrieve anything from the glove box.

The neighbourhood was strangely quiet, it was like everyone was staying inside, trying to figure out how it was that The Big One that was expected to hit Wellington had hit Christchurch instead. It was something Alice was still trying to get her head around.

In the evening, with aftershocks continuing, Olivia and Jack insisted Alice sleep under the table with them, so Ben and Chloe each got a bedroom. It was a restless night, full of rumbling and shaking, clammy children and stray limbs. Alice's head hurt and her mouth felt disgusting, a post-quake hangover. Alice extricated herself from the children, tucking the blankets around them like swaddling, then climbed out from under the table. In the kitchen, she poured herself a glass of water and quickly drank it down before remembering that residents were supposed to boil water before drinking it, until the city's water supply had been thoroughly checked. Too late now.

She heard the thunk of the cat flap in the laundry, then a pathetic meow. The cat walked past his food bowl full of biscuits and up to Alice, rubbed up against her leg. She picked him up and buried her face in his fur, which smelled musty, like he had been in the crawlspace under the house. It was good to be home.

The Blitz

October 2010

When the English first settled the Canterbury region, they tried to make it look just like home, planting English trees and releasing English birds and animals. Although flat and laced with streams in an England-like manner, the Canterbury Plains on which the city of Christchurch was built are not another England, they are, in fact, the product of mountain building. The upward growth of the Southern Alps is countered by erosion and glaciation, wearing away at the mountains and washing them down rivers and out towards the sea, piece by tiny piece. The finer soils of the Southern Alps are blown onto the plains by a regular, dreaded foehn wind that blows from the northwest. Two mighty braided rivers meander wide riverbeds, flanking the city, one some fifteen kilometres north, the other fifty kilometres south. Closer in, two spring-fed rivers flow from west to east, meeting in an estuary that empties out to the sea, the surrounding land soft, wet swamp overlying the river gravels. Then, south of the city, rise the Port Hills, the eroded remains of an ancient volcano cradling the city in a one-armed embrace. The contrast then is this: the swampy soils of flat parts of the city, soaked from a rainier-than-usual winter, and the hard volcanic rocks of the Port Hills.

A month after the big September quake, the people of Christchurch were getting used to living with cracks in houses, waiting for insurance processes to get properly underway and sleeping sporadically, plagued by hundreds of aftershocks that came at all times of the day and night.

Southeast of the city, tucked into a loop of the Heathcote River, a tributary cuts across the land. The area had been farmed by the early settlers, and the last farmer died in the old farmhouse shortly before the Second World War, leaving it and the land to his son, Bill Moorhouse. Bill returned from the war with an English bride, Marjorie, and a young daughter, and in the building boom of the 1950s, set himself up as a builder. He subdivided the land, in stages to avoid flooding the market, and kept the best of the land for himself and his family, raising a son and three daughters in the old farmhouse.

After Bill's death in 1990, Marjorie had a new house built further along the stream, in her favourite spot. Bill had been planning to sell off the land before he died, and he and Marjorie had argued about it. When Marjorie finally moved into her new house and began planning its garden, she gave up the pretence of missing her late husband.

The house had been well built, designed by her son Gerald to take advantage of the beauty of the land, with views towards the stream along the back of the house and plenty of views towards the hills along the front. The house was timber framed with wooden weatherboards and a steel roof and like many of that construction, it had performed well in the September earthquake. Bill had remembered the great earthquakes of the 1920s and 1930s and had drilled into Gerald the need for houses to be built on strong, stable ground. That was why Gerald had suggested his mother build further back on the section, not right up near the stream. Her garden stretched away to the stream, blending in with the old oaks, where monarch butterflies spent each winter, lining the bare branches, their folded bodies like thousands of unnatural leaves quivering in an unfelt breeze.

Marjorie had heard visitors refer to the old oaks as ancient, but nothing was truly ancient here, a thought she kept to herself. Never give people too much information about you, that was a rule Marjorie lived by. She gathered as much as she could about them, but never gave away too much about herself.

Marjorie had turned ninety a few days earlier and soon the house would be teeming with family. It was her tradition, a springtime gathering of all her children and grandchildren, although in recent years, she had allowed her daughters and daughter-in-law to take responsibility for preparing the savoury dishes. The desserts, though, were Marjorie's domain, and she had spent the last two days and much of the morning baking and preparing dishes. Now it was time to relax for a few moments and enjoy a cup of tea.

Her grandson Andrew, Gerald's son, had arrived ahead of the rest of the family, bringing along his teenage daughter, Alice, who Marjorie hadn't seen since she was a tiny girl. Her hair had darkened considerably since, to the same colour as Andrew's, and Marjorie's own when she had been young. Alice was blue-eyed, not the blue that changes, but clear and intense. She was taller than Marjorie and her daughters, something Alice had inherited from her mother's side of the family. Alice sat down on the sofa across from where Marjorie was sitting. Andrew asked if they wanted something to drink and went off to fill their requests.

'I remember when you were a little girl,' she told Alice. The girl seemed surprised. 'You came here with your father, and I took you down to the stream and showed you the butterflies.'

Alice looked out towards the back of the garden, confused. 'I think I do,' she said. 'Would they be there now?'

'It's the wrong time of year,' Marjorie said. Their conversation was interrupted by the arrival of more family, but soon after, Marjorie saw Alice walking towards the stream, looking up into the trees.

They weren't able to speak again until later in the afternoon, once most of the family had left and those who remained were cleaning up in the kitchen. Alice had brought Marjorie a cup of tea and was sitting across from her once again, sipping at a cup of coffee.

'They're a bit unnerving,' Marjorie said. 'This lot.'

Alice started to protest, but Marjorie cut her off.

'Don't worry about what they think of you,' Marjorie said. 'Their world is rugby and building, and a woman doing an engineering degree, well they don't know how to handle that.'

Alice laughed. 'Engineering's not so different from building.'

'It's the woman part they're uncomfortable with. As innovative as this family prides itself on being with regard to building, they're in the dark ages when it comes to women.'

'It's different from my mum's family,' Alice said. 'They're so proud of having a girl doing engineering.'

'That must be a lot of pressure,' Marjorie said, peering at Alice, daring her to brush away the scrutiny.

Alice met her gaze and seemed to drop her guard. 'Sometimes it is,' she admitted. 'But they're really supportive, almost too supportive sometimes and I wish they'd just let me help them with the cooking.'

'That's a better reaction than I had when I said I wanted to go to nursing school,' Marjorie said, smiling. 'My father said what was the point, I was just going to get married and have babies.'

'Did you?' Alice said, then laughed nervously. 'Because obviously... I mean, did you go to nursing school?'

'I did,' Marjorie said. 'I was a nurse in the war, until Suzanne was born. It was rare for a woman to keep on working after she was married back then, but during the war, it was all hands on deck.'

Marjorie made sure to invite Alice to come around any time. The girl's company was a refreshing change, she seemed able to talk to people of different ages, unlike Marjorie's other great-grandchildren, who mostly seemed bored, anxious to get away from family gatherings as quickly as possible.

Later that night, Marjorie was alone in the house, which had been tidied within an inch of its life by her daughters and daughter-in-law. All very dutiful women, always asking if she was all right, making sure there was nothing she needed to do for herself, she could just relax and enjoy her twilight years. They actually used that term, 'twilight years', as though death was simply a dimming of light, a fading into nothing. Bill had died suddenly, away from their sight, so they didn't really know the truth of it, that death is messy and ugly, and the common habit of romanticising death is all that protects those who encounter it from insanity.

From where Marjorie was sitting, she saw clouds coming over the hills from the south, piling up, then rapidly moving towards the city, bringing with them a wind that tore at the magnolia bush outside the window. The sky darkened with cloud, and she could see the rain like a veil, coming down on the hills and on the houses between her and them. Soon rain started to pick away at the window, getting louder and louder until she thought it might hail. She stood to check, but there was nothing settling on the lawn. The sky flashed and then thunder rolled across the city, a boom that spread, then broke up. It was a nice change from the rumbling that had been coming from under the hills in recent weeks.

One grandson, Tony, had wanted to move in with Marjorie after the September earthquake, not because his house was damaged but because, he said, he didn't want her to be afraid. Marjorie knew, though, that Tony was seeing a business opportunity and was planning to rent his house to those whose houses were uninhabitable. Although she approved of his initiative, she wasn't about to allow him to gain a foothold in her own home.

Marjorie had convinced her children that she would be fine on her own, she had lived through the Blitz, she said, and the earthquakes were much less frightening. Eventually, they accepted that and left her alone to the peace of her own house. But she was scared. It was unnerving waking in the night to a rumble coming from beneath the hills, hearing it before feeling it, then hearing the sound of the house's joints creaking. The Blitz was personal, the Germans dropping bombs on them, wiping out families, neighbourhoods, livelihoods. And through the years, everything she had faced was personal, someone trying to take business from the family, someone trying to take advantage of one of her children or grandchildren, to get one over on the family. She could face those things, see the enemy, figure out a strategy, a way to turn the tables and get one over on them. But this quake business was impersonal, she just happened to be sitting atop a part of the earth that was breaking, slowly but inexorably, assuming a new shape, oblivious to the tiny beings scurrying around on the surface.

She had told her family she was sleeping well, and that was true, until there was an aftershock. Then she was wide awake, not waiting with dread for the next quake, but awake and thinking about her family, past and present, worrying about what the future held.

Marjorie knew she didn't have much time left. She needed to make decisions about how her holdings would be distributed once she was gone. The question was: How did she want to be remembered? What sort of future did she want to set up for those she was leaving behind? She wasn't sure. She had made too many compromises over the years to feel truly comfortable with the past, overlooked the decisions Bill had made that had disadvantaged others. Yes, he had made those decisions, but she had done nothing to stop him, because she didn't want to lose everything.

There had been the Drakes. Greg was a chippie and he and Bill had known each other from school. Bill had given him work over the years, but Greg had a drinking problem, as many did after the war, and he found it difficult to work consistently. Money was increasingly tight and so Bill offered to buy his house and land. It was a lovely piece of land at the bottom of the Port Hills, west of the city, land that had not yet been developed into housing. It wasn't a great price, but it was enough to get Greg and his family out of the hole they were in and into a smaller property. What Greg hadn't known was that the land was going to be rezoned, and Bill was able to exert pressure on his mates in the council and get it rezoned quickly once the sale was complete. Had Greg held on for another couple of years, the zoning change would've gone through and he would have been able to subdivide the land himself. Instead, it was Bill who made a killing on the subdivision and development of the land.

Until the earthquakes started, Marjorie hadn't thought about Greg Drake for at least a decade. His son had come to see her once, in the 1990s, shortly after Bill died. He was angry. Knowing his parents' financial position, the son said, Bill should have used his influence to push through the zoning change and let them profit from the sale of the land. They wouldn't have ended up in their pokey, damp flat, Greg angry at being betrayed by a man he had thought of as a friend. It ate him up, his son said, and his health had suffered. Their retirement would have been happier if they'd had the opportunity to profit from the land, their land, instead of seeing it line the pockets of a man who had more than he needed, more than he would ever need.

Marjorie apologised. It was the polite thing to do, after all. She told him she was never privy to any business dealings, which wasn't true, but he wasn't to know that. Nor was he to know that it was Marjorie who first became aware of the Drakes' financial problems and encouraged Bill to ask questions, subtle questions meant to draw Greg out so he would confide in Bill.

Then there had been Stan and Suzanne. When Stan Watson first started working for Bill, Marjorie had recognised that his charm hid a cunning nature and she had resolved to keep an eye on him. He could be good for the business, but he had to be reined in. Unfortunately, Stan knew how to play Bill and before Marjorie could encourage him to do otherwise, Bill had promoted Stan over the other workers and entrusted responsibilities to him that Bill had previously been reluctant to let go of. Marjorie was looking after the books then and had noticed that materials they were buying in were being charged out at inflated prices, not the usual markup, but actually stated as being something they weren't. It would increase profits, but it had to be subtle or it would ruin the company's good reputation. She wouldn't let that happen, she dreaded being poor again, and she worried about the day when a particularly canny client would notice and call them out on it, she could see it all crumbling away.

She needed to find a way to control Stan, and it wasn't long before she found her way in. Suzanne was working in the office, and Marjorie encouraged her to try out the fashions of the day, the miniskirts, the big hair, the dramatic makeup. She was a pretty girl, with Marjorie's petite build but lighter colouring and the thick blonde hair of Marjorie's own mother. Soon she had the attention of all the workers, and a few encouraging words from her mother made her realise that her father's trusted foreman was handsome, that his ambition would provide her with a good life. Marjorie envied the girls of the 1960s. Although they had few choices, they had far more than she had at their age. In an ideal world, she would have encouraged a daughter to get an education and a career so she could support herself and not be dependent on a man, but she had to face facts, Suzanne wasn't that kind of girl, she was silly, easily flattered, and the few shiny presents Marjorie encouraged Stan to give her were enough to convince her that he was her shining knight.

Stan was ambitious and had a feel for what people would believe, but he was also a bully, a fact Marjorie hadn't recognised until it was too late. He enjoyed having power over those less powerful and took pleasure in forcing Suzanne into his mould, his idea of what a wife should be. Their son Tony was very like Stan, in both looks and temperament.

Suzanne was one of many Marjorie thought about late at night. The truth was it wasn't the quakes Marjorie was afraid of. It was the past, out there in the dark, waiting for her, the ghosts of those she had pushed and guided into making decisions that suited her during her life in this new country. She couldn't go back and change anything, but that didn't matter late at night, wide awake hearing the rumble fade into the distance.

There were some nights she couldn't get back to sleep at all, and what haunted her then was people from the deeper past, the people she had left behind when she married Bill and agreed to travel to the other side of the world with him. There were Walter, her first love, and her brother Edward, both dead in the trenches.

Andrew was like Edward. Edward had worshipped Marjorie, his glamorous big sister who had escaped the family home to a better life. When the war began, she encouraged him to go into the army. It was a way to get away from home, away from the angry drunk taking out the terrors of the previous war on his powerless family. Andrew had Edward's dark, thick hair and his eyes were the kind of blue that turned to grey when the light changed. Like Edward, Andrew had been soft and easily led. But Marjorie had encouraged Andrew to conceal that, to hide any weakness, any situation where someone would try to take advantage of him.

Marjorie's parents had been killed in the Blitz, but the others might still be out there, her other brother and her sisters. They had survived the Blitz, she knew that, but what of the years that followed the end of the war? What about their children, grandchildren, great-grandchildren?

The war had changed Marjorie, the grief of loss had squeezed her heart and made her hard. Had these earthquakes reversed the process? She hoped not. It would take another lifetime to undo the regrets the young Marjorie would have felt had she known the choices the older, grief-hardened Marjorie was going to make. And Marjorie didn't have another lifetime, she had, at most, a handful of years to decide what legacy she would leave behind.

Rubble Necking

November 2010

During the last months of 2010, the people of Christchurch became used to the aftershocks. Some mastered the art of sleeping through anything, others mastered the art of functioning adequately on interrupted sleep. A game arose, that of guessing the magnitude and location of an aftershock before the government's geological sciences agency could publish a quake report. This agency's website, Geonet, experienced more traffic than it ever had before, and tens of thousands of 'felt' reports were submitted to describe each individual's experience of a particular quake.

This is something people fail to understand unless they have been through a series of earthquakes: It's not the magnitude of the quake that determines how you experience it, it's how close to the epicentre you are. So although the July 2009 Dusky Sound earthquake in the southwest of the South Island was larger than the September 2010 quake, 7.8 to Darfield's 7.1, it was less damaging because it was far away from major population centres.

The Darfield earthquake, although it occurred in the countryside, was near a large urban area. As the months wore on, that urban area, home to 375,000 people, was shaken by repeated aftershocks. There were over 1700 individual earthquakes of magnitude three and higher from the initial Darfield earthquake until the end of 2010. Thirty of these were magnitude five quakes, and more than a few were very close to the city. Many of these quakes were centred under the townships of Rolleston, Springston, Lincoln and Prebbleton just west of the city, which was disconcerting for the residents of these quiet satellite towns, but they were also disturbing for the residents of the city itself.

One 5.0 aftershock just a few days after the Darfield earthquake was centred just south of the city, under the hard volcanic rocks of the Port Hills, between the port town of Lyttelton and Christchurch. Its motion was sharply up and down with little warning between the rumble and its shaking, unlike the quakes from Rolleston and further afield, and it occurred just before eight o'clock on a Wednesday morning. So close to the city, it was a brutal shock after four nights of sleep-interrupting aftershocks. An exhausted few packed up and left Christchurch at that point.

But most became used to the regular aftershocks, and learned to live with the interruption to their lives. Parts of the central city and badly damaged commercial areas were cordoned off, and fences went up around buildings that were regarded as too dangerous to be occupied. The people of Christchurch were regularly reminding themselves how lucky the city had been that the September earthquake occurred in the middle of the night, when most people were tucked up in bed asleep. One person had died from a heart attack that wasn't necessarily because of the earthquake, and two people were badly injured, one by a falling chimney, the other cut by glass.

One Sunday night, Alice's mother and stepfather, Lindsay and Kevin, went into the city for dinner with Lindsay's brother and his wife. Having Alice home was nice, Lindsay had missed her during her months flatting, missed the near-adult conversation during the days once Alice arrived home from school. Since the earthquake, it was almost the same, except that Alice's arrival times varied according to her timetable, and some days she didn't arrive home until ten o'clock. She was still on her restricted licence and determined not to lose it by being caught out too late.

One of the advantages of Alice being home again was that Lindsay and Kevin could go out, leaving Alice to look after the kids, spending a night at home studying once Olivia and Jack had gone to bed. Both children had been anxious following the earthquake and didn't like being away from their parents. They had become fussy about babysitters, and the neighbour's fourteen-year-old daughter was no longer a good option. She was showing all the signs of anxiety herself, and the last time they had left her to look after Olivia and Jack, it had been a stressful night, with both kids refusing to go to bed and insisting on sleeping with their parents. But Olivia and Jack seemed to feel safe around Alice, as though nothing could possibly go wrong with her there. She was a like a magic charm, and Lindsay and Alice had talked about that, wondering if they were thinking that way because Alice hadn't been there for the big one.

Lindsay and Kevin arrived in the city early so they could walk around and assess the damage. They had been into the city in the days after the first quake and seen the damaged buildings barricaded behind fences and cars crushed by falling brickwork. Now they parked well away from anything that looked dangerous and walked down to Manchester Street, where there seemed to be more damage than in other parts of the city. Manchester Street was just east of Colombo Street, the main street that ran through the city from the Port Hills all the way to the northern side of the city. Manchester Street had a lot of buildings built in the early years of the twentieth century that nothing much had been done with ever since Lindsay could remember. It was an eclectic mix of shops, cafés and services drawn to the street by the low rents offered on space in the old brick buildings.

One part of the street was closed off and soil had been piled up around a four-storey building that was being demolished. The intention to demolish had been fiercely argued, the building owner wanting it down, but heritage campaigners wanted it to stay and be repaired, a symbol of what Kevin mockingly referred to as the city's ancient history. His parents were English and he scoffed at the idea that a 105-year-old building could be regarded as 'heritage'.

Demolition had been underway for about three weeks and the building's guts were visible. Now, during the weekend when the equipment stood still and there were no workmen on site, pigeons could be seen roosting on the exposed beams. Lindsay and Kevin circled the cordoned-off area to get a good look at the building. Nearby there were shipping containers around other buildings, stacked to form walls and protect anyone nearby from falling masonry in case of an aftershock. One building, an old church, appeared to be open, even though blue steel beams braced up one wall. Mannequins had been painted completely white and anchored to the beams. One was kayaking down towards the ground, another was cycling upward and a third, a pony-tailed woman, tight-roped her way across a horizontal beam near the top of the tower.

'Very cool,' Lindsay said. She yawned and rested her head on Kevin's shoulder. There had been an aftershock in the night, a four-something at around one o'clock, and she and Alice had put a video on, unable to get back to sleep after comforting Olivia and Jack. Kevin, of course, had slept through it all. She envied him that. At least one of them was functioning on all cylinders.

Kevin checked his watch. 'It's nearly time, we should go.'

They walked around to Lichfield Street and walked up a lane that had been reduced to half its width by the fencing surrounding a badly-damaged building. Its façade had crumbled, leaving a pile of bricks on the footpath in front of it. Jason and Carla were waiting for them outside. Inside, the bar was busy, people had gone back to their normal lives, walking around whatever debris was in the way.

Jason and Carla looked exhausted. Jason was nearly a decade younger than Lindsay, and Carla even younger than that. Carla was closer to Alice's age than to Lindsay's. Lindsay had always felt ancient around her and found the gulf in their ages difficult to bridge. That had changed in recent weeks, Jason and Carla's house was badly damaged, and Carla was looking tired and losing weight from the stress of not sleeping and worrying about what would happen to the house. They had insurance, everyone did, but still, they had been planning to renovate the house in preparation for having children. Not that Carla was pregnant, that was proving elusive, but they wanted children, even though to Lindsay, Carla had never seemed particularly maternal. She worried that Carla was only wanting kids because Jason did. He loved his nieces and nephews, lavishing love and attention on them, but Carla always seemed a bit, well, afraid. But since the September quake, she had been good with Olivia and Jack, and had even had them laughing a couple of weeks ago when she and Jason had been around for dinner and there had been an aftershock. Lack of sleep seemed to force her to drop whatever barriers she used to have up when around Lindsay.

'Maybe we should stop trying,' Carla said. Jason and Kevin were at the bar ordering drinks. 'Wait until the house is fixed. Whenever that might be.'

'Have you been assessed yet?' Lindsay said, wanting to stay away from the subject of how often her baby brother might be trying to impregnate his wife. Carla had started down that path once before, and although Lindsay was pleased that the barriers had dropped, she sometimes wished that there hadn't been so many of them falling away.

'Not yet,' Carla said. 'They can't give me a time, just said it will be soon. And I'm sick of calling and being told the same thing.'

'You need to keep on them,' Lindsay said.

'But there are so many more people who are worse off,' Carla said. 'We don't want to be pushy. I don't want to be one of those pushy people looking to profit from the quakes.' One of her uncles was an antiques dealer, and he had been fielding endless calls from people wanting to replace glassware and crockery. 'He had one woman claiming a set would cost six thousand to replace, and he said it wouldn't even be worth sixty.'

'Pretty disgusting, really,' Lindsay agreed. 'Dad has a mate who's getting a new kitchen. It wasn't damaged, but he knows a guy who knows a guy, and you know how it goes.' Kevin and Jason were back at the table, putting down three beers and a coke.

Kevin nodded. 'It's who you know, and it's only going to get worse.' He told them about a big building company, Fletchers, that was going to get most of the EQC repairs. Of course, anything over $100,000 would go to private insurers, but many of the lower-value repairs would be worth a lot to Fletchers and their shareholders. 'And I've heard they'll be offering peanuts. So you know what'll happen, no decent builder will take up the work, but all the cowboys will flock to town to make a quick buck.'

Lindsay could feel Kevin jiggling his leg and was finding it unnerving. She reached over and put her hand on his knee. 'Sorry,' he said, smiling wryly. 'It just gets me angry, the way people are looking for a way to profit from all this. Looking for an angle.'

'C'mon, it won't be that bad,' Jason said. 'This is New Zealand, not Zimbabwe.'

Kevin shrugged. 'Well, maybe not. But it isn't looking good.'

Carla flicked a glance at Lindsay across the table. Yes, this line of conversation had to end. Lindsay and Carla both made a point of opening their menus and studying the choices. The sound of an aftershock rose in the distance, the building shook briefly and settled, ignored by the bar's inhabitants.

'It isn't looking bad, either,' Jason said.

'The steak looks good,' Lindsay said.

'It does,' Carla agreed. 'They do shoestring fries.'

'I love shoestring fries,' Lindsay said with excessive enthusiasm.

Kevin and Jason got the message and buried their heads in the menus and, after the waitress took their orders, Kevin dutifully changed the subject. 'Are you two going away for the summer holidays?'

'We were going to,' Carla said, 'but we don't know what's happening with the house.' She realised the opportunity missed so changed direction. 'What's it like having Alice back home?'

Lindsay grabbed hold of the bone thrown her. 'It's great,' she said. 'I think the time away's done us good. The kids love having her back, and it means we can go out a bit more. Well, when she's there, that is. She spends a bit of time at the library. And with Andrew's family.' Lindsay filled them in on Alice meeting the other side of the family.

'You all right with that?' Jason said when she had finished. Carla shot him a look, puzzled.

Lindsay shrugged. 'It's up to her, and I understand her curiosity. There's ways she's like them as much as she's like us.'

Jason raised an eyebrow. 'Really?'

'I mean, she doesn't look like us, does she,' Lindsay said. 'She has Andrew's colouring, not ours, and when she was a baby I could always see resemblances between members of his family more than ours.'

'There is that,' Jason agreed, 'but you're talking about surface things. She's like Dad, thoughtful, analytical, figuring out where the pieces fit, how things work.'

Kevin was jiggling his leg nervously beside her once again. Alice had never called him Dad and it had taken her a while to accept him, but he was the closest she had to a father. He said he understood her curiosity, but Lindsay worried that he felt he might be replaced by Andrew. Kevin also worried whether or not Andrew could be there for Alice, whether he had, as Kevin put it, 'grown a spine'. Andrew and Kevin had never met, but she had told him about their marriage, the reasons for its disintegration, as best as she could understand them, anyway. He understood, or said he did, why she hadn't made any real effort to keep Alice in contact with Andrew's family. Lindsay put her hand on his leg again and he stopped jiggling.

'Well that may be true,' Lindsay said, 'but whatever the case, she needs to figure it all out for herself.'

'She will,' Kevin said. 'She's a smart girl. She'll figure it out.'

They moved on to small talk for the rest of the meal, and after dessert wandered around the city looking at the damage. All had grown up in Christchurch, and places they had taken for granted were different now, broken and fenced off. 'I love that place,' Carla said, as they walked past a sandwich shop that was fenced off, its ceiling partly collapsed inside. Its façade had collapsed, a long pile of bricks on the footpath. 'Loved.'

'Honey chicken sandwich on white bread with coleslaw,' Lindsay said. 'I used to get one if I was in town for the afternoon.'

'They're in Northlands now, I think,' Carla said. 'But it's not the same.'

'No,' Lindsay said. 'Nothing's the same any more.'

When Lindsay and Kevin arrived home, Olivia and Jack were asleep in bed and Alice was sleeping on the sofa. Lindsay draped a blanket over her, then quietly moved through to the kitchen, where Kevin was sitting at the table planning the next week's work. She poured two glasses of whiskey, sat down across from him and sipped at hers. The whiskey had become a habit since the quakes started, it helped Lindsay to get to sleep and stay asleep. Sometimes.

'Do you think we're doing the right thing?' she asked.

Kevin turned away from the laptop to look at her. 'You think we should stop with the whiskey?'

'No, with Alice. Encouraging her to see more of Andrew. His family.'

He shrugged. 'It's not like we're pushing her at them,' he said, turning back to the laptop. 'And if we stopped her, that wouldn't be right.'

Lindsay nodded, sipping. 'I just hope she doesn't get hurt.'

'Drink your whiskey,' Kevin said, 'and get some sleep.'

'Maybe we should stop the whiskey,' Lindsay said. 'It's getting expensive.'

A faint rumble in the distance grew louder and the house gave a brief shake.

'Three point two,' Kevin said without looking up from the laptop. 'Rolleston.'

Quiet

December 2010

It was finally quiet. The rush of winding up work for the year, the stress of preparing for Christmas and having the house full of family on Christmas day, it was all finally over. It was Boxing Day, the day of rest, for the menfolk at least. The women were off shopping in the city, picking up Boxing Day bargains. Gerald had never understood the motivation, facing the madness of post-Christmas shopping only a day after finally seeing the fruit of the madness of pre-Christmas shopping. Michelle, their daughter-in-law, had picked up Sylvia an hour earlier. He did not expect to see them again until the afternoon. Hopefully late in the afternoon, which was very likely if Sylvia went home with Michelle to see the children, to spoil them with any extras she might have picked up in the sales.

Gerald was enjoying the quiet. He had already been awake when a four magnitude quake had rolled through at just after two in the morning. The quakes had tailed off the last few weeks, and it was getting unusual to have a four. That morning, there were a couple of threes, then another four inside half an hour, then the earth fell quiet once again, until eight o'clock, when Gerald and Sylvia had been eating their porridge, drinking their coffee.

These quakes felt close, but they weren't coming from the hills, he knew the sound of those. No, these ones were coming from the other direction, not the west, which everyone was used to, but the north. When Michelle picked up Sylvia, she said the burst of quakes had been right under the city.

Michelle looked tired. She was finding the quakes stressful, and the kids picked up on it and were frightened, which stressed her more, perpetuating the cycle. Sylvia had tried to talk to her about it, but she said it wasn't a problem, she was controlling her fear, the kids didn't notice. But children do, don't they? Certainly he and Sylvia were aware of the goings-on in the families they had grown up in, well before anyone gave them credit for that level of understanding.

Gerald was at the dining table, slowly going through the newspaper, enjoying the freedom of not having to be anywhere, do anything. In six months he would be old enough to retire, to have every day be like this. How long before he was bored? He didn't know, and he hadn't yet made a decision. Sylvia wanted him to sell up the business, but he found the idea of letting it go too much to contemplate, at least right now, anyway.

Gerald thought about what his grandchildren's lives would be like in this broken city, with the blocked off streets and the demolitions. Paradise for a boy who loved diggers, which Andrew and Michelle's boys did. Gerald would make a point of taking them into the city during the school holidays to see the excavators, to see how they tear at buildings, piece by piece, gradually chewing them up into pieces small enough to be taken away. It would have to be soon, the Manchester Courts demolition was nearly complete, and there was nothing else of real significance coming down after that.

This time of the earthquakes would probably be a tiny blip in their lives, the rebuild would be over before the young ones reached high school. For Alice, Andrew's oldest, though, it was disconcerting, she had told Gerald that. This had been her first year at university and she had flatted near the city for the first three terms so had spent more time in the city than she ever had before. She liked it, the cafés, the gardens, the river, and she had become used to it. Would she stay in Christchurch? he had asked. Short-term, yes, she said. She wanted to finish her degree, which would be another three years, but beyond that, she didn't know whether or not she wanted to stay in Christchurch.

Gerald's mother had taken a liking to the girl, and he wasn't sure he understood why as he didn't think Marjorie liked anyone. She approved of people, if they served some purpose, but generally she didn't give any indication of actually liking someone, even her own children, and Gerald's father, when he had still been alive.

He thought Alice should leave, find a nice city, finish her degree in Auckland, or even Australia, although he hadn't said that aloud. It wasn't the earthquakes or the effect on her early adult life, it was the city itself, the undercurrent of something rotten. Whenever he brought this up to Sylvia, she laughed. 'What do you expect from a city built on a swamp?' she said. 'We're all sinking into the rot.' It wasn't that he no longer found the city beautiful, he did, it was that he found it disturbing.

Just the day before, Christmas Day, a family in the low-income suburb of Aranui were woken when what was referred to in the newspaper as a homemade bomb was thrown through one of the windows of their house. Earlier in the month, police said they had found the place where a prostitute was murdered a couple of years ago. He knew the place, the land was next door to the radio clubrooms, back when he had still been doing ham radio. Christchurch was the site of too many disturbing crimes, and he wondered what it was about the place that drew the people who could do such brutal things.

Gerald closed the newspaper, made himself another coffee and went through to the lounge, where the day's sun was pouring through the windows. He sat down in a chair facing out onto the valley and started reading the mystery novel Alice had given him for Christmas.

He was well into the first chapter when he heard another quake, the approaching rumble, then the shaking of the house. Glasses and cups in the kitchen jostled against one another. A good one, and from the city again. He returned to his book, but in a couple of minutes another quake rolled through. Gerald looked out down the valley and could see the power lines along the street swaying. He thought of Sylvia and Michelle in the city.

He had a cellphone, it was necessary for business these days, but he hated the things and had powered his down at the close of business on Thursday afternoon. He powered it on and texted Sylvia, asking if she was okay. She quickly texted back that she was, but Michelle was upset and wanted to get home to the kids. He texted Sylvia to say he would pick her up.

There was a steady flow of traffic going out of the city but not much to impede his progress on the way in. He could see a few streets blocked off, occupied only by police and firemen. He parked down by the Botanic Gardens and walked in to the city to meet Sylvia at the end of the City Mall, under the Bridge of Remembrance. The mall was closed off and there was a fire appliance parked on the tramlines. Firemen and police littered the mall and people outside the cordon were discussing whether to stay and wait in the hopes of continuing their shopping.

Sylvia said she was fine, but really she was a little bit on edge. There had been three quakes since the first one, bricks falling off buildings and some shattering glass, but nothing for about twenty minutes. He talked her into a walk in the gardens, it would help her to wind down. She had become more relaxed about the quakes as the weeks wore on, but at the start, she had trouble sleeping and ended up weepy and easily confused. A trip to the doctor sorted that out, and a few days on sleeping pills had given her the rest she needed to get back into a routine.

Gerald and Sylvia walked along the river on the side opposite the hospital. Patients were outside, enjoying the fresh air. It always puzzled Gerald to see patients outside enjoying the fresh air while also smoking. The river was full of ducks and their ducklings, the usual mallard and grey ducks, along with the larger paradise ducks and their brown and white-striped ducklings. The gardens were full of people enjoying the warm summer weather, mostly couples and families with small children. It was sad to not see very many families with older children, but he supposed the older children were with their friends or at the malls. He hoped that was not his grandchildren's futures, to be alienated from their parents past a certain age. He and Sylvia had tried to keep talking to their children when they were growing up, and although there had been rough patches, there hadn't been anything too dramatic, except from the wider family.

There were too many people in the gardens, Sylvia said, she was ready to go home.

At home, Gerald made them an omelette for lunch. There were more quakes while they were eating, just threes, once again, but they disturbed Sylvia. After finishing lunch and a cup of tea, they went for a walk around the park near their house.

They had worked hard at having a peaceful family, at teaching their children respect for themselves and for others. The main issue had been when he decided to break away from the family business, the construction business his father had started. Gerald had only become a builder because he wasn't interested in school and when he reached fifteen years of age and told his parents he wanted to leave, his father had said he could, but only if he had a job. He had nothing lined up, so his father insisted Gerald go and work for him. It wasn't long before he found he enjoyed the work, the satisfaction of planning something, choosing the right materials and working towards a finished result, getting everything right. But in Gerald's late teens, he noticed his brother-in-law, Stan, was in the habit of cutting corners. Nothing that would make a house fall down, but Stan wasn't being up front with their customers about the choices being made. Gerald wasn't happy about it, but he knew his father would do nothing, the bottom line was as important to Bill, if not more so, than the quality of the finished product. By the time Laurel was born and Andrew was starting school, it was bothering Gerald. Quality was getting lower and lower and it wasn't about craftsmanship any more, it was about squeezing every last cent out of a build.

Gerald and Sylvia had spent many late nights after the children had gone to bed discussing what to do, coming up with a solution that wouldn't create a rift in the family. A lot of the cousins were similar ages and Gerald and Sylvia wanted their children to grow up with their wider family. It built a sense of family that neither of them had growing up. Gerald's father was the only one of their parents who had been born in New Zealand. Sylvia's parents were ten-pound Poms who had emigrated when she was just five years old and she had only vague memories of all the family they had left behind. No, however Gerald solved the problem of the declining quality of builds, it had to be done subtly.

The solution was to start up his own building company, Moorhouse Architectural, specialising in more high-end builds, especially in the hills around Christchurch. It was a market Bill and Stan weren't interested in, too many risks building on hills, fewer opportunities to make a profit. But Gerald had framed it as an extension of the family business, one for which he was willing to take all the risk. That is, he wasn't asking them for any money. It worked, and Gerald was able to build houses his way, without worrying about when a client would make claims about being ripped off. It was a relief, it lifted a burden from Gerald's shoulders he hadn't realised was so heavy.

Running his own company gave him and Sylvia the freedom to let their children spend time with their cousins while they were growing up without having to worry that everyone was too much in each other's pockets. Of course Lindsay's unexpected pregnancy had disrupted the family. Alice had been the first great-grandchild on both sides of the family, and all the new grandparents were torn over being in love with baby Alice and worrying about Andrew and Lindsay being too young. But that was the thing with children, you could encourage them to take responsibility for their actions, but you couldn't do more than that, they had to make their own choices.

Andrew and Lindsay knew each other through mutual friends while they were in high school, which was when they started dating. Both were doing first year law at university when Lindsay became pregnant. Gerald and Sylvia had offered their support for whatever Andrew and Lindsay wanted to do. Little Alice was a good baby, and they were upset to lose contact after the divorce. It was good to see Alice again, all grown up.

Boxing Day was the usual day for the family to pack up and go away for a holiday, and it sounded like Alice would be joining them in Central Otago for a week. It would be good for her, to meet some of the others, have a bit more time to get to know them properly. As much as Gerald and Sylvia wanted to spend that time with her, they had decided to stay in town, to enjoy the good weather and the quiet. They would see Alice plenty in the new year, especially as it sounded like she would stay at home rather than go flatting again. Lindsay and her second family were just five minutes' drive from Gerald and Sylvia, and now that Alice knew where they were, she could stop in whenever she liked.

After the Boxing Day quakes, there weren't many aftershocks at all. The city was quiet, the weather stayed hot and the skies were clear. Gerald and Sylvia spent their mornings in the garden, their afternoons inside reading and their evenings walking around the neighbourhood or up in the hills. Was this what retirement would be like? It wouldn't be too bad, although in winter he would have to spend more time indoors. Christchurch just wasn't amenable to gardening or walking from May to August, so a third of the year. But he deliberately tried not to think about it too much in those last days of 2010, he just wanted to enjoy the quiet while it lasted.

Looking Up

January 2011

Seismic activity tailed off quickly after the Boxing Day aftershock, and by early January it was quiet again. The days were hot and people were relaxing, trying to forget the upheaval of the past few months. The city had been lucky, in spite of what they had all been through, no one had been killed. Repairs would get underway in the new year, and the first anniversary of the quake would show how far the city had progressed. Things were looking up.

Alice spent a week with Andrew's family in Wanaka, a holiday town in the Central Otago region. Andrew and Michelle had a house there and it was big, two wings, four bathrooms, a swimming pool and plenty of land, where some of the kids in the family had pitched pup tents. It was Alice's first real chance to meet her relatives, she had been too nervous that first time she had met the family at her great-grandmother's house, when she had spent more time exploring the grounds than she had spent actually mingling.

Three of the second cousins staying at the house were close to Alice's age, all still in high school. The girl, Charlotte, was thirteen and self-absorbed, always on her phone reading and texting, looking up every now and then, but thumbs still going. Alice texted plenty, but she knew how to be around people. Well, more than Charlotte seemed to, she had no skills other than her thumb skills. Her mother would ask her to do something and she would have to be told two, three, four times, then would get up, huffing, and stomp off to do whatever her mother had asked. Only usually she would return in a minute or so complaining for one reason or another. The washing wasn't done yet, so she couldn't put it out, or the meat was still thawing, so she couldn't put it in the marinade. She had long dark hair, as thick as Alice's, but she made a point of straightening it every day, even if they would be spending the day on the lake or up a hill somewhere.

'Just leave me here,' she said to her mother one morning. 'I can just read for the day.'

Her mother insisted Charlotte was going with her family. Both parents seemed determined to do everything together. Each night, though, the parents left the kids to their own devices and walked off in the direction of the lake, hand in hand, like they were newlyweds. What was going on there?

Nathan was fifteen and into rugby in a big way. He resented the holiday away from home as he had wanted to stay behind. He had touch rugby he wanted to keep up with and, seriously concerned about losing fitness, spent his days running or climbing up hills or swimming. When he was back at the house, he was eating: bacon and eggs for breakfast, followed by a weetbix chaser, a half a loaf of bread made into sandwiches for lunch, and repeat servings from the barbecue each night, followed by double portions of dessert and then, before bedtime, another serving of weetbix. Alice had a good appetite, but felt like a fussy eater comparing the contents of her dinner plate with his. It was difficult having a conversation with him, as Alice didn't know much about rugby. 'Family full of women,' Alice explained. They were sitting on the grass outside the house eating dinner.

'No men at all?' he asked. He was gnawing a chicken drum clean, and it quickly joined the remains of another three on his plate. He picked up another drum.

'No,' Alice said. 'I have an uncle and an aunt, and my grandma has loads of sisters, and they mostly have girls. My uncle has only one boy cousin.'

'Don't the women get married?' Nathan said.

'Yeah, they do, but the husbands are pretty quiet,' Alice said. 'Or they're off fishing or watching rugby. They seem to live separate lives. The women in my family can be a bit overbearing.'

'What do you mean overbearing?' Nathan asked, chewing away at his chicken.

Alice shrugged. She felt like she was saying too much and that maybe she had strayed into being disloyal towards her mother's family. She loved the aunties, but sometimes found them too loud and pushy. Big family get-togethers were rare, and Alice wasn't sure if it was because her grandmother's sisters all lived outside of Christchurch or because it was difficult to have a gathering where there wasn't at least one row. Andrew's family, though, were polite to each other, saying please and thank you, and the conversations took place at a much quieter volume than in Lindsay's family. 'They know how things should be done,' Alice finally said, 'and they're not shy about letting everyone know how they should do things.'

Nathan laughed. 'So everyone's in charge?'

Alice nodded. 'And no one knows it. Recipe for chaos. Family get-togethers are noisy, not like this.'

'There's only one boss in this family,' Nathan said, speaking more quietly than he had been before.

'Who's that?'

'Who do you think?' he said and when she continued to look puzzled, 'Grandmother Moorhouse. Haven't you noticed how all the adults defer to her?'

'I've only been around them at her house once,' Alice said. 'I thought they were all so polite because she's old.'

'No,' Nathan said. 'It's cos they're all terrified of her.'

'But she's tiny.'

'I don't mean that she'll beat them up,' Nathan said. 'But they all want the land, so they don't dare do anything to offend her.'

Alice must have looked puzzled, because Nathan continued. 'She owns that big block of land, river outlook, goes down to the old farmhouse. It's all prime real estate, and subdivided would be worth millions. Whoever she leaves it to will clear the site, sell it off and make a fortune. Sorry, my mum's a real estate agent, she knows what everyone's properties are worth.' Properties, not homes.

'So they all try to keep her happy?' Alice said.

Nathan nodded. 'And they're all polite to one another, because great-grandmother expects everyone to get along. Pick a fight, not a fist fight, I mean start an argument or something, and you're in her black books for months.'

'And it just works out like that?'

'Mostly. As long as no one has too much to drink. Might want to stay away if they start cracking open too much wine. Not pretty.' He shot a glance back at the family gathered around the house, then got up, took their plates and headed back to the house. Alice turned to watch him go. At first, she had thought he was a bit dumb, but clearly there was more going on his head than just rugby. Interesting.

The cousin closest to Alice's age was Sean, he was Charlotte's brother. He had just finished high school and was going to be studying law. He didn't seem terribly interested in the subject, it sounded like something his parents were pushing him towards. They were both accountants, and, he said, thought law would be a good career choice. If his parents were making the career decisions in the family, Alice wondered what they would push Charlotte towards, and whether they would have any luck at all in getting her going in whatever direction they chose for her. Sean was gentle, easy-going, as relaxed as Charlotte was tightly wound. 'She's been like this since Mum and Dad got back together,' Sean said when Alice mentioned it. Their parents had separated for a couple of years and this was their first summer back together.

'Why?' Alice said. 'Are they fighting a lot?'

'No, nothing like that,' Sean said. 'I don't know what the story is, she's just determined to be awful.'

Thirteen was how old Alice was when Olivia was born. She remembered how invisible she had felt during the last weeks of Lindsay's pregnancy. Life was going to change for the second time, and she felt like she was still adjusting to the first change. She didn't particularly enjoy the first months after Olivia was born, too much crying, too many disgusting things she had been able to avoid thinking about before. Once Olivia became more interactive, Alice found it was actually pretty cool having a baby sister. But she had to work at it, not keeping to herself, making the effort to be part of the family in a new way. It was never going back to how it had been when it was just her and Lindsay, but when she thought about getting Olivia to laugh, watching her try new foods and how excited she got when someone said Dad was home, Alice decided things were actually pretty good.

Maybe it was like that for Charlotte. Things had changed and maybe she had become used to it. Then they had changed again. It would have been frustrating, and then, as her parents had separated once before, she was probably wondering if they would be doing it again.

'Must be confusing,' was all Alice said.

'Maybe,' Sean said. 'But that doesn't give her the right to make everyone miserable.'

'Looks more to me like she just wants to be left alone.'

'Yeah, well, Mum's determined to do the happy families thing, so that's not going to happen.'

Sean had brought along a card game called Monopoly Deal. Alice hadn't played it before, but it was easy enough to pick up and a good way to pass the time. At the end of each day, when the evening meal was over, Alice, Sean and Charlotte would sit and play hands. Nathan would always deal in, but had a tendency to be easily distracted, and most often ended up abandoning his hand, which went back into the bottom of the deck. It was still fun just the three of them, and by the end of their week together, Alice had exchanged cell numbers with them and connected on Instagram.

Andrew's wife Michelle was nice, if a bit overburdened with children. There were four of them, her half-brothers and half-sister. Alice had trouble thinking of them that way. Six months ago, she had only Olivia and Jack, now she had three times as many siblings and her life was starting to feel very crowded. The girl, Matilda, was the baby, she was only four, little enough for Alice to pick her up and carry her, for a short distance at least. At first, Matilda was shy with Alice, would barely say a word, but by the end of Alice's week there, Mattie was climbing onto her lap after dinner, telling her about her day. She noticed, also, that Mattie's acceptance of her was softening Michelle's attitude towards her.

Michelle and Andrew had met in Auckland, when he moved up there for work. Alice had met her a couple of times when she and Andrew first married, but Alice had been so young then that her memories were vague. When Alice had met Michelle and her half-brothers and sister after the September quake, Michelle had introduced Alice to them as their sister, which was nice, but she had been cool with Alice, as though she was unsure what space Alice could occupy in her family. She hadn't been nasty, but she would leave Andrew and Alice to talk rather than trying to join in the conversation. She wasn't sure how to read that, whether Michelle was just trying to give them space or deal with some lingering resentment of being reminded that she wasn't Andrew's first wife.

The three boys never seemed to stop long enough to have a conversation. They were like puppies, pushing each other around and wrestling. One day, Alice went with Andrew, Michelle and the children on a walk up a hill. The three boys, between eight and eleven years old, raced up the hill while Andrew, Michelle and Alice slogged their way up, Andrew carrying Mattie on his shoulders. Andrew was ahead of Michelle and Alice.

'How are you finding the family?' Michelle said.

'Different from my own,' Alice said. It seemed the most diplomatic answer, and she didn't want to get into discussing her own family's flaws as she had with Nathan a couple of nights earlier.

'Gerald and Sylvia are great,' Michelle said. 'They'll always do the right thing by you. But watch out for the others, they can be sharks.'

Alice didn't know what to say and her shock must have shown on her face.

'I'm sorry,' Michelle said. 'Just sometimes it bugs me that all they talk about is money, and the next deal, and how to make more money from all the money they already have.'

'They certainly talk about money a lot,' Alice agreed. 'My grandad says the more money people have, the more they have to worry about.'

'Well if worrying is indicated by talking, then they're all very worried,' Michelle said. She laughed. 'I'm sorry, they're not that bad, really, it's just that there's so many of them.'

'Your family is small?'

'Yes, it's just me and my brother.'

'Mum's family is pretty big, but most of them live outside Christchurch,' Alice said. 'Until a few years ago, it was just me and Mum a lot of the time, and I found it hard getting used to her getting married again, and then them having kids.'

'And now you have four more,' Michelle said. 'But at least they aren't all moving in with you.'

Alice didn't know how to reply. It was the most open Michelle had ever been with her, and she didn't want to say the wrong thing and end up shutting her down. 'I like them,' she said. 'Mattie reminds me of my sister Olivia. Olivia's a bit older, but this age is great.'

'She's taken a real shine to you,' Michelle said. 'I hope you'll be okay seeing more of them, because Mattie will need all the help she can get against those three.' She smiled at Alice, and for the first time, Alice felt welcome in Andrew's second family.

They had rounded the last bend and reached the final leg up towards the top of the hill. Andrew was ahead of them, just reaching the top, Mattie clinging on to his shoulders. They could hear the three boys, yelling and whooping, and found them at the top running around, chasing each other up and down the slopes, into and out of the scrub that lined the hill. Andrew was yelling at them to come back, but they weren't listening, they were off, like hounds after a rabbit. Andrew had put Mattie down and she ran towards Michelle and Alice. Michelle scooped her up into her arms and gave her a kiss. Alice walked over to where Andrew was surveying the view to the west, out over the lake and the mountains. He pointed out Mt Aspiring and asked if she skied. School trips only, she said, but she liked it.

'We do a family trip every winter, you'll have to come along. There's great skifields down here.'

Michelle came over and handed Mattie to Andrew. 'She's getting cranky,' she said. 'We'd better get back down and get these kids some lunch.' The boys' sharp hearing picked up the mention of food and they roared up the hillside and clustered around their parents, throwing out suggestions.

'We're going to go broke once all of these are in their teens,' Andrew said, and Michelle and Alice exchanged a look. Yes, there it was, money once again.

'I'll start down with Mattie,' Alice said. Andrew handed her the keys and Mattie climbed onto her back.

As she started off, she heard yelling, much louder than the boys had been a few minutes ago, mixed in with crying. She turned and looked back up the hill, where Andrew was trying to keep the two oldest boys apart as they flailed their arms at one another. The youngest had tucked himself up against Michelle and was crying. Whatever had gone on didn't matter, it had happened before and it would happen again. She turned and continued down the hill. There were definite advantages to having siblings you didn't live with.

12:51

February 2011

Alice had just crossed the road and was walking along the river towards Andrew's office when it started. The sound of the quake began only a moment before the shaking. Alice crouched down gracelessly, her bottom hitting the ground hard, and she put her arms over her head. Later she wasn't sure if she had gone down out of instinct or if she had been pushed down by the force of the shaking. It was violent, up and down, up and down, the roar overwhelming, and she couldn't hear anything but the quake and the sounds of buildings being shaken apart, the street breaking up. The cars parked on the road beside where she crouched were rocking back and forth, side-to-side.

The quake passed, the sound of it replaced with sirens and people shouting, some crying. The river roiled as silt started rising up from the force of the quake, and Alice stood up, her legs barely holding her up. She looked up to a nearby building, where people were starting to pour out, some crying, most desperately tapping at their phones or making calls, trying to get ahold of family. Across the river, a building had collapsed, awkwardly lopsided, and Alice could barely think about the implications, that there were people in there. What about the other buildings? Like the one Andrew worked in. It was hard to see, hazy, and she didn't understand why. She needed to pull herself together. She started to move towards Andrew's building but tripped on a crack in the pavement that hadn't been there moments ago, grazing the palms of her hands and dropping her phone, which skittered across the footpath. She retrieved it and started back along the road, too shaky to run. Her breathing was heavy and fast, and she tried to calm herself down, giving big, slow puffs. She wasn't calm enough to text, so shoved her phone deep into the pocket of her jeans.

Water was bubbling up from the street, thick and dark with silt. She remembered the sinkholes from the September quake and skirted the edges. There was an aftershock and she crouched down again, then told herself to stop it. There are always aftershocks, they're not as bad as the main quake. But then what was this? This was way worse than the September quake.

She saw Andrew coming out of the building and ran up to him, threw her arms around him.

'You're all right,' he said, and held her tight.

'Yes, I'm all right,' she said. She started to cry, and he held her, told her it would be all right.

'Text your mum,' he said. 'She'll be worried about you. But let's get away from the buildings.' He guided her back the way she had come, and across the river they could see the building that had collapsed, the top three or four stories pancaked, its central tower leaning to one side. She stopped to look across at the collapsed building when there was another big quake, the ground surging under their feet and all around them people screamed and buildings shook, chunks of brick, concrete and steel clattering. She didn't know whether to crouch down or run and just ended up half-crouched, walking in a circle. She felt Andrew beside her, the pressure of his arm across her back, moving her along the road and away from the disaster unfolding across the river.

They stopped in Victoria Square, which was full of people who had the same idea: stay away from the buildings. She tried calling her mother, but the network was overloaded, so she sent a text and hoped it would get through quickly. She needed to hear back, to quell her fear.

Andrew couldn't get a call through either, but he did receive a text from Michelle. She was fine, but the house was trashed, and she was going to pick up the kids. He texted back saying he was fine, but there was no answer, so he didn't know if his text had gone through. Aftershocks continued to roll through.

He had walked into the city that morning, he said. She had parked in the Farmers building, so they decided to go there so they would be able to get around, depending on the roads. But it was too dangerous to go into the building, a man outside said, and Alice and Andrew realised her car was no longer an option.

'You can come with me,' he said. 'It won't take me long to walk home, and we can see about getting you home from there.'

She shook her head. 'I haven't heard from Mum yet, I need to get home.'

They stood, not speaking. It was difficult to actually part ways, not knowing what would happen next. He nodded. 'Stay away from buildings,' he said. 'Walk down the middle of streets.'

'You, too,' she said. They said goodbye and that they loved each other, and then went off in the direction of home, Andrew to the north, and Alice to the southeast.

She felt like she was walking through a war zone, or as close to a war zone as someone living in this part of the world might experience without getting on a plane. Alarms continued to go off in buildings and shocked, scared people, some with cuts and many of them crying, were picking their way along the streets, keeping to the middle as much as they could, moving out of the way of cars moving slowly between the debris on each side of the street. Bricks, pieces of concrete and glass were everywhere, and the fronts of some buildings had fallen away completely, slumped onto the road, crushing cars. She could hear sirens in the distance and building alarms nearby, never stopping. Aftershocks caused dust to billow from buildings as they collapsed further.

She heard her name. It was Emma, whose parents lived down the road from Alice's family. They had been in school together, but had gone to different high schools and drifted apart. Emma had left school at sixteen and was now working in a bank. She was crying and hugged Alice tight. 'You're covered in dust,' Alice said, make a small effort at rubbing some off her.

'So are you,' Emma said.

Alice looked down at her clothes and saw Emma was right. She thought she could smell smoke.

Emma was living at home again since the September quake, she said, and that's where she was going now. Alice put her hand in Emma's and they started walking again.

At the intersection of Manchester and Lichfield, the red dome of the triangular building on the corner had come off and lay upside down in the middle of the street. Normally if she walked home from the city, she would go up High Street, but it was a mess, and a policeman was directing people to go up Manchester Street towards Moorhouse Avenue.

Before long, they were outside the CBD. Moorhouse Avenue was packed with vehicles moving so slowly that Alice and Emma were passing them. Two queues of traffic going towards the city parted way to let a ute through. A woman was walking forward, saying something to the drivers, and they all cooperated to make a third lane so the truck could pass through.

Alice and Emma walked past the stadium, where the ground was wet, covered in silt, gutters full of the stuff. Walking through Charleston was a strange experience, like the world had been twisted. There had been a lot of liquefaction here, water was still streaming in places, and houses lurched at strange angles. It was oddly quiet, very few people were moving around.

They crossed another main road, where traffic was heavy, moving slowly. But they noticed that drivers were being polite, letting cars turn in from the neighbourhood's roads.

Their street was covered in silt. They walked down towards their houses, looking to see what damage neighbouring houses had sustained. The further they went down the road, the more silt there was flowing out onto the road and down the gutters.

They reached Alice's house first, which looked shut up tight. There was a silt hump in the driveway, water bubbling up from the cracked surface. She asked Emma to come inside, but Emma had heard nothing from her family and was anxious to get home and see how they were. They said their goodbyes, hugging each other tight.

Alice had to shove the front door open, not because there was something behind it, but because it just didn't fit the frame any more. She left it open and inspected the house.

The power was off so she flicked the mains off at the switchboard to avoid a fire when it came back on. The house was a mess, worse than it had been the day of the September quake. The existing cracks were worse and more had joined them for company, although, thankfully, no plaster had actually fallen down. Everything in the kitchen was awry. The refrigerator and oven had shaken away from the walls and food from the pantry and the refrigerator lay on the floor, together with the shattered contents of the cupboards. There was a note on the whiteboard, from Lindsay, saying she was fine and that she had gone to pick up the kids. She was walking, the note said, the garage door was stuck. How long they would be?

Outside, the backyard had a layer of silt that might have been as deep as a foot. She had thought her days of digging silt were over after her stint in the student volunteer army in September, but if it was like this here, it must be way worse in the places that had liquefaction in September. Their chimney that had survived the September quake had cracked at the roofline and was hanging off the flue in one heavy piece. That would have to be taken down, Alice wasn't sure she would feel comfortable sleeping in the house if an aftershock could make that thing come through the roof. Then she thought about the physics of it and realised the real threat was to the neighbour's driveway, which would be blocked completely should the chimney come down.

Alice's phone had been fully charged when she went into the city, so she visited the Geonet page to see what the quake was. A 6.3, with its epicentre under the tunnel to Lyttelton. It had been nearly six months since the September quake, and the six magnitude aftershock people had waited for in those early weeks had finally come. Now they had the aftershocks of this monster to deal with, and there came another one, a rumble from the hills and then the shaking of the house. Everything that was broken in the kitchen clattered together. She wanted to know more and was tempted to visit the news sites, but she didn't know when power would be back on, so she resisted the urge.

It had been about an hour since the quake, probably more. Lindsay's note had given no indication as to when she had left to pick up the kids. Alice assumed it would have been right after the quake, so why wasn't she home by now? She decided to walk towards the school to see if she could find Lindsay there or on the way back. There were several ways Lindsay could go, Alice just had to pick the right one. She left her own note on the whiteboard, forced the front door shut once again and locked up.

At the end of the street by the river, the liquefaction was much worse. A sinkhole had opened and claimed four cars. Three men were pulling one of them out. An idiot had decided to do donuts on the silty water coming up from the street, they told her, and the road had collapsed out from under him. They were going to extract their own cars, but would leave the idiot's as it was, tilting precariously on the edge of the gaping hole.

She picked her way along the footpath until she reached the river, then walked along the river to Olivia's school. Parents were hurrying their children into cars and the teachers looked stressed. Alice found Olivia's teacher, who said that Lindsay had picked Olivia up about twenty minutes earlier and she was then going to pick up Jack. His kindy was further towards the hills and Alice ran there, hoping she would be able to catch up, but she had missed them and there were at least three different ways they could have headed back home from the kindy.

Alice couldn't decide what to do. Her grandparents, Lindsay's parents, lived about two kilometres away, and she could go there, but there was no guarantee they would be there. She decided to walk back home but stopped by to see Marjorie, as the way home went past her house. Marjorie was sitting outside in the garden, on a seat looking out over the stream, sipping a cup of tea.

'You have power?' Alice said.

'No, dear, I had a jug full of water and a little gas burner your grandfather set up after the first quake. Would you like a cup? A cup of tea is always good for the nerves.'

As if to reinforce Marjorie's offer, a boom sounded in the distance, then rumbling from the hills became louder and louder until the ground started shaking and they could see the ground rolling. She was glad they were outside, away from anything that could fall on them. Marjorie was strangely calm, and Alice suspected the poor woman might be utterly terrified.

Alice accepted the offer and went inside to help Marjorie get the gas burner on. She told Marjorie about the city, that Andrew was fine and had been walking home to his family when she last saw him. Marjorie hadn't heard from anyone.

It didn't take long to boil the water for a single cup of tea, and Marjorie topped up her own with more hot water. Marjorie's kitchen wasn't terribly messy, she had been using bungee cords to keep her cupboards shut since the first quake, and looking closely, Alice noticed that the ornaments in Marjorie's lounge were blu-tacked to the shelving. Still, furniture had been shaken out of place and there were some cracks in the plaster that Alice hadn't noticed the last time she was there. In fact, she had been impressed then at how well the place had fared.

They sat out in the garden sipping their cups of tea while quakes continued to roll through.

'There's a radio in the third kitchen drawer,' Marjorie said. 'There are batteries in the drawer too. I was going to put them in, but I couldn't get my fingers to work.'

Alice brought the radio outside and tuned it to National Radio. A report said there had been deaths and building collapses, fires and people trapped in buildings. It was very bad. The cellphone network was running on backup power and people were asked to use it sparingly. Alice texted her mother to say where she was, giving the address.

They were listening to the mayor saying the communities on Banks Peninsula hadn't been heard from when one of Marjorie's grandsons arrived, Tony. Alice had only met him a couple of times and their conversations had been brief.

'Grandmother,' Tony said. There was no hug, no kisses. 'Alison, isn't it?' he said, turning to Alice.

'Alice,' she said. The way he had said it made her think he knew perfectly well what her name was.

Tony had been working during the quake, he said, and had made it home to check on his family, who were all fine, just scared. He was on his way out to the seaside suburb of Redcliffs, to check on his mother. Tony said he wanted Marjorie to go with him, then go back to his house along with his mother. They shouldn't be alone for a night that was bound to be full of aftershocks.

'I won't be going anywhere,' Marjorie said. 'I can stay here, and Alice has already said she'll stay with me.'

Alice quickly turned to look at Marjorie, whose eyes innocently reinforced the lie that had just come out of her mouth.

There was some discussion over whether Alice should go home to 'her own family', which Alice resented Tony saying, she was part of their family, too. She decided to play along with Marjorie's lie. 'Our house is too dangerous to stay in tonight,' Alice said. 'The chimney has cracked and could come through the roof in an aftershock. We'll have to see to that before we can sleep there.'

Marjorie smiled at Tony, satisfied that the argument had been won. Tony checked Marjorie's emergency supplies and said he would be back in the morning.

'Don't worry about me, dear,' Marjorie said once Tony had left. 'I'll be fine here on my own. I just don't like the idea of all the tears and hysteria. Tony's wife is high-strung, like that wife of Andrew's.'

To Alice that seemed a bit unfair. Yes, Michelle could be tense, but she relaxed once you got to know her. It was probably the tension that was making Marjorie snap, be unkind. 'I can stay,' Alice said. 'And I'd prefer to, since I've said to Tony that I would.'

Marjorie was quiet a moment. 'I think I'd like that.'

Alice was going to walk home and see if her family were there, then she would collect some things and come back to Marjorie's for the night. When Marjorie learned that Alice's car was stuck in the city, she insisted that Alice take hers. She wouldn't be going anywhere, she said, and even if she wanted to, the thought of what the roads were like would quickly change her mind.

Alice drove Marjorie's Suzuki Swift slowly, uncertain of what damage there had been to the road. The main roads were still nuts and Alice crawled along. She had the radio on, reports said people had died, 'multiple fatalities', including some from buildings falling on buses. Alice remembered enough from discussions about earthquake engineering at university to think that should not have happened, and she wondered why a building that dangerous hadn't been caught in the checks after the September quake. But this quake had been so incredibly strong, were 6.3 quakes supposed to be like that? Could any building withstand that?

Power was out for most people, and phones were down. People were being told to get out of the central city and Civil Defence had declared the highest level of disaster. There was another strong quake as she crossed the railway lines, and she felt the car lift up, then the wave passed and the cars in front of her rose up, then sank back down. Freaky.

She thought about Marjorie's calm. She knew there was fear lying beneath it, could see that in the way she was so anxious to not be at her grandson's house. Maybe she should try to talk Marjorie into going and staying with someone. Maybe she could stay with Gerald and Sylvia, Andrew's parents.

Lindsay and Kevin were home, along with Olivia and Jack, who threw themselves into Alice's arms, telling her how scary it was during the quake. Lindsay and Kevin were packing. They were going to stay with Kevin's brother in Timaru, they didn't want to keep the kids here with no water, no power and no indication as to when they would be back on. Lindsay's parents and grandparents were okay, but were going out to stay with Lindsay's auntie in Amberley, north of the city and well away from the disaster of the quake. Lindsay's sister Sonya and her kids were going to Dunedin to stay with Sonya's ex-husband. That would be uncomfortable, but was preferable to staying in the city. Jason and Carla were taking Carla's mother to stay with relatives outside the city. Was anyone staying?

'How long will you be?' Alice asked.

Lindsay stopped what she was doing. 'You're coming with us, aren't you?'

Alice didn't know what to say, it hadn't occurred to her that they would leave, but given the lack of power and water, it made sense. 'I went to see Marjorie,' she said. 'I said I would stay with her. Tonight at least. She'll be alone otherwise. And then there's uni.' University had started for the year just the day before, she was supposed to go to a lecture after lunch with Andrew, and her books, that she had paid so much for, were now stuck in her car in the city. When would she get her car back? Would she? Did it matter, given that people had died? She started crying and shaking, and Lindsay hugged and shushed her.

'It's all right,' Lindsay said. 'It's going to be all right.'

'I'd offer you a cup of tea,' Kevin said, 'but I'd have to dig the barbecue out of the garage, and there's quite a few things in the way of it.'

Alice sniffed and wiped her eyes. 'It's ok,' she said. 'I had one before. It didn't really help.'

'There's no water, Alice,' Kevin said, 'and that means no toilets. We don't know how long until it's back on.'

Alice didn't want to leave Marjorie by herself, but she also understood their concerns. She didn't think she could talk the old lady into leaving her house, but maybe a night of aftershocks would make a difference. They agreed that if things got too bad, Alice was to ignore Marjorie's objections and pack her and her things into the car and take her down to Timaru to meet up with them. They would make contact with Marjorie's family from there and sort things out.

'Look at us plotting a kidnapping,' Alice pointed out.

'Civil Defence emergency,' Kevin said. 'It's allowed.'

Kevin's van was packed, and he had packed their own household emergency supplies into Marjorie's car: water, batteries, torches and plenty of food. They said their goodbyes. Lindsay grabbed her phone charger out of her own car and gave it and her phone to Alice. 'Text me on Kevin's,' she said. 'I'll text you when we get there.'

Marjorie and Alice prepared a cold dinner from the perishables in the fridge. Everything from the freezer would probably be defrosted by morning, and Alice thought about cooking it. If she was still here in a couple of days' time and the power wasn't back on, she might have to go back home and extract the barbecue from the garage.

Lindsay texted when they arrived in Timaru. It had taken them close to four hours for what was normally a two hour trip. The traffic flowing out of Christchurch had been heavy, Lindsay said, people carrying trailers stacked with stuff. People were evacuating. It was like the apocalypse.

Alice had a restless night in the double bed in Marjorie's spare bedroom. There were aftershocks through the night. Just as she felt herself drifting off to sleep from the last aftershock, there would be another. There was another sound as well, one she would come to find oddly comforting in the days that followed, the sound of helicopters flying over the hills. It meant there was still a world outside the city, that not everything was broken.

There were two toilets in the house and before going to bed, Alice and Marjorie had agreed to use one each, only for peeing, which they figured they could get away with for a day or two, whatever the condition of the pipes might be. They would have to dig a hole in the yard to use as a makeshift toilet, which Alice would do in the morning. Now that was a discussion Alice had never expected to have with anyone, much less a tiny ninety-year old woman. But, as Marjorie said, she had been a nurse in the war and she had seen it all.

Alice woke to a big aftershock. She felt like she had only just fallen asleep, unrested and weary. She powered up her phone and saw that it was only six o'clock. She lay there staring at the unfamiliar ceiling, trying to remember what it felt like to be refreshed and rested. She wondered what the day ahead held. More big quakes? Would there be power? Water?

Another aftershock prompted her to get out of bed. She decided to go for a walk, maybe even run, she had the right clothes and shoes and it would do her good to just try to relax and get her head in a better place for tackling the day.

Apart from the aftershocks the house was quiet, and Alice went out through the back door, closing it softly and locking it with the spare set of keys Marjorie had given her last night.

It was cool outside and Alice picked up her pace to warm up. There was a park just a few hundred metres from Marjorie's house and there was no one around but Alice. It was still dark, but the sun was starting to come up in the east, colouring the sky pink and orange. She headed along the track towards the river, the bulk of the hills dark against the navy blue sky, the same hills that yesterday had caused the deaths of at least a hundred people. She picked up her pace to a slow jog, then when she got to the river she sprinted, watching out for cracks in the footpath. She ran until she felt her heart pounding, her breathing heavy, then pushed herself further, to stop herself from crying. She reached Opawa Road, where she stopped, leaning on the bridge, and she started crying, gasping for breath and trying to make sense of the deaths of so many people.

Insomnia

March 2011

In the days after the big quake, scientists talked about what they called 'seismic lensing'. The quake's epicentre had been under the Port Hills, which are made of hard volcanic rock. Seismic waves had reflected off these hard rocks, intensifying them. The shape of the hills had then focussed the seismic waves, directing them north towards the city, magnifying the quake's destructive power.

The electricity had come on at Marjorie's the day after the big quake and water was back on the day after that, on the Thursday. Kevin had come up from Timaru on Thursday, bringing petrol and more water. He and Alice went back to their house to check it over, but there was still no water, so they were limited about what they could do. He had asked Alice to go back to Timaru with him, but she said she was doing fine, that she wanted to join the student volunteer army helping in the suburbs. Kevin packed more of the family's belongings into the van and headed back down to Timaru.

Now, nearly three weeks later, Marjorie had cooked dinner and they ate while watching the news. Marjorie was an excellent cook and it was only the exercise Alice was getting every day as part of the student volunteer army that meant she wasn't packing on the weight. The first few days she had been shovelling silt, but now it was deliveries, running all over town making sure people had food, water and other supplies. It was easier getting petrol now, not like the Mad Max days just after the quake.

The city had been cordoned off all the way out to the four avenues that framed the CBD, and the military was manning the cordon. What was even stranger than seeing the New Zealand military on the cordons was seeing soldiers from another country, Singapore. There were also light armoured vehicles patrolling the streets inside the cordon. Outside the cordon, helicopters patrolled the suburbs to deter looters. There were comments on Facebook saying that looters should be arrested and locked up in the Grand Chancellor, a hotel that was one of the tallest buildings in the city and thought to be in imminent danger of collapsing. Driving towards the city down Ferry Road, Alice could see the Grand Chancellor, which had slumped in one corner, like a giant that had been punched and fallen down on one knee. It was disturbing, when driving out of the city, she would see it in her rearview mirror when she checked the traffic behind her. It was like a stone angel from *Doctor Who*, sneaking up on her when she wasn't looking, waiting for her to blink so it could advance towards her, catching her to drain her of all her energy. What energy? She needed more sleep.

It was Friday night now, and she had the weekend to try to catch up on her sleep and get ready for the resumption of lectures on Monday. A lot of buildings still needed to be checked, but marquees had been set up for lectures and some local businesses were letting the university use their meeting rooms. She would try to wind down a bit over the weekend, and maybe go down to Timaru on Sunday. Lindsay and Kevin were still there, and her old flatmate Ben had been in touch as well. Last year had been his final year, so there was no need for him to come back up to Christchurch and experience the whole tent city thing.

For ninety years old, Marjorie was doing well. It was the Blitz, she told Alice whenever Alice brought it up, going through something like that, you never forgot the experience, so you always knew how to make do. Most of Marjorie's family had left the city. Those with little kids were worried about providing them some stability, and Andrew and Michelle were staying at their holiday house in Wanaka and had already enrolled their kids in a school there. They intended to stay for at least a term. Gerald and Sylvia were in Sydney, staying with Laurel, Andrew's younger sister. Their house on the hill was a mess, the roof tiles were all askew, and the day after the quake Gerald and Andrew had strapped blue tarpaulins over it to stop too much rain from getting in. The winds had been heavy and the tarpaulin wouldn't necessarily do a good job for long, but given the state of the place inside, Gerald said he wasn't sure it mattered. Gerald had signed up to Facebook and had told Alice that Sylvia didn't want to go back to Christchurch. Alice wondered how many other people were feeling that way.

Neil and Heather, Alice's other grandparents, were all right, but their house was damaged and it didn't seem like they would have water for a while. They had moved in with Heather's parents, whose house had new cracks and more liquefaction in the yard, but it was liveable. Lindsay's brother and his wife had lost their house, it had been badly damaged by liquefaction in the September quake, but this quake was much worse. The house had slumped so much it was difficult to walk around in. Jason and Carla had retrieved some clothes and were staying with Carla's mother in her damaged but liveable house north of the city. It was like that everywhere, families doubling up, picking the most liveable house and making do.

But a lot of people had left the city and the streets were empty. The jammed roads and crazy traffic of the day of the quake had given way to a few cars kicking up dust on the damaged, rumpled roads. Some roads were particularly bad. Going along Aldwins Road towards Eastgate Mall was like a rollercoaster, a huge hump in one lane changed into a dip, while the adjacent lane did the opposite. Around the city, roadworkers were starting to smooth out the silt humps, but given how many there were it would take a long time. It was dusty when the wind picked up, and the army guys on the cordon had to wear dust masks some days. Other days, when it rained, gutters full of silt backed up, flooding streets.

Before the quake, this big quake, not the September one, Alice had been a nervous driver, staying on her learner's licence for two years, only gaining her restricted licence just before she started at university. Now, though, she was used to driving over bumps and into dips and keeping a close eye on following traffic in case she had to dodge an especially large dip or pothole.

Dinner was finished and they were washing the dishes. Marjorie had a dishwasher, but everyone was still conserving water, so they were doing dishes in the sink using as little water as possible. Marjorie boiled the jug and made cups of tea and they sat back down in the lounge to watch Campbell Live. Alice felt herself slipping off to sleep, in spite of the hot cup of tea in her hands, when it was announced there had been a big quake off the coast of Japan, a 7.9. There was a clip of the Tokyo skyline, buildings swaying.

'That doesn't look nearly as bad as what we had,' Marjorie said. 'I think I'd be all right with just a bit of swaying.'

There was footage of a newsroom, which showed some juddery shaking, but nothing as bad as they remembered from the 22nd of February.

'It's far away,' Alice said, 'and they're built for it.' She felt callous for just dismissing it that way, but she was thinking of the collapsed CTV building. She had heard from someone in the student army that the Japanese search and rescue workers who had come to Christchurch were saying that the deaths in Christchurch were from a manmade disaster, not a natural one. She had told Marjorie that, and Marjorie said she heard on the radio that the media in Japan were asking a lot of questions, especially since so many Japanese students had died.

They kept watching, long after their tea had grown cold, as footage showed a black, oily-looking tide full of debris advancing across coastal towns, picking up everything in its path. The quake had been upgraded to an 8.9, a monster. Alice remembered the Indian Ocean tsunami when she was 12 or 13. What she remembered the most about it was going to bed with the death toll at a few thousand, then waking up the next morning to hear it had gone over 100,000. Sure, the Japanese could build super-strong buildings that could withstand an enormous quake, but what could you do about a tsunami?

Although she was exhausted when she went to bed at ten o'clock, she couldn't sleep. She was waiting for another quake, it had become like she needed one before she could feel the day was over and she could drop off. It was well after two o'clock when one finally came through, and by then Alice could feel her head tightening with a headache that she hoped wouldn't still be there in the morning. The house stopped shaking and the rumbling faded into the distance. She could hear Marjorie down the hallway, snoring lightly, and then Alice finally slipped into sleep.

The sun was shining brightly through the gap between the curtains when she woke up. Saturday. Stay away from the internet, she told herself, she didn't want to know, yet, how many people had died.

She could smell baking. She wandered through to the kitchen, where Marjorie was pulling a batch of scones out of the oven. It was eleven o'clock.

'I left you to sleep in,' Marjorie said. 'And I thought scones would be nice for a late breakfast.' There was a bowl of whipped cream on the dining table, along with a big slab of butter and two types of jam. Alice smiled. Marjorie was old-school food-wise, none of this low-fat eating. Milk was full fat and there was no cutting the fat off meat in her house. Alice would go for a run afterwards, to work some of it off. Marjorie was going to spend the day in the garden, she said. They had been eating Marjorie's summer vegetables, which were getting scarce, and so Alice would have to go to the supermarket today. A supermarket. The nearby one was a wreck, fenced off and silt all through the carpark. One of the few remaining neighbours said it was a write-off and would be demolished. The nearest supermarket was in the city on Moorhouse Avenue, just on the edge of the red zone. Later Alice would go and wander the aisles along with the rest of the walking dead, seeking fresh vegetables and other supplies.

After her late breakfast, Alice went for a run, following the river, looking at the damage to houses. She needed to go back to Lindsay and Kevin's and check that it was all right. There had been looters in the suburbs, breaking into houses and stealing valuables, including appliances and hot water cylinders. Scum. She would go over to the house later, in the car, on the way back from the supermarket.

There were two dairies near Marjorie's house, but both were in bad shape, brick buildings with a lot of damage, one with a partially-collapsed canopy. Both were fenced off. Further down the road, there were cars parked in front of the tiny mall, which housed about half a dozen shops. There was a café down the back, could it be open for business? There was also a doctor's office, but Alice didn't think there would be so much traffic for that. Proper coffee! Alice had been to that café before, she came in occasionally and they had good coffee, baking done on the premises. But it had never done great business, tucked at the back of a row of shops on a low-traffic suburban road. Alice checked her jacket pockets and found a ten dollar note.

The café was full of people, more than Alice had seen in the rest of the suburb on her walk. It was like normal life in here, except all the people looked worn out, some with crazy hair. Some of the women wore no makeup, one had made an attempt and really shouldn't have, the dark line of her eyeliner was shaky and broken along both eyes. But Alice couldn't blame her for trying to do something to feel normal again.

She ordered a triple shot long black, to go, because there were so many people there Alice didn't stand a chance of getting a seat. While she waited, she asked the owner, who was working the till, how it was they were still open. The building had no damage, she said, and once they had the power and water back on, there was no reason they couldn't open up.

'Business is good!' Alice said, trying to contain her excitement. Maybe caffeine wasn't a good idea. But it would be normal to have a long black, and after everything that had happened in the last two weeks and watching the footage of that tsunami coming ashore the night before, Alice desperately needed to do something normal.

'A little too good,' the woman said, wiping a stray bit of hair away from her forehead. 'If you know anyone who wants a job, tell them to come see me.' She handed Alice her coffee.

'I will,' Alice said. She walked home, sipping what she thought was the most delicious coffee she had ever tasted.

Poos

April 2011

They had their very own portaloo, on the grass verge right in front of the house. Lindsay had always avoided the things when they went to the fireworks displays held in the Botanic Gardens or the annual agricultural show day. But now, there it was, right there, every time she went up the driveway or looked out the front window. Another reason to go back to Timaru.

The first reason to go back was that they weren't going to get any action on their logburner for at least a month, and April was certainly having its cold, wet days. Kevin had demolished the top part of the chimney after the February quake, taking it down to the roofline and leaving a pile of red bricks alongside the house. Oh well, might be useful in the garden, should she ever be interested in working in the garden again. They still hadn't done anything about the silt that had filled the back of the garden, it was about half a metre deep along the fenceline, and on the opposite side of the fence, in the neighbour's driveway, there was an enormous hump that the poor guy had to drive over to get onto his property. He was well into his seventies, and his house was badly damaged. It had slumped from the liquefaction, and Lindsay didn't think he should be living there. No, he had told her, he wasn't leaving. He had lived in that house for fifty years, no earthquake was going to chuck him out.

The logburner. The Government had a programme in place, fast-tracking heating for damaged houses. She had called EQC the first time she was in Christchurch after the quake and someone had come out to take a look at their logburner to measure up its replacement and to try and talk her into a heat pump instead. They would only have to wait two weeks, instead of six, the guy said. But what happened if the power went out in winter? There had already been power cuts in different parts of town, it would only get worse in winter as the subtle damage to the electricity network became apparent under heavier loads. And if they got a heat pump, what would they do with all their firewood? They had ordered a load last spring, when prices were cheaper, which is what they did every year, and if they replaced the woodburner with a heat pump, all that wood would just sit there, along with the silt in the backyard, doing what exactly?

Lindsay desperately wanted to wash the dust off the house. A lot of silt had been dug out of properties – not their silt, of course, but a lot of other people's silt – and the City Council had taken it away, but there was still enough drifting around to make a mess. The stuff was everywhere, roads, cars, buildings. The cat was leaving silty deposits wherever he sat, despite Lindsay's best efforts to keep him brushed and clean.

There was no point washing the house or the car because both would quickly be dusty again. The night before, Alice had shown her a video of some teenage boys skateboarding in the city. It ended with a shot of a lone skateboarder drifting down the centre of an empty city street, dust blowing up around him. The first shot had made Lindsay start to cry. It was the old brick buildings in Woolston, she loved those buildings, had always hoped someone would do something with them, make them a proper retail area. But that wouldn't happen now, it was obvious they were past rescuing. In another shot, skateboarders were jumping the cracks along Fitzgerald Avenue, where the northbound lanes had slumped towards the river. One of them hit a crack and came off, falling into the crack, which was deeper than he was tall. The abandoned, damaged city was certainly a skateboarder's paradise, and she admired the fact they were getting out and exploring. She was too afraid to go near the city, to have a proper look at it. The thought made her start to cry, and she didn't want that, she was afraid she wouldn't be able to stop. She had lived in Christchurch all of her life and all the places familiar to her weren't there any more. But in her mind, they still existed. To go and see their gone-ness would just be so final, it would make everything real. She wished she could be 'resilient', a word she was hearing far too much of. Those skateboarders, now they were resilient, adapting to how the place was, rather than being like her and missing something that could never be put back.

There was also no point wanting to wash the house or water the car or the garden because there were water restrictions. It was still unclear what the earthquake had done to the city's aquifers, whether they were being polluted by sewage leaking from broken pipes, and everyone was being asked to conserve water. So no car washing or garden watering. It had annoyed her to see a neighbour a few doors down washing his car, even leaving the hose running as he soaped it up. She wanted to get in his face and tell him how inconsiderate he was being, not thinking about anyone around him and the fact that they, too, would like to wash their cars and houses, water their gardens and just enjoy a little bit of normality. She hadn't, and it scared her that what had stopped her was that she had Jack with her. She didn't want to be that type of person, who took their frustrations out on everyone unfortunate enough to be in her way. She needed to get away. But she had been back less than a week. And if she did go, she wouldn't want to come back.

Lindsay and Kevin had discussed staying in Timaru, enrolling the kids in school there. Even if Kevin's current jobs had been interrupted, they would need to be completed eventually. Things were starting to happen repair-wise and soon there would be more work. Kevin needed to be in Christchurch for that. She didn't want to be away from him, she would miss him, and the kids would miss him. And now that they were back in Christchurch, Alice had come home. Alice had come home! She had missed her baby so much, and so much was going on with her. Ben for one thing. And she had decided not to go back to university, to leave it for a year or so and see about work, earning some money. When Lindsay pointed out that a lot of people had lost their jobs because of the damage in the city, Alice told her she already had a job, she was working at a nearby café. There was an open café? They should go!

Lindsay was easily distracted. Alice quickly got her back on track, saying she would be able to help with the kids. Lindsay was doing a lot of paperwork related to the damage to the house, and she needed the extra support, Alice said. That was true. Plaster cracks subjected to repeated earthquakes continued to shed powder. She considered duct taping them up, but then couldn't be bothered because there was no duct tape and she would have to go to the supermarket, but then she remembered she hadn't been able to find duct tape the last time she went looking for it in a supermarket, and so she would need to go to a hardware store to get some and she couldn't think where there was a hardware store that was open, that still existed.

So there they were, living in a broken house with broken pipes, three adults and two little kids, one who they had struggled to toilet train just two years earlier. Olivia and Jack didn't like the portaloo idea at all, even if it was right in front of their house. Lindsay wondered how people with kids coped when the portaloo was several houses a way, especially little ones who sometimes don't plan their toileting all that well.

'The pipes take our poos away and make sure they can't make anything dirty,' she explained. 'But they're too broken for us to use.' 'But the toilet flushes,' Jack said. 'And the poos go away.' 'It might be going, I don't know, to a bad place.' A bad place? Really? She didn't want to have to explain sewerage backing up, flowing on people's sections. She tried again. 'The pipes are broken and the poos could get into the river and kill all the fish.'

'There aren't any fish in the river,' Jack said. 'Alice told me that. She said the river is so dirty from all the businesses that hardly anything can live in it and that's why we never see any fish.'

Lindsay shot the filthiest look she could manage at Alice, which, given her state of mind, was probably pretty bad. Alice just raised a single eyebrow. Lindsay remembered the first time she had done that, when she was just three weeks old and feeding, the way Alice had looked up at her and cocked her tiny little eyebrow. She had inherited that from her father. Lindsay had never been able to master the eyebrow cock and felt, sometimes, like something was missing from her emotional repertoire because she couldn't master that single querying mannerism. As a baby, the eyebrow cock had been sweet, but now it was infuriating. How dare Alice try to foster a sense of environmental awareness and responsibility in her children? Why had she left university? Why was she working in a coffee shop? They hadn't had that conversation properly yet, Lindsay had been distracted by... something.

The portaloo was fine during the day. Mostly. Hot days were smelly days, even if the loo had been pumped out just that morning, and there was one day, their second day back, when Lindsay found herself lurching out of the portaloo retching, the combination of the smell and the heat so overwhelming that she hadn't bothered to properly zip up her pants and just stumbled up the driveway and back into the house.

Fortunately, Olivia was back at school, so that was one less portaloo-averse person for her to worry about during the day. But there was no way she was going to expect her kids to go out to the portaloo at night.

For nights, there was the chemical toilet. The City Council had distributed chemical toilets free of charge to parts of the city that had badly damaged pipes. But with three adults and two children in the house, the chemical toilet filled up quickly and had to be emptied at the poo tank that had been installed down the road, about twenty houses away. There were chest-high poo tanks dotted all over the neighbourhood and sucker trucks coming around regularly to empty them.

Kevin emptied the chemical toilet every night when he came home, before getting in the shower. Because he truly believed in hygiene, he had a set of protective clothing just for that job. He put on his wet weather gear: raincoat, waterproof pants, gumboots and elbow-length plastic gloves, spread a tarpaulin set aside specifically for the chemical toilet in the back of his van and carried the chemical toilet out to the van. He drove down to the poo tank and emptied the toilet, then drove home, restored the chemical toilet to its rightful place in front of The Toilet That Should Not Be Used and proceeded to soak his raincoat, his pants and his elbow-length gloves in a dilute bleach solution. So that they would not get gastroenteritis. Then he would get in the shower. Each morning, before he went to work, he would take his raincoat, his waterproof pants and his elbow-length gloves out of the laundry sink and leave them on the clothesline to dry during the day so he was ready to repeat the whole process again when he came home from work. Lindsay thought he was being over the top. But, he argued, no one in the family was getting sick, so it was working. She hadn't heard of mass gastro outbreaks elsewhere in the city due to poor chemical toilet hygiene, but she decided it was best to keep silent on that.

The chemical toilets were just camping toilets, and it seemed the City Council had cornered the market on them, buying up every available chemical toilet In The World and distributing them, free of charge, to certain parts of Christchurch. Sachets for treating the contents of the toilet were being distributed regularly so that households could treat their own waste. Lovely. And they were lovely, the blue crystals in the sachets were an intense blue, like that of a Ceylon sapphire.

Lindsay needed to sort out Jack's bedroom. The walls had been damaged, there were so many cracks along them that she and Kevin wondered what the room was trying to spell out, what message it was trying to deliver. Leave Christchurch? The plaster in the closet was cracked and crumbling, coming loose and was all over the place, on Jack's clothes and in his shoes. She hoped she would be able to rescue them. The shoes, maybe, but she didn't think she could ever wash the clothes enough to feel they were free of plaster dust. She hated the way the stuff felt on her skin, like it was sucking the moisture out, and she didn't want to take a chance on leaving enough embedded in Jack's clothes that it irritated his skin. Jack was sleeping in the second bed in Olivia's room and they were niggling at each other, in spite of the fact that they had been just fine sharing a room in Timaru for the last few weeks. But now that they were home, they were getting territorial with one another. She could hear them arguing with each other over what they were going to watch on TV, then Alice interrupting them and making them watch her pick. That was *Finding Nemo*, which she had loved as a kid, and both Olivia and Jack loved it too. But then they were arguing over who got to sit where, and so Alice separated them, one to either side.

It was warm outside, so she opened the window to air the room out, which took more than a little effort, and she had to be careful, she didn't want to break the frame or the glass, because then she would have to get a glazier in and that would be just another thing on the list of things that needed to be done. The windows were tending to stick on that side of the house, and Lindsay worried if that meant the frames had been twisted. Did that mean there were problems with the foundations? Kevin hadn't said, but there were a lot of things he wasn't saying about the state of the house. She wished he would just tell her, the worrying about what might be was getting to her. If it was bad, at least she would know, and be able to deal with it. After all, they had insurance, if the house was so badly damaged that it needed to be rebuilt, the insurance would take care of all that, as well as where they would live while the house was being rebuilt. But they hadn't yet been assessed and didn't know if they would be going over the EQC's $100,000 cap.

It was a dry day, so Lindsay stripped Jack's bedding, threw the sheets and duvet cover in the washing machine and put the duvet inner and pillows on the washing line to air out, careful to keep them away from Kevin's toilet emptying gear. She pulled the red rubbish bin up alongside the open window of Jack's bedroom to make it easier to toss out the rubbish. It was heavy, all that broken plaster, and with the exposed laths Jack wouldn't be able to use the closet, so she used a bungee cord to tie the doors shut. She vacuumed the floor and wiped down the walls, which resulted in the room smelling much less dusty, but she really wanted to air it another couple of days, then give it a good vacuum again before setting it back up for Jack.

From the lounge, she heard the end of *Finding Nemo*, then some music. She checked in on the three of them. Alice was playing videos off YouTube on the laptop, just funny things that were making Olivia and Jack laugh.

'We're going to go for a walk,' Alice said. 'Just down to the river, then I'll come back and make dinner.'

Lindsay said that would be fine, just to make sure they all had jackets on and to be back in time for dinner. Lindsay went outside to bring all of Jack's bedding back in and was distracted by the state of the garden. It would do her good to put in a few minutes pulling out the weeds she could see from the kitchen window. A few minutes turned in to half an hour and she had cleared the beds at the back of the house, which she couldn't actually see from the kitchen window but that she always thought about. Because they were right there, under the window she was looking out of. She went out to the washing line and grabbed the washing.

If Alice wasn't home, Lindsay didn't know what she would do, trying to keep up with the house, the kids, the paperwork and the sheer exhaustion. She would be struggling to cook, that was for certain, and resorting to takeaways.

Cooking was pretty much Alice's thing now, she had learned a lot from her great-grandmother in the weeks she had stayed with the old woman. Lindsay had always found the great-grandmother aloof and disapproving, and Andrew had been almost frightened by his grandmother, at the very least, intimidated. But Alice and the old woman had clicked, and Lindsay wasn't sure if she felt comfortable about that. There was something cunning about her, and Lindsay didn't want Alice to pick that up, or be exploited by it.

Alice had become especially good at vegetables, roasting them or braising them in stock and butter. Lindsay had never eaten such flavourful vegetables, and even Olivia and Jack were getting better at eating their veggies. Lindsay had never been much of a cook, she was too busy trying to work and raise Alice and then, when she married Kevin, keep the house going while also taking on the books for Kevin's company. So she hadn't had any skills to pass on to Alice, for which she felt negligent, but she was too tired to dwell on it for long, she had things to do. There was always something more to do.

The logburner for instance. Damn. It was nearly five o'clock, she needed to get on to that today, to find out when they would be able to heat the house properly. It was supposed to take only six weeks and it had been more than that. She found the paperwork and dialled the number.

After being passed around to two different organisations, Lindsay still didn't have an answer. The second man she talked to took her number and said he would check it out in the morning and call her back. She hung up, then realised she didn't have his name, so she couldn't follow up if he didn't ring her back. Damn. She would have to start again in the morning.

The phone rang again. Hopefully it was the guy, calling back to make sure she had his name and number. But no, it was the police, calling for Alice. Her car had been retrieved from the carpark building she had left it in on the day of the February quake, she would need to bring proof of ownership and ID to get it back. Well it was something.

After dinner, Lindsay put Olivia and Jack to bed in Olivia's room for what she hoped would be the last time. Tomorrow she would air and vacuum Jack's bedroom once again and set it up for him, his books on the shelves, and she would get some crates to stack his toys in. Maybe one of the supermarkets in the city would have something. She hoped so, because there really wasn't anywhere else to try, unless she wanted to drive north to Rangiora or south to Ashburton.

Alice was in the kitchen, putting aside a plate for Kevin and putting it into the oven, which she turned on to low. He was having to go out of the city for work, nothing was happening nearby. He was on a job near Rangiora today. Maybe Lindsay could ask him to go to The Warehouse out there, or the Farmers, find something for Jack's room. She hoped he would be home soon, there was still the chemical toilet business to go through and all the cleaning up after that. So much to do, all the time.

'Why does Jack want to learn how to skateboard?' Lindsay asked Alice.

Alice laughed. 'I showed him that video,' she said.

'He said he wants to take his scooter down the driveway next door, see if he can jump the hump,' Lindsay said.

They both started laughing, then Lindsay pictured tiny little Jack coming off his scooter and disappearing into a crack. She burst into tears. Alice put her arms around her, and Lindsay started really crying, sobbing, feeling her nose blocking up, her sinuses swelling. She would have to stop, but she couldn't seem to.

Kevin's van pulled up, and Lindsay and Alice tried to pull themselves together, but when he came inside, he could see Lindsay had been crying.

'What's happened?' he said.

'Jack wants to learn how to skateboard,' Lindsay said. 'He wants to jump the hump next door.'

Alice suppressed a giggle, wiping at her eyes.

Kevin gave them both an odd look. 'Suppose I'd better do the loo.'

'I've done it,' Alice said. 'I did it when Mum was putting Livvy and Jack to bed.'

Lindsay hadn't heard a thing. Alice was doing so much for them and it wasn't right. Lindsay was the mother, and now, when everything to do with the house and the quake was just getting to be too much, her lovely daughter had stepped up and helped them out. She started crying again.

'Mum?' Alice said, while Kevin stepped forward and put his arms around Lindsay, which just made her cry more.

Muntsbury

May 2011

The night of the big quake, Gerald and Sylvia had moved in with Andrew and his family. After a couple of days, Andrew and Michelle and the children had gone to stay at their holiday home in Wanaka. At that point, Sylvia said there was no reason to stay in the city, it was gone, everything they had known all their lives was gone and she'd had enough of the regular aftershocks. Gerald agreed, and Sylvia packed in less than an hour, proving to Gerald just how desperate she was to go.

They had flown over to Sydney to stay with their daughter Laurel and her husband. The house was big, they were made to feel welcome and there was no reason for them to leave in a hurry. Gerald's staff in Christchurch were able to keep up with the emergency repair work that came their way and so there was no need for him to be there, for a few weeks anyway. It was good to be in Sydney, spending more time with Laurel than they had been able to for the decade she had been there. The weather was good and the city vibrant, full of life.

Gerald had made contact with the insurance company shortly after the February quake and they had said the process would be slow. That didn't really worry him too much, there was so much damage in Christchurch, he understood that there was a very long queue. Several of them. But by May, Gerald was starting to hear unsettling news from his contacts in Christchurch about how assessments were being carried out by people with no building background. He didn't like the idea of their house being assessed by an ex-policeman when it needed to be assessed by a structural engineer. Then there was the new Canterbury Earthquake Recovery Authority, CERA, and the legislation that went along with it. The Minister for Earthquake Recovery had been given extraordinary powers and to Gerald that meant only one thing: there was going to be more bureaucracy than ever.

He decided to take matters into his own hands with regard to their house. It was clearly a write-off, but he had not yet had any indication as to when EQC or his insurance company would assess it. He decided to engage an engineer, and now, nearly three months after the big quake, he was back in Christchurch to go up to the house with that engineer, a man called Robert.

It was unnaturally quiet on Huntsbury Hill. Or, rather, all the noise was natural. He could hear birds nearby, and that was it. The day was clear but cool, a slight breeze blowing from the east. Had he not just come back from Sydney, he would have considered it warm. He could get used to that warmer weather.

He met Robert at the house in the morning, and Robert worked until well past lunch time, taking measurements and photos, asking about the materials used to build the property. Gerald could remember every beam, and made sure Robert got it all down right.

In the time they were outside, Gerald didn't see any activity in the surrounding houses, and there were no cars going up and down the road. The hill really had emptied of people.

When the inspection was finished, Gerald was at a bit of a loss. He was staying with his mother and his flight wasn't until the next morning, but he wasn't quite ready to go back to her house and be mothered again. Or what passed for mothering on Marjorie's part, which involved being fed delicious baked goods while having your life's decisions scrutinised and judged. Sylvia should be where her husband was, Marjorie had said when he tried to explain to her how Sylvia felt about Christchurch. Gerald should make her come back to Christchurch with him.

Marjorie had always made sure their material needs were well met. They were always fed well and clothed adequately, but those domestic activities had seemed to Gerald, as he grew older, more his mother proving something rather than showing she loved them. Maternal was not a word he had ever associated with her, and feelings were never discussed. He couldn't explain to her the grief Sylvia felt over what had happened in Christchurch, that she felt that it was too difficult, at sixty-three years of age, to start building a new life in a completely changed city. Gerald understood, he was struggling too, but it all seemed beneath Marjorie, she couldn't seem to understand what all the fuss was about.

Alice had stayed with her for nearly two months, since the night of the February quake. It was the first time she'd had someone in her house for more than a couple of days since she had it built after Gerald's father died. Marjorie seemed to almost enjoy Alice's company and had taught her some cooking and baking skills, Alice had told Gerald. It surprised him, that she was being grandmotherly, for the first time he could recall. Of course she had knitted and sewn for all the grandchildren, beautiful, intricate pieces, but there was no affection in it. It had been, again, Marjorie proving something, although Gerald could never figure out what that something was.

No, he couldn't figure her out, after all these years.

Gerald texted Alice, and she told him where she was and said he should drop by. He hesitated. He hadn't seen Lindsay in over a decade and wasn't sure how she felt about Andrew's family. There was only one way to find out, so he texted that he would be over soon.

Alice hugged him, followed by Lindsay.

'It's lovely to see you, Gerald,' Lindsay said. 'You look well. Quite tan actually.'

Alice shut the door behind him, shoving it back into the warped frame with a loud bang. They all walked through to the kitchen, which was at the far end of the house. Gerald and Alice sat down at the table while Lindsay stayed standing.

He smiled. 'You're looking well, too.'

'Very nice of you to say, but I'm tired and I'm looking it. Would you like a beer?'

'We're celebrating,' Alice said. 'We're allowed to use our toilet again.'

'I've already had two beers,' Lindsay said. 'Alice is about to start on her second. Have you had lunch? I'll make you a sandwich.'

'Sure,' Gerald said. 'That would be lovely. But no beer, thanks.'

Lindsay started making him a sandwich, snacking on the bits of salad, meat and cheese as she put it together. It had been about a decade since Gerald had seen Lindsay and overall she was looking good for her age, but she was right, the tiredness was showing. She had dark circles under her eyes, her hair was dishevelled and her clothes untidy. The Lindsay he remembered from when she had been married to Andrew had cared about how she looked, even when suffering the sleepless nights new parents experience.

She placed the plated sandwich in front of him on the table and sat down across from him, taking a sip from her beer.

'Delicious,' he said, chewing on the first bite of the sandwich. 'How's things here? Any progress?'

Lindsay shook her head. 'Still trying to get our woodburner replaced. Major cockup at the hub, they came and did their assessment, all their paperwork and then nothing happened. I called and called for a couple of weeks before they finally tracked our file down, it had been sitting on someone's desk. We should get it by June sometime. We were down as urgent because we have small children, I'd hate to think how long elderly with serious health problems are waiting.'

Gerald nodded. 'Certainly hearing a lot of that sort of thing. Not feeling too confident about things going smoothly.'

'What's the house like?' Alice said.

Gerald told them about the engineer's visit, that he still had to do his report, but that it was his view that the house was beyond repair.

'That's the place you built?' Lindsay said.

'Yes,' Gerald said. 'It's very strange to see the place so quiet, no cars going up and down the hill. I wonder if anyone's living up there.'

'If you go back after dark,' Alice said, 'you'll be able to tell from the lights. When I've been past early in the morning, there's hardly any lights. People are calling it Muntsbury.'

Gerald repeated the word, puzzled.

'Munted,' Alice said. 'It's the new word for Christchurch. Huntsbury Hill's munted so now it's Muntsbury.'

'Munted,' Gerald said.

'Your house is munted,' Alice said. 'Though I doubt it's a term you'll see in your engineer's report. How long will it take?'

'A few weeks,' Gerald said. 'Then we'll see what EQC has to say.'

'Will you come back?' Alice asked. 'How's Nana feeling about Christchurch now?'

'Well she wouldn't come back with me this time,' Gerald says. 'She misses the family, but she's not ready to come back yet.'

'I can understand that,' Lindsay said. 'I'm getting used to how it is here, but there's at least a couple of times a week I want to go back to Timaru.'

Alice shot a glance at her mother, gave a slight roll of her eyes, then quickly looked away.

'Makes me laugh,' Lindsay said, oblivious to Alice's expression. 'I've always hated Timaru, I had an aunt and uncle down there when I was growing up and we used to go down every Christmas. I just loathed the place then, and now it's like my paradise.'

'I'm used to it here,' said Alice.

'That's because you've never gone away for more than a day or two,' Lindsay said. Then to Gerald, 'She runs around the cordon.'

'I don't want to go in one day and be shocked,' Alice said. 'If I stay away, that's what will happen and so if I go in a couple of times a week, it's like a gradual change, not something that's going to make me run away.'

'There's nothing wrong with running away,' Lindsay said, 'when a place is trying to kill you.'

Alice was about to fire something back at her mother when the phone rang, saving them from what Gerald had the feeling was a long-running discussion. Lindsay stood up and answered the phone, then left the room.

'How are you doing, Alice?' Gerald said.

'I'm okay,' Alice said. 'I think I'm used to not sleeping now.'

'I want to say thank you for looking after Mother,' Gerald said. 'I think she enjoyed having you there, and if there was any place open to go out and eat, I'd offer to take you and your family out for dinner.'

'Maybe one day?' Alice said. 'When we have restaurants again.' Her voice was quiet and she seemed unbearably sad, especially for someone who wasn't yet twenty.

'One day.'

They were both silent, unsure of what to say next.

'It will happen, Alice, the city will be rebuilt.'

'I know that,' Alice said. 'But there's so much to do before they can start. And they don't seem to want to start while there are still quakes.'

'There is that,' Gerald said. 'People are inventive, though, they find ways to get things done. You watch and see, people are starting to think about what they can get done, it will get started.'

She nodded, unconvinced.

'Why didn't you continue with your studies?' Gerald asked. 'You seemed very keen on engineering.' He had asked her the question in messages, but she had never answered.

She was quiet, her hands folded in front of her, resting on the table. 'Did you see anything about the coroner's inquest into the CTV deaths?'

'No, we don't have much coverage of things over in Sydney.'

She was thinking, collecting her thoughts. 'That building shouldn't have collapsed, all those people shouldn't have died. I heard that after the quake, when all the SAR people were still here. I heard the Japanese search and rescue people said this wasn't a natural disaster, it was a man-made one. And it made me think about engineering and what it involves.'

'You mean being responsible for people's lives? That's what the training is for, Alice, that's why it's a four-year course, not your standard three-year science degree.'

'No, it's not that. It's that engineers were involved. The week I was back at uni we were talking about it, people wanted to talk about it, as if there was something wrong with the buildings that collapsed, if some engineers got it wrong. All those people dying might be some engineer's fault.'

'Local council, too, it's not just all on the engineer. There are checks and balances built into the system.'

'I get that. But I'm not sure I want to be part of it. Part of a system where something might be wrong with the system.'

Gerald was silent. Young people had this idea that the world was perfect, and then when they realised it wasn't they were indignant. He and Sylvia had talked about this many times over the years, that part of getting older was the gradual realisation that there was something very wrong with the world. For Alice, the goalposts had been set high, her maternal family had recognised her intelligence and told her she could do anything. Possibly they believed that was the case. But, Gerald knew, the world wasn't like that, and he viewed growing up as the process of adapting to the way the world is while trying to keep some sense of having a moral centre. Had he kept his? He wasn't always sure. Another part of getting older was that he was increasingly aware of how little he knew. But he did know one thing, Alice was not the same girl she was before the February quake. Then she had a lightness about her and the same eager curiosity she had as a small child. She was interested in people, interested in learning things. Now it was like everything was shut up inside, and it was reflected in what she posted to Facebook: photos of wrecked buildings, wrecked streets, links to quake-related videos. No more people, which there had been plenty of in her Facebook feed before the quakes started.

'Something's wrong with every system,' Gerald finally said. 'But that doesn't mean you have to be wrong.'

'I'm not sure what that means,' Alice said, and her eyes filled with tears. 'All I know is that I couldn't stand people wanting to talk about it all the time like it was an intellectual exercise. It was like they forget that they were people with families.'

'Did you know anyone who died?'

'No, no one I knew,' she said. 'A girl from school lost her mum, and Mum's optometrist was in the CTV building.'

'You could leave, you know,' Gerald said. 'Or just get away. Come and visit us for a couple of weeks, go somewhere, do something different, get away from all the damage.'

Alice glanced down towards the other end of the house. They could hear Lindsay on the phone.

'I need to be here,' she said quietly. 'There's a lot for Mum to do about the house, and Kevin's having to work outside the city, it's hard on them, I can help out here.'

'What's happening with the house?' Gerald asked. Clearly the place was still habitable, but there were a lot of plaster cracks. Then there was the front door Alice had to force open and shut when Gerald arrived. It kept changing, she and Lindsay had said, sometimes too loose, other times they couldn't get it open at all.

'EQC assessed it just before the February quake,' Alice said. 'They said it had done well and would be undercap. But now, who knows? It moves differently, not just when there's quakes, but when cars drive by.'

'You think there's foundation damage?' Gerald said.

She shrugged. 'There are a lot of cracks in the foundation. Some of the windows are stuck, and the front door. Sometimes it's easy to open, but most of the time it's stuck.'

'Changing from aftershocks?'

'Yeah, seems like it.'

'Foundation damage is pretty serious,' he said. 'It would mean a lift, and that's a big job. Maybe even a rebuild.'

'A rebuild,' Alice said, looking grim. 'I don't know how Mum would cope with that, she loves this place, she has big plans for it, all the renovations she's going to do once Jack goes to school. Well that was the plan. I don't know about now.'

Alice looked far older than she was, and it worried Gerald, she was taking on too much responsibility that she didn't necessarily have to carry.

'There are a lot of things to worry about in life, Alice,' Gerald said. 'And most of those things never happen. It's best to just focus on what's right in front of you now and do what you can about that.'

She gave a small laugh. 'You know, I've tried doing that, but I can't make myself stop thinking.'

'About what?'

'Those people in the city.'

'You can't do anything for them, Alice. They're gone.'

Later Gerald drove into the city and walked around the cordon. It was a different kind of destruction in the city compared to that on the hill he and Sylvia had lived on for the best part of three decades. On the hills, the houses had been shaken and twisted, their structures were distorted. Roof tiles were askew on roofs, windows were broken, some window frames were falling out of walls, some walls had fallen away showing the chaos inside. Munted. But the city's buildings were beyond munted, they looked like they had been shelled. He could see down Manchester Street, where buildings had collapsed, revealing wooden framing that had splintered into kindling, chunks of wall linings, piles of bricks on the ground below or on the canopy between the ground floor and the first floor. Chaos. People had died in there, and Gerald understood Alice's sadness. It was difficult to think about those lives lost, the network of people affected, the grief multiplied, amplified, every single one of them wondering why it was the person they loved who was in the wrong place when the quake hit.

Did Christchurch have a future? He had reassured Alice that it did, but what he hadn't told her was how uneasy he was feeling about the layers of bureaucracy that had been put in place. CERA was a government department, which meant the recovery was being driven from Wellington by people who had little or even no local knowledge. Yes, the Minister for Earthquake Recovery was a local, but he was still a politician, and in Gerald's experience, politicians were more talk than action. Christchurch was a city that needed action.

Double Blow

June 2011

Following the September earthquake, Fletcher EQR was set up to manage repairs for EQC. EQR was part of Fletcher Construction, one of New Zealand's largest and most well-known construction companies. If a property had only minor damage, the homeowner would be paid out. But properties with more serious damage up to the EQC cap of $100,000 would go into the Canterbury Home Repair Programme, run by Fletcher EQR.

The reasoning behind having Fletchers manage repairs for EQC was to protect homeowners from construction cowboys, a problem that occurs in many areas following a disaster. Because the volume of work is so high following a disaster, people whose skills are normally not up to scratch are able to obtain work. EQC wanted, they said, to minimise the risk of shoddy repairs that was bound to occur if homeowners were left to manage their own repairs.

Within weeks of the announcement of the formation of Fletcher EQR, some of the region's builders were saying that Fletchers wasn't offering reasonable rates and that they wouldn't be having anything to do with earthquake repairs carried out through Fletchers.

EQR hubs were set up throughout Christchurch and repair work began in earnest late in 2010, interrupted only briefly by the February earthquake.

In June 2011, Lindsay and Kevin finally had an appointment with someone from the local hub. Lindsay was excited, they had been living in a cracked house for nine months. She knew that repairs wouldn't take place before winter set in, that was too much to hope for. But at least with the assessment process underway, they could have confidence that this would be their only winter in a broken house.

Mike, the project manager from the hub, arrived at nine o'clock, right on the dot, with two guys. Mike was young, late twenties, no older, clean shaven with an open, friendly manner. Lindsay was happy at the idea that he would be managing their repair. One tradie looked like your usual tradie, the other looked a bit dodgy. If they hadn't had an appointment and had showed up on their own while Lindsay was at home alone, she would not be inclined to let them in. Mike introduced them both, but later Lindsay could only think of them as Tradie and Dodgy. Dodgy's hair was long and straggly, Tradie's was shaved, his pink scalp peeking through the stubble.

The two guys were about to set off to do... who knew what. Obviously they had a plan before they got there. Kevin asked Mike the project manager about the scope, he wanted to know whether raking and filling the cracks was going to be good enough to fix the walls and ceilings, especially since the walls and ceilings in a couple of rooms were in pretty bad shape. 'Next quake comes,' Kevin said, 'and they'll just crack in the next weakest place.'

Tradie and Dodgy changed trajectory, Dodgy muttering something to Mike. Then they were off out of the still open front door.

'Where are they going?' Lindsay asked. Mike excused himself and followed them out, saying he would be back in a few minutes.

Kevin and Lindsay stood, Kevin jiggling, Lindsay gnawing on a thumbnail, exchanging worried looks. When Mike came back in, he explained that the guys weren't willing to quote on the work because there was no certainty they would get it.

'That doesn't stop them from quoting,' Kevin said.

Their time was valuable, Mike explained, they couldn't waste time quoting for work they were not likely to be doing.

'We're not saying we don't want the work done, because we do,' Lindsay said. 'We're just asking if it's right to just patch up the cracks, especially in here.' She gestured up at the fractured ceiling in the lounge.

Mike explained that it would be best if they were passed back to the hub for a full assessment. Lindsay felt tears stinging her eyes, they had already been waiting over nine months, nine months living in a cracked, plaster-dusty house, trying to keep surfaces clean, and she was sick of finding plaster dust in the cookware every time she took something out of the cupboards. And then Kevin was agreeing! She couldn't believe what she was hearing.

Once Mike was gone and the door was closed, Lindsay rounded on Kevin. 'Why did you let them leave?'

'Calm down,' he said.

Lindsay stalked off into the kitchen and stood at the kitchen sink, staring out into the backyard. She heard Kevin walk through and take a deep breath.

'Did you really want those guys working on our house?' he asked. 'They're obviously being paid peanuts if they can't afford the time to do a proper quote, and if they're happy to work for peanuts they probably aren't any good. And even if they are, they might be pushed into cutting corners.'

She nodded. Kevin had been hearing things about the work being done on EQC's behalf, that the quality was poor, they had talked about that and knew they had to be careful about their own house repair.

'I thought they were here to assess the damage from the February quake,' Kevin said. 'That they were here expecting to get started on the work isn't good, it means they're skipping the assessment stage.'

Lindsay started to cry. 'It's been so long,' she said, trying to keep from choking on her tears.

'I know,' he said, holding her tight. 'But it's better we get properly assessed, and Mike did say it would be a month, six weeks max. That's not long in the scheme of things.'

She nodded and wiped at her tears. 'Probably three to six months, more like.'

'Maybe,' Kevin said.

Although what Kevin had said made sense, Lindsay had trouble sleeping that night and all through the weekend. What if they couldn't get people to do the job right? What if they were going to end up with a bad patch job, like some of the people Kevin was hearing about at work? Paint flaking off after a few months, cracks appearing in walls that hadn't been repaired properly.

The following Monday, Lindsay still hadn't had a decent night's sleep, so instead of running her usual Monday errands, she went home after taking Olivia to school and Jack to kindy and flaked out on the sofa reading a book. Well, really, she was reading the same page of a book over and over again, her attention span wasn't great. She gave up around noon and decided to get some cooking done, to get ahead for the week, have some things in the fridge to heat up quickly. Chicken soup and a spaghetti bolognese.

The chicken soup was on, simmering away on the back of the stove, and Lindsay was chopping up the onions and garlic for the spaghetti bolognese when she heard a quake approaching, a loud rumble, then a big shake. She dropped the knife and crouched down by the kitchen cabinets, covering her head with her arms. The kitchen cupboards flew open and disgorged glasses and bottles that smashed, splashing her and a good part of the kitchen with balsamic vinegar. She heard the knife block on the window sill fall onto the bench, and knives shot out of it and clattered onto the floor, just missing her where she was crouching. But it wasn't like the September and February quakes, it was a small mess, a handful of objects, the knives, the bottle of balsamic vinegar, some glasses and a coffee cup.

The quake passed and Lindsay stood up, her legs wobbly. The pot containing the chicken soup had shimmied off the hotplate and pushed up against the back of the stove. The direction of the quake had pushed things on that side of the kitchen back, which was good, otherwise she would have a fresh pot of chicken soup all over the kitchen floor. She placed the pot back on the hotplate and turned the hotplate off. She would go and get the kids, once she was calm enough to drive. Once she had cleaned up. She walked unsteadily through to the laundry and retrieved the dustpan and the mop from the cupboard.

Her phone went. It was Alice, texting to say the quake was a 5.9 centred out towards Sumner, under Evans Pass. Alice was on her way home, her text said, and she would pick up Olivia and Jack. That was good, Lindsay didn't feel calm enough to go out. And it would give her a chance to make sure she caught all the broken glass.

Kevin was working away from the city that day and while normally he texted her after any big quakes, he had left his phone at home that day, he had no way of getting in touch with her, and she had no way of knowing if he was okay. But, she told herself, he was north of the city, the quake was to the southeast, of course he would be fine. He might not even know there had been a quake, depending on where he was. She told herself not to worry, he was fine. Alice and the kids would be home soon, and Kevin was well out of the quake zone. But what if something had fallen on him? She tried not to think about that.

She mopped the balsamic vinegar from the kitchen floor and filled a bowl with chicken soup. She was carrying the bowl of chicken soup through to the lounge when she heard another quake coming. She headed for the doorframe between the hallway and lounge, balancing the bowl of hot soup, determined not to drop it, not to have another mess to clean up today. It was a bigger quake than before, and given the last one was a 5.9, this one had to be a six. Hadn't they had enough? Somehow she managed not to spill her soup, although some slopped out onto her hand. She steadied herself and licked the soup off her hand, then set the bowl down on the coffee table. She heard the cat crying mournfully and followed the noise through to Alice's room and tried to coax him out from under the bed. But he just backed further into the corner, letting out deep howls. Where was Alice?

In the kitchen, two more glasses had been thrown onto the floor, but nothing else. So just shards of glass to sweep up before two little kids arrived home. She retrieved the dustpan from where she had stored it only minutes before and swept the mess up. She was emptying it into the rubbish bin when she noticed that the driveway was wet, muddy water running down from the back of the section, not as much as during the February quake, just a trickle. Liquefaction once again. She walked down to look and sure enough there was a new layer of silt on top of the one they hadn't yet cleared from February. At least the new round of liquefaction meant the City Council would be collecting it from the roadside once again. They had missed the February collections and hadn't yet dug out the silt as they had no idea what they were going to do with it.

Alice's car came up the driveway. Olivia and Jack jumped out as Alice pulled to a stop and they rushed Lindsay, telling her about being in the car during the quake, how Alice had just belted Olivia in and gotten back in the car when the quake hit. They saw the ground rolling, they said, and the trees shaking, and the car had been bouncing, like it was dancing. She hugged them both and they all went inside, where the phone was ringing. Alice ran for it, told whoever it was that they were all home and okay, then handed it over to Lindsay. 'It's Kev,' Alice said.

Lindsay asked when he would be home. About half an hour, he said. She should make sure all the water bottles were filled, he said, he was hearing on the radio that power was out in some parts of the city, water too, and there had been a lot of liquefaction. Again. There was more at home, she told him.

When he arrived home, they left Alice with Olivia and Jack and went to check on Lindsay's parents, then her grandparents. Both places had done reasonably okay, less mess than February, a slight worsening of existing damage. Lindsay's mother Heather was furiously trying to scrub coffee stains off a wall. When the second quake hit, Heather had a cup with milk and instant coffee sitting on the bench by the jug. It had been tossed onto the floor and had splashed up the wall, where it had seeped into existing plaster cracks.

'That's not coming off,' Lindsay said. Like so many in Christchurch, she was used to living with damage, although coffee stains in cracked plaster were a type of damage she hadn't seen before. But her mother kept scrubbing at the stains, determined to get them off the wall.

By the time Kevin and Lindsay arrived home, Alice had the kids asleep in bed and was watching the day's news. Someone had caught video of dust clouds coming off the cliffs in the seaside suburb of Sumner when the second quake hit, and a stone building had collapsed at Lyttelton, the historic timeball station that had been used to set ships' time when they came into port, in the days before radio signals were used. Then there was footage of more damage in the central city. Fortunately, people working on demolitions had evacuated after the first quake, so there was no one in the buildings that suffered further collapses. Alice had a serious look on her face that made her look a decade older.

'This is why people shouldn't be trying to save historic buildings,' Alice said, 'they're too dangerous while we still have quakes.'

Lindsay was worried that Alice was getting too wrapped up in the building collapse inquiries. They would be going on for months, and Alice was reading news reports about them most days, telling Lindsay about how the people shouldn't have died. She was right, it seemed a lot of people had died who shouldn't have, but Lindsay thought that shouldn't be the concern of someone as young as Alice.

Lindsay mentioned this to Kevin when they went to bed.

'She cares,' Kevin said. 'That's good.'

'But you can't take on all the world's burdens,' Lindsay said. 'That drives a person round the bend.'

'She is looking very tired lately,' Kevin said. 'What do you want to do?'

Lindsay shrugged. 'I tried suggesting that she gets away. Andrew's mother is over in Sydney, maybe she should go over for a break.'

'Isn't she staying with relatives? Would they have room?'

'Apparently the place is huge, there would be enough room for all of us,' Lindsay said.

'What did she say when you suggested it?'

'She says she needs to be here.' Lindsay was quiet a moment. 'I don't like that she feels like she has to be here for me. I mean, I am coping. Mostly. And it's not her responsibility.'

Kevin was quiet, and Lindsay wondered if he was considering debating with her whether or not she actually was coping.

'Do you want to stay here?' she said, and she felt him shuffle in discomfort. 'I don't mean going back to Timaru now, I'm okay with being here. I mean long-term. Do you want to stay in Christchurch?'

He was quiet. 'I don't know,' he said, and that surprised Lindsay, because she had thought the answer would be yes, that this was their home. She had only broached the idea to let him know that she might not want to stay here forever. She sat up and looked at him, feeling a small burst of hope in her heart. The hope of escape, of getting away from this wrecked place. He must have seen it in her eyes, because he proceeded to elaborate. 'Those EQR guys the other day, working for not much of anything. Stuff like that going on isn't going to be good for the city. I'm not sure there's going to be work for people who refuse to cut corners.'

'Is it that bad?' Lindsay said.

'Maybe. Maybe not. I've heard of some guys being let go, there's not enough work unless you're in with EQC or the insurance companies.'

'Could you look for work with one of the insurance companies?' Lindsay said. Now he had her worried, they needed to keep money coming in, and it had been pretty tight in the couple of months after the quake. She thought things were picking up.

He shrugged. 'I don't know, might be better than what's going on with EQC.'

'But?'

'I'm hearing things.'

'What about?'

'Rebuilds suddenly switching to repairs.'

'Well maybe that's what they're finding out when they take a closer look,' Lindsay said.

'But this is on badly damaged places,' Kevin said. 'There's something not right about it, and I'm starting to wonder if this is going to be a good place for Olivia and Jack to grow up. I mean, think about it, the rebuild is going to cover their formative years. Is this really what we want them growing up thinking is normal?'

'They're a lot better with the quakes,' Lindsay said. Ever since Lindsay had been making serious efforts to deal with her own anxiety over the ongoing quakes, Olivia and Jack had been handling them better. It was now more a game, which was good. They were developing resilience. Though she still hated the word, she had come to realise that trying to protect them from everything bad was a bad strategy, that what they needed was to learn how to cope, how to bounce back.

'Yes they are,' Kevin said. 'But in ten years they'll each be looking at what kind of work they're going to get, and I have a feeling the standard of workmanship is going to be dropping.'

'So not a good place to pick up a trade,' Lindsay said. 'University might be a better option.' She didn't want her children taking up trades. Yes, the work was steady, everyone needed homes and cars and so on, but she had seen the physical toll. Her father had spent his working life as a mechanic, which he was now paying for with his bad knees and back problems, and it wasn't uncommon for painters and plasterers to have shoulder problems. Kevin was nearly forty and although he didn't have anything of that sort going, he still had more than two decades of work to get through, and who knew what would happen. No, she wanted her children to go to university, get degrees, not have to ruin themselves physically to earn a living.

'What if they're not cut out for university?' Kevin said. 'What if it's too expensive by then?'

Lindsay didn't want to have this discussion. 'It doesn't matter what they do,' she said. 'I suppose the question is do we want them growing up in Christchurch if the rebuild goes wrong?'

'It's going wrong now,' Kevin said.

'I don't want them growing up in a dysfunctional city,' Lindsay said. She felt her voice catch and tried to stop from crying. 'They should know what normal is.' She swept her arm in an arc, meaning the broken city a few kilometres beyond their bedroom window. 'Not this, not this broken place that keeps having quakes. Two big quakes today. How many more sixes can we possibly have?'

Kevin put his arm around her and kissed her hair. 'I don't know,' he said. 'In my head I know it can't go on forever, but at what point do we say let's go? Maybe this is the point. We can't do anything until the house is fixed, but maybe we can start talking about possibilities.'

Lindsay nodded, sniffing back tears. 'I'd like that,' she said. 'I'd really like that.'

The Icing on the Quake

July 2011

After the February earthquake, the people of Christchurch adapted to living with a city that had a red zone, that part of the inner city that was cordoned off and guarded by the army because it was too dangerous for people to go in there without a good reason. Then, in June 2011, the Government announced a new red zone, the residential red zone. This was land that was so badly damaged that the Government said it was uneconomic to repair. It could be repaired, but to do so would be so astronomically expensive and would take so long that residents' lives would be disrupted for at least seven years, if not more.

Instead, the Government would buy the damaged land and owners could either sell their house to the Government or negotiate a settlement with their private insurance company. Once the red zone offers were accepted, all those houses would be cleared, those neighbourhoods would disappear, their people dispersed to other parts of Christchurch, or even further afield.

Alice's uncle Jason's house had been red zoned. He and Carla had planned on raising a family in that house and now the neighbourhood they had chosen for their future family was just going to disappear.

Despite the emotional impact, the residential red zone announcement seemed like good news, it would mean that people had a way out financially and they didn't have to wait years for their land to be fixed up. They could move on, go and live somewhere else. Some were unhappy that the settlement value used would be the 2007 rating valuations. It was four years later, and the New Zealand property market was growing quickly, so how could a 2007 value paid out in 2011 possibly be fair? Many New Zealanders rely on capital gains from property sales to increase their personal wealth, so the idea of foregoing four years of potential capital gains by accepting the Government offer was not a palatable one. If a homeowner had made expensive improvements to the property and could not prove those costs through building consents or receipts for work carried out, they stood to lose a good deal of money.

Then there was the actual value of people's insurance policies. A full replacement policy would give the homeowner the opportunity to buy a new section and build an equivalent house, but taking the red zone offer would not give many people enough money to put them back in an equivalent property. The Prime Minister had said, in making the red zone announcements, that the Government was committed to getting things right for people, but how could things be right if people were being offered less than the value of their homes?

Jason and Carla were over for dinner. They had come in the afternoon and watched a movie with Olivia and Jack, who had since gone to bed after having their dinner, what little Lindsay could get them to eat of the chicken and vegetables Alice had roasted.

Jason and Carla were still living with Carla's mother in the north of the city and hadn't decided what to do. Their red zone offer wouldn't give them enough for a house the same size unless they went out of the city, as far as Rangiora or Kaiapoi, over twenty kilometres north. But they had to decide soon if they were going out there, Jason said, property prices were skyrocketing with the all the red zoners looking for something to buy. Some red zoners wanted to stay where they were, while some wanted to get as far away from the quakes as they could. If Jason and Carla wanted to stay in the city, they would have to buy a smaller place or take out a bigger mortgage. Neither was a palatable option if they were going to have children any time soon. They were talking about Rangiora or Kaiapoi, but neither of them seemed convinced.

'I would miss the hills,' Carla said. 'And the rivers.'

Their families were in town and they didn't want to be away from everyone. If they had kids, they wanted those kids to grow up near their grandparents, not a forty-five minute drive away.

'Is your mum staying?' Alice asked. She hadn't seen them since soon after the February quake, when she had helped Jason dig out all the silt that had come up around his mother-in-law's house. She wasn't too happy about the idea of staying at the time.

Carla nodded. 'The house can be fixed, and Mum doesn't want to leave her garden. And it's where Dad lived.' Carla's eyes teared up.

Alice got up from the table and went out to the kitchen to get dessert while the others cleared the table.

Carla's father had died a few years before the quakes started, but for some reason the quakes had sharpened her grief rather than distracting her from it. Alice and Lindsay had talked about that, how her dad's absence was getting harder for her, not easier, and Alice knew Lindsay thought less of Carla for it. But wouldn't the father you loved be even more missed during the difficult times? In the months since the February quake, especially, Alice had spent more time thinking about her family than she ever had before, thinking about how things worked in her family, on all sides of it. Maybe if Carla's father were still alive, she would talk to him about where she and Jason would move to, maybe not having him to run ideas past was part of her inability to make a decision one way or another? She understood Carla's exhaustion.

'It's going to snow tonight,' Lindsay said as they started eating dessert.

'I would miss the opportunity to see snow on the hills,' Carla said. 'I don't want to be away from the hills.'

If their where-to-live problem seemed difficult, it looked simple when compared to the situation one of their neighbours found themselves in. Jason said the guy had decided to take the Government offer on the land and negotiate with his insurance company over the house. But when he contacted the insurance company, they said his house was repairable and they were going to pay him out on that basis.

'How's that possible?' Kevin said. 'The land is going to be cleared.'

'Exactly,' Jason said. 'But the insurance company said it's not their problem, the house can be repaired so they'll pay out as much as it costs them to repair it, no more.'

'That seems cruel,' Alice said, and everyone nodded. 'It can't be legal.'

'I wouldn't be surprised if it is,' Lindsay said. 'There's something in policies about government destruction not being covered and this would probably qualify.'

Another family, Carla said, were in the same boat, only their insurance company had already told them, before the February quake, that their house was a rebuild. Once the red zoning was announced, they had changed their mind. It was now a repair and the payout was going to be much smaller.

'That's dodgy,' Kevin said. 'There's no way something written off by one quake is suddenly fixed up by another one.'

Jason shrugged. 'Who knows, maybe if these quakes go on for long enough, everyone's houses will magically jiggle back into shape? Yeah, right.'

'At least they have an offer,' Lindsay said. 'Have you talked to Mum and Dad?'

'About the section?' Jason said. 'No, have they heard something?'

Neil and Heather had a section in the Heathcote Valley, near the epicentre of the February quake. They had been planning to build a new home on it, where they would spend their retirement. The plans were drawn up and they had been talking to builders, but since the September quake, everything had been on hold. There had been rockfalls on the hills in the February quake and, as a result, quite a bit of land had been white zoned, meaning it could end up red zoned, including Neil and Heather's section.

'Nothing,' Lindsay said. 'But they were talking to someone else who has a section up there and they reckoned there wouldn't be an offer. No insurance means no EQC cover, which means no offer.'

'You don't know that, Lin,' Kevin said. 'The guy was just speculating, they could still get an offer. And they still don't know that they'll be red zoned, it could go green.'

'But when the offers were announced, how Brownlee talked about them wasn't promising,' Alice said. Gerry Brownlee was the Minister for Earthquake Recovery, in charge of CERA and, therefore, the one heading up the land zoning decisions. 'He said the Government's first priority was helping people who had helped themselves by getting insurance. That's not the way you talk about people you think should get compensation. I don't think they'll be offered anything, given that attitude.'

'Why didn't they have insurance?' Carla said, looking confused.

'Can't insure bare land,' Kevin said. 'So what Gerry said was a bit cruel, really, considering there was no way they could get insurance and now the Government's taking their land.'

'That sucks,' Jason said.

'Yup,' Lindsay said. Everyone was nodding.

'And it kind of makes Brownlee's attitude a bit disingenuous,' Alice said.

'In what way?' Lindsay said.

'Well surely he knows you can't insure bare land,' Alice said.

'You would hope the Minister for Earthquake Recovery would know that,' Kevin said.

'Right,' Alice continued. 'So why's he say it unless he's being deliberately manipulative, laying the groundwork for the day when it's clear that no offers are going to be made on empty land?'

'Him saying that now won't make the landowners any happier later, when they don't get offered anything for land they can't do anything with,' Lindsay said. 'Mum and Dad certainly wouldn't be happy.'

'No, not for them,' Alice said. 'But for everyone else. Because if he paints them to the public as irresponsible, then they won't have public support. If they have to go to court.'

They all stared at her. Alice wondered if she should have kept her thoughts to herself, that maybe she was reading things the wrong way.

Jason said. 'I wouldn't have thought that was possible in New Zealand three months ago, but hearing what our neighbour's insurance company told him, I'm starting to think it's realistic.'

When Jason and Carla were leaving, it was starting to snow, big flakes turning the ground white. Alice and Lindsay stayed outside, sitting on the doorstep under the eaves, watching the snow fall, the ground getting whiter and whiter.

'Livvy and Jack will love it in the morning,' Lindsay said.

'It'll be their first real snow, won't it?' Alice said. 'The last was the year before Jack was born, and Livvy's too young to remember that.' It was the first really big snow Alice could remember. There had been a big snow the year Alice was born. Lindsay had told her about the power being out and the stress of trying to keep tiny little Alice warm in the cold flat they were living in. It was one of the few times she talked about those years being married to Andrew.

Lindsay nodded. 'Hopefully the power will stay on, but at least we have the fire back.' The replacement fire had finally been installed a couple of days after the June quake, and Lindsay was relieved. No matter the state of the house, at least they would be able to curl up in front of the fire. If there were power cuts, they would be warm.

'I wonder what the city will be like,' Alice said. 'If the snow settles, I might go in and see it.'

Lindsay looked at her, she seemed about to say something. Alice knew Lindsay thought her city visits were an unhealthy obsession, but Alice saw it as better than going in and being shocked at the drastic changes. This way she would get used to it, slowly. But in that moment, sitting on the steps, Lindsay was oddly self-controlled about expressing her opinions on Alice's choices lately. For one thing, she hadn't said a word about Alice not seeking something more than the coffee shop job. She seemed to appreciate Alice's help around the house, but never said anything to confirm Alice's suspicions.

'Let's go inside,' Lindsay said. 'I'll make you a hot chocolate.'

They sat in the kitchen sipping their hot chocolates, watching the snow falling in the backyard, increasingly steady. The cat dashed in through the cat flap, trying to shake the cold off his paws. They laughed. He looked so indignant.

In the morning, the city was covered in a blanket of snow. *The Press* website put up pictures of the city, broken buildings draped in snow. It looked pretty rather than sad for a change, and it wasn't long before someone on Facebook was passing around a snow-related meme: The snow is the icing on the quake.

For Kevin and Lindsay, though, the extra weight of the snow on the roof showed up problems with the house. The roof was leaking in four places and Kevin spent the morning in the roof space checking what tiles were broken and putting plastic sheeting up to stop the water from coming through. They would need to get a roofer to look at it, he said, once the snow had gone.

'Get onto EQC?' Lindsay said.

'Only if you want it done in about a decade,' Kevin said.

After helping Kevin with the roof, Alice wrapped up warm and told Lindsay she was going to see Sonya. She packed half a dozen of the cheese scones she had made that morning into a plastic container and stuffed the container into a plastic bag in case it started to snow again.

Sonya was Lindsay and Jason's sister, the typical resentful middle child. Although she had been having more contact with the family since the quakes started, something had gone wrong a couple of months ago and no one was talking to her. Or she wasn't talking to anyone, it was hard to tell which way it was. Alice tried her best to stay out of whatever it was, to stay in touch with Sonya, not because she particularly liked Sonya, because she didn't really, but she wanted to keep in touch with her cousins, Cody and Ella. They were eleven and eight, a little bit older than Olivia and Jack.

As comfortable as Alice was driving on the city's cracked and slumping roads, she wasn't comfortable with the idea of driving on snow and ice so decided to walk to Sonya's. It was two kilometres away but it took about twice as long as usual walking on the soft snow.

The power was out at Sonya's, and she was slow to answer the door, wrapped in a polar fleece blanket, wearing track pants and thick socks.

Sonya usually kept a tidy house, but over winter she seemed to be losing the plot a bit. Twice Alice had been around and found all the dishes dirty, piled into and around the sink, none of the clothes washed, the house dusty. The quakes were getting to everyone in different ways and with Sonya it seemed to be the erosion of her normally good household habits. Each time, Alice had helped her get everything back under control and then Sonya would cope fine for a few weeks before losing control again. As she followed Sonya down the hall into the lounge, Alice could see that the deterioration was starting once again. The washing basket in Sonya's bedroom was overflowing with clothes and towels, and more towels lay piled on the bathroom floor.

Sonya and the kids were camped out in the lounge in front of the fire. Cody and Ella leapt up from where they had a bunch of cars their grandparents had bought them set up on the floor. They mobbed Alice, who gave them big hugs.

'We have power,' Alice said to Sonya. 'You could come round, watch a video with us.'

Cody and Ella looked at Sonya hopefully. She shook her head. Clearly being confined to one room of the house with two children forced to find non-television means of entertainment for the entire day was preferable to spending time with her family. What would she do once it became dark but the kids weren't tired enough to go to sleep?

Alice got a cutting board and jam and butter from the kitchen and served up the scones in front of the fire. They had lost their warmth, but that didn't stop Cody and Ella from scoffing a scone each. Had Sonya fed them anything that morning? Alice looked around the lounge. There were dirty cereal bowls stacked on the television cabinet, so, yes, she had. It was something.

Alice played a couple of games of Monopoly Deal with them, playing badly to let them win. Cody won the first and Ella was on the verge of winning the second when the power came back on. It was a relief, Alice was wondering how to tactfully pull something together for lunch, since Sonya didn't seem motivated to go out to the cold kitchen and do anything for them. Having power would make that easier.

'What are you going to do for lunch?' Alice asked.

'Hadn't thought about it,' Sonya said. 'Not hungry.'

Alice suggested making a soup, and the two of them went through to the kitchen, which Sonya started heating up with a fan heater. The house was cold, uninsulated, like so many houses in Christchurch. Sonya had been in the house for a couple of years, it was a rental, but with the quake damage it was colder than ever. She would have to move out when her landlord had repairs done, which would be September, she said.

'What will you do?' Alice asked. There were some potatoes and onions that were looking a bit past it, but they would be fine in a soup. There were some more vegetables in the fridge and freezer and some stock cubes in the pantry. It would be enough.

'I don't know,' Sonya said. She was on the verge of tears and started peeling the carrots in a way that made Alice worry for her fingers. 'Rents are so expensive, I don't know what we'll do.'

Alice wanted to suggest her grandparents, but they hadn't heard from Sonya for weeks, and so that probably wouldn't go down too well. To her surprise, Sonya brought it up herself.

'Do you think Mum and Dad would have us?' she said so quietly Alice wasn't sure she had heard properly.

'Definitely,' she said.

Sonya sniffed back tears.

'Would you like me to ask them?' Alice said.

Sonya nodded.

Alice made enough soup for dinner as well as lunch. She had lunch with them and another game of Monopoly Deal, then walked back home. It was colder and the footpaths were freezing up. She was looking forward to spending the rest of the day in front of the fire reading.

'How are they?' Lindsay asked when Alice got home.

'Power's back on now, they'll be fine. But they have to move out in a few weeks. I said I'll ask Grandma and Grandad if they can stay with them.'

'They've already said yes,' Lindsay said.

'But she wouldn't agree if she thought we had all this planned out for her,' Alice said. She hung up her jacket and scarf and went through to the kitchen to put the jug on to boil. 'Want a coffee?' she called back to Lindsay.

'Please,' Lindsay said, coming through. 'I'm not sure I like you being cunning,' she added.

Alice pretended she hadn't heard. She could imagine the argument that would follow, how you had to be on the level dealing with people, not manipulative, people deserved to be given the benefit of the doubt. She handed Lindsay a coffee and took her own through to the lounge to sit in front of the fire. Alice didn't think people were evil, not many of them, anyway, but she couldn't see the value of giving everyone the benefit of the doubt. If there was any icing on the quake for Alice, it was that she was seeing more clearly how the world worked, that it wasn't the cosy place her mother wanted it to be, where people looked out for each other and businesses and governments kept their promises.

Compromise

August 2011

Alice woke with an aftershock hangover and had trouble making her eyes open. Her alarm had been going for a minute or so and it had intruded into the dream she was having, a dream that quickly faded as she looked around her half-dark bedroom. Had there been an aftershock in the night? Was that why she felt so awful? She would have to check Geonet. But that could wait. She had promised herself the night before that she would get up and go for a run that morning, that was the reason for the alarm. She wasn't working and she was going to relax for the day, potter around the house and try to pull herself together. The bed was warm, the room was not, but she had promised herself she would go out.

She forced herself from bed and into her running clothes, which she had set out on the end of the bed the night before. She had been running regularly in the months following the February quake, but winter had made it harder. Following the snow days, the footpaths were icy and she didn't want to slip and hurt herself. That would just be too depressing. Even when it wasn't iced over, it was dark in the mornings, which was when she preferred to run, and the footpaths were a nightmare. Dips, bumps and snags everywhere. She felt sorry for elderly people who were used to walking around their neighbourhoods. No footpath anywhere was smooth, no road was even. The roads were so hard on vehicles that mechanics were doing a roaring trade. Alice's Grandad Neil was seeing a huge increase in business: tyres needing replacing, suspension needing redoing. He reckoned windscreen businesses were flat out from all the stone chips flying around as roads were patched up and with all the big trucks hauling demolition waste out of the city.

Driving around Christchurch was an adventure of the worst kind, and Alice could always spot a non-local. They were the ones who still bothered trying to drive around potholes, bumps and raised manholes, whereas the locals knew that if you missed one hazard, there was another waiting a matter of metres away. As work proceeded on the roads, the diversions were increasingly bizarre, road cones marking out convoluted S-shapes where the cars were meant to follow. She had driven on more than one road where the footpath had actually been made into road so road crews could deal with whatever seriously bad thing had gone on under that particular road.

It was cold outside, but not frosty, and Alice walked towards the river, then broke into a slow jog, following the course of the river towards the hills. Her breath plumed out in front of her as she pushed forward, making herself keep going. This had been much easier a few months ago.

The weekend before, Alice had been invited to a family dinner. Andrew was back in town and he had asked if she wanted to meet up at his cousin's house. Rebecca and her husband Dan were Sean and Charlotte's parents, making Sean and Charlotte Alice's second cousins. The three of them had gotten along well and planned to get together again soon. All of them were finding Christchurch depressing, with their normal routines disrupted, many of their friends gone and the homes they were used to living in broken and cold.

Alice hadn't seen Andrew since soon after the February quake, although they had stayed in touch by text. He and Michelle were still living down south. Although Andrew came back to town regularly, his visits were brief, he was mostly there to catch up with his colleagues, who were working in a makeshift office set up in an old villa just outside the red zone cordon. It wasn't big enough for everyone and some people were working from home, which is what Andrew was doing a lot of the time.

Michelle refused to come back to Christchurch, Andrew said, and he had decided it was best for the children to finish out the school year in Wanaka and then see about coming back. They weren't the only ones from Christchurch doing something similar, he said, another family they knew was also in Wanaka and their children were going to the same school as Andrew and Michelle's children.

Rebecca and Dan's house was on a hill in the suburb of Redcliffs, in the city's southeast. Sumner was the beach suburb and Redcliffs was the one before it, nestled on the southern side of the Avon-Heathcote estuary, just before its outlet to the sea. Redcliffs had been in the news after the February earthquake because its primary school was beneath a huge cliff that had collapsed in the earthquake. Although no one in the school was hurt, there were houses behind the school, right beneath the cliff, and some of the residents who were at home that day had died. Redcliffs School was now using another school's campus over in Sumner, quite a long way for the local kids to go each day.

Rebecca and Dan's house had a lot of damage in the February quake and even more in the June quake, which had been nearby and shaken those eastern hill suburbs badly. It was hard to say which one had done more damage, Rebecca said, but they thought it might be June. Did it matter, though? Surely EQC would see how much damage there was and put them overcap? It might be more complicated than that, Andrew said. There was a court case, one of the private insurance companies had taken EQC to court over whether EQC should pay an overcap payment for each earthquake a householder had claimed on. Rebecca and Dan had made claims for three quakes, one each for September, February and June, so nothing was likely to happen with their house until that court case had been concluded.

There weren't many people left living in their neighbourhood, where a lot of the houses were obviously twisted and not fit to be occupied. There were rumours that parts of Redcliffs would be red zoned due to the risk of rockfall in future earthquakes. Rebecca and Dan were feeling like the process would never get going, they hadn't even been assessed yet. Red zoning would, at least, allow them to move on, even if they did lose money in the deal.

Alice had learned something interesting about the Moorhouse family that weekend. She knew they were what her own family considered wealthy, but Marjorie, apparently was quite the landholder. She had a tonne of rental properties, and Andrew and Rebecca had been talking about them, how most of them were repairable but there were a handful that looked like they were going to be put overcap. Once that happened, Andrew would deal with the insurance company on Marjorie's behalf. Alice had been thinking of Marjorie as a little old lady with a nice home on the river to spend her retirement in, when it turned out she had this extensive property portfolio.

'Grandmother has always had an eye for a good investment,' Andrew said when Alice asked him about these other houses. 'Pop was into commercial property, but after he died, she sold them all off, she had been trying to convince him to do that for over a decade, she could see the writing on the wall.'

What writing was that? Alice had asked. As the suburban malls grew in the 1980s, retail in the city started to suffer, which meant the city as a whole started to suffer. Returns on central city commercial buildings declined. Many buildings were old and required expensive updates, especially ones that were regarded as heritage. And as long as those buildings were in poor condition, they couldn't attract corporate tenants willing to pay higher rents, they could only attract retailers who were struggling, who couldn't afford to pay much. Marjorie could see that rents were only going to go down and she didn't want to waste money on expensive upgrades. Residential property values, on the other hand, were only going up, so Marjorie had moved her money into residential properties and Tony, another grandson, managed those properties for her.

Tony was currently working for EQC, which meant, Andrew said, that Marjorie's rentals were getting through the system quickly. That sounded dodgy to Alice, although she didn't say so. But she did say she thought the speed with which someone was dealt with by EQC should be based on need. If someone couldn't live in their damaged house and was having to rent, while also paying a mortgage, shouldn't their needs take priority? It shouldn't depend on who you knew to get things done following the earthquake.

Alice wasn't sure, but she thought Dan, Rebecca's husband, might feel the same way. At that point in the conversation, he had left the room, saying he was going to check on lunch. But there was a grim look on his face, his mouth set in a firm, disapproving line.

Later, after dinner, they were sitting in the lounge drinking tea and coffee when Dan's views became apparent. The adults were talking once again about how repairs were being prioritised. Alice said it should be older people first, like her great-grandparents, her mother's grandparents. They had been living in their house near the Avon ever since she could remember. The house had a lot of cracking, but the foundations seemed to be okay for that part of town, they were far enough away from the river that the ground had held up well. But they were in their eighties and their health wasn't great, so surely they should be prioritised. Dan was nodding away as Alice described their situation.

'Unfortunately,' Andrew said, 'it's those who make the most noise whose houses are getting done first, those who use their connections.'

'But it shouldn't be like that,' Dan said. He was flushing, only slightly, but because of the earlier conversation about Marjorie's rentals, Alice was watching him closely. 'We could make lots of noise and insist our house gets fixed first. But we can live in our house.'

'But why should we wait if we can get things done more quickly by just asking Tony to push us along in the queue?' Rebecca said, jumping in. Clearly this was an ongoing discussion.

'What if we're behind Alice's great grandparents in the queue,' Dan said, 'and us jumping the queue means that those eighty-somethings have to sit in the queue for six months longer.'

'It wouldn't be six months,' Rebecca said. 'Not if we were right behind them.'

'No, but think about everyone who can jump the queue – because of someone they know – going ahead and doing it. Then those old people who have no someone-they-know are stuck for months or even years. Six months is nothing to us, we're young. But to them, six months might be, say, only a quarter of the time they have left. How would you feel being asked to give up twenty-five percent of your remaining life so someone with a mate in the right place could get their work done before yours?'

'They're older, they're classed as vulnerable,' Rebecca said. 'It doesn't work like that. We're not in the same queue.'

Across the room, Sean was silently jerking his head at Alice. Charlotte was already headed out of the room towards the kitchen and so Alice swallowed down the last of her coffee and used her empty cup as an excuse to leave the room.

Sean and Charlotte were on the balcony, which looked out over the estuary past the rock formation that used to be known as Shag Rock. This pillar stood on the southern shore of the estuary mouth, a sentinel over ten metres high marking the end of the estuary suburb of Redcliffs and the start of Sumner beach and the wide Pacific Ocean. In the February quake, Shag Rock had been shaken apart and was now a third the height. It was starting to be known as Shag Pile.

'That argument's been going on for months,' Sean said. 'Ask the family for help, Mum says. No, Dad says, we're doing things the right way.'

'Do you think if you know someone who can help you and you ask them to help that that's the wrong thing to do?' Alice said.

'No,' Sean said, while Charlotte's answer was an emphatic 'Yes.'

'The difference is that we agree to disagree and leave it at that,' Sean said, pointing back and forth between him and Charlotte. 'The world's not fair, and if you know someone who can help you, why shouldn't you take advantage of that?'

'Because it's taking advantage of who you know and it affects the less fortunate,' Charlotte said. But she laughed, without intention of prolonging the discussion. 'We should go for a walk.'

Sean looked at Alice questioningly. 'Whaddya think? Go get ice cream?'

'I'm game,' Alice shrugged.

They told the others, who, it seemed, barely noticed. Andrew was too busy trying to play referee between his cousin and her husband.

The neighbourhood was mostly dark, the bulk of the hills looming up behind them and they walked down the hill past all the empty, broken houses. They walked along the road in the direction of what had been the suburb's supermarket, careful to dodge dips and kinks in the footpath. The wind was cool and had the scent of rain in it. Alice shivered, wishing she had brought a thicker jacket.

The supermarket had been demolished and the site was bare, but fenced off, nothing happening. They stood at the fence and peered in. 'There's nothing to do around here,' Charlotte said. 'Except go get ice cream and walk around looking at ruins.'

'At least the quake left the dairy standing,' Sean said. 'Best ice cream cones in the city.'

'Given the state of the city, that's not too difficult,' Alice said.

They ordered their ice creams and started walking back towards the house. There were few cars on the road, it was the wrong time of day to be going anywhere. Post-quake people went to work, then went home. There just weren't enough reasons to go out any more.

'We should do something,' Sean said.

'We are doing something,' Charlotte said, 'we're walking and eating ice creams while trying not to kill ourselves on the footpaths.'

'I mean one night, a Friday or something. Get a video, maybe something old, so none of us have seen it.'

'That's not a bad idea,' Alice said. She was going to Timaru that weekend to see Ben, but that didn't happen every week, they could get together the following Friday. Sean and Charlotte asked if they could watch something at her house and she said yes without thinking to ask Lindsay and Kevin first. She felt sorry for Sean and Charlotte. Clearly their parents argued a lot, and knowing that made Alice grateful that in spite of the stress of living in a broken city, Lindsay and Kevin were still getting along, even if there were more sharp words than there had been before the February quake.

What Alice had been thinking about the most since that evening with Andrew's family was how commercial properties in the city had been allowed to stay in a dangerous state. There was a documentary from 1996 someone had uploaded to YouTube soon after the February quake. It talked about how much damage liquefaction would cause in Christchurch in a quake and how dangerous some of its old buildings were. It surprised Alice that the risk had been known about so long ago, and yet nothing had been done. Building owners hadn't been made to upgrade the buildings, the City Council couldn't force them to do so. But if they wanted to make changes to modernise the building and make it more appealing to tenants, they had to upgrade them so they were less quake prone, which could be very expensive. That meant owners tended to leave their buildings as they were. People had died because some of those buildings weren't upgraded, because people had put their own financial welfare above the risk their buildings posed to people's lives. She hoped lessons would be learned, that out of the Royal Commission would come changes to regulations that meant people couldn't just leave their buildings in a potentially dangerous state. She didn't want to live in a place where profits were valued over human life.

Background Noise

September 2011

Charlotte had fallen asleep on the bus and missed her stop. As soon as she jolted awake, she realised she was too far, so she got off at the next stop. She was all the way around in Sumner and although, on the face of it, Sumner wasn't too far from home, the wind was picking up and it was dark. She thought about waiting for the bus going back the other way, but that wind was cold, the best way to keep warm was to start moving.

The way home was along the road between Sumner and Redcliffs, where broken houses hung dangerously off the edges of a cliff that had collapsed. A long line of shipping containers had been set up to protect the road from rockfall, stacked two high, the gaps between showing rock and splintered pieces of houses. The shipping containers narrowed the road so there was barely room for cyclists and none for walkers. Charlotte had to pick her way along at the very top edge of the beach. It was slow going, lights from cars coming from the city shone in her eyes, meaning her vision never really adapted to the darkness. As nice as it was to not have to be at school until lunchtime each day, getting home well after dark and heating up her dinner and eating alone were wearing thin.

There had been a lot of liquefaction at her school, which was just outside of the city and near the Avon River. That was the February quake, and since school started up again in March, Charlotte and her classmates had been travelling to another school, all the way on the other side of the city. That was the case with a few of the city's high schools, damaged schools were sharing sites with undamaged schools. The undamaged school's students would attend from early in the morning until lunchtime, then the damaged school's students had the campus until the early evening. Other schools had gone back to their own sites after a few months, but it seemed Charlotte's wouldn't be back on site until next year, which meant she had another three months of going all the way over to the other side of town. She was lucky to get home before half six each night. It was grossly unfair.

She texted her mother to say she had missed her stop and where she was in the hope that her mum would come and pick her up. Fat chance, though, her mum was so wrapped up in getting new offices set up and there would, no doubt, be something urgent and picking up Charlotte wouldn't even cross her mind. Charlotte felt invisible, like she was just furniture in the background. Charlotte texted Sean as well. Maybe he would come and get her, maybe he was on his way home and picking her up was just a slight detour. They were getting along better lately. Still, if Sean was already warm at home, fat chance of him shifting himself to come out and get her.

It was Sean's first year at university, and he had kept going, in spite of the interruption caused by the February quake. At first, students had their lectures in tents and sometimes in offices opened up to them by local businesses, but eventually a temporary village had been set up. Sean had thrown himself into his studies, determined not to be disadvantaged by the post-quake situation. He was more serious about everything, which, for some reason, meant he was less likely to pick on Charlotte. That was the only post-quake change Charlotte was pleased about. In every other respect she found it hard going on with life, travelling all the way across town to go to school, living in their strange, empty neighbourhood, driving past collapsed cliffs, seeing half-houses dangling from them, walking up the hill past twisted, empty houses. She had started reading *The Hunger Games*, but she was already living in a dystopian world, why would she want to escape into one in her reading?

A couple of weeks ago, Sean had been happy to take Charlotte to the mall when she wanted to spend the vouchers she had received for her birthday. They had met up with their cousin Alice and had lunch at the food court. Charlotte wasn't the mall-going type, but there wasn't anything else to do in Christchurch, so it was good to do something other than staying at home or walking around their shattered neighbourhood. Alice was more Sean's age than Charlotte's, there was something like five years between her and Charlotte, but the three of them got on well. They talked about what the city had been like, what they missed. Before the February quake, Charlotte was bussing into the city after school, then catching a connecting bus home. Often she would spend an hour or so wandering around the city, checking out the buildings and laneways. Sean wasn't such a fan of the city, but he tolerated Alice's nostalgia, which meant Charlotte could speak about her own. That wasn't the case at home. Whenever she said something about missing the city, her parents would say something about how old and tired it had been, the quakes had done Christchurch a favour. That horrified Charlotte, because people had died, there was nothing favour-ful about what had happened in the city that day.

To Charlotte's surprise, Sean texted back right away and said he would pick her up. Was something going on? A couple of minutes later, she recognised his car moving past when he tooted the horn at her. He had to go further on to turn around and she thought of backtracking to find a place where he could stop without annoying other drivers, but there wasn't really anything, she was in the middle of the kilometre-long no-stopping stretch. But there was only one car behind him when he stopped and she quickly jumped in so they could get going.

Charlotte cranked up the heater, it was freezing outside. But it seemed the car had only been running a few minutes, so all that achieved was blowing cool air on her. She flicked it back down again. He had been home already, but had come out to pick her up.

'What are you grinning about?' Sean said, glancing over at her.

'Nothing,' Charlotte said and suppressed her smile.

It was supposed to snow, Sean told her, which was good and bad. Good because it meant Charlotte wouldn't have to do the trip across town to school the next day. Bad because the house was cold, wind came in through the gaps in the walls and there had been leaks in the roof after the last snow. Also bad because her parents might stay at home for the day, and they would just end up arguing over when they could make some progress on their insurance claim, over how long they could stay in the house in the state it was in, over whether they should spend some of their own money to make it more liveable and, finally, over whether her mother should ask someone in her family to help them out. That always ended with her father saying no, they would sort it out themselves and it would only be a few more months, they would be seen by an assessor and then repairs could get underway.

Charlotte's uncle Tony, her mother's brother, was a builder and had picked up work for EQC as an assessor. They could ask him to push their claim along. Her mother's uncle was also a builder and, she said, if her father didn't want Tony doing anything about the house, they could ask Gerald and he would help them out the next time he was back in Christchurch. No, her father insisted, there were other people in greater need and they would wait their turn.

'Do you really want our children growing up thinking this is normal?' her mother would ask. Charlotte wondered why she didn't notice that her children were pretty much grown up already.

'Do you want our children growing up thinking they deserve better than other people?' he would counter.

'It's not like that,' her mother would reply.

'Yes, it is,' her father would say. 'There's too much of who-you-know going on in this town and we aren't going to be part of it.'

They had been back together since soon after the September quake, and now they argued more than they ever had before. Charlotte wished they would separate again, and maybe the house would be quiet for a change, a peaceful quiet, not that stony quiet that fell between arguments. Mornings were great, her parents would go off to work, Sean would go off to uni, leaving Charlotte alone until ten-thirty, when she had to get on the bus for her long trek across town. But now she had the evening to get through, and it was unlikely to be peaceful.

'You wanna go somewhere?' she asked Sean. 'Just for a drive around.'

He glanced at her and there was, she thought, pity in that glance. What was he thinking? 'I have to study,' he said. 'Tutorial tomorrow.'

She said nothing.

'Maybe we should get a video Friday night,' Sean said. 'See if Alice wants to come over.'

Charlotte shrugged. That was most of the week away. If her grandmother were home, she could ask to be dropped off there, but Nanny wasn't living at home any more. Her house was damaged and she was moving around the South Island, staying with different members of the family. Charlotte had tried to teach Nanny how to text, but she was hopeless. For one thing, she powered her phone off when she wasn't using it. Even on the day of the February quake when they had been having lunch in the city, Charlotte had to stop her from turning the phone off after sending a text message to different family members: Charlotte & I fine, will head home. They couldn't hear back from people, Charlotte tried to explain, and know that they, too, were fine, unless they kept their phones on. Still, Nanny didn't get it.

Their father was in the kitchen and pulled a plate from the oven as Sean and Charlotte came inside. Sean went straight back through to the lounge while Charlotte sat down at the dining table and started eating. There was a folder full of papers on the table, so tonight was going to be an insurance night. Her father sat down across from her.

'How was your day?' he said, giving her what she supposed he meant as an encouraging smile. She shrugged. What was there to say, given that all the time they had was between now and whenever her mother arrived home. She had thought, when her father moved back home, they would be able to talk more. It had been like that when her parents were separated. Although they only saw each other once a week, he encouraged them to talk, run things past him. He said he wanted his kids to speak their minds, that then he would know what they were thinking about. Charlotte was pretty sure her mother didn't see things the same way, she certainly never seemed interested in what Charlotte had to say. She might ask, but she was never really listening. But when he had moved home after the September quake, he and her mother were all tied up in 'putting their marriage back together', like it was something that had broken in the quake, they just needed to get it assessed properly, then they could figure out a repair strategy and get it scoped and costed. What would a scope of works look like for the repair of a marriage? These were terms they used when talking about the house, and this utilitarian, systematic approach was polluting their marriage.

The garage door opened and her mother's car pulled up the driveway. Her entrance was greeted with a curt, 'I'll get your dinner out of the oven', no hellos, no glancing kisses. Charlotte took her meal through to the lounge, where Sean had books and papers spread out over the coffee table.

'Hey,' he said, only raising his head to glance at her as she sat down on the sofa, her plate on her lap.

'Hey,' she said back and started eating. He was back into his study, and she wondered if he would be finished any time soon so they could, you know, just talk. Even the TV would be welcome company, but she didn't want to interrupt Sean's study.

After Charlotte finished her dinner, she texted her friend Lucy. They had gone to school together but ended up at different high schools. They hadn't seen each other in weeks, Lucy's school had also done the site sharing thing, but she had been going in the mornings, not the afternoons, so there was never a chance to catch up during the week. But now her own school was back to normal, the other school's repairs were finished and they had gone back to their own site. Charlotte had thought she might get to see Lucy more often, but that hadn't happened.

Nothing back. She'd had nothing back in days and had no idea what she had done to offend Lucy.

She flicked through her Instagram feed to see what was going on with everyone. The usual selfies, photos of food, rubble, nothing interesting. She sighed and tossed her phone off to one side. She could hear her parents in the kitchen, voices raised. Insurance nights always ended like this. Non-insurance nights were just silent.

After the September quake, her dad was around at their house within half an hour. Hugs and kisses all around, he had been so worried that he just climbed over the debris at the flat he had moved into and drove right over. They cleaned up the house together, went to check on Nanny together, then on aunts and uncles, the other grandparents and the great-grandparents. He stayed with them that night, sleeping on the sofa, and made them pancakes the following morning, all of them bleary-eyed from the night of aftershocks. In the weeks afterwards, they saw more of him, then, that November, he moved back in.

The summer had been odd. They had all gone down south to the big family gathering, which they did almost every year. Her parents put on a show of being a family again, which annoyed Charlotte, because they never left her alone to do what she wanted. And the long conversations she had been having with her father during the separation were gone. She had taken to getting up early each morning and going for a run, just to get some truly alone time.

On their last day there, Sean had made a big deal about wanting to do his own thing for the day while their mother had planned out where they would have breakfast, lunch and dinner.

'I just want to swim and lie in the sun for the day,' Sean said.

They took him seriously and left them both to their own devices for that last day. That annoyed Charlotte even more than the constant coddling because she had been saying the same thing for the last week and they had taken no notice at all. Was she invisible? Did she have a mute button she didn't know about? Only once the precious son spoke up did they take notice. It wasn't fair. But they did ease off once they got home and for that Charlotte was grateful. They planned little trips for the rest of the holidays, day trips or one or two nights away, and they made a point of letting Sean and Charlotte have time to themselves. It was good and Charlotte started the school year feeling like she was part of a real family, more like a real family than she could ever remember anyway.

Then the February quake hit and the panic of not knowing everyone was okay until late in the day was surpassed by the grind of trying to keep going in a house with no power and no water. They left the city, went to Nelson for three weeks to stay with one of her dad's brothers and his family. Again, that was a family time.

It was when they came back to Christchurch that things started going downhill. Her parents were trying to get the house assessed and fixed, but they struggled to even get people in to patch up the place and make it more liveable. There were cracks everywhere, the floors were uneven and it was difficult to get windows and doors open and shut. Charlotte couldn't close her bedroom door properly until her dad planed off some of the bottom of it.

Their house wasn't as bad as many in the neighbourhood, which was almost deserted. They were on a hill and the hills had been shaken badly in the February quake. Nearby, cliffs had collapsed onto the buildings below and people had died. When they first came home, there were only three other families living on the street, which had thirty-seven houses. Some were badly damaged. One had slumped, crumpling the garage door, another had its front door twisted in the frame. Eventually, people moved back into the neighbourhood to the point where about half the houses were occupied, but the June quakes had done even more damage to the hill suburbs and some families had left once again. There were fourteen occupied houses, including their own. Charlotte thought she had seen someone at the window of a fifteenth, but she didn't want to check too closely, there were rumours of squatters living in abandoned houses throughout the city.

Charlotte flicked through her Instagram feed again and saw that Alice had posted a photo from their summer holiday, her three younger brothers wrestling on the grass outside the house. There were other people in the background and Charlotte recognised herself sitting against a tree with a book. Only she wasn't reading, she was looking off into the distance, towards the hills. She remembered that day, it was the last, when her parents left her and Sean to their own devices for the day. It was a lonely picture of her, so far away from everyone and staring off into the distance. No wonder she didn't have any friends.

Alice's caption said she continued to be amazed that her brothers didn't break each other. Charlotte tried to think of something funny to say in reply, but her brain wasn't cooperating, so she just hearted the photo. Lame. She texted Alice instead, asking if she was still working at the café. Idiot, she thought as soon as she sent the message. Of course Alice was still working there, they had only seen each other two weeks ago. Yes, Alice replied, asking why. Charlotte couldn't think of anything to say. Her phone warbled again. It was Alice, saying she would see them Friday night. Sean must've asked her around for a video, like he had said earlier. Well it was something to look forward to.

She went through to the bathroom and flicked on the light to look at herself in the mirror. She wasn't breaking out horribly like some of the girls at school, which was a relief. She had followed the hair straightening trend for a while, but lately she had just let it do its thing, leaving it to curl and letting it just hang down. No one noticed one way or the other. She pulled her hair up and back from her face and wondered what it would be like to have short hair. It would be easy enough to find out, there were scissors around somewhere. But what if it turned out awful? No, she wasn't going to risk that, she'd get someone to do it, someone who knew what they were doing. She would find some photos, she decided, and go to the mall before school the next day, or the day after if it snowed. Then she would go home and see if anyone noticed. She decided to keep her expectations low.

Opportunity Knocks

October 2011

It was spring again, but a very different spring from that of a year ago. Then people had felt a sense of relief, that they had survived the big one, that their houses had survived the big one, mostly intact. Assessments were getting underway, repairs would follow and then it would all be over.

Now eight months after the February quake, the sense people felt was grief, for the people who had died and the city that was no more, barricaded off from the general population, army sentries on its entry points. Not armed, of course, this was New Zealand and it wasn't wartime, but it felt the way England had felt after the war, people going about their lives only partly awake, avoiding the devastated buildings, coping with life in the damaged ones.

Before the February quake, Marjorie would regularly go into the city to shop at Ballantynes and have lunch in their café. She had done so for many years, decades. She had been in Christchurch long enough to remember the 1947 Ballantynes fire, in which forty-one employees had died. The city was in mourning following that tragedy, too.

Soon Ballantynes would be reopening, at the centre of a new development, a temporary mall built of shipping containers. That was a couple of weeks away, and Marjorie had arranged with her daughter Suzanne to go into the city then and have a good look at the place. Marjorie had not been near the city since the quake, she had seen a ruined city once before, she didn't need to go looking too closely this time. But a return to Ballantynes would be a welcome dose of normality. Marjorie had missed the place, the quality of the service, not like those modern stores where a person could go in looking for something only to end up searching for staff interested in serving them. Not so at Ballantynes, where the sales ladies would ask her what she was looking for, quiz her on her tastes while giving her a discreet visual inspection and then go off and find what she wanted. Now that was service!

Some of the family were still living away from the city but many had returned, and with them Marjorie had returned to her weekly baking ritual. Friday was baking day and then over the days that followed, various family members would drop by to check on her. There was always something for them to have with their cup of tea, and she made sure there was enough to fill a tin they could take away. Her chocolate eclairs and cream horns never made it out of the house, but the date loaf, banana cake, chocolate cake, chocolate chip biscuits and gingernuts were made to be taken away, so they would have reason to remember her fondly. It kept her busy, and she was happy to have the family back in the city.

While most of the family were still away, she had taught Alice her recipes, passing on what her old neighbour had taught her when she first arrived in New Zealand. When Marjorie left home, she had no domestic skills, and when she and Bill started their life together in New Zealand, she struggled to figure out how to keep a house. Her nursing training had taught her the housework basics, that wasn't the issue. The issue was food that was too often ruined and thrown out to the chooks or the dog. A neighbour had taken pity on her, teaching her to cook and bake. The woman had lost a son in the first world war and seemed impossibly old to Marjorie then. Of course, she was probably a couple of decades younger then than what Marjorie was now.

Now Marjorie was passing on those recipes to Alice, savoury and sweet. The girl had been experimenting and Marjorie was pleased at the variations on the old standards she was coming up with. She had the same knack for baking that Marjorie's daughter Judith did. Judith was a baker by trade and ran a successful catering business. Although Marjorie could have suggested to Judith that she give Alice a job, she wouldn't do that to the girl. Judith was always losing staff. She would complain about how difficult it was to find and keep good staff, but the truth was that Judith was not easy to get along with, shrill and demanding, expecting perfection when she hadn't put in the effort to make her expectations clear. No, Alice was better off where she was now, even if a job with Judith was a step up from working at a coffee shop. And Alice was better than that, she had more in her than just being a baker, if only she could get past her grief for the city and the people in it.

In some ways, the war had been easier than this disaster business. There was an enemy to fight against and that kept people going. But in this post-earthquake situation, there was nothing to fight against, there was just keeping going, and without that enemy to rail against, it seemed many were just giving in. Alice was in danger of that, although recently she had told Marjorie she was thinking of leaving Christchurch. Most of her friends were gone and her boyfriend was thinking about going over to Sydney for work. Alice was happy with her decision to not continue with her studies that year, she said she couldn't imagine keeping up and doing well given everything that was still happening in Christchurch. If she wasn't going to go back to university next year, she needed to figure out something to do, she couldn't work at a coffee house indefinitely. Maybe Sydney would be a good change, Marjorie had told her. The girl needed to get out, if the city was going to drag her down with it, she needed to get away to place where she could make something of herself.

Marjorie had just pulled a rack of biscuits from the oven and put another one in when she heard a knocking at the front door. It was her grandson Tony, who had come from work, a fact made apparent by his high visibility vest and EQC identification hanging around his neck. The high vis vest had become like a badge of honour for people working on the rebuild. In fact, it had become so ubiquitous that criminals took to wearing them, showing up at people's houses claiming they were there for inspections when, in fact, they were seeing if there were any valuables in the house. Later they would return and, if the owner wasn't home, break in and take what they wanted. Disasters brought out society's vermin: looters, thieves, bureaucrats and lawyers. Certainly the bureaucrats had come to Christchurch in large numbers, it was only a matter of time before lawyers followed. It was the way a modern society worked.

Tony had been working as an assessor, EQC had taken on people from all over the country and from Australia. They had taken anyone who could, at a stretch, be regarded as having the appropriate skills to assess properties, including ex-policemen. Alice had said she had even seen assessing jobs advertised through the university's Student Job Search service. Marjorie wouldn't be happy having her house assessed by anyone but a builder who knew what they were looking at. As for being assessed by a policeman, she was a customer, not a suspect. But she didn't have to worry about that, her house was well built and had suffered only a few cracks. Gerald had his engineer come through and they had sent his report on to EQC. Tony had used his connections there to see her claim settled quickly and Gerald had the required work done during the winter. The only difficult period was when Marjorie was shut out of her kitchen, but, fortunately, that hadn't gone on for long.

As for Marjorie's rental portfolio, having Tony in EQC had pushed most her properties along nicely and payouts had followed, allowing her to make her own decisions about how repairs were carried out. There were four properties that had more serious damage, and Andrew was handling the insurance side of things for her.

'I was in the area,' Tony said. 'So I thought I would drop by.'

That was unlikely. He wanted something, and she was curious, so she stepped back and let him in. He commented on the scent of the baking and she asked if he wanted a cup of tea. Of course he said yes. Through in the kitchen he sat down at the breakfast bar and helped himself to one of the biscuits cooling on the wire racks and asked after the cream horns. She would be doing those in the morning, she said. He shrugged and bit into the biscuit, started telling her about his work while she made the tea.

He moved on to telling her how his children were doing. He definitely wanted something, it was usually his wife who filled Marjorie in on all that. Tony was never one for paying that much attention to his children so he must have assembled the information as some sort of offering to his grandmother. Yes, he wanted something, and it wasn't just the biscuits. He reached for another one and she was tempted to smack the back of his hand but resisted the urge.

'What do you want, Tony?' she said.

He laughed, biting into the new biscuit. 'That's what I like about you, Grandmother,' he said, speaking around the biscuit. 'You always get right to the point.'

Just as you don't, Marjorie thought. 'Well then?'

'There's houses going overcap,' Tony said, wiping crumbs from his mouth. 'Some are being cash settled and people are sick of the quakes and of Christchurch, so they're just flicking them on, taking the payouts and getting out. There are only a few at the moment, mostly from September and ones really damaged in February, but it's going to be big and there are going to be less damaged properties coming onto the market.'

'And you see this as a good opportunity?'

'Sure. A foundation might need to be replaced outright under an insurance contract. It's a full replacement contract after all. But you could repair it to just be good enough to live in for a while. Rent out the place and once the rebuild is over, bowl the place and use the land for whatever. It'll be worth a fortune, and you've had all that high rent coming in during the rebuild.'

Tony had been managing her rental portfolio for over a decade. He was an efficient manager who vetted the tenants well and made sure they kept up with their obligations. He had gotten value for money out of her payouts and now her repaired rentals were full of people using their insurance company's accommodation allowance while their homes were repaired. Earthquakes were very good for the rental market.

Marjorie thought about what Tony was suggesting. It was a good opportunity.

'Do you have your eye on anything at the moment?' she asked. He would be in an excellent position to spot such properties and keep track of them using his industry contacts as they went through the settlement process.

'I've already picked up one for myself, an old lady who wanted to go into a rest home rather than go through the repair process, so it's not too badly damaged, I'll be able to do it up easily and rent it out,' Tony said. 'I'd like to get a couple more like that, but I thought you'd like to get in as well, too good an opportunity to just let go to waste.'

'How much are they going for?' Marjorie asked.

'Around land value,' Tony said. 'Some places that are less damaged for a little more. Now, anyway. I expect that will change as people twig on to what a great opportunity they are.'

'Is there any dealing with the insurance company?' Marjorie said. Insurance companies were expensive and frustrating to deal with. Getting one's full entitlement always involved lawyers, and Marjorie was happy to have avoided that with her own house and was fortunate enough to have a grandson who was a lawyer who could deal with all that for her more seriously damaged rentals.

'No, as-is-where-is houses are sold with no claims attached, the owner doesn't pass on the settlement, you just get the place, damage and all,' Tony said. He reached for another biscuit, his third. 'It's like just buying the land but you get a damaged house with it. Advantage for the owner is they get to move on, no worries about demolition costs or foundation costs blowing out. The only snag is that banks aren't lending for as-is-where-is houses, you have to have cash.'

She said nothing, just watched the last of the biscuit as it disappeared into his mouth. 'It's not a bad idea,' she said at last.

Tony agreed to pull together some information for her and bring it over in a couple of days. He didn't want to leave it too long, he said, too many good opportunities out there, too good to be missed. Marjorie, though, knew she would be doing her homework.

No point buying land that dictated expensive foundations, any money she made renting it out would be lost trying to build on it in the future. The Government was going to be tightening up requirements for building on some land types, and she wanted to avoid buying those properties.

Marjorie put some of the biscuits into a tin for Tony to take home for his family. It was expected, after all, and it was something her neighbour had taught her all those years ago: feed people and they will do what you want them to do. That wasn't how the old woman had phrased it, of course, she had said that the way to people's hearts was through their stomachs. But Marjorie wasn't terribly interested in their hearts, except to the degree that good baking warmed their hearts and made them more likely to do as Marjorie wished them to do.

Once Tony left, Marjorie had her dinner and settled down in the lounge with a cup of tea to watch the news. She wasn't really watching, though, she was thinking about the property portfolio she had built up and why she was now considering adding to it. She was ninety-one, logic should dictate that she stopped. But she had never been able to resist an opportunity to make money, especially given she had so much expertise available to her in the form of two motivated, competent grandsons.

Tony was like his father in that he was willing to put the interests of the business above the needs of the customers, unlike Gerald, who thought that looking after customers' interests generated loyalty and built a good reputation. The family business had thrived under Tony's father's leadership, whereas Gerald's business had stayed small, he never had more than a dozen men working for him.

The family business had thrived even more after Stan died and Tony took over. Tony was smarter than his father and didn't take the risks Stan had. Tony didn't hire the best workers, they wanted too much money, but he didn't hire the worst either. He expected his workers to be competent, but not inspired, and anyone who took too much time on a job was quickly encouraged to move on. The same went for anyone whose work had to be done again.

The rapid ramping up of the EQC had been another opportunity, and Marjorie had encouraged Tony to put his most trusted foreman in charge of the family business, just for a time, and to take on a role with the EQC. He was drawing a good salary and he was making contacts that meant that once he left, the family business would benefit considerably from the work sent their way.

Andrew, on the other hand, could not be directed so obviously. His parents had instilled in him the golden rule about doing unto others and Andrew had, for a time, struggled with the way the real world worked versus how Gerald and Sylvia told him it should work. These days, though, that notion of the golden rule was just a distant memory for him, something that only became an issue if he was spending too much time around his parents. But they were away in Sydney, with Gerald making monthly trips back to the city to keep his business going. Andrew was seeing little of them, which was good, given the environment in the city and the discussions that would go on between Gerald and his son, about how the Government should do the right thing and help the people of Canterbury move on from the issues caused by the quakes.

When Andrew said to Marjorie that he wanted Michelle and the children to come home after the February quake, she had suggested he let Michelle's anxiety run its course in the peaceful mountain surroundings of Wanaka, it would be better for them as a couple in the long run. Their own house was perfectly habitable in spite of the required repairs and staying in Christchurch for work would allow him to ensure the work was carried out to a good standard. He could go down to Wanaka each weekend and spend time relaxing with his family. Too much family time made Andrew soft, he began to question his priorities.

Studying law had been an excellent choice for Andrew. It gave him a foundation other than his parents' foolish altruism, a framework that helped him understand better how the world worked. He had a good mind, had trained himself well to follow the logic of the law and had learned to hold his own under pressure.

Since the earthquakes started, though, Andrew was getting soft again. Marjorie wasn't sure if it was the quakes themselves – the threat to life – or whether it was the renewed contact between Andrew and his oldest child. Alice's outlook was different from the rest of the Moorhouses, influenced by growing up in a more working class family. When Alice had stayed with Marjorie after the February earthquake, she had been up early in each of the days after the quake, out working as part of the Student Volunteer Army. She had decided after the February quake not to continue with her studies, a decision Marjorie would have talked her out of had she known it was in the cards. Alice needed to focus on building her career, her future, in spite of whatever was going on around them. Post-earthquake Christchurch presented untold opportunities for skilled, motivated young people. But Alice's decision was an emotional one, she was haunted by thoughts of the people who had died in the quake and what their families were going through in the aftermath.

Alice had a good work ethic, unlike so many young people today who preferred to simply 'surf the net', filling their minds with what, as far as Marjorie could tell, was pure nonsense. Marjorie had asked Alice what the appeal of the internet was and Alice had said cat videos. At first Marjorie thought the girl was being polite, that 'cat videos' was a euphemism for something unseemly, but then Alice showed her one of these 'cat videos', a series of scenes where cats interacted with people and with each other in ways that Marjorie supposed could be considered cute. But what a waste of time! Once you're over ninety, or eighty for that matter, you don't even think about wasting time glued to mindless videos. Marjorie's television came on once a day for an hour and a half, for the news at six o'clock through to whatever was passing for current affairs these days on one of the two main stations. Lately, though, she was considering giving up the television altogether, some of the so-called news items were truly mindless, part of the dumbing down of modern society, a society that had more information to hand than any previous generation and yet was less informed.

Gerald and Marjorie had discussed the Government's decision to red zone parts of the city, to buy people out of their difficult situation by taking over their claim with the EQC and their private insurer. Both saw the Government's apparently philanthropic conduct for what it was. The Government would, after all, get most of the money they paid out back from the EQC and from insurers. Whatever was going on, it wasn't the interests of the people of Canterbury they were serving, it was the Government's interests, which was to stay in power. This was virtually guaranteed for the election that was just over a month away, no nation whose second largest city had been devastated by a series of powerful earthquakes would vote the incumbent government out. No, the nation needed stability, even if the city of Christchurch had nothing of the sort. The Government was looking ahead to the election of 2014, which was clear from their promise to bring the nation back into surplus for that year. Their agenda was to look good, generous even, in the eyes of the rest of the nation, while minimising costs on the ground here in the city. That was apparent from what Tony had told her about the internal workings of the EQC and their cosy arrangement with Fletchers.

Gerald wasn't foolish enough to think the Government was being philanthropic, no, that wasn't his problem. His was being an idealist, thinking the world could work in a better way and hoping that one day someone would step up and do it right, form a government that was truly looking out for the interests of all its people, not just those of a select few. Marjorie, though, had lived through a war in which she had lost people she loved. Not that she told Gerald that, she simply stuck to her argument that no government could ever put aside its own interests and the interests of those who cosied up to them.

As far as Marjorie was concerned, governments consumed their citizens, especially those with less, the unfortunates who had weaknesses that opened them up to exploitation. No more was this true than in a war, when it was the sons of the poor, not the sons of the rich, who were sent to die. Or worse, who came back from wars broken, haunted for the rest of their lives by the horrors they had witnessed, sharing out their pain with those closest to them. She had been born into a poor family and had struggled to build a different kind of life for herself. She would never allow herself to go backwards, which was why she would continue to add to her property portfolio.

These quakes weren't over and although her properties had, by and large, fared well, there were four with major damage that would be passed over from EQC to her private insurer. Andrew would do his best, but insurance companies had a way of wriggling out of their obligations, minimising them, and Marjorie could lose money if they decided to play hardball. She needed to add to her portfolio, take on some of these written off properties, to ensure she wouldn't be worse off from the quakes. For that, she needed Andrew to assure her she was buying properties from which she could profit, and for that she needed him to be focused, his mind untarnished with worrying about his family and how they were coping in the aftershocks.

Demolition

November 2011

At the end of October 2011, the central city reopened to retail. The red zone cordon was still there, although it had been reduced to cover only a handful of city blocks. What opened was a new shopping mall, the Re:Start mall, made of shipping containers painted in bright colours and arranged into a shopping precinct. It was meant to be temporary, but it was something cheerful in a year when there wasn't much to be cheerful about. The containers had been set up in Cashel Street near the Ballantynes department store, which had completed its repairs and was ready to act as the anchor retailer, bringing people back into the city. For many, it was the first close look they'd had at their city for eight months.

Alice had gone into the city the afternoon after the container mall's grand opening. The mall was full of colour and vibrancy and, at the same time, unbearably sad. People had died here. Alice was disoriented, the shape the containers assumed was not that of the old, demolished mall but of laneways with courtyards. She kept trying to think of what had been there before, if she was in a spot where someone had died, and she thought of the people, remembering them from the coroner's inquests. The families of the dead had been into the city in the days before the container mall opened, they had been able to pay their respects. But could that ever be enough?

Now Alice was back in the city with her cousin Tyler, walking around the rubble, pointing out buildings that had not yet been demolished. Tyler was Kevin's nephew, and he was the same age as Alice. Ever since Lindsay and Kevin had gotten together, Tyler would visit her family in Christchurch for a week or so at a time and she would go and visit his family in Blenheim. After leaving school, he did a carpentry course and had been working for a builder since then. The previous week, he had decided to quit his job and move to Christchurch for the rebuild. It was, he said, the best opportunity for someone like him to really set himself up, he wouldn't be out of work for a decade. Kevin warned him it wouldn't be easy, and that he should've held onto his existing job and taken a few days to check out possibilities in Christchurch. But the cautious way was not Tyler's way, never had been.

Walking around rubble had become a habit for Alice. There was little else to do when she wasn't working or looking after the kids. There were no restaurants, no bars, at least not on the eastern side of town. Most of the Port Hills walking tracks were off limits, the only one near to home was too exposed for Alice, a fierce wind often came up over the ridge and she would end up freezing cold, in spite of the effort required to slog to the top of the hill.

Friends. There weren't many around. Emma, who Alice had walked home with the day of the quake, had stayed with her parents until after the June quakes, which had been the death knell for their brick house. Her parents had moved out to Rangiora to stay with Emma's brother and his family. Emma had been working for a bank in Riccarton since the February quake, but didn't fancy commuting all the way from Rangiora into Riccarton every day, so left for Australia.

Some of the people Alice had been at uni with the year before had chosen to transfer to another university and those who stayed on seemed worn out by the temporary lecture theatres, the confusion of a university that wasn't quite functioning as normal. What was?

Alice had warned Tyler the place was dead boring, but he said he'd be okay, she was there to keep him company. Alice wasn't so sure that was a good idea. She was used to the place, Tyler wouldn't be, he had a short attention span and when the dullness of the place drove him crazy, he would start driving her crazy.

The previous Friday night had been one of those times. Alice had been spending Friday nights with Sean and Charlotte for a couple of months. They would watch a video, at either her place or theirs. That Friday night, Sean and Charlotte had come around and Kevin and Lindsay had gone out for the night. Well, they had gone to visit friends for the night, there was little to go out to in the city, which was why Alice, Sean, Charlotte and Tyler stayed in watching a video. Which Tyler had complained about the whole time. Alice had picked the original *Jaws* because she thought it would appeal to him, but instead he fidgeted the whole time, swapping between sitting on the sofa or on one of the beanchairs. At one point, he sat back down on the sofa with a dramatic whump, knocking against Sean, who had a bowl of popcorn in his lap. The bowl upended and popcorn went everywhere, all over the sofa, between the cushions and down on top of Charlotte, who was sitting in a beanchair in

front of the sofa. They paused the movie and cleaned up, Sean
muttering about Tyler and Tyler complaining about how boring the
movie was, why couldn't they go out and do something?

'We can't go to a nightclub,' Sean spelled out, 'because there
aren't any. And even if there were, Lottie is fourteen, she's not
allowed in.'

'She doesn't have to go,' Tyler said. 'Just because we're going
doesn't mean she has to tag along.'

'Nice,' Alice said. 'Real nice, Ty. Just sit down, shut up and watch
the movie.' Which he did, quietly, but that was only because every
time he seemed about to open his mouth and complain, Alice poked
him in the ribs. In the end, the final battle between the shark and
Chief Brody kept his attention, but she couldn't get him to admit
that the movie was actually pretty cool.

'Your cousin's an idiot,' Sean had told Alice on the way out.

'Your cousin's a knob,' Tyler told her once Sean and Charlotte
were down the driveway and out of hearing range.

Although Alice and Tyler had always gotten along, it was
different now. The quakes had changed her whereas for Tyler, they
were almost entertainment. Alice had matured, or at least she
thought she had, but he was still the same as he had been at fifteen,
and he hadn't been particularly mature then.

One summer when Alice was still in high school, Tyler was
staying with them. They were fifteen and the next year would be
their first year of NCEA. Alice wasn't worried about herself,
although she would get stressed over the exams, but she was
worried about Tyler. He didn't like school, didn't like reading and
wanted to leave as soon as he could. But he had no plans for
anything other than hanging around his mother's house playing
games. When Alice brought it up, he accused her of being too
serious, of having her life too planned out. That wasn't true, she
would point out, she had no idea what she was going to do at
university. But you know you're going to university, he would say,
and she would feel like her life *was* too planned out, that maybe she
had just assumed she would cruise through high school and into
whatever course she chose at university.

She had decided not to go back to university this year for
reasons she barely understood herself. Lately, though, she had
found herself thinking about last year's courses, what she had
learned, and she realised that her interest in the subject was still
there. Maybe, given some time, going back to university would be a
good idea, the right choice. She had voiced these thoughts to Tyler,

she thought that he would understand as they had known each other so long.

'You should do a trade,' he said. 'Be a builder. Get your hands dirty.'

'I have no problem with getting my hands dirty,' Alice said. She had explained this to Tyler already, the reason she wasn't working for Kevin was that Kevin was having trouble picking up work. So much of the available work was tied up with Fletchers and although Kevin had registered for that work, he found it difficult to get any. On the jobs he did get, he had been pressured to cut corners. He said it was all about cutting costs, not about making sure people's houses were repaired properly, and when it became clear that there was unlikely to be more work coming his way, he made the difficult decision to let his guys go. So no, Alice wasn't working for Kevin. Kevin was barely working for Kevin. Apart from Fletchers, there wasn't much work going on. Insurers weren't offering insurance on building work because of the ongoing quakes, so for one reason or another, everything was stalled. Kevin had told Tyler it would be best to go back home, that if there was work for him there, it would be better for him to be there. Tyler, though, had decided that Christchurch was his big opportunity and couldn't see past his dream to the reality of the stalled rebuild.

It was over a year since the first quake, and Alice thought about how different her life was. If it weren't for the quakes, she would be nearing the end of the second year of her engineering degree and looking for a work experience placement. In the rebuild environment it would be interesting work. Or would she also experience the pressure to compromise that Kevin had experienced? She didn't like the idea of that because it was clear from the Royal Commission that cutting corners in an engineering sense meant risking lives, and she didn't want to be part of that.

Instead, here she was, in the city with her man-boy cousin watching a building being demolished. An enormous digger, nicknamed Twinkle Toes, was tearing away at a building some seven or eight stories high, dropping steel and concrete onto the site below. Tyler wondered what he would need to do to qualify to drive such a thing.

'I thought you were a builder,' Alice said. 'This is anti-building.'

'Yeah, but it's cool,' Tyler said. His hands were gripping the wire fencing, his eyes had a faraway glaze. She wondered if he was thinking of it as a video game. Actually, that wasn't a bad idea, a video game about building demolition that you won by making the building collapse faster.

No, she told herself, this wasn't a game. The rebuild was about people's lives, which were on hold while the bureaucrats worked at getting the rebuild underway. The rebuild would take off in 2012, people were saying. But what if they were still staying the same thing about 2013? Or 2014 even? Alice hoped that wasn't the case, she didn't want to move away from her friends and family, well family anyway, most of her friends had already left. But she also didn't want to spend years living in a broken city, finding things to keep herself amused. She wasn't attention deficient the way Tyler was, but, she had to admit, the place was getting tedious. Something needed to change, progress needed to be made, and all she was seeing lately was demolition. She kept telling herself demolition was progress, the first step in getting the rebuild underway, but standing outside a building site watching a giant digger tearing bites out of a sad, broken building didn't feel like progress. It felt like an autopsy. The city was being taken apart and hauled away, buried in a landfill north of the city. The old Christchurch was dead, this demolition process was about watching it decay.

Alice dragged Tyler away from the demolition and in the direction of the container mall. She needed to see something that would give her hope and as they wandered through the mall, looping through the laneways, she felt that sense of hope. The thinking that had resulted in the container mall could be applied to the wider rebuild, and if that happened, the city would be exciting, full of life, more than it had ever been before the quakes.

'Pretty lame,' was all Tyler would say. She wanted to hit him, punch him in the arm, but resisted the urge. That would be immature, something fifteen-year-old Alice would do. But that Alice was gone. She had been carried away with the debris of the city she loved.

A Shaky End

December 2011

After the building collapses in the February earthquake, the Canterbury Earthquakes Royal Commission was established to find out why buildings had collapsed, why people had been killed and injured. Public hearings started in November 2011. Until those hearings began, many in the city believed that it was the intensity of the shaking that had caused the building collapses, that such collapses were unavoidable given the ferocity of the February quake. Privately some may have considered that there were other factors, but it wasn't until the public hearings were underway that it started to become apparent the degree to which failures in communication and failures to address known issues had set up the situations in which so many people could die.

Following the first quake in September 2010, the city had a placard system in place sorting buildings into three categories in a rapid assessment process. Red placards were for buildings that were too dangerous to occupy, yellow for buildings that should only be entered on essential business and green for buildings for which there was no restriction on occupancy. After significant aftershocks buildings would be assessed once again. Of course building owners were keen to keep a green placard so their tenants could go about their business without interruption, and those with yellow or red placards wanted to be certain that the assessment was correct so they could go about their business, if circumstances made that possible.

As became clear from the early public hearings, there was often confusion about roles and responsibilities, who could say a building was safe to occupy and the criteria for determining so. One building that was regarded as safe to occupy collapsed in the February quake, its façade falling onto the road and killing a man sitting in his vehicle. In another case, a building that collapsed killing eighteen people had structural flaws that had been known about for twenty years, and the building had been known to be quake-prone as long as five years before its collapse. The building had been sold in 2009, but its new owner didn't know it was regarded as quake prone. His property manager did, but had never told the owner. Alice followed the news stories about these hearings and did a mental tally of how many people might have lived if people had been less passive about buildings known to be dangerous. If people knew of potentially dangerous situations, surely they would do something rather than assuming that someone else would be sorting the problem?

As far as Alice was concerned, the Royal Commission hearings were a depressing end to a surreal and stressful year. She thought she had dealt with the stress of the quakes pretty well, overall, but lately she had found herself crying at random things. Buildings disappearing she hadn't previously thought she had an attachment to, art works appearing on random walls around the city, paradise duck babies in the river going through the city. Little things, little hints of normality and beauty making appearances among the rubble.

She was looking forward to getting out of the city, to being somewhere else where she could work through everything she had experienced in the past year. Lindsay was, strangely, keen to stay. They had swapped roles lately, Lindsay being the mum once again and taking care of Alice. Alice said she wanted to go to the West Coast with Andrew and Michelle for a couple of days before Christmas, they were staying with Andrew's cousin Rebecca and her husband Dan at a house on a lake. It would the closest Michelle and the kids had been to Christchurch since February. It still wasn't clear when they would be moving back.

Sean and Charlotte were going over to the lake as well, and Alice was looking forward to spending some time outdoors with her cousins. Alice had been reluctant to bring this up with Lindsay in case she felt slighted because Alice would be spending holiday time with Andrew's side of the family, but Lindsay surprised her when she said she should go for longer, have a good break. No, Alice insisted, she would go over for two nights then come back in time for lunch on Christmas day.

'We'll go up Rapaki afterwards,' Lindsay said. 'Work off all that food.' Before the February quake, the Rapaki Track to the Summit Road had been the family's favourite trail up the hills, but since February, it had been closed because of rockfall. The track was opening up again the Friday before Christmas, the day Alice would be driving to the coast.

After coming back to Christchurch for a couple of days, she was going to spend a week in Timaru with Ben. She had told him she wanted to go to Sydney with him and they were going to make their plans.

As for the lake, the adults had gone over a couple of days earlier, and Alice was to pick up Sean and Charlotte and drive across to the coast. Although she got away from home at eleven, Sean and Charlotte hadn't even started packing, and they would be away a lot longer than her. She had brought them lunch from the bakery in Woolston, thinking that they would all just scoff that and get going. Not a chance. Yes, they did scoff their lunches, but it would be a while before they got themselves sorted. Alice settled down in the kitchen, made herself a coffee and started to flick through news websites on her phone while waiting for the two of them to get their act together. Nothing to see, it was close to Christmas and so the media had given up its usual pretext of reporting on serious matters.

Soon Sean came through and asked her what she was looking at.

'Nothing much,' she said. 'What's Charlotte doing? When will she be ready?'

Sean shrugged. 'She's on her phone.'

Alice texted Charlotte to hurry her up. Charlotte texted back a photo of her middle finger, then a selfie of her face twisted, her eyes crossed. 'You know, we should just leave her behind,' Alice said loudly to Sean. 'There's food here, she'll be fine.'

Alice knew Charlotte better now than she had last year. In the last few months, she and Sean and Charlotte had spent more time together, and Alice no longer thought of Charlotte as the selfish brat from last summer. She wasn't sure if Charlotte was no longer the same person she had been a year ago or if Alice simply knew her better. People had changed because of the quakes, Alice knew she had changed, maybe Charlotte had too. Alice asked Sean.

'I don't know,' he said, after thinking for a moment. 'She's easier to live with, those few months after the September quake she was a pain in the arse, angry over everything. So annoying.'

'Where was she during the quake?' Alice said. It was either something people talked about right away when they first met up after the February quake or it came out gradually, when someone was ready to talk about it. Alice tended to be in the first category. But Charlotte didn't talk about the quakes.

'At South City with Nana,' Sean said. 'The only thing she's ever said is that Nana screamed a lot.'

'You didn't hear from your mum for a while, did you?'

Sean nodded. 'It wasn't until that night, when she finally arrived home. She had left her phone in her office and couldn't go back in, so she just had to walk home. Lottie was really upset.'

Charlotte walked into the kitchen and slapped a half-full backpack onto the benchtop. 'You two ready?'

'That's all you're taking?' Sean said.

'Mum took most of my stuff,' Charlotte said. She poured herself a glass of milk and started drinking, giving herself a milky moustache. Charlotte's hair was a lot shorter than it had been. She had it all cut off without warning a few months ago, ended up sporting an edgy asymmetrical cut that framed her face and drew attention to her eyes, which were the same blue as Alice's. The interest in the edgy cut had lasted only a couple of weeks, it needed to be straightened every day to keep control of the curls, and she quickly decided to grow it back out. Longer was easier, she said.

'What've you been doing all this time?' Sean said.

'Filling up my iPod,' Charlotte said. 'Don't wanna get bored.'

Alice rolled her eyes, Sean rolled his back, while Charlotte sipped slowly at the rest of the milk. 'Let's go,' Alice said, 'before it gets dark.' She slung her handbag over her shoulder and walked purposely towards the front door. Sean followed.

'You're so serious now that you're nearly twenty,' Charlotte called after her.

'Leaving without you,' Alice called without turning back.

Charlotte flew out the front door ahead of Sean, who locked up behind them.

The day was warm and sunny, the sky blue and crisp. The roads were reasonably clear, despite being so close to Christmas, so they made good time to Springfield, where Charlotte started complaining about the lack of cellular coverage as the signal dropped away.

'Who are you texting?' Sean asked. 'Why aren't they doing stuff with their family instead of texting you?'

'No one,' Charlotte said. It was her friend Lucy, Alice guessed. Although Alice had never met Lucy, she knew a lot about her from the photos Charlotte posted of the two of them on Instagram, and would recognise her if she ran into her at the mall. Which was likely, Lucy seemed to spend a lot of time there. Alice was sure she hadn't been like that at fourteen, mall and clothing-obsessed. Maybe if she had, she would have better fashion sense now. Or maybe she was beyond help, it was difficult to tell, she hadn't yet developed those critical faculties.

'Well this No One will be okay with there being no signal,' Alice said. She sounded like her mother.

Charlotte huffed and from the driver's seat Alice could see her turn her head to stare out the window at the passing countryside. There was a smile on her face, clearly she was messing with them.

They were starting up the road towards Porters Pass. She was looking forward to the top of the pass, when the road swept down between the tussock-clad hillsides, it was like driving into a new world, the golden tussock low against the grey shingle of the eroding mountains. It was her favourite part of the road, a world away from the rubble and rough roads of Christchurch. Charlotte commented on the beauty of the pass, echoing Alice's thoughts.

The tussock-clad mountains started to give way to the rocky outcrops of Castle Hill. 'Can we stop?' Charlotte asked as they came up to the turn off to the Castle Hill walkway. 'I need to pee.'

'You know there's no coverage there?' Sean said.

'Don't stop then,' Charlotte said.

Sean rolled his eyes at Alice.

'I need to pee,' Alice said. 'And I'm sick of sitting.'

In spite of the sunny day and it being December, it was cold outside. It was high up in the mountains, after all, but it was still a surprise after all the sun burning through the car's windows. Charlotte quickly got back into the car and closed her eyes, leaning her head against the window.

'Aren't you going to pee?' Sean said, tapping on the window. Charlotte scowled, but didn't reply.

After going to the loo, Alice walked up to where Sean was reading an information board that marked the start of the track. The track went up to a bunch of rocky limestone outcrops. Alice had been up the track years ago, as part of a school trip. She didn't feel inclined to go for a walk at the moment, all she wanted was to get somewhere where she could have a swim. But she asked Sean anyway.

'Wanna go up?'

'Nah.' He shrugged. 'It would just annoy her, us taking so long. And then we still have over an hour in the car with her.'

They walked back to the car and got in.

'About time,' Charlotte said.

Alice and Sean said nothing. Sean connected his phone back up to the stereo and cranked up the volume. Charlotte may have been saying something about his choice of music, but it was simply too loud to hear.

Soon they were crossing the Waimak, then the road entered the southern beech forest that marked the point that had always said to Alice that it wasn't long until they reached Arthur's Pass. She turned down the music to ask if they needed to stop. Sean said yes, he was hungry.

'You had a pie two hours ago,' Alice said.

'It was a small pie,' he said.

'Charlotte?' Alice said, glancing back. Charlotte's phone had beeped a bit and she had her head down reading.

'There's been another quake,' she said, looking up. 'Can we stop?'

Alice pulled into the carpark at the railway station, a pit of dread in the bottom of her stomach. Again? A 5.9, Charlotte said, just over an hour ago. That would've been around the time they were coming down Porters Pass. Alice powered up her phone. She had a message from her mother saying they were all fine, her grandparents were fine. Alice tried calling home, but there was no answer. There was no answer at Neil and Heather's. Next she tried Marjorie, who reassured her it had been nothing really, she had lost a glass that had fallen off the kitchen bench. That was no surprise, all the old lady's knick knacks were still blu-tacked to their shelves, cupboards bungee-corded shut.

Sean and Charlotte were both talking on the phone, Alice couldn't tell with who. Sean finished his call, his mate Joe had been at Riccarton Mall where everyone had panicked and poured out onto the streets. People were tired, Joe had told him, people just looked like they'd had enough.

Charlotte was making another phone call. 'Nanny,' she said to Sean and Alice, while she waited for the call to connect. 'Are you okay?' she said when the call connected.

Alice and Sean could hear the muted buzz of Suzanne's voice on the other end. Sean gestured at her to put it on speaker, which she did. She was at the office, she said, closing up for the end of the year. She was working for Gerald, helping him out while Sylvia was still in Sydney.

'It wasn't too bad,' she said, but her voice was high enough in pitch that they could tell she had been scared. 'I'm just going to tidy up then go home and see what the damage is.'

They were just saying their goodbyes when they heard it, even over the phone, a rumble, and then Suzanne was screaming and they could hear sounds of furniture and equipment shaking.

'Get down, get down, get down,' they were yelling, and then the rumbling faded into the distance and Suzanne stopped screaming. They could hear her rapid breathing. They felt the earth swell under the car as the wave passed across the island. That would be a six. Once again, Christchurch had a five followed soon after by a six. It wasn't fair.

'I'm all right,' Suzanne said. 'A couple of things have fallen over, but it's not too bad.'

'Are you sure?' Sean said. 'Do you want us to come back?'

'No, I'm fine,' she said. 'You keep going, and enjoy yourselves.'

After a few rounds of reassurances, they disconnected the call.

'Do you think we should keep going?' Charlotte said.

'She says she's okay,' Sean said. 'She'd feel pretty stink if we went back.'

Charlotte nodded, but clearly wasn't happy about the idea of not going back. In fact, she looked like she was going to cry. 'Can we get something to drink?' she said, sniffing. 'Just stay here for a few minutes in case we hear back from anyone.'

'Okay,' Alice said, and started up the car. Just up the road they stopped at the general store where Alice and Charlotte ordered coffees, while Sean bought a pie, chips and a Coke. They rolled their eyes at him.

'Don't go flatting,' Alice said. 'Paying for your own food you'll never be able to afford your fees next year.'

There were a few more messages from people about the city, Alice ended up copying the same message and sending it in reply. Everyone they heard back from was fine, there didn't seem to be much damage, and by the time they finished their drinks, Charlotte seemed to feel better about continuing on.

An hour later, they arrived at the lake, where the four parents were sitting on the deck outside the holiday home, the women sipping from glasses of wine and the men from bottles of beer. Andrew stood up, waved her around the corner and started to walk off the deck in the direction of somewhere behind the house. Alice followed his directions and pulled her car up alongside the house, behind Andrew's and rolled down the window. He leaned in, the bottom of his half-empty bottle tinking on the car door, the smell of the beer coming off his breath and into the car.

'No quake talk,' he said. 'Shell and Rebecca are really upset. Rebecca wants to go check on home, but she also doesn't want to go back.'

'Okay,' all in the car said.

'We don't even say where we were?' Alice said.

'Nothing. We've agreed not to talk about it, it won't do anyone any good. The kids don't know, they were all running around so didn't notice it, and we're not telling them.'

They got out of the car and walked up the deck, said their hellos to everyone, air kisses exchanged with Michelle and Rebecca, glasses of wine (Alice), beer (Sean) and Coke (Charlotte) pressed into their hands.

'Swap ya,' Charlotte said to Alice only to be growled at by her father.

The younger children could be heard from behind the house, doing who knew what. Alice decided to finish the wine before she ventured out to see what was going on.

'When's dinner?' Sean said.

'He had a pie an hour ago,' Alice said. 'And another before we left. And chips.'

There was no talk of the day's quakes, which was easy before the children went to bed, but it led to some odd silences afterwards. It seemed no one in Christchurch knew what to talk about apart from the quakes any more, except for insurance, and that was also quickly ruled an off-limits topic. Sean broke out a Monopoly Deal deck, but couldn't persuade the adults to play, so it was just he, Alice and Charlotte, trying to be quiet so the children didn't get woken up.

Alice was worn out when she went to bed, in a room she was sharing with Charlotte and Mattie. Poor Sean was sharing with Alice's brothers and although that was peaceful enough once the boys had fallen asleep, it sentenced Sean to an early morning. Every morning.

Alice woke early the next morning and noticed Charlotte was already gone. Alice managed to dress without waking Mattie and sneaked out of the house for a run along the road. It was cool outside and the sky was still pink from the rising sun. The sky was cloudless, promising a sunny, warm day. Alice walked, then picked up her pace to a jog, continuing up the road, listening to the bellbirds calling from the bush lining each side of the road. It was so peaceful, the only noises natural ones, no dust in the air, no heavy traffic, no listening for the sound of a quake approaching from the distance.

She ran along the road to the next bay and walked down to feel the temperature of the water. It was cold, but not icy, it would be great for swimming as the day heated up. She thought about staying down at this little beach for a while, but she wanted to get back and help out with breakfast. She started back, running once again. As she came near the turnoff to the house, she saw Charlotte coming off the track that went up to a waterfall. She was wearing the clothes she had been wearing yesterday, black jeans and a t-shirt. Alice picked up her pace to catch up with her. Charlotte turned as she heard Alice running up behind her, and Alice saw that her face was red, she was sweating heavily.

'Did you run up there?' Alice said, impressed.

Charlotte nodded. 'And back down.'

'How far is it?'

'About ten minutes, maybe.'

'Wanna race?'

'Not now,' Charlotte said. 'Need to eat.' She took off towards the house, racing away from Alice. 'But I'll race you back to the house!' she called back.

Alice did her best to catch up, but she had already pushed herself and when she slowed down and began to walk, she found herself shaking, but whether it was because of the exertion or the year she had been through she couldn't be sure.

Part II: Broken City

There is a temple in ruin stands,
Fashion'd by long-forgotten hands:
Two or three columns, and many a stone,
Marble and granite, with grass o'ergrown!
— *Lord Byron, Siege of Corinth*

Towns find it as hard as houses of business
to rise again from ruin.
—*Honore de Balzac*

The Break Up

January 2012

Alice was stopped at the traffic lights at Eastgate, waiting to right turn into Linwood Avenue. In the car in front of her, a couple was smoking, exchanging a single cigarette. The man was in the driver's seat, would take a puff and hand it to the woman, who took her own puff and handed it back. Back and forth, back and forth, there was a rhythm and unity to the motion that spoke of familiarity. The green arrow came on and the woman held on to the cigarette as they right-turned. Alice followed their car around the corner, then into the turnoff to the mall.

She and Ben had argued the night before, well as much as you can argue in a series of text messages. But it was just a rehashing of the arguments they'd had in person during her last couple of days in Timaru. Now, after last night's argument, instead of staying with her and her family for a few days before leaving for Sydney, he was going to come up to Christchurch and fly out the same day.

The mall's two-storey carpark had been demolished soon after the quake and the space behind the mall was open to the wide blue sky. It was a huge improvement on the dull, crowded understorey of the carpark with its too-tight parking spaces and narrow aisles that she'd found tricky to back out of if there was a long vehicle opposite her. Of course that was a couple of years ago, when she was a relatively new driver, but the old carpark was gone now so she wouldn't have the chance to test her skills, to see if she had improved. She told herself she was being silly, you couldn't grieve for an opportunity missed to test your carparking skills, that was being over-the-top as far as the whole missing-old-Christchurch thing went. But she did miss driving up onto the top storey and looking out over the trees of Linwood towards the hills and the estuary. Today the sight would be amazing, the sky clear and blue, stretching out into the Pacific Ocean, not a cloud in sight.

The couple who had been in front of her at the lights were walking across the carpark to the mall, swapping back and forth what must now be the tiny end of the cigarette. Alice hated cigarette smoke, the smell of it made her think of closed, stale rooms and stained walls. Her grandfather Neil's mother had been a lifelong smoker and after she died, Lindsay had bought her house. That was when Alice was seven and when she and Lindsay moved in, they had cleaned it from top to bottom. The wallpaper in the lounge they had thought was a golden brown had turned out to be something else, only discovered when Lindsay tried to scrub a mark away. They scrubbed the whole wall and then the whole room back to its original colour, which was a nearly-white that they much preferred to the golden brown. The room seemed brighter for their effort, the house more theirs. Lindsay then hired a carpet cleaning machine, which sucked up murky water and, the second time around, less murky water. That would have to do, Lindsay decided at that point, there was only so much you could get out of old carpet. She would save for renovations, take up the carpets and polish the floors if they turned out to be native timbers, the house was the right age for it. They painted the walls, but they never got around to doing the floors.

It wasn't a great house, but it was what Lindsay could afford at the time. They had been living with Neil and Heather for nearly two years, Lindsay saving up money working as a receptionist at a doctor's office while Heather looked after Alice outside school hours. Alice had loved living with her grandparents, but, looking back, she could see how hard it had been for the adults. There were times now when Alice thought Lindsay was being too hard on Olivia and Jack, and she had to stop herself from criticising Lindsay's parenting of them. She wasn't the mother, she had to keep her views to herself. Instead, she made a point of giving Olivia and Jack a cuddle when they needed one, of being a good big sister, not another mother.

When Lindsay and Kevin decided to live together, it was his house that Lindsay and Alice moved into. Alice resented that, leaving the old one, it had been hers and Lindsay's project and at the time it felt like Lindsay was abandoning their project for something more interesting. In the old house, Alice had her bedroom exactly the way she wanted it, Lindsay had let her pick the wall colour, a pale purple that matched the pink and purple flowers of her duvet cover. She was ten when they left that house, and it felt like a death, like she was leaving her happy childhood behind.

In Kevin's house it was different, all of Lindsay's and Alice's furniture had to fit in with Kevin's tastes, which meant that Alice's opinions took a back seat. She felt left out, alone, and it had taken a long time for her to stop feeling that way around Kevin.

She felt that way now, alone and irrelevant, watching the smoking couple walking into the mall. Her destination was the supermarket whereas theirs was the main doors to the mall, so she veered off, making a point of looking away from their cosy familiarity.

During her time in Timaru after Christmas, she and Ben had talked about going to Sydney. After the December quake, she had been dead keen to leave. As the days passed, though, her certainty had faded and she had started to think about the things she would miss. Ben wanted to go right away, by the end of January, but she wanted to give notice at her job and say goodbye to people, not just rush away as though she was abandoning them to whatever the faults in the city were going to do.

Christchurch was a place full of fear and anxiety in the weeks after the December quakes. There were aftershocks, which was expected after a magnitude six quake, but after the deaths in February and over a year of regular earthquakes, the population was worn out and on edge. Then at the start of the year there had been a rumour going around that scientists knew there was a big quake coming, another one off the coast, further east than the ones just before Christmas. The rumours said this quake would generate a tsunami that some people feared would wipe out northern Christchurch and the satellite towns north of the city, where many of the city's residents had moved to get away from the quakes. To some, it seemed like the quakes were pursuing them, getting closer, and that there was nowhere they could go to escape them. In some ways that was true, there were few places in New Zealand that weren't quake prone, but fear and statistical risk were not things that mixed well together. That was what the scientists were meeting about, analysing the statistical risk and revising the aftershock forecast for Christchurch, they didn't have any secret knowledge of a coming apocalypse.

Although Lindsay didn't buy into the fear (so she said), she was worn out, and after coming home from Timaru, Alice started to feel like she couldn't leave, not yet. Maybe at the end of summer or in the autumn, she said to Ben. He couldn't wait that long, he said, there was nothing for him in Christchurch, no job prospects as long as the city centre was in lockdown, as long as there were still quakes and uncertainty about the future of business in the city. It was a conversation they had been having for months, and every time he said there was nothing for him in Christchurch, she resented it, because she was here, and he said he loved her, but it seemed he didn't rate her highly enough to keep giving Christchurch a go. He didn't understand why she wanted to stay here, to keep working in a café making coffees, he thought her mother would be fine without her. Alice couldn't let go, he said, she was too comfortable living at home, being a child.

Had Alice and Ben ever had that comfortable familiarity of the couple sharing the smoke? For a few months there, Alice thought they did, or were starting to. She would go down to Timaru to see him for a few days or he would come up to Christchurch. But that had been a few days here and there, and it was always just her and him, an escape from the stress of trying to cope with life in Christchurch. That feeling of normalness and ease had made her start to think about where they were going. Such a cliché, where they were going, and it annoyed her to start thinking along those lines, she wasn't even twenty yet. But it seemed like he was thinking along those lines, too, because he had started talking about going to Sydney together. There would be good jobs there, he said, they could get a flat or find someone looking for flatmates. She had been thinking about it more and more, and the quakes of the 23rd of December helped her make up her mind, another five followed by a six. It seemed like the whole quake sequence was never going to end and now every five would be followed by the anxious wait for the trailing six.

Although they had flatted together for half a year in 2010, Ben hadn't been around much until after he split up with his girlfriend. Then there was a month or so when he was spending too much time drinking with his boozy mates, which had been where he was at when the first quake came along. His near miss falling asleep on the sofa the night of the first quake had seemed to shake him out of that, and in the months after, they had kept in touch, getting to know each other better. She had thought she was seeing the real Ben for the first time and she'd realised she liked him.

Before the doublet of quakes, Alice had planned to spend a couple of days in Christchurch with Lindsay and Kevin before going down to Timaru to spend some time with Ben. But Lindsay and Kevin left Christchurch for Timaru on the day of the new quakes, so there was no point going home. Alice stayed on the West Coast with Andrew and his family for an extra couple of days, then drove straight to Timaru, bypassing Christchurch altogether. It felt good not going back, and as she drove the road from Springfield to Timaru, she enjoyed the beauty of the mountains and the rivers and felt alive again in a way she hadn't since the quakes began. Yes, it would probably be good for her to leave Christchurch.

In the end, she missed Lindsay and Kevin, because they went back to Christchurch before Alice arrived in Timaru. Alice was annoyed that Lindsay hadn't thought to let her know they were going back home and wondered if it was some subtle dig at Alice for spending Christmas with her *other* family. Although Lindsay never said anything against Andrew and his family, there was this feeling Alice picked up, of something Lindsay disapproved of. Lindsay hadn't just broken up with Andrew, she had broken up with his entire family, and Alice had missed out on knowing her grandparents and her half-siblings. Surely Lindsay understood that Alice wanted to make up for lost time?

She tried to put her complicated family situation behind her and concentrate on spending time with Ben and getting to know his family better. Ben's father worked long hours and Alice had never spent much time around him, but over the holidays, he had time off and it was the first time she had spent more than a couple of hours around him. As the days wore on, Alice started to see her own family in a different, better light as she saw how Ben and his father treated his mother. They expected his mother to wait on them, and would snipe at her when she did something they perceived as wrong, finding fault with the food, critiquing the way she stacked the dishes as she cleared the table or yelling through to the kitchen where she and Alice were filling the dishwasher, complaining that they wanted to start watching the video they had hired for the evening. Why couldn't they come through and help? Alice had spent time around Ben's mother before and Ben wasn't like that when his father wasn't around, he helped with the dishes and with the cooking. When the whole family was together, though, there was an undercurrent, something nasty, and Alice wanted to go home to escape the cool silences that seemed to roll in like fog. But she hung on until the end so it didn't look like she was trying to get away from Ben. Though she had been desperate to stay away from Christchurch after the last series of quakes, she was then relieved to be driving up the straight stretch of highway towards Christchurch and home. Aftershocks and her irritation with her own mother were preferable to whatever was going on in that family.

When she called Ben and told him she was thinking of staying in Christchurch until autumn, he said she was being a child, and the mocking tone he used with her had been the same one he and his father used when talking to his mother. Alice felt small, and then she felt angry and ended the call. He texted to tell her she had just proven how immature she was, and she had resisted the urge to text back, to keep the argument going. Now that would be childish and immature. But after a string of nasty texts from Ben, she had fired one back, and then another until finally he had said he would drive up and fly out the same day. And that, it seemed, was that.

Ben was right, she could be childish, but she didn't think she was being childish about wanting to be spoken to respectfully. And she didn't think it was childish to worry about her family, to want to be there for them to help them cope.

When Lindsay and Alice had first moved in with Kevin, Alice had held on to her resentment like it was oxygen. The nights Kevin cooked, she would pick at her food, pushing it around her plate. She would refuse to be drawn into conversation, giving only one or two word answers, or none at all if she thought she could get away with it. If she needed help with her homework, she would accept Lindsay's help but refuse Kevin's, and each morning she would take a cup of coffee through to her mother, but never one for Kevin. Neither Lindsay nor Kevin had ever brought it up with her, and looking back she could see that the decision had been made to let her work through it herself.

Back then, she could hear Lindsay and Kevin through in the lounge talking each night, after Alice had gone to bed. She couldn't hear what they were saying and at first she would get herself twisted up over the possibility they were talking about her. Then there was a night when Kevin had to work late and Alice couldn't fall asleep. She was waiting for the sound of that conversation, Lindsay and Kevin catching up with each other over what had happened during the day. Her mother was happy, Alice realised, she had someone to share her concerns with, and the sound of the two of them talking had become a comfort to Alice, a sign that no matter what had happened in the day, there was something comfortable and stable at the end of it that she could drift off to sleep to.

Alice had reached the supermarket, which was strangely quiet. There were plenty of people shopping, but they seemed worn out, drained of life from the endless quakes, the interrupted nights, the constant effort of trying to live a normal life in a broken city. Alice wanted to get through and get out quickly, back into the hot day and under the blue sky.

Alice was packing the groceries into the car when she heard her name. It was Kevin, waving at her as he walked across the carpark towards her.

'I thought that was your car,' he said, taking a shopping bag from the trolley and placing it in the boot. He had finished work early so he could shop for something for Lindsay. He wanted to surprise her with something for the kitchen, it was time to start replacing some of the crockery lost in the earthquakes. 'I could use your help. You're much better at picking what she likes.'

Alice burst into tears and Kevin put his arms around her, apologising for suggesting it was time to replace all the things that had been broken.

'It's not that,' she said. 'Ben and I broke up, I'm not going to Sydney.' She sniffed back tears and wiped her face. 'I'm stuck here.'

He said he was sorry and hugged her tight. 'Anything frozen in there?' he asked.

'No,' she mumbled.

'McDonald's?' he said.

She nodded. 'We can take some home,' she said.

'No, just you and me,' Kevin said.

She choked back more tears as she locked up the car. 'And then we'll shop for Mum,' she said as they walked across the carpark to the main entrance.

'And then we'll shop for Mum,' Kevin said.

Separation Anxiety

February 2012

The house was empty. Jack had turned five over the summer, which meant he started school with all the other kids at the end of January, and Lindsay was finding the house a bit too empty in the afternoons. Sure Jack had been going to kindy four days a week for the last six months before the holidays started, but the combination of the full-on kid time during the holidays and the empty house every day was making Lindsay tense. Lindsay found herself waiting, waiting and listening for the next quake.

The quakes before Christmas had come after months of relative quiet and had made Lindsay want to leave Christchurch all over again. Until that point, she had become used to being there, had accepted that they wouldn't leave the city any time soon, but then those quakes hit, one right after another, and she wanted to leave and never come back.

They had gone down to Timaru for Christmas, which hadn't been the plan, and it hadn't gone well. It wasn't Kevin's brother and his family, they were always happy to have them and their girls loved spending time with Olivia and Jack. It was that Lindsay hadn't really thought when she packed and they kept needing stuff she had forgotten. Toothbrushes, enough underwear for the kids, socks for Kevin, a hairbrush, birth control pills, the Christmas presents. By Boxing Day, Kevin, Lindsay and the kids were cranky and ready to go back to Christchurch. They packed up what little Lindsay had remembered to take with them and went home.

Alice's time with Ben hadn't gone well and Alice and Ben had broken up, whereas just a few weeks before they had been planning to move to Sydney together. Lindsay wasn't wild about the Sydney idea, she wasn't really sure Ben was the right kind of guy for Alice, but at least Sydney didn't have damaged buildings and regular earthquakes. Her separation anxiety would have been offset by knowing Alice was no longer in danger of being killed by some bit of building falling on her.

To make matters worse, Alice had signed up with a temping agency to get office work. She was hardly at home during the day any more, and Lindsay couldn't just pop down to the café to have a coffee with her (and make sure she was okay). With this new job, Lindsay didn't know where Alice was at any given time because her jobs took her all over the city. Not into the city, of course, that was still off limits, but if there was another big quake, Lindsay wouldn't know where Alice was. She was used to this with Kevin, finally, but now she had to adjust all over again with Alice. Lindsay had suggested to both of them that they use one of those tracking apps that tell you where someone's phone is. Alice had refused outright, walking out of the room in disgust saying the only thing that could possibly be worse was wearing a tracking collar and that she wasn't a kakapo or a takahe that needed to be babysat. Kevin's refusal had been more diplomatic, a kiss on the forehead and a promise to always let her know where he was working.

So it was just Lindsay, home alone with her housework, Kevin's bookwork and her fears, wondering if everyone was okay and, then, when the house might be fixed.

Following the debacle of the not-assessment where the tradies had refused to come back in the house last June, EQC had sent someone out for a proper assessment. They had concluded that the house had foundation damage that meant it was likely over the $100,000 mark. They had confirmation a few months later that they would be handed over to their insurance company and then there was a phone call from the bank asking Kevin and Lindsay what they should do with the money. There were two payments, one for each quake, and having those sitting against their mortgage made their monthly repayments much more manageable and reduced the stress of Kevin not having the work that had been expected as the rebuild got properly underway. But it didn't quite eliminate the stress of living in a broken house, wondering if it was becoming too normal for the kids.

There was also the problem of their 'technical category'. When the land zoning announcements had first been made in 2011, their land was green, which was fine, they would be able to repair their house, unlike the poor people stuck in the residential red zone, who were being bought out by the Government at what many saw as less than their properties were worth. There were also orange and white zoned properties then. Orange was flat land and white was the hills. Further investigations were required before a decision could be made one way or the other, red or green.

Green zone properties were fine and so repairs could proceed, but there was one complicating factor. The green zone had been subdivided into three technical categories that were about toughening foundation standards. It was only a problem, really, if you had foundation damage, which was most problematic on TC3 land. Lindsay and Kevin were on TC3 land, which meant they needed a geotechnical investigation before their foundation repairs could proceed.

They had soon received a letter from their insurance company and someone had come to check that the house was indeed damaged. That had been two weeks ago, early February. The guy who visited was there less than fifteen minutes. Lindsay showed him the cracks inside the house and where the foundation was crumbling. And that was it, he didn't go under the house or into the roof space. When she thought about it later on, she realised the insurance company hadn't made a specific appointment and the 'assessor' hadn't shown her any identification. Had he been casing the house? There had been stories in the news about fake assessors, people ripping off claimants, wearing orange high visibility vests to look official. She didn't want to say anything to Kevin, she felt stupid about not asking for the guy's credentials, but as the rest of the week passed and then the next without hearing from the insurance company, Lindsay was feeling paranoid. Every noise the house made might be someone trying to break in. Or the sound of the imminent collapse of the foundations? But she only really considered that last possibility when she hadn't had enough sleep.

She could relax now, on the assessment front at least, because that morning a letter had finally arrived from the insurance company saying the next step would be a full assessment of the foundations. But it was going to be a long process, the letter said, as there were so many claims.

Next week was the first anniversary of the February quake. Lindsay wasn't sure what she would do. Did she want to go to the memorial service planned in the city? Maybe watch it on TV? Or did she want to pretend it was just like any other day? Fat chance of that last option. She couldn't think of a single moment in the last year when she had actually forgotten about the February quake. It was all around them: the house was munted, the roads were wrecked, there were houses in varying degrees of muntedness all around them. She couldn't walk the kids to school without carrying out her own uninformed assessments of the status of the houses she passed, wondering how the people were doing, whether they were able to live in their houses or whether their accommodation allowance had run out, meaning they were possibly back living in their houses even if it probably wasn't a good idea to do so.

She didn't think she would ever forget the February quake, ever even stop thinking about that day. She had been working at the dining table, doing some invoicing for Kevin, with the stereo going in the lounge. Unlike all the earlier quakes, she hadn't had time to process the sound of the approaching quake before the shaking began. The stereo cut out as the power died and then there was just the up-and-down of the quake, the noise and her fear. She could remember feeling the panic at not being able to stand up to get under the table because the force of gravity kept pushing her back into the chair, then the fear of thinking the concrete tile roof was going to fall in on her as she sat in front of the laptop watching everything in the kitchen being tossed up and falling down. When the shaking slowed and the quake passed, there was the panic of wondering if Kevin and the children were all right, where they were, knowing Olivia and Jack would be terrified and wanting to rush to them as quickly as possible. But Alice, she had no idea where Alice was, at the university or in the city? She had lunch with Andrew every second Tuesday, was this Tuesday one of them? Was it Tuesday? Yes, it was.

No, she decided, she had no desire to relive that day by going to some memorial, she relived it often enough just going about her daily business. The names of the dead would be read out at the memorial, and Lindsay didn't want to hear about the people who had died, the number was too great, the grief associated with each name too intense. Even listening at home in the privacy of her own living room would be too much.

Lately, Alice had been telling her about the Royal Commission. Alice had been following newspaper stories and news reports, not just on the Royal Commission but on all the coroner's inquests that had been conducted last year. Mostly Lindsay stayed away from the news, there were just too many other things to be done. And she didn't like the idea of a witchhunt, it had been a terrible earthquake, stronger than anyone had expected, of course no buildings could withstand that kind of shaking. People like to find someone to blame, she told Alice, it helps them deal with the grief. Alice said she understood that, but that shouldn't mean that there weren't any failings, that there weren't some deaths that could have been prevented. It had been reported that the CTV building had not been up to code and that the police were getting advice on whether there should be a criminal prosecution. One hundred and fifteen people had died in the CTV building.

One building in which three men had died had been a church damaged in the September 2010 quake, then again in the Boxing Day quakes. The men were part of a team working in the church to get the organ out so the building could be stabilised before a decision was made on its fate. An engineer had proposed propping to make the building safe to work in, another engineer thought it would be safe to work in without the propping. A lawyer representing the families wondered if it was necessary to put people's lives at risk to recover an organ. These deaths bothered Alice because about the same time as the Royal Commission hearing, there was a building that had been added to CERA's ever-growing demolition list, a community museum. Some people were upset that no effort had been made to recover some of the exhibits, because they represented the region's history, its heritage. She spat out the word as though it was poisonous. 'Heritage.'

'As far as the February quake is concerned, I get it,' Alice said. They were at the dining table having cups of tea one night after getting Olivia and Jack off to bed. 'There was a plan to go into that building, keep the men inside safe. No one expected an aftershock to actually be worse than the seven point one. But now? Why on earth would anyone think it was worth sending people into a dangerous building to recover things? No one should be asked to take that risk. Would the people who want those things saved be willing to go in? Or send their sons or their husbands in?'

'Alice,' Lindsay said, 'I think you need to stop following all these inquiries.'

'No, Mum,' Alice said. 'Everyone needs to follow them, everyone needs to know, because all those people died and some of them didn't have to.'

Lindsay knew that was true, but she didn't like the idea of Alice spending so much time trying to get her head around what had happened. She started to cry. Alice got up from the table and walked around it to put her arms around Lindsay.

'I'm sorry, Mum, I didn't mean to upset you, I won't talk about it any more.'

Lindsay wiped her eyes. 'No, it's okay. I know it's wrong, that some of those people, maybe a lot of them, didn't have to die. But we can't change the fact that they're gone.'

Alice sat back down across from Lindsay. 'I know that,' she said. 'But people shouldn't forget. If people forget, then they start making the same mistakes again, things like thinking it's okay to send a crew of guys into a damaged building to do work on it when it's maybe safest to just tear it down. This whole risk assessment business, check this and then this and this and if your calculations say the risk is low, then it's probably okay doing something. But is any risk low enough? If there's the remotest chance of the bad thing happening, then the risk is too high. When you're talking about someone's life.'

Lindsay nodded. 'I see your point,' she said. 'But you can't fix the world. You can't think about everything that goes wrong in the world and, I don't know, stay sane. You have to stop thinking about these things.'

'I know that,' Alice said. 'But I don't think I should stop thinking about these things quickly. They happened here, right here.' She was tapping the dining table with her finger. 'We shouldn't stop thinking about them. They happened to people like us, Mum, people who went to work and thought they would be going home. It's not fair that I just go on with my life.'

Lindsay nodded. She kept to herself the fact that she disagreed. There was a difference between being aware of something and being burdened by it. She was afraid that Alice was too burdened by what had happened in the city and that it was hindering her ability to get on with her life.

In the end, she let it go. Alice was twenty now, still young, still working out for herself how the world worked. And Lindsay did trust her to work it out, she was, mostly, a sensible kid, and Lindsay wanted to treat her like an adult and show that she trusted her to form her own opinions.

In the mornings, though, when everyone had gone to work or school and Lindsay was back in the house by herself, she did wonder. Was she trying enough to help Alice through what she was feeling? Or was she lying to herself, saying she was letting Alice work it out for herself because the longer she spent doing that, the longer she would stay at home?

That was Lindsay's big fear, not that there was going to be another big quake and that someone she loved would die, but that Alice would open her eyes and look at the city around her in the light of her own future and decide to leave. Lindsay wasn't yet ready to lose her baby.

Marmageddon

March 2012

The big news wasn't that a fantastically high number of insurance claims had been settled, that a bunch of buildings had been rebuilt or that the city's roads would all be fixed up by the end of the year. No, the big news was the Marmite shortage. The factory that made all of the country's Marmite had been damaged by the quakes and had shut down for repairs. The manufacturer had tried replicating the recipe outside of Christchurch, but it hadn't worked out and now supplies were running out.

Panic buying ensued and Marmite was auctioned on TradeMe for ridiculous amounts of money. Ben had messaged Alice asking her to buy up as much as she could and send it over to him. Back in January when he had left for Sydney, she had gone out to the airport to say goodbye. They had made up, to a degree, said they were sorry about the things they had said to each other and that they would stay friends, keep in touch. He texted her for the first week or so, but now the only contact between the two of them was him posting photos on Instagram, which was no sort of contact at all because he was posting those to everyone who was following him. Alice waited a few minutes and messaged him back that the supermarkets had all run out, then unfollowed him on Instagram.

Alice was fine going without Marmite, she preferred the more bitter Vegemite. But Jack was a die-hard Marmite fan, he had Marmite on toast for breakfast at least a couple of times a week and he was forever asking Alice to make him little Marmite sandwiches for lunch. When Alice made Olivia and Jack sandwiches, she cut them into different shapes using cookie cutters.

'Stop spoiling them,' Lindsay would say. 'They need to get used to the idea that bread comes with crusts.'

But Alice kept making them sandwich shapes. She knew she wouldn't be there forever, that one day she would move out of home and begin her independent life once again, as she had done at the start of 2010.

When it first became known that Marmite was running short, Lindsay had tried to swap in Vegemite, but Jack had noticed and refused to eat it. Lindsay had then asked family members for their supplies and added them to her own one full jar and one half-used jar, tucking them away in the pantry, behind the tins of tomatoes and the three-bean salad that never got used. Alice had tried to get her to toss the three-bean salad out after the first quake.

'It's been there since before Jack was born,' she had argued. 'Maybe even before Olivia. Toss it.' Alice tried to remember if the bean salad had been around for longer. Possibly. Lindsay had a half-empty Vicks vapo-rub from 1991. It was older than Alice.

Now, eighteen months later as she pushed the tins apart looking for a new jar of jam, the tin of bean salad was still there, with a dent in it from the February quake. Wasn't there something about not eating tins that had been dented? She would google it later.

'Leave the Marmite for the kids,' Lindsay said. 'We might have to make it last for a while.'

'You tell me not to spoil them,' Alice said, 'and here you are hiding away this black gold. It's your precious.'

'One spread to rule them all,' Lindsay said, doing a Gollum voice that made her start coughing. Alice patted her back to help her stop.

Another thing that made March different was that Alice had picked up a full-time job. Woo-hoo! No more temping. It was okay for a couple of months, but Alice had been getting tired of having a day off and then suddenly not having a day off because someone's receptionist had called in sick and they needed a substitute. She was doing office work for one of the companies managing claims and rebuild work for an insurance company. It wasn't exciting, stimulating work, but it was regular, nine to five. It kept her busy and away from following the CTV hearings too closely.

The hearings found that the building didn't comply with the Building Code when it was built because its load-bearing columns didn't have enough reinforcing. Yet it had gotten past the City Council's consenting department. At some point, someone identified a flaw in the design and work was done to make the building stronger, although given what happened in the February quake, that work wasn't enough to save the building and all those lives. The saddest thing, Alice thought, was that quite a few people working in the building were uncomfortable about the building. But because they had to work, they kept going into that building, five days every week. If the quake had happened at the weekend, as the September quake had, so many people would still be alive.

Alice's grandparents, Lindsay's parents, were out of their house while it was being repaired. Their accommodation allowance was covering what they considered the extortionate amount of rent each week. They were right. The place they were in was about the same age as the one Alice had been flatting in before the first earthquake, less than two years ago. In fact, Alice's flat had an extra bedroom and, on that basis, qualified as a better house. But Neil and Heather were paying a full $200 more a week than Alice and her flatmates had paid. It had taken them six weeks to find it, going to see places and finding out they had been snatched up by someone who had turned up a few minutes earlier. It was crazy, the fierceness of the competition. At one place they went to, there were two other couples bidding on the flat, putting the rent up by $20 a week until the price was $100 higher than what had been advertised. Alice had told Gerald, her other grandfather, how much trouble they were having finding a place and he asked around. Someone he knew had a place whose tenants were a month away from moving out, and so Neil and Heather ended up getting that place before it was advertised.

Every now and then Alice thought about leaving home and going flatting again, but rents that high put her off. Lindsay had told her she could stay as long as she liked and things were good at home, but Alice couldn't stay forever. She was an adult now, and moving back home had happened because an earthquake wrecked her flat, not because she was incapable of being away from her family. And she worried about leaving it too long, that Olivia and Jack would become too used to having her there, she would be too used to seeing them so often, that it would be difficult moving away, even if it was to a place nearby. She decided she would find a flat when Lindsay and Kevin moved out of the house for repairs, whenever that might be. Foundation guidelines were being written for houses like theirs and would be published in April. They couldn't expect any progress until then, at the earliest, and realistically 2013 probably wasn't a bad guess. In the meantime, Alice saved whatever she could so she would be able to get a reasonable place and some decent furniture.

Everything about living in Christchurch was weird, it wasn't just the reaction to the Marmite shortage. Each weekday morning, Alice drove west over the rough roads littered with orange cones marking roadworks in various states of completion. Once she was past Hagley Park and driving up the overbridge onto Blenheim Road, it was like crossing into a different world, one where the roads were relatively smooth, compared to the east, and where buildings weren't falling apart all over the place. Before reaching the overbridge, there were regular gaps where buildings had disappeared or were in the process of disappearing, but not on the western side of town, where it was rare to see something being torn down.

Then there were the ongoing arguments around the rebuild. It was normal in a natural disaster, Alice had read, for things to not go smoothly. A region that had been affected by a natural disaster went through stages. The first anniversary of the quake a month ago had told the story of the heroic phase, where everyone pitched in to help people out. And Alice definitely remembered the honeymoon phase, being so glad to be alive when she woke up each morning that it was easy to look past how tired she felt, to drag herself out of bed and keep going on with what passed for normal life in a city that was still being shaken on an almost-daily basis. They were well into the disillusionment phase now, where people were worn out and snarky with the effort of keeping going for so long. That was manifesting itself in how people were feeling about those running the rebuild.

At the end of 2011, the City Council's chief executive had been given a pay rise that was higher than what Alice thought she might make each year by the time she was thirty, some $68,000. Given the city was facing an expensive rebuild and the rumours that there wasn't going to be enough insurance to cover repairs to council properties, people were angry about such a substantial pay rise. People protested outside the council's offices twice, asking for the chief executive and the mayor to resign. A few days later, the Minister for Earthquake Recovery referred to the Christchurch mayor as a clown, which seemed unbelievably childish to Alice, it was something Olivia and Jack would do. These people were responsible for getting the city back on its feet and, therefore, for Alice's future, should she decide to stay in Christchurch. Instead of working past differences and getting on with the job, they were all behaving like, well, clowns.

There were days when Alice wanted nothing more than to leave Christchurch. When it became too much, she would stop ingesting news for a few days, just focus on doing her job, spending time with her family and catching up with the few friends left in Christchurch.

One Friday night, Alice and Charlotte decided to take advantage of the good weather while it lasted and go for a walk instead of spending the evening watching videos. Sean had spent most Friday nights with them in the last few months, but since university started a month earlier, he had university friends to do things with. Fair enough, Alice thought, but she knew Charlotte was hurt. Over the summer, she had told Alice she was enjoying getting to know her brother, there were four years between them and until the February quakes had changed everything about their lives, she had always felt left behind, the annoying little sister it wasn't cool to hang around with. Charlotte said the girls at school were too superficial, always talking about boys and clothes and squealing in alarm at the tiniest of aftershocks. Their idea of fun, she said, was going to the mall, hanging out trying to out-normal each other by mocking anyone who looked different.

They had decided to stop in and see Alice's great-grandparents, the Bennetts, and then walk around the residential red zone. Alice had seen the damage to the houses around the Avon River east of the city, the pumps on the streets that stood in for the broken sewerage network in the months after the February quake, but she hadn't been through the red zone properly for months. The Bennetts, Heather's parents, lived a couple of streets away from the start of the red zone. Their house hadn't yet been assessed, but it didn't seem to be too badly damaged and they were still living in it, looking after their fruit trees, vegetable garden and chickens. Alice and Charlotte had dropped in and had a cup of tea, and had a shopping bag of fresh fruit and vegetables foisted on them, along with a carton of eggs.

'Your greats are pretty cool,' Charlotte said. 'The only great I have is the old lady by the river.' She stopped and thought for a moment. 'The other river.'

They had left Alice's car at the Bennetts' house and were walking the couple of blocks to the red zone, which meant they were headed towards the river. It was the suburb's proximity to the river that made the area so vulnerable to liquefaction. Over centuries, silt deposited by the Avon River built up, creating the soft, fine, waterlogged soils that liquefied during earthquakes. There were similar issues around the Heathcote River, the river that ran through the neighbourhood Alice lived in, but it didn't seem to be as bad there, even though it had been closer to so many of the big quakes.

The houses in the part of the neighbourhood they were walking through were occupied and looked like they had some damage, although there weren't the dramatic cracks and breakages of the houses in the red zone. But as they drew closer to the red zone, the roads became worse, more lumps and dips where silt had been forced upward and broken through the surface of the road and footpaths.

'They're certainly different from Marjorie,' Alice said. Grandma and Grandad Bennett were warm, affectionate people, always calling their children, grandchildren and great-grandchildren 'Love' or 'Pet'. Marjorie never shortened someone's name, it was always 'Alice', never 'Ali'.

'Is their house okay?' Charlotte asked. 'I saw some cracks, but it felt pretty even.' People in Christchurch had become amateur house assessors. Alice had been in places that were clearly out of level, giving the feeling of walking downhill to go from one room to another, then uphill to go back the way you came. Charlotte was right, there was none of that in the Bennett house, whereas at home, in Lindsay and Kevin's house, there was a subtle downhill tilt from west to east.

'Seems to be,' Alice said. 'But they're still waiting to be assessed. What did you think of Grandad?'

Charlotte thought a moment. 'It was funny what he was saying about the dog going into the river after the ducks,' she said. 'A bit risky, given there's sewage going into the river, I hope he washed her off properly.'

'Did you see a dog?'

Charlotte stopped and looked at Alice. 'No.'

'The dog died a couple of months after the February quake, Grandad's taken it really hard. He keeps talking about her like she's still around though.'

'So he was talking about something from last year? He seemed like he was talking about today,' Charlotte said. 'You think he's losing it?'

'I don't know. We've been noticing a few little things like that,' Alice said. 'A few odd things he's saying lately.'

They were at the river, walking along the crumpled road. The land was going to be cleared, but that hadn't started yet. People who were living in the red zone had been made offers and they had been given a few months to make a decision, and then a few more to move out. There were few signs of life in the broken houses, although there were plenty of signs of break-ins and vandalism: broken windows, doors ajar, a few graffiti tags here and there.

'Anyone would be feeling a bit out of sorts living so close to all this,' Charlotte said. 'It's just weird. Like a wasteland from a movie. Kind of creepy.'

They were walking past the entrance to a long driveway and Charlotte stopped. Alice turned back to look at her, to try to see what she had seen. 'There's someone living down there,' Charlotte said. 'She looked quite old, from what I could see of the back of her.'

'Poor thing,' Alice said. 'She's probably lived here for decades.' Alice's great-grandparents had lived in their house for over sixty years, it was where Heather had grown up. It would be difficult if they had to leave, even if it was only for a few months of repairs.

They started walking again. It was getting dark and they picked up their pace to loop back around to the car.

'You know what's really weird?' Charlotte said.

'What?' Alice said. She had no idea what was going on in Charlotte's head, they had seen nothing unusual in the last few minutes, just the ducks on the river and the broken roads and houses.

'That there are people leaving here, saying goodbye to their lives here. Why aren't we hearing more about it? Their stories. All I've heard about lately is the Marmite shortage. They're talking about it like it's the end of the world that we're running out of a sandwich spread. But here it really is.'

She was right. People's lives were being left behind. They could only take their furniture and their memories, everything else was left to the bulldozers. It really was the end of a world.

The Rise of the PMOs

April 2012

With over 100,000 damaged houses in the region, builders and other tradesmen were flocking to Christchurch to get their share of the huge volume of work that would be ramping up from 2012 onward. The organisation set up to manage EQC's repairs was Fletcher EQR, and to work for EQR, tradesmen had to be accredited. The private insurers could see the value in having a similar setup, it was a way of ensuring repairs were done properly. These project management organisations were also looking for staff, and anyone who didn't get work with EQC or EQR was being picked up by one of the private insurers' PMOs.

In the months after the February quake, before Sylvia had decided she was okay about coming back to Christchurch, Gerald had tried to run his construction business from Sydney. It was too hard, the bureaucracy was byzantine. Actual building work was impossible to pick up, properties needed to be assessed first and engineers and assessors were as rare as hen's teeth. A lot of business owners had to let workers go, and Gerald wasn't happy about the idea of being one of them. So he decided to stay in Christchurch three weeks a month and live with his mother. He could work his contacts face-to-face to make sure there was enough work coming in to keep his staff on and pay the bills. What he ended up doing was demolition and make-safe work in the CBD red zone, managing teams going into buildings to strip out the fittings before demolition or, if the building could be saved, to do the work required to make it safe to work in.

Gerald and Sylvia had talked at length about whether they would go back to Christchurch. Their house was a write off, it had been assessed and they were pretty much all the way through the settlement process with their insurer. They had plenty of options, including staying in Sydney. At first, that was what Sylvia wanted. Her view was that most of the family had left Christchurch, there was no one to go back for. But it wasn't long before various family members started heading back to the city to get their houses and businesses sorted and to resume their lives, lives that would one day get back to normal. She said that she finally realised that she and Gerald should be there to support them in whatever they ended up going through. As nice as it was spending time with Laurel and her husband, the truth was they worked all week and needed their weekends to themselves. Sylvia was starting to feeling like an intruder, always waiting for them when they arrived home, and if she went back to Christchurch, Gerald could really commit himself to the rebuild. He was keen to be part of it, to give something back to the city he had lived in for all of his life. Before the quakes started, he wanted to retire, but after the February quake it seemed wrong to just stop working. Now there was just too much going on to consider that. Maybe he could start thinking seriously about retirement in a couple of years, when the rebuild started winding down. And maybe that retirement could be in Sydney.

They found a house on flat land below the hill on which their ruined house sat. This house wasn't in bad shape, it seemed to be on stable ground. The family who were selling had lost a family member in the earthquake, the wife's or the husband's brother, Gerald wasn't exactly sure, but they wanted to get out of Christchurch and so Gerald and Sylvia got a good deal on the place. Its foundation had stood up well and there was only minor cracking on the inside, things Gerald could easily fix up in his spare time. Sylvia seemed happy to be back with Gerald, and unpacking the possessions they had been able to salvage from the house up the hill and deciding where to put everything in this new, smaller house made it start to feel like being home again. Going through some of the mementos they had collected over their decades together seemed to make her feel happier about being back.

Once the house was reasonably sorted, Sylvia offered to help Gerald out with the paperwork. He hesitated at first, the bureaucracy involved in getting anything done was confusing, and although Sylvia had dealt with the City Council on and off over the years, this CERA organisation was something else entirely. But she insisted, and she was good with paperwork and, more importantly, with people. If anyone could get things done it was Sylvia.

It was only a matter of weeks, though, before Gerald regularly heard her muttering over having to deal with CERA. That night, when he arrived home, she was trying to arrange passes into the red zone to carry out some work. She had organised passes for the same job weeks earlier, which had been the usual gruelling process, but additional damage had been discovered that required the input of an engineer. The work had stopped while that was organised and the workers' passes had expired. Now that the engineer had made his recommendations, Sylvia needed to organise a new set of red zone passes. More paperwork, it never ended.

Gerald kissed Sylvia on the cheek and left her alone in the office. In the kitchen, Alice was cooking. When she arrived, she said, Sylvia had been stuck on the phone with CERA and getting a bit too stressed, so Alice offered to take over the meal prep. She had sliced chicken breast simmering with mushrooms and red capsicum and two other pots, pasta and broccoli.

Gerald offered to help, but she said she was fine, the cooking helped her to wind down from her day's work. She was working for one of the newly-appointed PMOs as an office administrator. Hardly challenging for a girl as bright as Alice, but it seemed to be something she wanted to do, to help out with the rebuild. Gerald had thought of telling her to keep out of the insurance side of things, there was so much cost-cutting going on with repairs that he couldn't help but think the EQC and insurance side of the rebuild was not going to go well. But that was his old man's cynicism and he decided he should keep it to himself.

Gerald had decided a couple of weeks ago to finish up on their current lot of make-safe jobs and start looking for opt-out work. Some people wanted EQR to take care of everything for them, but others wanted more control, and those people could opt out of a managed repair and project manage their own repairs or contract someone like Gerald to do it for them. What that meant for Gerald was that he was less likely to have to deal with the bureaucracy that was bound to come with all the EQR repair work. Gerald could contribute to the rebuild without being strangled by all the red tape, and without dirtying the reputation he had worked so hard to build. It would take a few months before everything he already had going was finished, but in that few months he could line up something else for his guys to move on to.

Gerald's mother had taught Alice some of her cooking skills in the weeks Alice stayed with her after the February quake. It was nice seeing the old girl pass on something, and Marjorie was a good cook. Gerald wasn't sure what it was about Alice that his mother liked, she had never seemed to like her own daughters, or Sylvia. Of Gerald's sisters, Suzanne and Judith still wanted Marjorie's approval, tried to do things to look after their mother, to please her. Karen, on the other hand, made a point of saying she didn't care about their mother's opinion, but Gerald could see the sadness she carried, the sense of something missing from her life. He felt that sadness had a lot to do with Karen's poor choice in men, her careless parenting of her children.

With Alice, Marjorie was different. There was a level of care and consideration there that Gerald had never seen directed at, well, people. Gerald wondered what had prompted that softening.

It had been difficult losing touch with Alice. But Alice had remembered Gerald and Sylvia from the time they had taken her up to Auckland to see Andrew, while Andrew was still making time in his life for his little girl. There had also been visits in Christchurch before Lindsay had drifted away from them. But now Alice was back in their lives and having her in the house fussing around in the kitchen of their new home made it feel like more of a home. He would have to point that out to Sylvia later on, in case her frustrations at dealing with the bureaucracy were making her regret coming back. It was good to build new bonds with family, to look out for them as they worked their way through EQC and insurance issues. Not that Alice had those concerns, but the city was a strange place, the old boys' club was thriving in the frenzy for everyone to get a cut of the insurance funds pouring into the city.

On the surface, the establishment of Fletchers EQR and all the PMOs was about ensuring quality, making sure the people of Christchurch had a fair deal from the city's rebuild. Gerald had been dealing with bureaucrats for the whole of his adult life, and they were seldom that kind and caring. The arrangement gave the Government and the insurers the power to control the costs, minimise their outlay. One could argue that insurance companies were businesses, they had the right to try to contain costs, and Gerald agreed with that in principle. However, it was a dangerous line, it was too easy to compromise on quality for the sake of containing costs. There were already people complaining of poor workmanship and damage that had been ignored, and the rebuild was only just starting to crawl to the starting line. Sylvia was coming into contact with people who talked about similar things, from business contacts to neighbours and people she ran into while walking. Between them, Gerald and Sylvia were hearing about these shoddy, inadequate repairs too often for it to just be isolated cases.

Alice turned down the element for one pot and moved another off to the sink. Sylvia came through from the office and right away moved to help her, but Alice nudged her away, told her to relax, she had it all under control. And she did. Gerald asked Sylvia how the phone call had gone.

'I never even got through to the right person,' she said. 'I'll have to try again in the morning.' She asked Alice about her job. It was all right, Alice said, but she didn't like dealing with customers desperate for information.

'That's understandable,' Sylvia said. 'People have been waiting a year and a half now, if they've been waiting since the September quake.'

'It's sad,' Alice said. 'There's nothing I can tell them, and they sound so tired.'

'There's a lot to do,' Gerald said. 'Not everything can happen at once.'

Alice nodded. She was draining the broccoli. 'I get that,' Alice said. 'What I don't like is that the claim staff tend to talk about them like they're greedy. When they just want what they've paid for.'

It was good she could see beyond the insurance company spin: claimants are greedy and want more than they're entitled to. The policies people had claimed against were, by and large, full replacement policies, basically gold standard that allowed for reinstatement to an 'as new' condition. He doubted there were many people wanting more than they were entitled to, especially as what he heard most often when people talked about what they expected from their insurance policy was that the place should be put back to the way it was before the quake. That wasn't an expectation of a new house, that was an expectation that earthquake damage should be repaired. He wasn't convinced people were going to get that. 'There's a bit of that going around,' he said.

'I get that dealing with CERA,' Sylvia said. 'The staff talk like they're doing me a favour, they seem to forget that they exist to help the people of the city to recover, that's the purpose of the Act, the R in the act is Recovery. It wasn't enacted to keep them employed for five years.'

'Too easy to forget,' Alice said, 'even though it's in their name.'

'Comes from the top,' Gerald said.

'From the PM?' Alice said.

'Maybe,' Gerald said. 'But I was thinking more the Minister. He talks like the Government is doing everyone in the red zones a big favour by paying them out based on a five-year-old property valuation.'

'My aunt and uncle are in that position,' Alice said. 'It looks like they'll have to buy a smaller place and take out a bigger mortgage.' She lifted the lid on the pasta and used a wooden spoon to push a piece against the side of the pan to cut through it. She turned the hotplate off and lifted the pot off the stove.

'Which offer are they taking?' Gerald asked.

'The land and house,' Alice said, pouring the pasta water down the sink. 'They were going to take the land offer only, but there's been a lot of people whose houses have mysteriously changed from rebuild to repair. Things were getting too stressful, they've decided it's better to be able to move on.'

'That's not a silly idea,' Sylvia said. 'The bureaucracy is a nightmare and why prolong that if you don't have to?'

'The Minister should step in, iron out problems,' Gerald said. 'But any time anyone brings up an issue, he attacks. In Parliament the other day, Lianne Dalziel raised a question about people being out of pocket if they took one of the Government's offers, his response was to say she was grumpy because she wanted more taxpayers' money for her red zoned property.'

'That's just plain rude,' Sylvia said. 'She's the Opposition's spokesman on earthquake stuff, there's nothing wrong with her bringing up issues that affect a lot of people. At least she has some sympathy for the position people are in.'

'He does seem to resort to name-calling a bit quickly,' Alice said. She was mixing the broccoli, the cooked chicken and a splash of cream through the pasta. 'First a clown mayor, now a grumpy opposition MP, what will it be next? Sneezy and Dopey?'

Gerald and Sylvia laughed. But it wasn't funny. The rebuild was a serious matter, affecting the lives of thousands. The region needed leaders who could effectively deal with the problems that would arise, not ones who would lash out any time an issue was raised or criticism voiced.

The Last Five

May 2012

For the last five minutes, Charlotte had been watching the neighbour's house. She was home sick for the day, her throat sore from coughing, and had set herself up in the lounge on the sofa where she could watch the TV, the street outside and the estuary and ocean beyond. She had the TV, DVD player and AppleTV remotes lined up on the coffee table within easy reach in case she finally managed to decide what movie to watch, but for most of the morning and afternoon, she had been engrossed in the second book of *The Hunger Games* series, which she had started that morning. Charlotte and Alice had seen the movie of the first book a couple of weeks ago and she wanted to see how it turned out. It was past two o'clock and Charlotte was nearly done, but had been ignoring her own hunger for a good couple of hours. She put the book to one side to get up and make herself some two-minute noodles.

She was eating while staring out the window, thinking about how the soup was soothing on her throat and that she needed to make more effort to get up and drink more water. That was when movement caught her eye.

The neighbour's house across the road was empty, locked up, and no one had lived in it since February 2011, over a year ago. There was a woman standing in front of the house, looking around. She was dressed in black jeans and a long jumper, her long dark hair hanging like a heavy curtain, partly closed over her face. Although she was standing in one spot, she couldn't seem to stand still, moving from one foot to another, one fist up by her mouth, rubbing her face, while she looked around, up the street, then down the street. She didn't seem to think to look up the hill to the house looming above her, the one Charlotte was watching her from. She looked like she was on something, not that Charlotte really knew what someone who was on something looked like, it was her best guess based on seeing people hanging around the courthouse when she went to visit her mother at work in the city. Back when there was a city. And there was a woman who panhandled at the bus exchange that reminded her of this woman lurking outside the neighbour's house. One time the woman at the exchange had asked Charlotte for money, saying her boyfriend had stranded her in the city and she needed to catch a bus to get home. Charlotte told her she didn't believe her and quickly walked away, towards the portable building that served as the information desk. She told the guy there about the woman, and he said she was there every day and wasn't stranded. This reassured Charlotte, since the moment she had opened her mouth to say she didn't believe the woman, she hoped she was right, otherwise she had just made a bad situation worse for her by being unkind.

A man walked up the driveway from the house the woman was standing in front of and he and the woman quickly moved on to the next house. She stood at the letterbox while he shot down the driveway, looking around, up and down the street. Should Charlotte call the police? She put her bowl of noodles down on the coffee table and stood up to get the phone.

Charlotte was about to start dialling when she heard the approaching rumble. She froze, just stood there in front of the bookshelf on which the cordless phone and its charger sat. It had been a long time since she had taken cover during an earthquake. The house jolted and swayed, she heard glasses and crockery jiggling in the kitchen and the TV swayed alarmingly on the cabinet. The quake was from the northeast, had that under-the-sea feel that accompanied the quakes that originated offshore. It was strong, bigger than a four, probably a five. The motion stopped and Charlotte felt her heart racing. She just stood there for a minute, breathing deeply, then put the phone back into its cradle and walked through the house to check for damage.

Nothing seemed to be broken except for the pot that held The Last House Plant, the only survivor of all the quakes. Before the September quake, her mother used to have them all through the house, potted creeping figs, peace lilies, spider plants and different coloured African violets. She said she wasn't going to replace them until the quakes were over, it was just too hard to clean up. One plant that fell in the September quake had landed on a bunch of books that had slipped out of the bookshelves. They were still, over a year later, finding bits of potting mix in various books.

Charlotte wished her mother would start getting some more plants, they made the house feel full of life in a way it hadn't for over a year. Her mother had seemed softer then, now everything was about her job, the house and EQC. Maybe once Charlotte was feeling better, she would get some pot plants. When she was younger, she used to buy her mother plants from the supermarket, but the supermarket was gone now, and there was no indication as to when it would be rebuilt. There was a hardware store in Ferrymead that sold plants, and an actual plant shop on Ferry Road closer to the city, she would go to one of those.

This last plant was one of the African violets. It had been sitting on the window sill above the kitchen sink and had been tossed off and down onto the floor. Pieces of broken pot and dirt were everywhere, its lone pink flower peeking through. Charlotte found some newspaper, gently picked the plant out of the remains of its container, along with as much soil as she could scoop up, and wrapped it in the newspaper. She poured some water into the makeshift pot and placed it in the sink.

There was nothing else broken because they had become used to being vigilant. Dishes were never left on the bench where they could crash onto the floor and shatter, they were always stacked into the dishwasher as soon as they had finished eating off them. Books they were reading, things they were using, cups, plates and bowls, all were tucked away, put into drawers or pushed towards the backs of cupboards to minimise the possibility of them being lost, should there be another quake. So many precautions. Alice said her mother was the same way, and her grandparents, too. Charlotte opened up the cupboard and pushed her favourite coffee cup towards the back, where it was less likely to fall and break. Just in case.

Charlotte vacuumed up the last of the dirt and threw out the broken pot. Back through in the lounge, she started to compose a text to her mother and father, but then decided not to. Would they get in touch with her? They hadn't so far, and it had been nearly twenty minutes since the quake. She texted Alice instead, who was going to be coming over that night. Sean had said they would cancel, but Charlotte had been home sick most of the week, she was bored, she needed the company, and if Alice wasn't there, Sean would just study the whole night. Or worse, not bother to come home, just hang out with his university mates. She was almost better she insisted, no longer contagious, and they should stick to their Friday night plans.

Alice replied saying one of her co-workers had freaked out, her husband was working in the city and she couldn't get in touch with him. Charlotte looked on *The Press* website and a story said the city centre had been evacuated. The quake was a 5.2 under the sea near Scarborough, east of the city, about 20 kilometres from where Charlotte was. People were reporting things falling off shelves, but nothing worse. It seemed the shelves of Christchurch houses had been cleared, people were tired of picking things up, throwing them away, cataloguing what had been lost and putting in contents claims.

Charlotte settled back on the sofa, tucked her blanket around her and returned to her book. She soon finished it and decided to move on to the third one, it was too exciting, she wanted to see what happened next. She forgot about the suspicious man and woman across the road until her mother arrived home after five. One of the neighbours had been broken into, she said. The woman had come home from work early to check on the house and found the back door open. Had Charlotte seen anything? she asked. Charlotte hadn't seen the man and woman clearly and how could she explain not calling the police? Sure, there had been the quake and the clean up, but would her mother see that as a reasonable excuse? Not likely. She decided not to say anything.

'What's missing?' Charlotte asked.

'Doesn't look like anything's missing,' her mother said. 'But the back door has been kicked in.'

They must have been interrupted by the quake, then scared off. Served them right.

She was going back out, her mother said, meeting a friend for dinner, since Sean and Charlotte were going to be watching a movie and their father was working late. She asked nothing about the quake, nothing about how Charlotte was feeling.

It was different when Sean arrived home, with Alice arriving soon afterwards with Thai food she had picked up on the way. While they served up and started eating, they exchanged experiences. Alice's workmate had left work early to go into the city and find her husband. Everyone had tried to reassure her it was just a five, but she kept saying she was over it all, Christchurch, quakes, everything.

'I don't think she'll be sticking around,' Alice said. 'I wonder how many other people will feel they've had enough. My mum's not very happy, she didn't say it, but I could tell she wants to leave again. I just hope that's the last five we have for a while, or the last anything.'

'It wasn't a big deal at uni,' Sean said.

'Well it wouldn't be way over there,' Charlotte said. 'Not coming from off the coast.'

'It wasn't where I was,' Alice said, nodding. 'The building just sways a bit. It was only a big deal because Connie's husband was in the city and she was freaked out.'

'Did you hear anything from Mum and Dad?' Charlotte asked Sean. 'A call? A message?'

'No, nothing,' Sean said. Sean and Charlotte had been talking lately about how they were almost invisible as far as their parents were concerned. They were too wrapped up in paperwork, trying to get the house assessed, to get some idea of when their repairs would finally happen. They were seldom home at the same time any more, which was kind of a relief, as there was less arguing.

'Me neither,' Charlotte said. 'She didn't even ask if I'm feeling better.'

'She was home?' Sean said.

'For all of five minutes,' Charlotte said. 'Enough time to change. She said she's going out for the night.'

'Not still at work?'

'Nope,' Charlotte said. 'Apparently not.' She raised an eyebrow, he raised one of his back.

'What?' Alice said, looking back and forth between them. 'What's going on?'

Neither of them said anything at first, but then Sean told her. They thought their mother was having an affair, but they weren't sure who with. In fact, they weren't really sure, maybe she was just going and meeting a friend, a sounding board, someone she could talk to about earthquake and house stuff because she couldn't talk to their father about them. But if that was the case, if it was just an innocent friendship, then she would say who she was meeting, which she never did.

'You could sneak a look at her phone,' Alice said.

'Which would only give her something to use against me,' Charlotte said, 'whenever I object to her wanting to see the contents of mine. No way.'

'Then don't get caught,' Sean said.

'Hey, hang on,' Charlotte said, 'why all of a sudden am I doing this?'

'Forget it,' Sean said. 'We're probably just reading too much into things.'

Charlotte caught him shooting a look at Alice. He looked uncomfortable. Did he know more? Was he trying to protect her? She wished he wouldn't try to do that, she wasn't a child. And she had lived through hundreds of earthquakes and the city she had grown up in being destroyed. It was probably a change-the-subject look, because that was what Alice did.

'What do you miss most about the city?' Alice said.

'Going to the movies,' Charlotte said. She had finished her meal and got up to slide her empty plate onto the coffee table. She sat down again, tucking her blanket around her. 'I'm sick of the malls, I wish they'd do something about getting the Moorhouse Ave movie theatre open again.'

'Isn't that all coming down?' Sean said. 'The whole railway station?'

'Is it?' Alice said. 'I hope not, I like that old place.'

'I miss Drexel's,' Charlotte said. The place on Hereford Street served American-style breakfasts, and she had loved their pancakes ever since she could remember.

'There's the one in Riccarton,' Sean said.

'You mean in the mall?' Charlotte gave him a pointed look.

'It's not in the mall, it's just outside the mall,' Sean said. 'You don't have to go in the mall, you just have to breathe some of the god-awful mall air wafting out the automatic doors.' It was an old argument.

'I miss people not talking about insurance all the time,' Charlotte said, moving on to the next item on her list.

'What do you want them talking about?' Sean said. 'How evil malls are?'

'I don't know,' she said, shrugging. 'Just something else.'

'People are worried,' Alice said, her voice softer than Sean's, kinder. 'There's a lot of money at stake, some people could find they can't afford their house any more.'

'What would happen then?' Charlotte said. She pictured people living in tents in Hagley Park. Some people had done that at the end of last year, camping in the park near the hospital. It was part of the Occupy protest movement that had started in New York. Some people who no longer had houses as a result of the quakes had ended up there, which was maybe why the city hadn't moved them on as quickly as they did elsewhere in New Zealand.

'They would have to find a smaller place, one they could afford,' Alice said. 'Or rent.'

'What I can't believe,' Sean said, 'is people who didn't bother to have insurance.'

'It's expensive,' Alice said. 'Not everyone has loads of money to blow on insurance they might never need.'

'Well they take their chances, then, don't they?' Sean said. 'They can't go crying to the Government asking to get paid out because they couldn't be bothered to get a better job so they could have insurance.'

Alice had tensed up. 'Are you talking about red zoners?' she said.

Charlotte knew Alice's grandparents had a section that might be red zoned. It was a section they planned to build their retirement home on, now it looked like they wouldn't be able to do anything with it. Alice was worried about them, they had a lot going on, they were in a rental while their house was being fixed, and it looked like it was going to take longer than expected. But, it seemed, Sean did not know this. Things could get entertaining.

'There are some talking about taking the Government to court,' Charlotte said.

'The ones who didn't have insurance,' Sean went on, 'people with bare land.'

'People with bare land can't get insurance,' Alice said. 'It's just not possible. So it isn't a matter of negligence or stupidity, they simply can't get insurance.'

Sean stared at her, baffled. 'Then why do people talk like they could. The Minister does, and I've heard lots of people say the people who weren't insured shouldn't get anything.'

'It's not about insurance,' Alice said. 'It's about the Government taking their land. The whole insurance thing is a red herring, an excuse for not paying them out.'

'No, that's not right,' Sean said. 'The red zone offers let people move on, the Government steps in and takes over the claims with EQC and the insurance company so people don't have to.'

'What if the Government negotiates a better deal with EQC and the insurance companies than the people would've gotten?' Alice said. 'What if the Government gets more than they paid the original owner?'

'That won't happen,' Sean said. 'That's not how it's going to work. And besides, we're talking about people who didn't bother to get insurance, it's different.'

'So my grandparents, who have a section in Heathcote, didn't have insurance on the land,' Alice said, setting her trap. 'If it gets red-zoned, should they should just lose the land, lose the money they used to buy it?'

Sean hesitated. 'If they didn't have insurance, couldn't get it like you said, why should the Government pay them out for the land?'

'Why can't they build on the land?' Alice said.

'Because of the earthquakes,' Sean said.

'No,' Alice said. 'Because the Government red zoned it.'

Sean said nothing to that.

Alice went on. 'They're losing their land because the Government red zoned it, it's nothing at all to do with whether or not they had insurance. The Government red zoned it, the Government should compensate.'

She glared at Sean, waiting for his answer. Charlotte kept glancing between the two of them, waiting to see if Sean was going to get it. Finally, he nodded.

'I get it,' he said. 'Not about insurance at all.'

Alice nodded and sighed. 'I hope, Sean,' she said, 'that when you're no longer a baby lawyer, you do a better job of analysing the finer points of the law than you're doing now.'

Sean blushed and mumbled what might have been an apology.

Charlotte pulled her blanket up around her face, smiling behind it. The last five minutes had been thoroughly entertaining. It was the most fun she'd had all week. She tried not to giggle, but only ended up coughing.

Transit of Venus

June 2012

Lindsay had expected that the winter of 2011 would be the only winter they spent in their broken house, but as 2011 finished and 2012 began to drag on, it became clear there would be at least one more winter. Although they had been handed over to their insurance company months ago, it wasn't until May when someone came around to have a look at the foundation. The guy who visited pointed out cracks in the concrete ring foundation, different spots where it was crumbling away. He went under the house to check the piles and when he came back up the manhole, he said they looked mostly okay, there were only a handful that looked wonky. But the house would need to be lifted and a new ring foundation built. Kevin and Lindsay were given no indication about how long this would take. They had to wait for the insurance company to send them a scope of works before they could have some idea of timeframes.

'Once the geotech work is done, it won't be long,' Kevin reassured Lindsay. 'They know what they're going to do, we just need to be patient, wait a few more months, then we'll have a better idea of timeframes.'

'I don't know,' Lindsay said. 'Sometimes it feels like we'll see another Transit of Venus before we'll see our house fixed.'

Kevin laughed. 'Not like we'll see this one,' he said. The transit was the next day, but the city was smothered in grey cloud and the air was damp, threatening rain.

The previous Transit of Venus had been in 2004, and Lindsay remembered Kevin trying to explain it to Alice. Alice was still learning to accept Kevin then and had been torn between being fascinated and not wanting to show too much interest. They had both been disappointed that it wasn't visible from New Zealand and promised each other that they would be sure to see the 2012 one.

When Lindsay woke up the morning of the transit, it was starting to snow and soon the driveway was white. She got the fire going in the lounge to warm up the house. In the kitchen, Alice had made two coffees. Lindsay flicked the fan heater on and sat at the dining table sipping her coffee while Alice made porridge.

'You'll be careful on the roads?' Lindsay said.

Alice raised an eyebrow. Annoying. 'I'm going to go 70 down 50 kay roads and put an end to my miserable existence.'

'Okay then,' Lindsay said.

'Want some?' Alice said, filling a bowl with some porridge for herself.

Lindsay shook her head. 'In a little while,' she said.

Alice sat down at the table and started to eat while flicking through news articles on her phone. She looked up. 'You should get Grandma and Grandad over here today, it'll be cold in their place.'

Neil and Heather were still in their rental, which they hadn't expected for winter. Repairs on their house were going to take an extra month or so, only the contractor hadn't told them until a few days before the original completion date. They had frantically negotiated with their landlord for another two months in the place. The landlord turned away the tenants he had lined up for a six week repair, which Neil and Heather felt bad about. But, Lindsay told them, it was probably happening all over Christchurch, they weren't the only ones with repairs that didn't stick to the schedule.

'I think I'll do that,' Lindsay said to Alice. 'Even if school opens, I'll keep the kids home, and having Mum and Dad here will help them relax for the day.'

'Are you sure about that?' Alice said.

Lindsay laughed.

'You're right, though,' Alice continued. 'It will be good for them. Text Sonya, maybe you can pick up Cody and Ella, have them here for the day. It'll mean she doesn't have to choose whether or not to go to work.'

'Another good idea,' Lindsay said, full of cheer. 'You're firing on all cylinders this morning.'

Alice shrugged, scraping porridge from the sides of her bowl. She sucked the last of the porridge off her spoon and got up from the table. 'Three more days,' she said. 'Just three more days.'

A woman Alice had been working with had moved on, taking a job with Southern Response, and soon after she left, she had offered Alice a job as a claims officer. Alice would be trained for the job and she was keen to do something new, something that really helped with the rebuild. Filing and phone calls were, she said, killing her brain.

Southern Response was the organisation the Government had set up after bailing out AMI Insurance. AMI had a large number of earthquake claims, too many, and near the end of 2011, it announced it would not be able to cover all of them. The Government set up Southern Response to handle all of AMI's earthquake claims and sold all of AMI's other policies to another insurance company.

It was, Lindsay could see, a good opportunity for Alice, although she would still prefer that she go back to university and finish her degree. Engineering was a good profession to get into, Lindsay insisted, Alice would be able to work wherever in the world she pleased, be able to earn a good living. The insurance industry was all over the world, too, Alice had said. Who knew? Maybe she would rise in the ranks and end up running one. She was joking, of course. Lindsay hoped she was joking. There were too many rumours about insurers doing the dirty on people for Lindsay to feel comfortable with the idea of Alice making her future there.

One thing that especially bothered Lindsay was that when the red zoning was first announced, the Minister for Earthquake Recovery had said that most red zoned properties were rebuilds and that red zoning would allow the homeowners to move on. They wouldn't have to wait around for months or years for the ground to be repaired before the rebuild could take place. It sounded good in theory. Following the announcement of the Government offers, though, a lot of those properties had switched to repairs, which meant the insurance companies could pay out much less than if the house was classed as a rebuild. These repairs were fictional, the land was red zoned and repairs couldn't be carried out because the land could no longer legally be built on. The argument over repair or rebuild was simply over how much the insurance company would pay out. There was something nasty about the switch from rebuild to repair, and Lindsay didn't want her daughter working in an industry that had the whiff of something that nasty going on.

Kevin came through to the kitchen, made himself a cup of coffee and poured a bowl of porridge. Lindsay tried to persuade him to stay home for the day, given the snow, but he insisted it would be fine, he had a job to finish, he would run heaters, if necessary, to dry the place out.

'But if you stay home you can watch the transit of Venus,' Lindsay said.

'Not for real,' he said. 'Not with this cloud cover. Only online.'

'It's as good as the real thing,' Lindsay said. She didn't share his passion.

'It's nothing like the real thing,' Kevin said, irritated. 'It's the difference between repairs that will actually be done and those insurance companies say can be done because they know they'll never have to do them.' They had been talking about fictional repairs a few nights ago. Kevin had gone to school with a guy in that situation. His insurance company had an estimate of over $400,000 for a rebuild, but then they offered only $125,000 because they insisted the house was repairable. Even though the repairs couldn't legally be carried out. It defied logic. And morals.

Kevin brought in some more firewood and helped Alice to clean the snow off her car before both of them left. Lindsay decided to leave the children to sleep in, poured herself a bowl of porridge and made another cup of coffee. In the lounge, she wrapped herself in a blanket on the sofa close to the fire. If she was going to have a busy kid-filled day, she was going to have a quiet start.

Lindsay texted Sonya to say that if the kids weren't going to school, she could look after them. Sonya texted right back saying that would be great, she would drop them off on her way to work. Then Lindsay called her parents to let them know. No point texting Heather, she still wasn't used to carrying a phone around all the time, even though many older people now did, because of experiencing the stress of not knowing the whereabouts of someone they loved during one of the many quakes.

Lindsay loved the house they were living in. It was an old state house with native wood timber floors that they had planned to expose and polish. They had chosen the house for those features, although they hadn't been able to get underway with the renovations once Lindsay found she was pregnant with Olivia. The walls were old-fashioned lath-and-plaster, very cracked from the earthquakes. They were also uninsulated, and the house was colder since the quakes started, harder to heat. Now they were just hoping it could be repaired, and soon. It would be odd to move out of this place, into another and then back into this one. People just didn't do that.

Then there was finding accommodation. Her parents had faced bidding wars whenever they went to look at a place and, in the end, had only been able to find something because Alice had asked her other grandfather if he knew of any places that would be available. Lindsay didn't like the idea that it was who you knew that found you a place, but she also didn't like the idea of a bidding war.

She and Kevin had talked about leaving Christchurch during their repairs. Kevin could find work that wasn't insurance related and they would be able to stretch their insurance company's accommodation allowance further away from the city. But Kevin wanted to be close by, to keep an eye on the place during its repairs.

There was too much moving going on in the family. Jason and Carla had no idea where they would be living in a month's time. They had accepted the Government's offer on their red zoned property and had made an offer on a townhouse. But the paperwork on house sales in post-quake Christchurch was a nightmare. Inspections needed to be carried out to ensure all the repairs on the scope of works had been completed correctly and that there wasn't damage that had been missed.

Then there were Lindsay's grandparents, Heather's parents. Their repairs had been scoped and they were expected to be out of the house for eight weeks, although when was still unknown. The best thing would be for them to stay with Neil and Heather, but they didn't know where they would be, neither did Jason and Carla, and Lindsay and Kevin didn't have the extra room. No one liked the idea of Grandma and Grandad Bennett staying in a cold, damp flat or in one of the temporary accommodation villages. There were a couple of them in the city, one near Eastgate Mall not far from Lindsay and Kevin. But Lindsay had heard there were problems with drugs and drinking there. Maybe Lindsay and Kevin could make do for eight weeks, Olivia and Jack could share and Alice could have Olivia's room. Grandad would have trouble getting in and out of their shower, though. It was a string of problems she wasn't going to solve sitting in front of the fire digesting her porridge. Time to move.

Lindsay woke Olivia and Jack, telling them there was snow and so it was a no school day. Both jumped out of bed and for once she didn't have to push them to get dressed. They bundled up warm, rushed outside and right away started to pile snow up in the backyard. Sonya arrived with Cody and Ella, who quickly dumped their stuff in the house and ran off to help Olivia and Jack.

Lindsay's plan for the day was to get her parents to look after all the kids while she did some work. It would do her parents good, keep them busy, not thinking about their house and whether or not they would need to move again before finally getting home.

Heather made lunch for everyone and just as she and Lindsay were cleaning up and the kids had settled in the lounge playing video games, Kevin pulled up the drive. Too cold to keep working, he said. He talked the kids into going back out into the snow.

Soon Kevin and the children had made a giant snowball and were standing around it. There was a small stone embedded in the snowball and Kevin was moving his arms around like he was explaining something to them. They just looked puzzled. Lindsay wondered what was going on but then twigged. He had made his own transit of Venus, the stone was Venus moving across the face of the snowball sun.

It would be one hundred and fifteen years before there would be another Transit of Venus. The opportunity had been missed.

What worried Lindsay the most about how long it was taking to get their repairs scoped was that this was their second winter in a damaged house. If the insurance company didn't start taking action soon, the opportunity to get them back into the house before the winter of 2013 would be missed. They would then have to spend another winter trying to heat a damaged house, and Lindsay was already feeling too used to the house the way it was. Living in a damaged house was now normal.

A City on the Plains

July 2012

The Share an Idea campaign in the autumn of 2011 had given the people of Christchurch an opportunity to think about the future of their city in the months after the February earthquake, when they were facing a stark winter in damaged homes and a broken city. It had reminded Alice, as that first post-quake winter got underway, that the rebuilt city would soon start to take shape. Share an Idea promised a smart rebuild, harvesting the ideas of the city's residents to make something good out of the bad.

What appealed most to Alice was the idea of a green city full of parks and cycleways, one that made the most of the city's natural beauty, combining the enjoyment of the green spaces with the usual functions of a CBD. Residents wanted to see a city connected to Hagley Park, the Avon River and beyond to the estuary and the sea.

The City Council collected these ideas and used them to formulate a draft Central City Plan, which was submitted to the Government at the end of 2011. The Government rejected this plan and then, via CERA, created a group called the Central Christchurch Development Unit. The CCDU's initial assignment was to produce what was known as the 100-day plan, a blueprint for getting the CBD up and running that was so full of good ideas and promise that businesses would rush to put their development dollars into the rebuild of Christchurch.

The 100-day plan was announced in July 2012. There would be a new library in the centre of the city, a new, larger convention centre and a new stadium to replace the damaged one just outside the city centre. Another idea was to develop precincts to bring common activities together: an innovation precinct for technology companies, a justice and emergency services precinct, a retail precinct, a health services precinct and a performing arts precinct. Alice wasn't sure about the whole precinct business, it seemed a lot to ask businesses that had survived the earthquakes to move on because some government planner thought something else should be there. But what was exciting was the way green spaces would be used to frame a smaller city centre. The areas around the Avon River would be widened in places and a riverside park would be developed to connect to corridors of green spaces to the east and south of the city.

It was a city Alice wanted to live in and could see herself having a future in, something that had become more and more difficult as the year dragged on.

Alice wasn't enjoying her new job. She had been expecting that this job would be more challenging than her last one, but that the challenges would be balanced by the fact she would be helping people make progress on their claims. Her grandparents had found in their dealings with Fletchers and EQC that the people they talked to often seemed unwilling to provide the information they were asking for, and they didn't seem interested in pursuing answers for their customers. Alice was determined to be different, to find out for her clients the answers to their questions, to help them understand the process and feel that their claim was going in the right direction.

The system didn't work that way. Alice considered herself a reasonably intelligent, logical person, but the systems were impenetrable. But, she promised herself, she was going to stick with it, get her head around the systems and do her best to become an effective claims officer.

Alice had spent most of the last two months training and getting used to her new job, and her frustration continued to mount. By the time the 100-day plan was published, she was feeling that she was in a dark place, wondering what she should do, what options were open to her.

The plan was a bright light on the horizon, a promise that things would get better, the city would return to normal. No, not normal, because Christchurch had, in truth, been a bit dull before, but something new and vibrant, a place where there were always interesting things to do and see, any time of the year. The plan painted a picture of a shining city on the plains, showing off all that Alice loved about Christchurch, making the most of it.

But was it enough to keep Alice going? There was a lot of work to do to achieve the blueprint, land and buildings to be bought, buildings to be demolished and new ones to go up. It would be a few years before the plan began to be realised, but Alice would be in her mid-20s by then, the right age to take advantage of everything the new city had to offer.

This broken city was only for a brief time. The shining city on the plains was the future.

Fletchered

August 2012

In 2012, it became more common for shipping containers to appear on grass verges in front of houses, storing the house's contents while repairs were carried out. The Canterbury Home Repair Programme run by Fletcher EQR was in full swing. All over the city, people moved out of their houses, often taking weeks to sort through household goods accumulated over decades, taking only what they needed to get by for the few months they would spend in temporary accommodation. Some people moved in with friends or family, others into a rental property and some spent the duration of their repair living in motels. In Christchurch, it was becoming normal to move out of a house and then back into it again a few months later.

Back before the earthquakes started, Neil and Heather expected to make only one more move in their lifetime, from the house near the river where their children had grown up, into a new house built on a section two suburbs away. Instead, they packed up their old house, moving some of its contents into the rental they had arranged but packing the rest into the Bowens' garage.

Five months later, the work was finally complete and Neil and Heather went through with the project manager, who expected them to sign off the work. There were some things they weren't happy with, but the project manager said they had three months to complain. The lease on their rental was nearly up and in a few months, Heather's parents needed a place to stay while their own repairs were done. They decided to sign off the repairs and move back in.

A month later, the list of flaws was staggering, and their project manager was not returning their calls. What would they find given another month? So far, floorboards creaked throughout the house and some were starting to split, not all of the plaster work had been sanded back properly, the wall between the kitchen and the lounge was cracking, the door to the bathroom was constantly swinging open and, the latest thing, paint was flaking off the walls in two of the bedrooms.

Problems with their repairs were the last thing they needed, especially since they didn't yet know whether or not their section would be red zoned. There was, Lindsay had said, going to be an announcement later in the month, but deadlines had already been missed, so Heather wasn't holding her breath. Even if there was something soon, the whole process was taking far too long, it had been fifteen months since the February quake, nearly two years since the September quake, and they had talked about whether or not they needed to get a lawyer to pursue the matter for them, if something didn't happen soon. But then there were the problems with the house they were already living in. Would they need a lawyer for that, too?

They were disappointed, they had expected better, after the repairs to the house Sonya rented had gone so well. Sonya and her children had lived with them for the last four months of 2011. It had been a stressful time, full of loud arguments, followed by long silences, then a few days of peace before the cycle started all over again. Even saying nothing was regarded as an affront, and Neil and Heather had many late-night conversations discussing how to cope with the arrangement for the sake of Cody and Ella. Heather stopped trying to understand her younger daughter, she didn't know where Sonya's anger came from and why it was so often directed at her.

The day Sonya moved back into her repaired flat, Neil, Heather, Kevin and Alice helped her move back in while Lindsay took the four children to Willowbank for the day. 'We definitely have the easier job,' Sonya said sitting in her newly painted house surveying all the boxes. She was in a surprisingly good mood. Heather was trying not to be offended at the idea that Sonya's good mood was more about getting away from her mother than from getting back into her renovated flat.

The landlord had insulated the house while all the wall linings were replaced and it felt warm and dry, much different from how it had been before. The kitchen, bathroom and laundry had been replaced, not with new items, they were clearly early-2000s-style fittings.

'It's lovely,' Heather said, running a hand over the kitchen benchtop.

'From demolished houses,' Kevin said, placing his forefinger alongside his nose. 'It's who you know.'

'Better here than in the tip,' Lindsay said.

'Yeah, I know,' Kevin said. 'I'm just saying that not everyone has a mate who knows a guy who can get you a kitchen and bathroom cheap.'

A few weeks later, Neil and Heather had moved out of their house for repairs, their expectations high, riding on the good result for Sonya's flat.

Now Kevin was under their house in the crawl space, clad in disposable overalls, looking like a crime scene technician. Even though he was slender, he was finding it difficult moving around under there, they could hear him grunting and coughing as he moved along. Occasionally he swore as something went wrong. It was slow going. The house was starting to smell dusty, they would have to air it out once Kevin came back up through the manhole.

Finally he passed up the digital camera and the torch, then pulled himself up. Neil and Heather were silent as Kevin removed the coveralls, rolled them up into a ball. Heather tucked them into a plastic supermarket bag, which she tied closed.

'I'll put the jug on,' she said. She needed the distraction. If it was good news, Kevin would be telling them right away.

In the kitchen, they sipped at their coffees and Kevin showed them some of the photos from under the house. There were several cracks at different points in the foundation.

'We'll have to get someone to have a look but I think what they've done is glued the cracks on the outside, but not all the way through,' Kevin said. 'There's one just near the corner of the kitchen we should have a look at from the other side.'

They all went outside to the area Kevin had mentioned. There was a faint trace of the repaired crack beneath the paint that covered the skirting foundation. Kevin bent down and scraped away at the soil below the repaired crack, scooping out handfuls of soil and revealing that the crack continued below the ground, unrepaired.

Heather felt like she was going to cry and Neil spat out string of words, including a couple Heather had seldom heard from his lips.

'That's putting it mildly,' Kevin said.

'That's what this repair programme is supposed to be for,' Neil said. He put an arm around Heather's shoulder. 'To stop the cowboys from doing cowboy work like this. Instead we've got this, this, I don't know what you'd call it. Amateur hour.'

'I heard someone call it being fletchered,' Kevin said.

'Fletchered,' Heather said. 'It would almost be funny if it wasn't happening to you.'

'If it's any comfort,' Kevin said, 'I don't think you're alone.'

'No, that's no comfort,' Heather said. 'What do we do?'

They decided that Neil would call Fletchers on Monday, bypassing the unresponsive project manager, and let them know the work hadn't been done properly. Whether that would get them anywhere remained to be seen.

Kevin helped them go through all their paperwork, which went some way to getting their thoughts in order, but overall Neil and Heather weren't feeling very good about whatever process they would have to go through to get their house fixed. Properly.

Later, Lindsay and Alice dropped by with the rest of the grandchildren. Alice had picked Cody and Ella up from Sonya's earlier in the day, and they had been playing with Olivia and Jack for the afternoon.

'They have to be home by six,' Alice said. 'But that gives us time for an early dinner.'

Heather was pleased to see Cody and Ella, she had missed them once they moved back into their own home. Although Sonya seemed to be all right with them seeing more of their grandparents, it was still only about once a month. Not enough as far as Heather was concerned. They were lovely children who got along well with the younger Olivia and Jack.

There was mention of buying a couple of hot chickens, but that was drowned out by the children's requests for fish and chips. Fish and chips it would be.

Alice took the children through to the lounge to keep them amused while Kevin and Neil went to get dinner. Heather and Lindsay cleared the dining table of their EQC paperwork.

'What's the story with the house?' Lindsay said.

'Foundation's not been repaired properly, looks like,' Heather said.

'In what way?'

'Cracks glued on the outside only.'

They talked about options. Lindsay said one of the mothers at school had a house where all the plaster cracks on the inside of the house had been painted over. The repair of the cracks was on the scope of works, but it hadn't been done. 'You should get a lawyer,' Lindsay said. 'Let them take care of everything.'

'But that costs money, and we still don't know what's going to happen with the section. We may have to choose between a lawyer for the section or for the house.'

'I wish I'd stayed at uni,' Lindsay said. 'Finished my degree, then I'd be a bit more useful now.'

'I'm glad you didn't,' Heather said.

'But you were so set on me going to uni, making something of myself.'

Heather was quiet, considering if that's how it was at the time. 'There was an opportunity,' she said at last. 'University was still relatively cheap, I wanted you to take advantage of that.'

'The way you didn't,' Lindsay said. There was a hint of accusation in her voice, but it wasn't matched by her gaze. She looked amused more than anything.

'You know the sixties bypassed Christchurch,' Heather said. 'I think it was the eighties before girls going to university became a real option.'

'On this side of town anyway,' Lindsay said. 'What would you do? Right now, if you could have your very own university degree, what would it be?'

'Law,' Heather said. 'Definitely law. It would come in handy right now.'

Lindsay laughed. 'You and half the people in this part of town,' she said. 'That would make for some very crowded lecture theatres.'

'Has Alice said anything about going back to uni?'

'Not something we talk about,' Lindsay said. 'She gets defensive.'

'Because she feels you expect her to go back,' Heather said. 'She feels that pressure. Maybe the same way you felt that pressure?'

Lindsay shook her head. 'No, I'm not applying pressure. I just want her to do something that has a future. This job she has now, that's going to wind down, the rebuild's only going to last so long.'

Heather raised an eyebrow. 'Are you sure about that?' she said. 'If there are other places like ours, there's going to be years worth of work, repairs of the repairs, and so on.'

Lindsay shrugged and smiled at her mother. 'If I was Alice's age, would you want me building a career in the insurance industry?'

'No, I wouldn't,' Heather said slowly. 'But I would be very careful about letting her figure things out for herself.'

'You mean the way you're letting me figure out the raising of my own daughter for myself?' Lindsay said.

Heather knew she had gone too far. She felt something needed to be said, but she didn't know how to say it. That was the thing with Lindsay, they usually had a fairly easygoing relationship, until Heather stepped across a line she was never good at seeing. Whereas with Sonya, the line was clear, there was a very short list of topics they could discuss without entering the conflict zone.

'There's Dad and Kevin,' Lindsay said as Kevin's van pulled up the driveway.

Relieved at the end to the conversation, Heather went through to tell the others dinner had arrived.

That night, when Heather was trying to fall asleep she found herself thinking not of the house but of her daughters, and of what she had expected from both of them. When they were growing up, Heather was certain that she only wanted them to be happy, but now, looking back, she could see how she had, maybe, been a little heavy-handed in how she had tried to guide them. She could see this now, because she could see Lindsay doing the same thing with Alice. That was the difficulty of being the mother of daughters, how did you separate your own distant dreams for yourself from wanting the absolute best for them? It was difficult to balance seeing the pitfalls of their choices with knowing it was good for them to figure things out for themselves. It had been so much easier with Jason, he had always been interested in his father's line of work, and training as a mechanic had been a foregone conclusion. Heather had been more anxious about Jason making a mistake over who he married than over his choice of career.

Heather had always been prone to worrying, while Neil had been the bright, cheery one, able to make her laugh. Whatever they had gone through in the four decades they had been married, they had always been able to look forward to the future, to see that what was going on would pass.

Neil had been more and more quiet the longer they were back in the house. She had found herself more often in his usual role, trying to be light and cheery, making him laugh, making the future look bright. She found it tiring, she was running out of reasons to be upbeat and cheery. When he finally brought up the possibility that there was something more wrong with the house than the few items they had during the inspection, it was clear he had been thinking about it for some time, given the lengthy list of faults he described.

She tried telling herself the house wasn't important, in the end, her family was. That was true, her family was more important to her than anything else, but they did need a place to live that wasn't going to, in the long run, wear down their health and drain their finances. The house was demanding attention she would rather pour into her children, her grandchildren and her parents, and she didn't think there was going to be an easy solution. Nothing was easy, especially now that they had been fletchered.

Carpers, Moaners and Red Zoners

September 2012

Although the first land zoning announcements were made in June 2011, it wasn't until fifteen months later that the first red zone offers were made to people who didn't have insurance: fifty percent of the 2007 rateable value of the land. Some of these people had bare sections, which couldn't be insured so had no EQC cover. Others didn't have insurance for various reasons, from deliberately choosing not to have insurance to having missed payments due to illness or other difficult situations; these people were offered nothing for their houses.

Alice's grandparents finally received the news that their section was red zoned, but they hadn't received an offer. But the news of the half-price offers came on the heels of the discovery of the poor state of repairs to their house and both were looking stressed, like they hadn't had a good night's sleep in a long time. Alice and Lindsay decided to arrange a family dinner for the weekend so everyone could spend some time together, take their minds off what was going on with houses, land, city. Lindsay wanted to have a barbecue, but although technically September was spring, the weather was too unpredictable to guarantee a barbecue wouldn't result in one miserable man cooking meat in what passed for shelter just inside the open garage. Alice persuaded her to do a big roast meal instead, and arranged for Heather to do salads and Sonya and Carla to do a dessert each.

Alice was looking forward to having the family all together for an afternoon, even though it would be somewhat chaotic, squeezing all the adults around the dining table and keeping the children amused in the lounge. Kevin had set up a card table for the four kids in the lounge so they didn't have to endure all the adult talk. Hopefully it wouldn't rain so they could run around outside.

Then, just an hour before the others were due to start arriving, Sonya texted Alice to say she wouldn't be able to make it. There was no explanation, just that she wouldn't be coming, and her cancellation irritated Lindsay, whose dark mood started to grate on Alice. 'I'll go over, see what's going on,' Alice said.

'No, just forget it,' Lindsay said. 'I'm tired of being the one trying all the time.'

Alice insisted, she would be able to bring Cody and Ella back.

Sonya looked like she hadn't slept well. She was still in her pyjamas and hadn't taken off her makeup from the day before, her mascara and eyeliner dark smears under her eyes.

'I've hardly slept,' she said, turning away from the door and walking through to the kitchen. Alice shut the front door behind her and followed. Sonya had the jug on to boil and mixed two instant coffees. 'Cody and Ella are in their rooms, I've told them to do some reading, I need it quiet.'

'What happened?' Alice said. She sat down at the dining table.

'Up too late,' Sonya said. 'Couldn't stay asleep.' The jug finished boiling and Sonya poured the coffees, handed one to Alice, then sat down at the dining table.

'Anything in particular?'

Sonya shook her head, although Alice didn't know whether that meant there was nothing specific or that it wasn't anything Sonya wanted to talk about. Whatever was going on, Alice wasn't going to pry, it seemed to her that if people really wanted to talk about something that they would, if you spent enough time with them. That was certainly the case with Charlotte, now that she and Alice were spending more time together.

'Sometimes I think I need to get out of this place,' Sonya finally said.

Alice looked around. 'The flat or Christchurch?' she said.

'Christchurch,' Sonya said.

'What are you thinking about?'

'Dunedin,' Sonya said. 'It will be good for the kids to be closer to their dad, Cody'll be a teenager next year, can you believe it? He needs his dad. And I'm thinking about doing some study.'

Sonya worked at a clothing shop, a job she had been in ever since Ella had started school. Alice had never thought of her wanting an alternative. But these earthquakes had shaken people up, made them think about their lives, where they were, where they were going. 'What would you do?'

'I'm thinking nursing,' Sonya said. 'I should be able to get a student allowance, help with the kids, and they're at a good age for me to do some study, especially if we're near their dad.'

'When?'

Sonya shrugged. 'Just thoughts at the moment. A lot to do to get there.' She seemed overwhelmed at the thought of everything she would have to do to pack up and move. 'Probably just dreaming,' she mumbled.

'Well check it out,' Alice said, trying not to sound too perky and pushy, which is what Lindsay would do if she knew Sonya was making some plans for her future. Lindsay would push too far. 'You don't have to decide today. Hey can I take Cody and Ella? That way you can just rest for the afternoon?' Alice said.

Sonya thought about it for a moment, then nodded. 'That's probably a good idea.'

Both were quiet, sipping at their drinks. Sonya brightened for a moment. 'I did make a pav,' she said. 'You might as well take it, best it not stay here with me.'

'Will do,' Alice said. She finished her coffee. 'I better go, I still need to help Mum with the vegetables.'

Sonya went to get the kids and while they were getting their shoes and jackets on, took the pavlova from the refrigerator. 'You have any fruit?' she said. 'I forgot to get some. But I have a jar of passionfruit pulp if you don't have any.' She reached into the pantry and handed Alice a jar.

'This will be good,' Alice said. 'Save you a piece?'

'Sure, why not.'

At home, Neil and Heather had arrived and were in the lounge with Olivia and Jack, who were showing them their latest game on the Xbox. Cody and Ella hugged their grandparents then joined Olivia and Jack in front of the television. Alice went out to the kitchen to help Lindsay and Kevin. Soon Jason and Carla arrived, bearing a bowl of trifle. Carla lifted the edge of the plastic wrap and Alice sniffed. The scent of rum drifted out into the kitchen.

The roast was a leg of lamb that had been cooking slowly in the oven since first thing in the morning. A tray of potatoes and kumara had been added in the last hour, and everything was ready to be served.

Carla was the first to bring up the state of the city. Following their red zoning the previous year, she and Jason had bought a townhouse in Addington, one that had only minor damage. They had moved in just three weeks earlier. They had to increase their mortgage to afford the place and would have preferred a house with a yard for the children they wanted to start having, but overall they were happy with the place and putting off having children for a couple of years. She wasn't even thirty yet, Carla said, there was no hurry. They were more relaxed than they had been for a while.

The red zoning had been stressful and upsetting, but taking the Government offer had taken them out of a difficult situation, living in a badly damaged house in a munted neighbourhood. But it was over now, they were in a place they could make a home once again.

Carla said the roadworks around their house were crazy. 'Some days I wonder if I'll be able to get out to get to work,' she said.

'There doesn't seem to be much in the way of planning,' Heather said. 'Usually we have about half a dozen different ways into our neighbourhood, now we're down to two. It seems like the ones down the street aren't coordinated with the ones around the corner.'

'Will you take the offer?' Jason said without prelude.

'We don't know whether we're red zoned or not,' Neil said.

'But I thought they had decided all that?' Jason said.

'No,' Lindsay said. There was an edge in her voice, she was irritated with Jason for some reason. 'The flat land's been decided but the hills are still being worked on.'

'Even if we did have an offer,' Neil said, 'we don't know what we would do. It doesn't seem fair, we didn't do anything wrong and all of a sudden our land might not be ours to keep. We don't know who to complain to.'

'Well don't complain too loudly,' Kevin said.

'Or you'll get called carpers and moaners,' Lindsay finished. She laughed wryly, shaking her head.

'Who said that?' Jason asked. At Lindsay's disbelieving look he added, 'Sorry, I've been busy with the house, I haven't been following anything this last couple of weeks, I only know about the red zone offers because a guy at work, his grandparents have been offered fifty percent for their land. They're not insured.'

'Someone did a survey of TC3 residents,' Lindsay said. 'People like me and Kev, with foundation damage. They weren't at all happy with EQC and insurers, saying everything's taking too long. Anyway, the Minister wasn't happy about them complaining, said he was sick of all the carping and moaning.'

'From people who had time to buggerise around on Facebook all day,' Alice finished. The election the previous year had been the first she was old enough to vote in and she had thought long and hard about who to vote for, who she felt she could have confidence in to run the rebuild well. Nearly a year later, she was disappointed to hear someone who was supposed to be looking out for the people of the city talking about them that way.

'How many people were surveyed?' Jason asked.

'Nearly 700,' Lindsay said. 'So quite a decent chunk. Apparently there's ten thousand in our situation, on TC3 land who need new foundations.'

Jason asked what was going on with their claim, and Lindsay explained that they had their scope of works – the house would be lifted and the foundations replaced – now they just had to wait for the geotechnical work to be carried out.

'But there's only a couple of rigs to do the drilling for the whole city, 10,000 sites, so we probably won't hear anything until the end of the year.'

'Well at least you know what's going to happen,' Jason said. 'Not everyone does.'

'And we've avoided being fletchered,' Kevin said. 'So we're happy about that.' Alice saw Lindsay shoot him a look that said to shut up, but he ignored it and ploughed onward. 'I reckon that's what would've happened to us if we'd gone ahead with the work they wanted to do last year,' he continued. Alice felt Lindsay kick at him from under the table, but he ignored her. 'I think those guys from Fletchers were here to do the September work, they hadn't taken into account the damage from February. It would've gone ahead if we hadn't been asking questions, and now we'd be in...' Lindsay had kicked him again, hard enough to make him stop.

'... our position,' Heather finished.

Kevin's face turned red. 'Yeah. Though you didn't have a scope from September then, so possibly yours is just shoddy scoping.'

'I'll get dessert,' Alice said, getting up from the table.

'Can you help me clear the table, Kev?' Lindsay said, getting up and starting to stack the plates. Kevin got up and helped her, which resulted in a hushed conversation in the kitchen that Alice pretended not to listen to, consumed by getting the desserts out the fridge.

'This is supposed to help them get their minds off what's happened,' Lindsay said, 'not rehash the whole thing.'

'We need to talk through it,' Kevin said. 'It's complicated, they need to get their thoughts in order to decide what to do.'

Lindsay sighed and brushed her hair from her face. 'But that doesn't have to happen right now, does it?'

'Look at them, Lin, they're exhausted, we need to do something to help, even if it's just talking it all through, listening.'

'But...'

'And I think it would be good for Jase and Carla to know what's going on,' Kevin said. 'They're so relieved to be out of the red zone that they've forgotten that this is still going on for a lot of people.'

Alice handed a stack of bowls to Kevin and a handful of spoons to Lindsay. 'Right then,' she said, pointedly. 'Time for dessert, everyone can talk after.'

Once the dessert bowls were cleared, coffees and teas were served and the children were settled in front of a video. The adults started talking about Neil and Heather's house. They were having trouble getting EQC's attention because they had signed off on their repairs.

'We had to sign to move back into the house,' Neil said. 'I only signed because they said we had three months to complain, and we're well within the three months, but they don't want a bar of it. Because we've signed off, even though we were railroaded into it. So I don't know what to do.'

'I've heard about that happening,' Jason said. 'And about people's repairs being signed off by the contractors themselves.'

'That's dodgy,' Kevin said. 'Surely the police would be interested in something like that.'

'They'd have to double the police force to investigate all the dodgy stuff going on in the city,' Lindsay said.

'What I want to know,' Heather said, 'is why we're not hearing anything about this in the media, on TV. Surely it's the sort of thing Fair Go should be picking up?'

'Not going to get covered on TV,' Alice said. She had been silent up until then and everyone turned and stared at her. 'Look at who advertises, TVNZ isn't going to shoot themselves in the foot by doing nasty stories on their advertisers.'

'You heard this through that job of yours?' Jason said.

Alice hadn't wanted to say anything because she didn't want her job being drawn into it, but there it was, she had said something without thinking and now she felt like her job was fair game. She was talking to some very stressed people, and she was finding it increasingly hard to go to work each day, wondering if she would be able to do anything to make their situation better. She couldn't help but think of these people as being like her grandparents, paying their premiums for decades and yet not getting the response they had been promised. The rebuild was so slow to get going, it was hard to believe that it had already been two years since the first lot of damage was done.

'Even if the media was listening,' Neil said, 'we wouldn't go that route, we will not make a spectacle of our situation, at least we have a place to live. Give the attention to the people worse off than us, the ones who can't stay in their homes.'

'Dad,' Lindsay said, 'your repairs need repairs and you have a section you might one day be offered half the RV for. It doesn't get much worse than that.'

'We can still live in the place,' Heather said. 'It's not like we're paying a mortgage and rent like so many are. We'll just keep plugging away on getting the repairs fixed, and as for the section, let's see what the next month or so brings. There's one man talking about taking court action over the fifty percent offers. Maybe if we end up red zoned, we can be part of that.'

'Or at least keep an eye on it,' Neil said. 'See what happens.'

Everyone was quiet again. That decided, there seemed to be nothing else to talk about.

'Nice to have the supermarket back,' Lindsay said. Their local supermarket had been a rebuild after the February quake, so the closest supermarkets for the past year and a half had been in the city. 'Would never have thought three years ago that a new supermarket could make me so happy.'

'It is beautiful,' said Heather. 'That view of the hills is just so lovely.'

'I'm just happy not to go to Moorhouse Ave any more,' Alice said. 'A bit depressing seeing the old railway station being ripped apart.'

'Have to wonder,' Kevin said, 'it's taking them so long to take that down, if it's that strong, did it really need to be demolished?'

'Don't you remember?' Heather said. 'Gerry Brownlee wants all the old dungers gone!'

'So stop carping about it,' Lindsay said. 'You big moaner, or we'll settle your claim for fifty percent of its actual value.'

Everyone laughed, but half-heartedly. With the Minister for Earthquake Recovery so scathing of the people whose red zoned properties had been worst affected by the quakes, the future of the rebuild was far from shiny.

Mind the Gap

October 2012

The September 2010 quake occurred on the Greendale fault south of the small town of Darfield. During this quake, the fault did what faults famously do: it broke the surface, offsetting roads, fences and railway lines. The February 2011 quake, however, occurred on a different fault, one that did not break the surface, one running under the Port Hills south of the city. Although it left no surface scar, the February quake did deform the hills and surrounding land. The hills and the floor of the estuary were pushed up by the force of the quake, while some areas north of the estuary and in the east of the city sank by as much as fifteen centimetres.

Neither fault was known to exist before the Canterbury earthquake sequence began. In the months that followed the September and February quakes, scientists swarmed over the land, collecting as much information as they could about the network of hidden faults in the region. This wasn't simple curiosity, but was an attempt to understand how at risk the region was, what faults lurked beneath the river gravels, building up tension, ready to rupture.

These investigations found that there was a poorly-formed connection between the two faults several kilometres underground. The Port Hills fault extended far enough west to almost touch the eastern end of the Greendale fault. This almost-touching point corresponded to an area that had become known as The Gap, the area near the satellite towns of Prebbleton, Rolleston and Lincoln. It was an area that tended to have a lot of aftershocks whenever there were quakes elsewhere in the region. Scientists theorised that if the September 2010 earthquake had run along the gap, rupturing the Port Hills fault, the quake generated would have been a 7.3 magnitude quake rather than the 7.1.

'Is that much of a difference?' Marjorie asked.

Alice was setting the table, telling her about something she had read recently. Andrew and his family were coming around for dinner and Alice had arrived early to help Marjorie with the cooking. Michelle and the children had been in Christchurch for the week, they were still living in Wanaka, but Andrew and Michelle's house had been repaired, the number of quakes had dropped right off and Michelle had finally agreed to come back to Christchurch. Not right away, but at the start of 2013. The children would finish the school year in Wanaka.

The leg of lamb and vegetables were in the oven and more vegetables were on the stove.

'It's not just a little bit stronger than a 7.1,' Alice said. 'It's twice the energy, so there would've been a lot more shaking, more damage.'

There was a knock at the door and Marjorie went through to the living room to open it. Alice would just knock and then come in, but the rest of the family always waited for the door to be opened for them. It was a formalism that Marjorie had been unable to train into the girl ever since she had stayed with her after the February earthquake. At first, she had minded, it was her own home after all, but she had become used to it from Alice, who seemed to want nothing from her other than to get to know her, to know the family's history and to understand how she fit in.

It was Andrew and Michelle and their four children. Andrew leaned in and kissed Marjorie on the cheek.

'Grandmother,' he said.

'Come in,' she said, stepping away from the door. Andrew and Michelle stepped over the threshold and Michelle leaned in for the obligatory kiss on the cheek, holding off to one side a bowl that held a salad covered in clingfilm. Marjorie took the bowl from her and started walking through to the kitchen. The children spilled past the adults, pouring into the living room through to the kitchen beyond, where Alice scooped up the youngest, the girl, in her arms, kissing her on the forehead and squeezing her tight. Andrew and Michelle followed Marjorie through to the kitchen while Alice's siblings told her what they had been up to.

It was a pleasant afternoon. Andrew's children were well-behaved compared to some of her great-grandchildren and they never complained about vegetables or played around with their food. After dessert, Michelle and Alice cleared the table and filled the dishwasher while the children played outside and Marjorie and Andrew discussed business.

Marjorie's rental properties that EQC had put overcap were still caught up in the assessment process with the insurance company, which Andrew was handling for her. He had received a scope of works back on one of them, plus an offer of settlement. She had a choice: let the insurance company carry out the repairs or take the money and organise the repairs herself. It was tempting to let the insurance company do the work, if there was more damage discovered, the risk would be theirs and they would bear the costs. If she organised for the work to be done and more damage was discovered, she – meaning Andrew – would be stuck negotiating with the insurance company for money to cover that new damage while work ground to a halt, her property sitting there earning no rent while the insurance company's bureaucracy contemplated what to do. It was tempting to just let them get on with it. But the building industry had gone mad and there were rumours of poor quality work and good builders struggling to get work. Marjorie and Andrew decided that he would engage an engineer to do their own scope of works, that was the best way to ensure all the damage had been captured.

Then she moved on to the matter of properties she was interested in buying. Marjorie had bought three damaged properties in the last year. Tony had organised for minor repairs to be carried out and had then found tenants. Not a difficult job in a city that had lost thousands of houses, and she intended to buy up more of these as-is-where-is properties.

'Next year, I expect TC3 properties will start to come onto the market,' Marjorie said to Andrew. 'I'm curious to see how much ground works will cost, do you know anyone?'

'Shouldn't you be slowing down, Grandmother?' Andrew said. 'TC3 land will require a lot of work to get them suitable to rebuild on. I think you're better off sticking to TC2 and TC1 properties.'

'Possibly,' Marjorie said. 'But I would like to know what's involved.'

'Fine,' Andrew said. He seemed harried, but Marjorie knew he would never say no to her, he had always been eager to please his grandmother. 'I'll look into it on Monday, but I think it will be some time before it's worth buying anything TC3, not with all the geotech work that still needs to be done.'

TC3 properties were those on the most liquefaction-prone land and if a TC3 property had foundation damage, a geotechnical investigation had to be carried out before replacement foundations could be designed and built. There was simply not enough equipment in the country to carry out this work quickly and EQC and geotechnical engineering companies were slowly working their way around the city, carrying out both shallow and deep investigations. Marjorie had seen a drilling rig on a nearby property, one near the river that had visible cracks in its ring foundation.

Michelle came back inside, carrying the girl, Mattie, who was rubbing her eyes. 'She's getting tired,' she said. 'It's probably time to get her home.'

Andrew set about rounding up the other children and getting them to say their goodbyes. Alice left soon after, saying she would drop by later in the week, after work one night.

Marjorie was relieved to have the early finish to the evening. She had been in the habit of staying up late most of her adult life, but lately she was retiring as early as eight o'clock some nights. The family leaving early meant she didn't have to let them know how tired she was, she didn't want to be seen to be slowing down. She was still keeping up with the garden, but lately she had been thinking about getting someone in to take care of the housework. She didn't want to ask one of her daughters, she would feel obligated to them, and she didn't like to think about how they might try to collect on that obligation. Karen was a real estate agent and had made it clear that she wanted to be the one to sell any properties Marjorie decided to part with.

Before Alice had switched to the topic of the gap between the Greendale and Port Hills faults earlier that day, she had told Marjorie there were some in her family having problems with insurance and the stress of living in a broken city. It was difficult, Marjorie found the roads and always-changing detours gruelling. Until recently, she had driven into the city every Thursday to do her supermarket shopping, enduring the jarring roads, the diversions, the indignity of shopping at an inner city supermarket. Thankfully her local supermarket had reopened a few weeks ago, and Marjorie no longer had to worry about anchoring her handbag to her shopping trolley to prevent it being stolen.

Alice seemed overly concerned with her family's mental health. Mental health was not a term Marjorie had heard of when she was young. She understood the concept of shell shock, after all she had grown up with it. Then, in the war, she had seen men fall apart from seeing too much of the horrors of war. She had lived in a city under siege and seen the neighbourhood she grew up in destroyed, her family home obliterated, and she had been just fine. But really, back then, most people just got on with it rather than having breakdowns. It was the weak ones who resorted to alcohol and violence, weak men like her father.

Her father had returned from the first world war and married a woman who had lost the man she truly loved. Marjorie was born soon after, and brothers and sisters followed, her fellow witnesses to her father's rages, victims of his bullying. Nursing school had allowed her to escape as soon as she turned eighteen, and the others soon found their own ways out. Her parents were the only ones killed when the terrace was bombed.

For Marjorie, her family had died when Edward was killed, even though she still had another brother and two sisters. Before Marjorie left England, she would run into Gwen and Charlie occasionally, and they would ask if she had heard anything from Lizzie. Even if she had, she wouldn't tell them, that would only result in her being drawn back into it all. When she, Bill and Suzanne left England for New Zealand, she saw no reason to get in touch and let them know. After all, they would only judge her for the expedient decision marrying Bill had been. Rather than risking her two worlds colliding and blowing her new one apart, she had told Bill that her whole family had been killed in the Blitz.

Lately, listening to Alice talk about her mother's side of the family, Marjorie had thought more about Gwen, Charlie and Lizzie. They were all younger than her, they could still be alive. What had they made of themselves? Had their parents' legacy dragged them down or motivated them, driven them to do anything but be like their parents? It had certainly motivated Marjorie. But there was a whole world between her and them, even if they were still alive, a gap that could not be bridged, not without shaking apart the life she had spent the last sixty years building. She wouldn't let that happen. Instead, she would keep wondering, keep telling herself she had done the right thing by getting out of England, getting out of her family.

The Best Teacher

November 2012

Until September 2010, Wellington was the city New Zealanders expected to be hit by a devastating earthquake. In February 2011, those outside Christchurch watched the television news as the horror unfolded, and while Christchurch struggled to get on the road to recovery, the rest of the country did its best to learn lessons from the Christchurch experience. What to do, what not to do.

As bad as the 2010 and 2011 quakes were for Christchurch, a large quake under Wellington would be worse. Roads in and out of mostly-flat Christchurch remained open in spite of the February quake, but that would not be the case for not-so-flat Wellington. Wellington's main routes in and out went over hills and up valleys and so were likely to be cut off in a quake. Power and water supply would also be interrupted as they tended to follow those main routes in and out of the region. Some suburbs would be cut off, not for days, but for weeks and months. People in those areas wouldn't have power or water and would be reliant on helicopters and barges for supplies. In short, what had happened in Christchurch following the February quake would be repeated in Wellington, but on a larger scale and for a longer period of time. Wellington needed to learn from the Christchurch experience, build more redundancy and strength into their systems and be prepared. It was a need that was difficult to ignore as long as Christchurch was still fresh in people's minds.

One mistake Lindsay hoped Wellington would learn from was the CTV building. Buildings needed to be built properly and any issues found needed to be dealt with, not brushed under the carpet as too hard or, worse, as not worth doing because it cost too much. As much as she hadn't wanted to believe that human failings had led to the building's collapse, in the end it was undeniably clear that was the case. There were so many mistakes leading to those one hundred and fifteen deaths, and no one had stepped up and taken responsibility for the part they played in the building's collapse. The engineer who had designed the building didn't have experience with multi-storey buildings. His boss failed to supervise him properly and then when City Council officials expressed reservations about the design, he pressured them to sign it off. After the September and December 2010 quakes, the council's inspectors failed to pick up the state of the building. The Royal Commission heard that some people working in the building had felt unsafe after the Boxing Day quake, and some were actively looking for other jobs in order to get out of the building.

Lindsay hated the saying about experience being the best teacher. To her that meant one's life would be littered with mistake after mistake after mistake. It was best to learn from other people's mistakes, something she tried to teach her children. But it was a difficult thing to teach children when even adults made short-sighted decisions, postponing upgrading a building because they didn't want to spend the money, not thinking about the consequences of that building killing people in a large quake. Valuing life more than money, perhaps that's what she needed to focus on with her children, teaching them to value life and people more than things. But was she teaching by example when so much of her present life was taken up with worrying about when the house would finally be fixed? She constantly felt that she was failing as a parent, not spending enough time just relaxing with Olivia and Jack, leaving it to Alice to be the fun adult in the house. Lindsay tried not to be consumed by worrying about things, tried to remind herself that childhood was short, to enjoy every moment. Look at Alice, after all. Her childhood had passed so quickly, she was twenty now, working full time, and Lindsay struggled to remember where all those years had gone. She tried to learn from that and make the most of these years with Olivia and Jack, but most of the time she was simply too tired.

The second winter in their broken house had passed with more massive power bills, over $400 in June and July, in spite of Lindsay's efforts to not use the heaters when she was home alone during the day. She was just so cold, sitting in the lounge with the laptop doing Kevin's paperwork, not moving enough to keep herself warm.

At least the insurance process was going well. The insurance company's PMO had prepared a scope of works and organised for a geotechnical engineering firm to carry out investigations on the state of the land. The firm had made a series of appointments to carry out the investigations that would be required and the first had been the day before. Lindsay had not known what was involved, otherwise she would have kept Jack home so he could see the rig that they brought onto the section. It was yellow and on caterpillar tracks, with two spiral plates that drilled into the ground. A rod was then forced down into the ground and a series of measurements taken. They had drilled at two spots, one in the backyard and one in the front yard.

Seeing the rig at work would have made up for Jack's disappointment at not getting the teacher he wanted next year. Julia had been Olivia's year 2 teacher, and she was one of those teachers who had a way with little kids, could always make them laugh. She never discouraged the kids from asking questions, never became annoyed at the Why? Why? Why? of teaching six-year-olds. She was good at explaining things in a way that made sense to them without being patronising, and this made the children like her and want to be in her classroom. When she told them to do something, they did, because they wanted to please her. A few days ago, Jack had found out that the impending birth of Julia's first child meant she wouldn't be teaching next year. She wouldn't be teaching him. It wasn't fair, he said. Olivia got to have Julia as her teacher, why couldn't he?

No, life wasn't fair, it didn't always go the way we wanted it to. That was a difficult lesson for children to learn, and Lindsay was glad Jack was starting to learn it over something as trivial as who his teacher would be next year. There were plenty of good teachers at the school, it was unlikely Jack would end up with someone he didn't like.

Life certainly wasn't fair for the families of the people who had died in the CTV building. There had been no accountability, no police prosecution, no professional censure for the engineers who worked on the building. Lindsay remembered going into the city for the first time after the February quake. The cordon had been reduced and it was possible to see the remains of the CTV building, its scorched lift shaft standing there like some grim memorial, the space around it utterly bare. It was awful, and Lindsay was relieved to hear it had been demolished. Even now, over a year after the lift shaft demolition, Lindsay tried to avoid that part of the city.

Lindsay was glad Jack and Olivia were too young to understand what it meant that so many people had died and that no one had taken responsibility for what had happened. It was hard enough to bear as an adult.

That night as Lindsay and Kevin were getting ready for bed, she asked him about the CTV building. 'How do you feel about no one being accountable for the CTV building?' she asked him.

He had just removed his t-shirt and he paused to look at her before tossing it into the washing basket. 'Don't think about it,' he said, his mouth a grim line that said he did think about it. Was that his answer? Or was he telling her to stop thinking about it? He took off his jeans and socks and tossed them into the basket, grabbed a pair of boxer shorts from the drawer and went through to the bathroom.

Lindsay changed into her pyjamas and tucked herself into bed. She was reading a novel about a missing woman, but she felt she was making little progress, reading the same paragraph over and over again. One day, maybe, she would get back to her old reading habits, ripping through a novel in a few days, instead of weeks. One day when she stopped feeling so tired all the time.

She heard the shower stop, then a few minutes later Kevin came through and climbed into bed. He leaned over to kiss her gently on the cheek and she sniffed the light perfume of soap and shampoo. She looked at him questioningly.

'I hate it,' he said, his voice strained, full of emotion. 'So many people died and they didn't have to, and no one steps up and takes responsibility.'

Lindsay put her hand over his but said nothing.

'I hate this place,' he said. 'I hate what it's teaching our kids. How are we supposed to teach our kids to take responsibility for their actions when one hundred and fifteen people died and no one answers for it?'

'We teach them that,' Lindsay said, 'we can teach them to do the right thing, even if it seems no one else is.'

'But we're fighting against the tide, Lin,' he said. 'There's so many bad jobs being done, people being short-changed, and hardly anyone steps up and takes responsibility.'

'We'll go,' Lindsay said. 'When the house is sorted, we'll go somewhere else and we can forget about what's going on here.'

He nodded. 'That would be good.'

185 Chairs

December 2012

In the suburb of Riccarton west of the central city, it was easy to
forget there had been earthquakes, especially if you were on the
stretch of Riccarton Road near the busy Westfield Mall. Cars were
pulling in and out of the mall carpark and people were walking
along the streets and going in and out of the mall. Further along
Riccarton Road towards the city, there were gaps where buildings
had been demolished, but that wasn't the case around the mall, and
Alice could understand why Emma had chosen to stay in Riccarton,
if she was dreading seeing the city as much as she had said in her
messages.

Although Emma's parents' house had been badly damaged in the
September and February quakes, it was still liveable. In the June
2011 quakes, though, its brick walls had finally collapsed, exposing
the inner rooms to the outside and sending her parents out to
Rangiora to live with family. Emma decided at that point that she'd
had enough of earthquakes and had moved to Australia. In
Melbourne, she had met Dave, and now, a year and a half after she
had last been in Christchurch, she had brought Dave home to meet
her family and to see the city she grew up in.

Her parents didn't know she was back yet. She wanted a couple
of days on her own to adjust, she said, and she and Dave were
staying at a motel.

The complete destruction of her parents' house, although
distressing, had the advantage that there was no arguing over what
needed to happen to the place. It was clearly uneconomic to repair
and was one of the first rebuilds in the neighbourhood. Over winter
and spring, Alice had watched the construction of the new place.
She had run past it each morning, watching it slowly take shape,
the old house demolished and the site prepped, the foundation
being marked out and then poured, the framing going up, the roof
going on. That experience contrasted with what she was seeing in
the city. Instead of coming down slowly, piece by piece, this house
was going up, emerging from the ground, and Alice felt a thrill

watching its progress. It said there was a future for the city, something beyond devastation and demolition. She would have felt that thrill even if she didn't know the family who would be moving back in, and she looked forward to the day when it was her own family going back into their repaired home. She wouldn't be moving back in with them, of course, that was her mental deadline for leaving home, when Kevin and Lindsay packed up and moved out for repairs. Their insurance company had put together a scope of works and Kevin and Lindsay had a meeting with a project manager scheduled in a few weeks, which meant their repair would probably get underway sometime in the new year.

'Your parents' house looks great,' Alice told Emma. They had met for brunch at a café near the mall. 'From what I've seen of the outside. How are they feeling about it?' They had moved back in two weeks earlier.

'Really happy,' Emma said. Their coffees arrived and they ordered their meals.

'We'll stay with them from tomorrow,' Dave said. 'Once Emma's had a chance to see the city.' He sounded uncertain, as though he was unconvinced of her reason for not going right to her parents' place.

'Dave doesn't get it,' Emma said. 'He's seen plenty of pictures of the city, but I don't think he understands...'

'No I don't,' Dave interrupted, frustration in his voice. 'I know that.' He shot Emma a look while sipping at his coffee.

Emma just shrugged, scowling. It must be difficult, Alice realised, to explain how you felt about a place that had been irrevocably changed, even to accept for yourself that the place you had known was gone. It was something Alice didn't know about, she knew without a doubt that the old city was gone, she lived with the reality of it every day. But for Emma, the true state of the place as she had experienced it after the February quake had faded. When she talked to Alice about the city, she talked about the city she had grown up in, she didn't like to talk about the city as it was now. Alice thought she understood Emma's hesitation over going home, her parents were back in a new house, the one Emma had grown up in was gone. But they were used to it being gone, she wasn't.

Their food arrived and tucking into it gave them an excuse to change the topic of conversation. Dave was a software developer, he said, he worked for a website development company. He was the same age as Emma and Alice, and he was from Melbourne, where they were both living now.

'My parents are kiwis,' he said. 'Went over in the eighties.'

'They ever tempted to come back?' Alice asked.

'Nah,' he said. 'They come back every now and then to see my grandparents, my mum's parents, but usually they come to us. They like it better in Aussie. Warmer. Have you ever been over?'

'To the Gold Coast,' Alice said. 'With my grandparents when I was eleven. We did the theme parks and Sea World, which was cool.'

'You should come see Melbourne, it's a great place.'

'It is,' Emma agreed. 'Christchurch could learn a lot from it.'

'People have mentioned Melbourne when they've talked about the rebuild,' Alice said. 'The laneways, things like that. It sounds like they're going to try to work that sort of thing into the city, and the container mall is a bit different, not your usual New Zealand retail area where you have a row of shops on one side of a street and another row of shops on another. It's very cool.'

Emma looked unconvinced.

They were finished eating. The waitress came and cleared their plates, asked if they wanted anything else. No, they said. Emma said it was time to go and see the city, but the expression on her face was one of someone facing their execution.

'C'mon,' Dave said, putting his arm around her as they walked away from the café. 'Just do it!' She shrugged his arm off. No, he didn't get it, Alice could see. But how could anyone who hadn't been here?

They walked down to where Alice had left her car in the mall carpark and drove into the city. Alice parked by the Botanic Gardens, it would be a good spot to return to after seeing the city, a part of the city that looked like it always had.

Alice led Emma and David in towards the city, skirting the red zone to Victoria Square. Both were mostly quiet, staring through the fencing to the wrecked sites beyond, Dave asking the occasional question and Emma or Alice giving only brief answers.

Victoria Square had opened only a few weeks earlier, when the cordon shrank to allow access to it. Efforts had been made to restore the gardens in the Square and it looked good, like the city Alice remembered. On the other side of the river, though, the wrecked town hall sat on the riverbank, its fountain stopped, its pebbled concrete walls jutting starkly into the sky. Had it ever looked attractive? She couldn't remember.

'Whoa,' Emma said. She was staring off past the town hall to where the Crowne Plaza hotel used to stand. It had stood twelve stories high diagonally across the northwest corner of Victoria Square. Now blue pallets had been stacked on the site to form much lower walls, to make up a pavilion that would be used for events over the summer months.

'There used to be a hotel across the end of the Square,' Emma explained to Dave. She turned to Alice. 'When did that come down?'

'Over winter,' Alice said. 'Took five or six months, I can't remember.'

They continued along the river, past the PGC building site, where eighteen people had died. Alice had been across the river from it during the February earthquake, although she said nothing to Emma and David, she didn't want to talk about it.

'Is that the CTV building site?' Emma said.

'No,' Alice said, 'that's over that way.' She pointed towards the centre of the city.

'Is that the one where all the people died?' David asked.

'CTV? Yes,' Alice said. 'One hundred and fifteen people. The designer didn't have enough experience with multi-storey buildings and it didn't meet the Building Code. Shouldn't have been approved by the City Council. The council was under pressure to approve it, and so they did.'

'Who was applying pressure?' David said.

'The guy who ran the engineering firm,' Alice said. 'But it wasn't just him, it was a whole string of mistakes. The guy who supervised the build wasn't around enough to do a proper job and then later when people recognised there were flaws, no one did enough to make the building safe.'

'Is anyone being charged?' David asked.

'This is New Zealand,' Emma said. 'No one gets held responsible for anything.' The bitterness filling her voice surprised Alice, Emma had never talked to her about the people who had died or the enquiries into the building collapses, but obviously she had been following them from Australia. 'Can we get there?'

'If we keep going this way,' Alice said. 'But first, I want to show you something.' She led them further along the river, past the families of mallard and paradise ducks. There was even a white-faced heron, its blue-grey plumage sleek and lovely as it moved along the riverbed.

They crossed to the other side of the river and stopped on a dry patch of grass. Covering the grass were chairs, office chairs, lounge chairs, dining chairs, wicker chairs and even a beanchair and a wheelchair. All were different, but all were painted the same crisp, clean white. They were laid out in rows, marching across the grass to form a square.

'There's a hundred and eighty-five of them,' Alice said, her voice quiet. Traffic shushed by in the background. 'One for every person who died in the February quake.'

David reached for Emma's hand and she let him take it. He squeezed it tight. 'I get it,' he said.

Keeping You Moving

January 2013

Alice had finished work at the end of 2012 feeling worn out with the difficulties of dealing with claimants who only wanted to get back to their normal lives. But there was a process to go through and the systems in place sometimes didn't make sense. The systems would change, though, when it became apparent something wasn't working, and then there would be more training, more getting up to speed with how they were meant to do things from that point on. Things were getting better.

Alice had taken two weeks off work over the Christmas and New Year break and now it was the second week of January and her first day back. She had promised herself she would go back to work refreshed, with a good attitude, ready to do her best for the people she was dealing with. But what faced her that morning was plenty of emails to clear, anxious claimants wanting to know what was happening with their claims, but she couldn't give any answers, too few people were back from their holidays and there was simply no one to follow up with. She fired off emails to various people anyway and made notes to herself to call them the next week. That was the best way to get something done, make contact by phone, otherwise emails were too easy to ignore.

She felt fatigued, almost as tired and flat as she had felt when she had influenza a few years earlier. Her ankle itched and she reached down to scratch it, then scratched it even more viciously. Sandfly bites. Alice had gone tramping with Andrew and his two oldest sons, Andrew's cousin Rebecca and her children, Sean and Charlotte. Andrew and Rebecca had gone on family tramps as teenagers and they had wanted their children to experience the same thing.

The track the seven of them went on started just off the main highway towards Arthur's Pass. There was a carpark tucked into the trees just before the road bridge that went over the Waimakiriri River. They had left their two cars in the carpark and started up the track late one morning.

The first part of the track looked down bluffs onto the riverbed, where purple and blue lupins were flowering. The day was hot and the sweet perfume of the lupins drifted up the bluffs, a cloud of dizzying sweetness. The forest was beech forest and small, round beech leaves littered the track. Spongy mosses grew on either side of the track, soft little pillows that sank when stepped on.

The track went uphill for about five hundred metres then looped down across a stream that ran down a wet, mossy gully, rocks towering above the track. The track looped back over the bluffs and they were soon in a rhythm, going steadily along. Alice stopped to take off her long-sleeved top, the day was getting hotter and she was starting to really sweat. The others marched on ahead of her and in the still silence she could hear a high-pitched peeping. She peered off into the trees to see if she could locate the source. There, about shoulder height on the downhill side of the track, two tiny birds were hopping up the trunks of trees. She called to Sean, who turned and came back.

'Riflemen, I think,' Alice said, pointing. Sean took his lens cap off his camera and took as many shots as he could. He hoped to get a decent one, he said, but it would be difficult because they were so damned fast.

The others had stopped and come back. 'I can hear more,' Liam said. He was the oldest of Alice's half-brothers, thirteen now. He was looking up the hill off the other side of the track. 'There,' he said, and there was another one, closer. Sean took more photos.

'I hope you brought a spare card,' Charlotte said, 'or there'll be no space left for any interesting stuff we see further up.'

They spent a few more minutes watching the tiny birds going up and down trees. The feathers on their upper bodies were a rich olive colour, which surprised Alice, she had half-expected a drab grey-purple. Then she realised why, she had only really seen riflemen before on the old two dollar notes her mother had kept when they had been replaced with coins, before Alice was born.

'We better get a move on,' Rebecca said. 'We'll never get there at this rate.'

The beech forest ended and the track started to drop down to the riverbed. The river meandered through a wide valley, alternating water-filled channels and shingle beds. The track went up through a grassy field that was growing on one of the shingle beds where water had not flowed for many years, orange markers picking out the path. They headed up towards the bush-clad mountains, a strong wind coming down the valley making them work, although the uphill incline was slight.

About an hour later, the track went up a steep bluff. At the top, they had to climb down one-by-one, but once they were past that, it was an easy walk to the first hut. It was a small tin hut, only six bunks with a fire and a tiny kitchen. There were seven of them, but they were prepared, they had brought tents as even if the hut was empty at least one of them would need to be sleeping outside. Two bunks had already been claimed, so they decided they would all tent. The weather was warm enough and there wouldn't be much rain overnight. The only hazard of sleeping outdoors was the sandflies that descended on them when they stood still for more than a moment.

Back in Christchurch in the airconditioned office, Alice missed the fresh air of the mountains, the open spaces, the river flowing off into the distance, its separate ribbons meandering across its wide stony bed. She scratched furiously at another sandfly bite, this one on her knee. Out there in the mountains, nothing was expected of Alice except that she keep her legs moving. Here, though, back in real life, there was a whole list of issues to deal with and none could be solved as easily as just smacking a tiny black fly into oblivion. She was expected to have the answers that would help claimants make major financial decisions, decisions she had never made for herself. She had never owned property, had never made an insurance claim, she was simply a bystander in the whole process, watching her family work through their claims, making what she hoped were the right noises when they were frustrated over how long the process was taking. She knew how frustrating the whole process was for her family, so she tried to always follow up with the claimants she dealt with, even if there wasn't much she could tell them.

Someone was saying her name, snapping her out of her thoughts. 'Ali?' She looked up at the shape standing over her desk. It was Kylie, another one of the claims officers. 'We're going to the ale house for lunch, first day back and all, wanna come?'

'Sure,' Alice said. 'Give me a minute to finish up what I'm doing.' She didn't have anything more to do right at that moment, but it would give her a chance to pull her head together. Some fresh air would be welcome.

Lunch at the pub was less boring than sitting at work through her lunch break waiting for emails that weren't going to come until next week at the earliest. Her co-workers talked about their holidays and not liking being back, it seemed that's the way everyone felt coming back to work the first day of each working year, flat and worn out. Only Jessica was enthusiastic, but she was enthusiastic about everything insurance, she planned to make her career in the industry. She seemed to believe the ads with the catchy songs, the ones that said insurance helped people recover from disaster, that it kept people moving. It looked to Alice more like insurance slowed people down and held them back, but maybe that was just the post-holiday fug she was enveloped in that was making her feel that way.

The job was fine for now and she would stick with it for another year or two. Southern Response would only be around for another couple of years, their only purpose was to settle claims, another insurance company had taken over the other policies. Although she had found it difficult getting used to the way things were supposed to be done, she was starting to feel more on top of things, more like she was contributing something positive to the rebuild.

That didn't change the fact that she still wished it was the holidays. Alice missed the outdoors, the clean air free of fumes. Throughout the earthquakes, she had escaped into running. It cleared her head, helped her to sleep better. It had kept her sane. She would go for a run after work that night. It would be good for her to get into that space where nothing was expected of her but to keep her legs moving.

Two Cities

February 2013

Early in 2013, the media reported that the Minister for Earthquake Recovery had ignored his officials' advice over how much to offer the owners of red zoned vacant land. CERA had recommended that these people should be offered the full 2007 rateable value, the same as those with insured properties. The Minister, however, said that recommendation wasn't an actual recommendation but 'initial thinking'. The fifty percent offer was made to avoid the 'moral hazard' of the Government acting as a safety net for the uninsured. It just made Alice's grandparents feel like they were being punished for not having insurance that didn't actually exist. No insurance company in New Zealand offered policies for bare land.

Alice was discussing the state of the city with her grandfather, Neil. It was late Friday afternoon and the second anniversary of the February quake. She had texted Charlotte to say she didn't feel like doing anything that night, but then found, on her way home, that she wasn't quite ready to go home. She had detoured to Neil and Heather's instead.

'I read this book a couple of years ago,' Alice told Neil. 'It was about these two cities that co-exist, they occupy the same space, but the citizens of each city choose to ignore the crossover. A kind of mental conditioning.'

'You mean you see the city as being like this?' Neil said. 'Like the divide between east and west?' If you lived on the western side of Christchurch, you could almost forget there had been an earthquake. But if you drove over to the east, it was a different story. The roads in the east were still a mess, there were road cones and road works everywhere, red zoned land was being cleared and there were temporary stopbanks along the lower reaches of the Avon River, near where the land had dropped in the quakes, making houses more prone to flooding.

'Kind of,' Alice said. 'But I was thinking about me going to work and there are people there who don't really have an idea what it's like for people still living in broken houses or dealing with roadworks all the time. They stay over the western side, never even go into the city. And then there's the city we live in and the one Gerry Brownlee thinks he's rebuilding.'

'The one full of carpers and moaners, you mean?' Neil said, an eyebrow raised.

'Yeah, that's the one,' Alice said, laughing. She stood up and walked over to Neil's bookshelf, ran her fingers along the spines of all the books. 'Recommend anything?' she asked. 'What's this guy like, Ian Rankin?'

'A bit dark,' Neil said. 'Set in Edinburgh.' He stood up and reached for one of the books in the series. 'This one,' he said. 'It's not the first but it's a good starting place.'

Alice flipped the book over and read the back of it. It would be good to have something to bury her head in for the weekend.

Some of Alice's workmates had finished before lunchtime so they could go to the memorial and have the rest of the day off, but Alice stayed on. She didn't want to go to the memorial and be reminded of that day. And it annoyed her that after two years there still wasn't actually a memorial for the families of the dead to visit. The 185 chairs were poignant, but the installation had happened in spite of, not because of, the efforts of those in charge of the rebuild.

Those who remained at the office were silent at 12:51, and Alice had found it difficult not to start crying. She wondered how long it would be until she stopped feeling the sting of that day.

'Stay for dinner?' Neil asked. 'Your grandmother's making plenty.'

Alice thought a moment. 'Okay,' she said.

'Let your mum know,' Neil said, getting up and walking through to the kitchen. 'Ali's staying for tea,' she heard him say.

'Don't need to,' Alice called after him, following him through to the kitchen. 'I was going to go out with Charlotte but texted her earlier to let her know I'm having a quiet night.' She asked her grandmother what she could do to help.

'Nothing, love,' Heather said. 'All under control. At least something is. Are you not feeling well, is that why you're not going out with Charlotte?'

'No, I'm fine,' Alice said. 'Just felt a bit odd because of today. The anniversary. So what's not under control? What's happened?'

'Nothing really, just been talking to your mum today about the engineer's visit. Sounds all backwards, what's happening with them.'

At the end of 2012, Kevin and Lindsay had finally had the geotech work done. They had a scope of works and once the geotechnical report was done, their repair would be a major step closer. It looked like 2013 would be their year. But then their new project manager had made an appointment. This project manager told them that their foundation didn't need replacing, that technology had advanced so considerably that the cracks only needed to be glued. Kevin and Lindsay had objected, and the project manager had agreed to get a structural engineer to look at the foundation. That was fine, they said, they would wait to see what the structural engineer's report said.

They were surprised to receive a revised scope of works only a week later, before the structural engineer had visited. The scope no longer said their house would be lifted and its foundation replaced, now it said they had a number of cracks that could be glued. A few days later the structural engineer visited, along with the project manager. The engineer poked his head down the manhole, didn't bother going under the house, and after the visit, Kevin went outside to clear the letterbox. The project manager and the engineer were in front of the house discussing how the cracks could just be glued. Kevin came back inside, disgusted. The engineer was just ticking off the project manager's opinion, Kevin said, wasn't doing a proper assessment at all.

'The engineers are supposed to determine the strategy, not the project managers,' Alice said. 'The way their one's been done is real cart before the horse stuff.'

'I'd say more arse backwards,' Neil said.

'Language, Neil,' Heather said.

'I think they need a lawyer,' Alice said. 'Someone who can make sure their claim's done right.'

'Lawyers cost money, love,' Neil said. 'But I think you're right, it might be the only way to get their claim back on track.'

'That's what Mum thinks, too. But Kevin's not willing to accept that, says to just wait and see what the geotech report says and go from there.'

'How long will that take?' Neil asked.

'A few months?' Alice shrugged. 'All the sampling was done in December, so maybe April, May at the latest.'

'Everything takes such a long time,' Heather said. 'Including this chicken.' She had taken the chicken out of the oven to see if it was done, but the juices were not yet running clear. She touched the chicken, pulling her fingers back, then touched it again, keeping her fingers on it. 'It's barely warm,' she said. She checked the oven, then threw the oven mitts on the kitchen bench in disgust. 'I switched the oven off instead of putting it up when I put the chicken back in half an hour ago. Dinner will be a while.'

Neil moved towards her, gave her a peck on the cheek. 'Been in Christchurch too long, love,' he said. 'Turning off the oven before the chicken's cooked. Bit like Kevin and Lindsay's engineering report.'

Heather and Alice laughed. 'I'll put it back, it'll be about half an hour, can everyone wait?'

Neil and Alice nodded.

'So Ian Rankin,' Alice said. Neil and Heather were in better moods than they had been for a while. They had been struggling to make progress with getting their repairs looked at, but had recently been given the name of a foundation specialist who could look at their place. They would have to pay for it, but it seemed worth it, if it could cut through all the red tape they encountered every time they tried to get EQC or Fletchers to look at the state of their repairs.

'Ian Rankin's a good choice,' Neil said. 'Lots about corruption in his books.'

'I've never thought of New Zealand as a corrupt place,' Heather said. 'But lately...'

'We've always known about the old boys' network,' Neil said. 'That's a kind of corruption.'

'That's not corruption,' Alice said. 'Corruption's bribes, kickbacks, that sort of thing.'

'In every situation there's always someone who has an advantage,' Neil said. 'One group that prevails. But when it's always the same group of people having the advantage over everyone else, that's corruption.'

Alice thought about that for a moment. 'One group exploiting another,' she said. 'Setting up the system to do so.'

'Think about your mum and dad's project manager,' Neil said. 'Kevin said he seemed very matey with the structural engineer. Assume the project manager gets a bonus for reducing costs. Do they?'

'I don't know,' Alice said. 'Some of them are pretty motivated to keep costs down. But that's more because we know we're dealing with taxpayers' money, I don't know what it's like for the private insurers.'

'Well let's just say a project manager does get some kind of bonus,' Neil continued. 'So it's to his advantage to get a structural engineer who is on his side, going to say what he wants them to say. He picks his mate, gives his mate the business. If he does this with all the houses he's managing...'

'Homeowners don't get the repairs they should get, but the project manager gets his bonus and the structural engineer gets the insurance company's assessment work,' Alice said, nodding. It was corruption, but it was a different way of thinking about it than she was used to. It was a way of looking at matters that she certainly wouldn't be bringing up at work, where some of the staff felt that any homeowner who questioned their repair strategy was expecting a gold-plated mansion from their as-when-new policy. If her grandad was right, project managers and other PMO staff would be motivated to keep the insureds' expectations low.

'Do you think Gerry Brownlee's corrupt?' Alice asked. 'That he's getting some sort of kickback from, I don't know, Fletchers? Insurance companies?'

Neil thought about it for a few moments, paused to speak, then paused to think again, choosing his words carefully. 'No, that would be too simple an explanation,' he finally said. 'I think he's incompetent. The way he shoots off his mouth is not the mark of a strong thinker.'

'Well he's certainly not concerned with people,' Heather said. 'He's supposed to be our minister, the Minster for Earthquake Recovery. Anyone who questions why things are being done the way they are or points out some detail the Government has missed gets called a name. Ignored. Put in their place.'

Alice nodded. 'Did you hear what he said about Kevin McCloud?'

'Grand Designs Kevin McCloud?' Heather said. It was her favourite show, and it surprised Alice that given the state of her house she could still watch other people building their dream homes, because it was looking less and less likely that Neil and Heather would get their retirement home built. The issue of the fifty percent vacant land offers looked like it was going to court, but even if they did get 100 percent in the end, they couldn't afford a section in Christchurch on a payout based on 2007 values.

'Yes, him,' Alice said. 'He said a great city needs to be built with local input. But Gerry dismissed him as a tourist.'

'A tourist who's more qualified to talk about architecture than that... that... old dunger!' Heather said, huffing.

'You shouldn't call people names, Nana,' Alice said. 'It's the last refuge of the ignorant.'

'That's profanity, love,' Neil said. 'Your grandmother is perfectly correct.'

Later, on her way home, Alice stopped the car and pulled over. She walked up the road to the roadworks, where the road was reduced to one-way traffic by a series of the orange traffic cones that were everywhere in Christchurch. For the first anniversary of the quake the previous year, people had decorated some of the road cones, putting flowers and decorations in their tops. In Alice's neighbourhood, there had been purple agapanthas in many of the road cones, the long-stemmed flowers were common in the neighbourhood. But this year, the custom had really taken off and most of the road cones Alice had seen that day had flowers in them, of many different varieties. These, though, were something else. Someone had brought bouquets of yellow, orange, white and pink lilies, red roses, freesias and carnations and decorated all the cones on that stretch of the road. It was thoughtful and beautiful, and Alice hoped that this was one part of the rebuild that would persist, no matter how many years passed. Yes, there would be far fewer road cones in the city in the decades to come, but the custom of putting flowers in them for the February anniversary was one mark of the quakes that should endure.

Splitting the Bill

March 2013

When people think of earthquake damage, they think of what the shaking does, how it causes buildings to break up and collapse, all the above-ground damage. What people don't really think about is what goes on below the ground, where the shaking can push groundwater up through the soil, the process known as liquefaction. Liquefaction damages foundations, roads and underground pipes, undermining structures, destabilising them from below. Liquefaction was a huge problem in Christchurch, especially in the east, and the extent of the damage to what was referred to as the city's horizontal infrastructure was immense.

In 2012, it became known that the city's horizontal infrastructure – its roads, pipes, drains and the sewerage system – had been vastly underinsured. This was a consequence of the local council's need to balance what it charges ratepayers with what ratepayers get in the way of services. Insurance is invisible, an apparent pouring of money down the drain, until a claim needs to be made. One way of minimising the cost of insurance is to cut the amount of coverage, which had been the case in Christchurch before the quakes started. It's a gamble to reduce one's insurance cover, one that pays off as long as nothing happens.

At first, the bill for repairing the horizontal infrastructure was estimated to be about two billion dollars. But damage to underground services is often invisible, it doesn't necessarily result in water pipes bursting and water flowing all over streets or sewerage flowing back onto properties. It's not until a camera is put down a pipe that it can be known how damaged it is. What was determined during 2011 and 2012 was that many of the pipes on the eastern side of the city were full of silt. And cracks. A great deal more of the city's pipes would need replacing than had been thought in the immediate aftermath of the earthquakes.

By early 2013, the bill for the city's horizontal infrastructure had been estimated at nearly four billion dollars, nearly twice the initial estimate. But who was going to pay for it? It was usual in

New Zealand for local government and national government to split the bill for underground services. In Christchurch, the question looming was exactly how this would be split. If the city itself had to assume responsibility for the lion's share, where would this money come from? The city's ratepayers were already facing regular rates increases. Would the Government agree to spend more? Good questions, especially considering it was no big secret that the Government wanted to get the country's budget back into surplus before the next election. Helping out Christchurch would put the Government's promise of a surplus at risk. How would the Government balance the needs of one city with those of the rest of the country?

Gerald thought he knew. It was two years since the February earthquake and he wasn't impressed at the pace of the rebuild. Sure, at the start of the year people were saying this would be the year the rebuild really took off, but would it? The same had been said at the start of 2012, and yet here they were again, a significant part of the central city still cordoned off, the bureaucracy around getting into the city still a swampy mire.

Fortunately Gerald no longer needed to deal with that, he had enough repair work that he could step away from the pre-demolition work he had been doing in 2012. His company was doing repairs that fell within the EQC opt-out range of below $100,000, and enough claims of that value were being settled that Gerald had been able to keep on his existing staff. He had even been able to take on half a dozen more. Often a homeowner wanted to do something extra to the place, make their settlement money go further or put in some of their own money. These were the happy people, the ones free of the overwhelming weight of working through an insurance claim, the ones who felt that they were the captains of their own ships once again.

The private insurers tended to want to manage repairs and rebuilds through their project management offices, this was a way of containing costs. But Gerald was staying away from PMO work, the rates offered weren't nearly high enough to do the job properly, and pressure was being applied to the contractors to just do the job on the scope, they were encouraged to ignore damage discovered during repairs. Gerald had taken on one builder, a guy with two young kids, he was stressed out, not sleeping. He had been working for a company contracted to a PMO and had a camera full of photos showing damage to a property he was working on. He had shown his boss the photos, asked what to do, whether they should get onto the project manager about getting the work added to the scope. No, his boss insisted, the job would stop, possibly for months, given the pace of producing these scopes of works, and if they stopped jobs every time they discovered unassessed damage, no one would get paid and they would all have to bugger off back to wherever they came from.

Sylvia and Gerald's sister Suzanne were running the office together, an arrangement that had worked well in the past. Lately, though, Suzanne had been complaining to them about how much time Alice was spending with her grandchildren.

'They get along,' Gerald or Sylvia would say, 'what's wrong with them spending time together?'

'She's a lot older than them,' Suzanne said.

'She's a year older than Sean.'

'She's five years older than Charlotte, and Charlotte looks up to her. It's not good,' Suzanne insisted. She was out of her townhouse for repairs, staying with Rebecca and her family, so seeing Sean and Charlotte every day, rather than once or twice a week. Charlotte was Suzanne's favourite grandchild, and as she had grown into a teenager, Suzanne had started to feel that she and Charlotte were no longer as close as they had been. Charlotte had been born soon after Suzanne's husband Stan had died, and Suzanne had offered to babysit when Rebecca decided to go back to work. Looking after Charlotte and Sean would take her mind off Stan's death, she had said.

'Is she a bad influence?' Gerald asked one day.

'Yes, she is,' Suzanne said. She was decisive in her statement, clearly she had been thinking about this.

'She has them drinking? Doing drugs?' Gerald said, trying not to laugh. He knew very well that what Suzanne disapproved of was that Alice encouraged Charlotte's interest in art. Different art installations were popping up all over the city, and Alice, Sean and Charlotte tried to see as many as they could. They were young people, after all, with no obligations, why shouldn't they get out and do things?

'You know what I'm saying, Gerald,' Suzanne said. 'Charlotte has a bright future ahead of her, if she applies herself, and your Alice...'

'She's not my Alice, Suzanne,' Gerald interrupted. 'She's her own person.'

'Your Alice encourages her to spend her time daydreaming and doodling, when she should be studying.'

'Surely an interest outside of studying is not a bad thing, Suzanne,' Gerald said. 'The girl can take a break every now and then.'

'Well if she decides to do some arts degree because of your Alice, I won't be helping her with her university fees,' Suzanne said. 'My contribution towards my grandchildren's education is so they can make something of themselves, not muck around being artful.'

It wasn't worth continuing with the discussion, Suzanne would just get wound up and infect the whole office with her black mood. But it concerned Gerald that Suzanne wanted such a level of control over the choices her grandchildren made.

Suzanne herself hadn't had many choices in life. Their mother had always treated her children as disappointments. Suzanne had grown up quiet, pliable, trying to guess what her mother wanted of her, but never getting it right.

Gerald had never liked Stan, didn't understand why his father had kept him on. Yes, he was a good with customers, charming, but when Bill's back was turned, Stan took every opportunity to bully the younger workers, including Gerald, if he thought he could get away with it. And most of the time he did get away with it, he was subtle, cunning, little digs about the boss's son being given more leeway than the other apprentices. Gerald hadn't been particularly interested in being a builder when he left school, but his father had insisted he do something. Stan's presence had motivated Gerald to work hard at picking up the necessary skills, and that improved focus had revealed to him a job he loved, that of crafting something, taking the raw materials, imagining a result and doing his best to achieve what was in his mind's eye. Yes, Stan had made Gerald a better builder, but that didn't in any way result in Gerald liking Stan, or even respecting him very much. He kept silent because his father's opinion of the man was so high, whereas that of his son was low. But Stan's continued presence in his father's business was a significant factor in Gerald deciding to set up his own building company. He hated the bullying, the subtly dishonest manner in which Stan conducted business and the continual reminder that his parents approved of Stan's tactics.

Stan's courtship of Suzanne had happened so quickly that it was only when they became engaged that Gerald became aware of it. Looking back, he could see how their mother had helped the relationship along, encouraged them to be discreet. Marjorie knew Gerald felt protective of his sister, and she also knew that he didn't like Stan. But once they were engaged and Suzanne had hung her hopes on a future with Stan, there was nothing Gerald could do. He had asked her if she was sure marrying Stan was what she wanted. He had tried to put into his voice a seed of concern so that if she did have doubts, she would hear it, hang onto it and know that he would support her if she wanted to change her mind. Her reply had been an enthusiastic yes, that of a girl in love, seeing a perfect future stretching out before her.

Suzanne continued working in the office after she and Stan married, but once she was pregnant with Rebecca, Stan insisted she stop working, stay at home and get ready for the baby. Of course that was in an era where baby clothes were made, not purchased, so there was plenty for Suzanne to do to prepare for the arrival of their first child, Bill and Marjorie's first grandchild. Gerald knew it hurt Suzanne that their parents didn't disguise their disappointment in that grandchild being a girl. But the second was a boy, Tony, which pleased both grandparents no end, although all Marjorie had said to Suzanne was that she had taken her time. There had been four years between Rebecca and Tony.

Gerald had met Sylvia by that point and married her when Tony was a few months old. Suzanne had managed to hide her misery well, she always put up a cheerful front with the family, but Sylvia was sharp and it was when they were engaged that she said to Gerald there was something badly wrong in that household. He knew that, he said, although in truth, it was only her saying so that forced him to finally admit it. It was soon after they had become engaged and they were trying to decide where to live. At first, he and Sylvia had discussed finding a place in the city's northwest, nearer to her family than to his. Then, after they discussed Suzanne's situation, Sylvia said they should find a place near Suzanne, so they could help out. It made Gerald love her even more, although they were never able to be much help to Suzanne, not until after Stan died.

Suzanne had lived with a controlling, abusive husband for three decades, and once Stan died, she had gone back to work and built a new life for herself. Gerald admired that about her, that she had never looked back, never felt sorry for herself. Even in the first year after Stan died, she hadn't fallen into despair, she had just thrown herself into caring for her grandchildren. Once Charlotte started school, Suzanne started working for Gerald part-time, helping Sylvia out in the office. It was an arrangement that worked well, until recently.

Suzanne wasn't one to talk about what went on inside the family home, a habit ingrained after thirty years with Stan. Gerald and Sylvia had only been able to pick up snippets of what life was like for Suzanne living with Rebecca and her family, but those snippets suggested it was stressful. Rebecca and Dan's marriage had never been a happy one, and the earthquakes had put more strain on them than ever. One thing Suzanne did talk about was how stuck they were in their situation with EQC, despite the fact that their house was clearly badly damaged.

In New Zealand's two-tier insurance system, if a house's damage was under the cap of $100,000, EQC handled the claim. But once it was overcap, the house should be passed on to the homeowner's private insurer, along with an overcap payment. Unfortunately, more than one earthquake event had damaged houses in the region, which meant there were multiple claims on the same house. The EQC and private insurers needed to figure out how to split the bill. The process was called apportionment and involved, firstly, figuring out how much damage had been done. Once that was decided, the second step was to figure out how to split that up among the different quakes that claims had been made for. If the value of the damage from at least one quake was over the cap, the claim would be passed on to the homeowner's private insurer.

Rebecca and Dan had made claims for each of the four major quakes, and it was EQC's job to figure out how to apportion the damage. It seemed obvious that their house would eventually be passed on to their insurer, but until EQC made a decision, nothing could happen. This was, no doubt, the source of the stress Suzanne seemed to be experiencing while living with them, and why recently she seemed so interested in controlling the choices her grandchildren made.

She had been the same at work since moving in with Rebecca and Dan. Gerald had discussed with Sylvia what they could do about Suzanne's black moods, and Sylvia's response had been that they should be patient, that this would pass and Suzanne would go back to being the old Suzanne, the one they enjoyed working with. Gerald knew she was right, but he still didn't like it. He wasn't worried that Suzanne would affect the smooth running of the office, he was worried that she might try to interfere with the decisions Sean and Charlotte made, the same way Marjorie had interfered in the decision Suzanne had made in marrying Stan. Interfering in other people's lives often had unforeseen consequences, consequences borne by the other people, seldom by the interferer. Gerald wondered if his mother ever felt guilty about the situation she had pushed Suzanne into. He doubted it, he had never seen any evidence of that sort of softness in Marjorie.

Marmageddon's End

April 2013

'How much longer is Nanny going to be staying here?' Charlotte asked her mother. Rebecca had put all the breakfast dishes into the dishwasher and was waiting impatiently for Charlotte to surrender the last item, the plate that held her toast. Charlotte had pointed out that she could do that, get everything in the dishwasher and get it going before she left for school, but Rebecca insisted on doing it herself. It was like Charlotte was a small child, incapable of pressing some buttons. Had Rebecca seen kids with phones and tablets these days? They knew more than the adults.

'She'll be gone by the end of June,' Rebecca said, her voice heavy with tiredness. 'It won't be much longer now.'

Charlotte took another bite of her toast, chewing slowly, savouring the bite of the dark spread mixed in with butter. The Marmageddon crisis had ended a few weeks ago and just in case there was another shortage, Charlotte had bought a couple of big jars of Marmite and stored them away in her bedroom. Just in case, because you never knew in Christchurch when something was going to disappear and, once gone, when it might return. Charlotte picked up her second piece of toast and before she could bite through the first corner, her plate was gone, disappeared away into the dishwasher. Then her mother disappeared out the back door into the garage, gone for the next eight hours at least.

Usually her mother didn't get home until late evening. Too much to do at work, she would say. Although Sean and Charlotte had thought a few months ago that their mother was having an affair, they had come to the conclusion that she was simply throwing herself into work, it was preferable to going home and facing the fact of the house, living with the damage, not being able to move their claim forward.

The earthquakes had taken the city from her, it had been cordoned off for months. Years. Soldiers stood guard at the main points through the cordon, keeping everyone out of the city. Their city. The cordon had gradually been reduced in the months since the earthquake, but there were still parts of the city mere mortals couldn't get into. That was supposed to end in winter, and Charlotte wondered what it would be like to be in there again. The February quake had happened in her second year of high school, and the city was, then, still relatively new to her, part of her journey to and from school. On her way home, she often postponed getting her connecting bus and walked around to see what was going on. She was just starting to get her bearings, get familiar with the old buildings. She had watched the demolition of the Manchester Courts building in a kind of stop motion: five afternoons a week she would go past and see progress, what walls were being taken down, what innards were being exposed.

The earthquakes had also taken Charlotte's parents from her. To be strictly correct, the September earthquake had given them back, her father had moved back in and they played at being happy families for a while. The February quake had opened up a few cracks in that happy family unit, but they were just minor ones, they were all pulling together, putting aside their bad tempers from lack of sleep, from the difficulties of living in a broken city with a broken sewerage system. But the June quake had opened those cracks wider, and at the same time, her mother was trying to deal with EQC, getting their house assessed, getting some idea of timeframe for repairs. The arguing started again.

Charlotte had a late start at school that morning so she had the house to herself for a few minutes. She considered not going to school that day, she could fake an email to the school fairly easily. All it would take was an email from her mother's email account on the family computer. Charlotte could watch for replies and delete them so Rebecca would never know. It was tempting, but she couldn't guarantee her mother wasn't checking emails during the day. If she was caught, her parents might decide she needed to go and spend her school holidays with relatives, so they could keep an eye on her, 'get her back on track' was probably what they would say. She would end up in Ashburton with her father's sister and her three cousins, all younger than her, watching videos, one after another, day after day. Even Ashburton suffered disappearing building syndrome. Although it was an hour away from Christchurch, some of its buildings had been damaged in the first earthquake, the Darfield one, and some had been found to be earthquake prone and were being demolished.

Apparently you could cook with Marmite, that's what Nanny had told her the other morning, and Charlotte was going to have a go, google some recipes and try them out at the weekend. It was going to be her school holiday project, ten ways with Marmite, something to amuse her while she studied, because that was all she was doing during the school holidays. Her parents couldn't afford time off work, because all their spare time was going into their dealings with EQC, and Sean had already had his mid-term break, it was almost finished, just when Charlotte's was about to start.

Charlotte would miss her grandmother when she went home. At school, it was a running joke, how long would someone be out of their house while repairs were done? No one knew, it was never as fast as the builders said it would be. But Suzanne's repairs were going to plan, they were being carried out by Uncle Gerald's company, so of course it was on schedule. Maybe once Nanny went home, Charlotte could go and stay with her. It would be peaceful, and although Suzanne was stressed over being away from her home and having to live with more people than she was used to, she wasn't verging on crazy. Not like Charlotte's mother, who bounced between yelling, crying and painfully uncomfortable silences. Other girls at school talked about how stressed their parents were over insurance issues, and for once Charlotte had something in common with them. So many of them seemed to be going through life invisible to their parents, and that was certainly the case for Charlotte.

One side effect of the stress at home was that Charlotte was studying a lot and getting better grades than she ever had before. She had done well in NCEA Level 1 last year and was determined to do even better this year. What else was there to do? Staying in the lounge and watching TV wasn't an option, there simply wasn't enough on the actual television stations to hold her attention, even if she could ignore the insurance discussions going on in the kitchen. In her room, headphones on, studying, it was the only way to get away from those tense discussions. Sean was escaping to the university library and his girlfriend's flat. Not that their parents knew about the girlfriend. Not that he was hiding it from them, they just weren't paying attention.

Charlotte had tried learning about insurance so she could understand what her parents were going through. And maybe she could learn enough to help. She had read about the concept of 'good faith', which meant a person buying an insurance policy had to be honest about the things that made them riskier to insure and about what had happened when they made a claim. For the insurance company, good faith came at claim time, when they were supposed to treat the insured fairly. There was an imbalance of power at claim time, Charlotte could see that. Insurance companies had money and lawyers and experts, plus a thorough understanding of the ins and outs of the insurance policy, which your average person didn't.

Charlotte's parents' problem wasn't their insurance company, it was EQC and getting over that $100,000 cap. Their house had been assessed several times and each assessment came back different. The first one had said they would be overcap and passed on to their insurer, but then, because they had claims in for four earthquakes, the damage was divided between those four quakes and they were undercap for all of them and they would stay with EQC. Her parents were trying to argue that the February quake had been the most damaging one and would surely put them overcap. It was confusing, not just for Charlotte, but for her parents and, apparently, for the people at EQC because, Rebecca said, she was never told the same thing twice.

Charlotte had asked her grandmother if there was anything Uncle Gerald could do to make her parents' insurance claim go better. After all, Suzanne's repairs were going well because Gerald was in charge. Suzanne had only said, 'Oh sweetheart,' pulled her close and kissed her on the top of her head. 'People like me are the lucky ones, our damage isn't much and there isn't money to be made off us, so EQC's willing to let us go.'

Charlotte was puzzled. 'I don't understand.'

'If this house stays undercap, Fletchers gets all the work,' Suzanne explained. 'It's worth a lot of money to them.'

'But it's wrong,' Charlotte said. 'They have an insurance policy.' It was something her parents said often, that if only they could get passed over to their private insurer, things would start going smoothly.

'There's a lot of things wrong in the world, sweetheart, and not much anyone can do about them.'

A Chill Wind

May 2013

Lindsay and Kevin had recently heard from their insurance company's project management office again. The last communication had been in February, when the project manager visited with the structural engineer. This was the cowboy project manager who had slashed their original scope of works, changing it from having the house lifted and its ring foundation replaced to just gluing the cracks. There had been nothing from the PMO since then, but Lindsay and Kevin had decided to wait and see what the geotech report said. Work on their house could not move forward without the geotech report.

Then, in May, they heard from a new project manager, who arranged a visit to discuss the next steps in their repair. Although Lindsay and Kevin were happy that the cowboy was no longer their project manager, they had questions to pose to the new guy.

There were two of them at the door that morning, and Lindsay quickly ushered them inside. It was freezing outside, snow was predicted for parts of the South Island, including Christchurch, and it certainly felt like it would be happening today.

The new project manager was the younger man, called Kurt. He was in his thirties and reserved, but he seemed intelligent. There was no attempt at charming them, which was a relief. The first project manager had been charming, or thought he was. This new one, Kurt, shook hands with Lindsay and Kevin and then introduced the second man, who was about sixty. His name was John and, Kurt said, he would be their project manager as Kurt was moving on to a new role. Kurt was training John, who had just joined the PMO after a couple of years with EQC.

Kevin welcomed them inside and as they walked into the lounge, he shot Lindsay a look that said he was worried. Kevin wasn't impressed with EQC, he had heard too many bad things.

Lindsay and Kevin sat on one sofa while Kurt and John sat on the other. Kurt was about to start speaking, but Kevin got there first.

'We're not happy with the latest scope of works,' Kevin said. He reached across to the coffee table, where Lindsay had stacked their information. He picked up their copy of the scope. 'The first scope had the house being lifted and the ring foundation replaced, this just glues the cracks,' he said, waving the sheaf of paper.

Kurt and John exchanged glances that Lindsay could not interpret. Were they mentally slotting them into the difficult customer category? Or were they sympathising? Had the previous PM been replaced because there were issues? Lindsay was briefly hopeful that the previous scope would be reinstated, that they wouldn't have to fight to get their damage properly repaired.

Kurt made no comment on the suitability of the second scope, but he did say he and John would do a new assessment, take some floor level measurements.

'We've been waiting for the geotech report,' Kevin said, as they started to stand up. They sat back down again. 'The work was done last year, but the report seems to be taking a long time and it doesn't make sense to decide what's done to the foundation without the geotech report.'

'After all,' Lindsay added, 'we're TC3 and we need foundation work, which requires a geotech investigation. It seems backwards to decide on a repair strategy without the geotech report.'

Kurt tapped on his tablet and after a few moments told them the previous PM had cancelled the geotech report after his first visit.

'That's before the structural engineer visited,' Lindsay said, irritated. 'He's decided he can glue the cracks without waiting for the engineering report, and that's backwards.'

'Well let's have a look around and take some measurements,' Kurt said.

Kevin and Lindsay had drawn up a layout of the house when they first moved in, to figure out what renovations they would do, and it was coming in handy as various people went through the house carrying out assessments. Kevin handed them a copy of the layout and went around the house with them while Lindsay stayed in the lounge, by the fire, trying to quell her sense of unease. After a few minutes of becoming more agitated, she went through to the kitchen and started preparing vegetables for dinner, peeling potatoes, kumara and carrots, chopping broccoli. She became so engrossed in distracting herself that she soon realised she had done enough vegetables for two nights. Oh well, that's what refrigerators were for, after all.

'They're off, Lin,' Kevin called from the front doorway. Lindsay wiped her hands dry and went through to say goodbye to the men. She and Kevin stood on the front steps and watched them walk down the driveway. The wind had picked up and its chill bit through Lindsay's jumper, making her shiver. She rubbed her arms, and they continued watching the men. When the two project managers were out of sight, Lindsay and Kevin walked back inside and shut the door. In the kitchen, Lindsay boiled the jug and made Kevin a coffee.

'You not having one?' Kevin said.

'My stomach's agitated enough,' Lindsay said. 'I don't like this.'

They walked through to the lounge and sat on the sofa nearest the fire.

'I don't either,' Kevin said.

'They didn't even go under the house. Did you tell them where the manhole is?'

'Yes, I did,' Kevin said. 'They said they didn't need to go under, so I didn't bother suggesting they go up into the roof.'

'I don't get it,' Lindsay said. 'They were going to lift the house and now they're not and they don't have any explanation for it.'

'They're trying to stick us with a cheap repair, that's what's going on,' Kevin said.

'We need a lawyer,' Lindsay said. She knew this wasn't what Kevin wanted to hear, but her suspicions the last few months had been confirmed when their new project manager said their geotech report had been cancelled.

'We'll call up, ask about the geotech report,' Kevin said. 'See what happens.'

'But they've said it's cancelled, what's the point of that? We need to get someone involved who knows what they're doing.'

Kevin closed his eyes, he was thinking. Lindsay kept her mouth shut, pushing wasn't the way to get her point across.

'We'll keep getting as much information as we can,' Kevin said at last, 'then we'll know what we're dealing with. Until then, a lawyer is jumping the gun.'

Lindsay nodded, although she didn't agree. 'I'll call up about the geotech report,' she said. 'But I'll call the insurance company, not the PMO.'

'Good idea,' Kevin said. He swallowed back the last of his coffee and set his cup on the coffee table.

'I used to feel sorry for people who've been red zoned,' Lindsay said. 'But in some ways they're the lucky ones.'

Kevin raised an eyebrow.

'Not my parents, I don't mean them, but people like Jase and Carla, they've moved on, they're in their new places.'

'You're right about that,' Kevin said, 'but they do have a bigger mortgage, red zoning didn't give them enough to get back the equivalent. That's set them back some.'

'That's true,' Lindsay said.

'But are most red zoners better off?' Kevin went on. 'Or are there more like the O'Loughlins, who've had to get lawyers to get what they're entitled to?'

A decision had been handed down in the O'Loughlin case in April. The O'Loughlins had a red zoned house and their insurance company offered to settle based on the repair of the property. The court ruled that insurers could do this because the red zoning process could not be regarded as damage that the insurer had to pay for, even though repairs could not legally be carried out. However, the court did find that the O'Loughlins' insurer had not met their obligations, because their fictional repair involved a strategy that had a high likelihood of failure and had not, in fact, been carried out by the insurer's experts. In effect, the insurer was trying to get the O'Loughlins to accept a repair strategy that was not realistic and not likely to be attempted if their house actually could have been repaired.

'Did they say anything about the foundations as you went around?' Lindsay asked.

'No, they just pointed and looked,' Kevin said.

'At least they can see how crumbly it is,' Lindsay said. 'Surely they won't go away thinking that can be patched.'

Kevin shrugged. 'Hopefully,' he said. 'But I don't know.'

Kevin put his arm around her and she snuggled into him. Outside drops of rain started to hit the windows, blown in by the chill wind. 'It'll be okay,' Kevin said, kissing her cheek. She nodded. 'Really, it will.'

A New Normal

June 2013

It was a strange thing, being excluded from going into the centre of the city you lived in, but it was normal life for the people of Christchurch for over two years following the February 2011 earthquake. The original red zone cordon had gradually been reduced. Each time, Alice had come into the city to walk around the newly-moved barriers, peering in to see what was going on, what had changed. She was never the only one, there was always someone else with a dazed expression, trying to make sense of where they were, what they were seeing. It helped Alice to know she wasn't the only one feeling dislocated. She knew the demolition and rebuild would take years and that there were people who had decided they would avoid the city centre until then. But Alice preferred to be shocked bit by tiny bit, gradually demolishing her idea of what a normal city was and replacing it with this new transitional city.

Finally the last of the cordon was coming down. Officials held a ceremony to stand down the army troops who had manned the cordon since February 2011, but Alice, Sean and Charlotte wanted to avoid all of that. It seemed put on by people from outside the city, the Prime Minister and other politicians down from Wellington, the officials from CERA. Yes, City Council officials and local Ministers of Parliament would be there, but it seemed more like the locals were guests rather than the hosts.

The rebuild was feeling more and more like something being imposed on the city by Wellington rather than being done by the people who were supposed to be running the city. There were political things going on, tensions between the City Council and the Minister for Earthquake Recovery, and there were rumours that the Government would take over the City Council and put commissioners in place. Sean and Charlotte said they had enough of seeing people play happy families at home, they didn't want to see it on what should be a relaxing afternoon in the newly cordonless city. Alice understood, the tension between their parents was getting to them both.

Sean had talked to Alice about wanting to leave home. He was 21 and he wanted to go flatting for his last year at uni, but he didn't want to leave Charlotte home alone, dealing with their parents by herself. Alice could relate, she should be flatting as well, but she didn't want to leave her family, not if she could help around the house and so reduce some of the pressure her mother and Kevin were feeling. She felt sorry for Olivia and Jack, their happy, fun parents had been replaced by stressed, angry people who had trouble relaxing. Alice was the fun one now, who read to them at night and made them laugh.

Alice, Sean and Charlotte went into the city late in the afternoon, parking down by the hospital and walking along the river into the city. A month earlier they had debated whether or not take a red zone bus tour, but that seemed wrong, being shown around your own city, told a history that might not match your own experience, and seeing it from bus height rather than the eye level they were used to. They had decided to wait until the end of June and do the self-guided option.

Apart from the days after the container mall had opened, Alice had never seen so many people in the city since the big quake. People weren't in a hurry, they were stopping to look, to figure out what had been where they were standing, thoughtful and quiet, some teary. The day was warm and dry for midwinter, no rain threatening, no chill wind to put people off. It was like the city had put on its best winter weather to welcome its citizens back in.

It was disconcerting knowing what street she was on but trying to convince her brain that was where she was. They stood on the corner of Hereford, Colombo and High Streets, looking up the tramlines and through to Cashel Mall, turning, trying to take it all in. A sculpture of a sheaf of wheat rose from the stone paving, starkly silver, towering above them. Alice couldn't remember if it was there before the quakes. Of course it had been, why would they put something like that up now when there hadn't yet been any memorials to the people who had died in the February quake? Maybe the sculpture hadn't been noticeable because of the buildings. But now there were hardly any buildings, so the wheat sheaf stood out.

Near the wheat sheaf stood a shiny new sign, about as tall as Alice. It had photos of the building that used to stand on the corner of High and Hereford Streets and said that it had been built in Venetian Gothic Style. Sean was reading it, puzzled.

'Why mark this one?' he said. 'But not all the others?' He was turning again, still trying to get his bearings, figuring out where the building in the photo had stood. He read off one part of the sign. '"What architectural styles or features do you like on High?"'

'Well this rubble grunge motif lends a kind of end-of-the-world ambiance,' Charlotte said in a posh accent, crooking her arm like she was sucking smoke from an old-fashioned cigarette holder. 'But I do wonder if the architect has considered the functional aspects of the design. The day-to-day uses, you know.'

'The signs were for the Rugby World Cup,' Alice said. 'Don't you remember? They started turning up all over the city at the end of 2010. There's one down on Moorhouse pointing the way to the stadium.'

Sean nodded. 'Of course,' he said. 'I'd forgotten all about that.'

'I haven't had KFC since the day of the quake,' Charlotte said in a soft, faraway voice, the posh one gone. She was looking up Colombo Street to the spot where the red and white KFC shop used to stand. The site was clear, the whole shopping complex that once filled it gone, pounded into rubble and trucked out of the city. 'I got out of school early and came into the city, had some KFC and then walked up to South City, met Nanny and then it hit.' It was the first time she had mentioned what she had been doing the day of the quake to either Alice or Sean. They both glanced at each other over the top of Charlotte's head. Had Charlotte lingered in the city just a few minutes longer, she would have been on Colombo Street, where a building collapsed onto a bus.

'Which way?' Sean said.

The old green-blue BNZ building that had been demolished to half-height pointed the way towards Cathedral Square, but Charlotte had already shot off up Hereford Street. Alice and Sean followed and stopped where she had stopped, peering in through the murky windows of a café. There were still cups and plates on the tables, dried food on them. The food cabinets held what could not really be described as food, not after more than two years.

'That's disgusting,' Alice said. 'It must stink in there, or do you think it's beyond that?'

'Let's not find out,' Charlotte said, quickly walking off back towards the Square. 'There's probably rats in there.'

In the Square, people were milling around fencing that kept them from getting too close to the gothic cathedral that marked the centre of the city. A few people held up cameras, but more just stared. There was steel bracing holding up the front of the old church, although it was difficult to tell if the bracing was actually doing anything, so much of the front of the building had fallen away. Inside, pigeons lined the wooden rafters.

'Wow, what a mess,' Charlotte said. 'Pigeon central.'

'Were there pigeons before the quakes?' Sean said. Alice and Charlotte shot him a look that said he was stupid. 'Well of course there were, but I don't remember ever seeing any. Maybe it's like the birds on the river and rats and stuff and the quakes have given them the opportunity to really take off.'

'Probably,' Alice said. 'It's pigeon paradise in here for a few years at least.'

'Vermin always thrive in a disaster,' Charlotte said. 'Rats, pigeons, lawyers.'

'Oooooo,' Alice said, 'that's harsh.'

'But accurate,' Charlotte said.

'She's right,' Sean said. 'Lawyers are going to be very busy in Christchurch for some time.'

'You shouldn't be so happy about it,' Alice said, poking him in the ribs. He oofed and poked her back. 'Or so proud about being classed with the vermin.'

They walked around the fencing to get a good look at the whole building, which looked better from the back and sides. The front, though, was a mess, crumbly stone and roof tiles breaking apart. In the days after the February quake, it was thought that people had died in the cathedral. There had often been tourists in there, walking up to the top of the spire, and people had wondered if they would have been able to get back down in time, once the shaking started. Luckily, though, no one had died there, although a woman working in the cathedral had been injured and needed to be helped out of the building.

The fate of the cathedral was unknown. The Anglican Church wanted to demolish the building and replace it with a modern church. But there were some in Christchurch who saw the cathedral as the heart of the city, symbolic of the city's English origins and, therefore, worthy of restoration, regardless of the cost. The issue was in court, a heritage trust had been formed to stop the demolition. Like so many things in Christchurch, the issue of what would happen to the cathedral was going to take a long time to settle. A temporary cathedral was being built a couple of blocks away and would open in a few months. It was made of shipping containers with roof beams of lengths of cardboard tubing and was being called the 'cardboard cathedral'.

Later, while drifting off to sleep, Alice was still trying to make sense of the city. She had become used to not going down certain streets, to running into fences blocking her way. Allowing extra time to get places and changing which way she would go at a moment's notice had become normal. There had been a time in 2012 when she could drive across the city from east to west, but then she couldn't drive back the same way. To go back east, she had to drive south and then out of the CBD to Moorhouse Avenue. Now it was all open and back to normal. No, not normal, because nothing was normal any more. It was a new normal, one that would, in a few months, be replaced by another one, and then another one.

Part III: Jaded City

Put not your trust in princes, nor in the son of man, in whom
there is no help.
— *Psalm 146:3, King James Bible*

Nothing is illegal if one hundred businessmen decide to do it.
— *Andrew Young*

To argue with a man who has renounced the use and authority
of reason, and whose philosophy consists in holding humanity
in contempt, is like administering medicine to the dead, or
endeavoring to convert an atheist by scripture.
—*Thomas Paine, The American Crisis*

Accreditation Lost

July 2013

The largest earthquake to occur in New Zealand since the 7.8 Napier earthquake was the 2009 Fiordland earthquake, also a 7.8 but not nearly as destructive to human settlements as the Napier quake had been nearly eighty years earlier. This was because of its location, near Dusky Sound in the remote southwest of the South Island where there are few towns and, therefore, few houses to damage and people to injure. Everyone forgets about this quake, because although it was felt throughout the South Island, its location meant there were no injuries and only minor damage.

The Opunake earthquake in July of 2012, though, is remembered by more people, coming as it did towards the end of the Canterbury earthquake sequence, when the nation's awareness of just how damaging quakes could be was at its peak. This quake was off the western coast of the lower North Island and was felt throughout the country, especially in Wellington. This quake was a 6.5 but, again, because of where it was centred, there were no injuries and only minor damage.

In July 2013, there was another major quake, this time off the coast of Marlborough, in the Cook Strait. This 6.5 occurred at five o'clock on a Sunday evening and it was near enough to several population centres for people to notice it. There was damage, in both Marlborough and Wellington, and a few minor injuries. The region was haunted by aftershocks in the week following and its inhabitants came to feel they understood what Christchurch was going through. But that quake didn't destroy Wellington, or even Seddon, the small Marlborough town nearest to the epicentre. Although Christchurch people appreciated the show of fellow feeling on the part of those further north, they still felt that people outside of Christchurch didn't really understand what they were experiencing.

The fanfare that had followed the 100-day-plan in 2012 had not been met with much in the way of action. People were becoming suspicious of the promises of both local and national government, especially after the City Council lost its accreditation for issuing building consents. Yes, in the middle of the biggest building project the country had ever seen, the local government entity responsible for issuing the majority of the required building consents lost its ability to do so.

The messy way in which the loss of accreditation unfolded did nothing to boost the confidence of the ratepayers and other residents of Christchurch. The qualifying authority had informed the council at the end of May that it had a month to remedy the situation and keep its accreditation. The council's chief executive chose not to tell the mayor or the city councillors. It seemed he hoped to fix the problem before anyone higher up the food chain found out. When the Minister for Earthquake Recovery found out, he called a press conference to announce this dire state of affairs, which was embarrassing to the mayor and the councillors. The end result was that the Government appointed a crown manager to achieve what the chief executive had not been able to: put the consents department in order. The chief executive resigned and the mayor announced he would not run for re-election later in 2013. This political earthquake took place in the last weeks of June and the first week of July and it was three weeks into the month when the Seddon quake reminded the country that Christchurch was not alone in being vulnerable to seismic activity.

Alice watched all this unfold and began to think seriously about whether she wanted to stay in Christchurch, or New Zealand for that matter. It wasn't the risk of earthquakes that bothered her, she had become used to them, she knew how to protect herself to give her the best chance of surviving a quake, and she also knew what she would do to keep her own house safe, when one day she had one. What made her want to leave was the bureaucracy and behaviour of those who were supposed to be running the rebuild. She had seen six-year-old Jack behave more maturely over disclosing to his parents something he had done wrong than the City Council's chief executive had behaved over the building consent issue. That he wasn't sacked on the spot astounded Alice. Lindsay and Kevin worked hard to teach Olivia and Jack to take responsibility for their actions, but there seemed to be none of that accountability for decisions at local government or even national government levels. Why do your best to make good decisions if there are no consequences for the results of the bad ones?

But leaving the city wasn't an option for the short-term. Before she could even consider moving somewhere else, she had to get herself some qualifications, though what in she did not yet know.

She was frustrated with herself. She was still in the claims officer role and she had been asked if she wanted to move up, into roles with more responsibility. But she was increasingly uneasy about whether the system she was part of was actually helping people. It seemed to create more problems than it solved, dragging out claims instead of moving them closer to settlement.

One thing they were taught at work was that your average person didn't understand their insurance policy. And that was true, most people didn't read their policies and didn't understand how insurance really worked. Although Alice had been working in the insurance industry for a year now, she was still getting her head around it all. One thing that bothered her was that almost everyone in the city had full-replacement-as-when-new policies. That meant their house was supposed to be put back to the state it was in when it was new. But so many of the repairs that were being proposed seemed to be patch-up jobs that barely put properties back to their pre-earthquake state. Alice could understand patching broken foundations if the policy imposed a limit on how much could be spent on repairs, but these policies didn't.

Alice knew she didn't want to keep doing that job, but she was holding on until the end of the year. She was thinking about going back to university and continuing with her engineering degree.

The other issue that was wearing Alice down and making her think about what direction she was going in was the situation her grandparents were in with their red zoned land. Although they had been red zoned nearly a year before, Neil and Heather still hadn't had an offer, not even a fifty percent one. A group calling itself the Quake Outcasts was taking the Government to court, asking for a judicial review into whether or not the red zoning and the buy-out offers were legal. People she worked with talked about the Quake Outcasts like they were losers who had forgotten to insure their properties, said they should just take what they were offered and move on. But Alice knew, from her grandparents' position, that just accepting the offer and moving on felt like being cheated, having something stolen from you. If the court case didn't go favourably for the Quake Outcasts, Alice thought, it meant that there was something seriously wrong with how the law was applied in New Zealand. She wondered, on and off, whether she should consider a law degree, then one day she could help people like her grandparents, making sure they got a fair deal. But that involved being part of the industry, insurance and law, and she wasn't sure she wanted to immerse herself in all that more than she already was.

Alice had talked to Gerald about her doubts about the industry, about being part of it, and he had asked if she wanted to move on. She did, she said, but she didn't know what to do. It was good to be able to talk to Gerald about it, he didn't try to push her in any particular direction, as Lindsay tended to. But sometimes she felt some guidance would be welcome, from Gerald anyway.

'Let's look at what you're good at,' Gerald said when she suggested this to him.

She thought about that for a moment. 'I can type, answer phones, keep files in order, arrange meetings and site visits.'

'You're good with people,' Gerald said. 'Good at communicating. So something where you're figuring out what people need. I could use someone like that.'

'Doing what exactly?' Alice gave him a weary look, he was simply humouring her, his hopelessly flaky granddaughter who couldn't find herself a real job, a real career.

'I'm serious, Alice,' he said. 'Not all people are. Don't underestimate yourself, you deal with people well, and that's definitely something you should factor into whatever you choose to do. Now when I hire people,' he went on, 'I look at their qualifications, but that's not the main thing. I want to know how good they are at solving problems, because that's what most jobs are about: investigating problems and coming up with solutions. So think long and hard about what problems you want to solve and that's where you will find your career.'

'I don't understand,' Alice said. At primary school and high school, people always asked what you were going to be when you grew up: a fireman, a doctor, a policeman, an engineer. What you liked to do didn't really seem to come into it.

'You don't have to figure it out today,' Gerald said. 'Just try thinking about it in a different way.'

'One thing I don't want to do is choose something just because it's convenient.'

'What do you mean?'

'Well I'm doing this insurance stuff now, because that was the opportunity I had from working for the PMO. But staying with SR would be like marrying a man standing next to you in the queue at the coffee shop because you decide you want to get married,' Alice said. She wasn't making sense, she knew. There were opportunities around her, but she didn't want to wake up in twenty or thirty years and find she was doing it just because it had been convenient.

'That's a completely different decision,' Gerald said. 'One that should never be decided on the basis of convenience. But a job, that can always be changed. You learn some skills, such as how to deal with people in difficult situations, and you can take those skills into different jobs.'

'But that's not what you did,' Alice said. 'You became a builder because your father was a builder. Don't you wish you'd done something different?'

'I started out a builder for convenience, that's true,' he said. 'But I didn't have to stay there. I liked it, which is why I stayed, why I built up my own company. But I've done a lot of different things, from working for other people to running my own business. You could look for another job, something different that gives you a chance to build some different skills. You're young, Alice, you have no responsibilities, you can experiment. You're still stuck in the university year way of thinking, your life doesn't run from February to November each year, so maybe try something different, a few months doing one thing, a few doing another. Think differently. Find out what you like doing.'

What problems did she want to solve?

Thanks Very Much, It's Been a Lot of Fun

August 2013

The 26th of August 2013 was to Heather the most wonderful day in a very long time. The High Court ruling was in on the Quake Outcasts case and it had gone against the Government. Although Neil and Heather still hadn't had an offer on their section, the court's instructions to the Government were to make a different offer on vacant land. The fifty percent offers had been labelled an abuse of power and had been set aside. It was wonderful!

However long it might take, the section saga was at least a step further ahead. That was certainly not the case with the repairs to their house. Their initial attempts to complain to Fletcher EQR about the quality of the repairs had been fobbed off. They had signed off on the repairs, they were told, it was too late to change their minds. But they had drafted a complaint, which had been 'investigated' and closed. Next they had followed up with a report from a foundation specialist they had engaged to assess the house. He had spent half a day at the house, taking measurements and photos, and he had picked up issues that no one had before. Now the report was with EQC, it was just a matter of waiting. The High Court ruling gave Heather hope that reason would prevail, as long as they were patient, as long as they stuck to their guns.

When Neil arrived home, they had dinner and afterwards he and Heather went for a walk around the park. Although it was still winter, the days were starting to get longer and warmer, and the world was looking brighter to Heather. She said as much.

'It's not all over yet,' Neil said. 'We haven't even had an offer.'

'I know that,' Heather said. 'But it's just nice to have forward movement, even if it's only a tiny half step. It's something.'

'It's not much,' Neil insisted.

'No, but it's something, and the way things have been the last couple of years, I'll take what I can get.'

'Okay,' Neil said. 'I just don't want you being disappointed if there's no more progress for quite some time.'

'I'm quite prepared for that,' she said. 'I'm just happy to be a tiny bit further along the path.'

Her elation was short-lived because there was an article in *The Press* the next morning saying the Government would appeal the High Court ruling. Not only that, the Prime Minister said the Government might just walk away from the vacant land owners. She called Lindsay.

'Did you read it?'

Lindsay had. 'Unbelievable.'

Heather read from the webpage. '"Thanks very much, it's been a lot of fun. If you don't want to take the offer, that's where it's at." That, that... man.'

'Mmmmm hmmmm,' Lindsay said. 'I hate the way he refers to it as uninsured land, as though land can be insured.'

'He's either the most misinformed man in New Zealand or the most devious. I cannot believe they keep trotting out this line about us being careless over not being insured. We can't get insurance on land!'

'Did you read the bit where he said it's not easy for the Government?' Lindsay said.

'I did,' Heather said. 'That man is an arse. Does he think it's easy for us here? Sitting and waiting, not knowing when our house is going to be seen to? Not knowing whether we're going to have our land taken off us, not knowing how much we'll get for it?' Her voice had risen and had an edge to it that verged on hysterical and she tried to rein her feelings in, only to feel tears roll down her cheeks.

'I'm coming over Mum,' Lindsay said. 'Okay?'

Before Heather could object, Lindsay had disconnected the call.

Heather tried to calm down, to think of something else, but wherever she went in the house there was a reminder, whether it was a new crack forming in one of the walls because their foundation hadn't been repaired properly, paint flaking or bubbling on the walls or stacks of paper documenting their claim.

Ten minutes later, Lindsay arrived. Heather was pacing the kitchen, still clutching the phone, her hands red from the pressure she was applying. Lindsay gave her a hug and took the phone off her. Heather was trying her best to not start crying again.

'I'm sorry,' she said, sniffing back tears. 'I had this little ray of hope that something, just one thing, might be sorted out sometime soon, and now it's gone.'

'I know,' Lindsay said, rubbing her back. 'It's so unfair. Unjust.'

'Yes, unjust. They just do what they want and won't listen to anyone, they don't care who they hurt.'

Lindsay insisted that Heather spend the day with her. They would go out to lunch and Heather could help her around the house, pick the kids up from school later.

They drove to a complex of old tannery buildings a couple of kilometres away. The buildings were in an industrial part of Woolston, with large trucks rumbling along the roads. A gelatine factory nearby was notorious for a smell that on hot days made the area smell like damp, rotting fish. The river passed through this part of Woolston and the tannery buildings were along the riverbank. The owner had planned to demolish one building to use as a carpark and restore all the tannery buildings, turn them into an arcade full of shops and cafés. But the June 2011 earthquake had set him back, shaking bricks from the buildings he was planning to restore, and the only functional building he was left with was the one he was planning to demolish. He turned that building into a pizza bar and café and brewed beer on site. The Brewery drew people from all over the southeast. It was a welcome distraction from the quakes, something new from old in a city where so many of the old things were being torn down and replaced with nothing.

The restoration of the old tannery buildings had continued throughout 2011 and 2012, and recently the first set of shops had opened up. It was the first time Heather had been there since shops started to open. Lindsay held open the heavy door for Heather. The tile floors were a beautiful checked pattern, bordered with zigzagging blue, cream and red tiles, the colours rich and warm. The two of them walked into the main part of the arcade and looked up and down. The shop frontages were large wood-framed windows with stained glass along the top. Wrought-iron light fittings ran the length of the arcade and above the shops were balconies that pointed up to the glass ceiling, held up by intricately patterned beams. Late morning sun streamed through the ceiling.

'This is lovely,' Heather said, trying to catch every detail she could. She couldn't remember anything quite so beautiful in Christchurch.

'I'm starving,' Lindsay said. 'Let's get something to eat, but let's come back and have a proper look after.'

They went to The Brewery at the front of the complex and after coffees and a shared pizza, walked back through the shops, enjoying the newness of them. The tannery complex was similar to an arcade Heather and Neil had once visited in Melbourne, something built in the early 1900s, when people still cared about craftmanship and beauty. This new arcade certainly outdid the too-large malls that had come to litter Christchurch's suburbs in the last thirty years. When she was a child, shopping had been done in the city or out at New Brighton, and Heather had never really warmed to the idea of modern mall shopping.

'It's lovely to see someone get on and do something,' Heather said. They were standing at the end of the main arcade, looking down it, past the shops they had been meandering through. 'So little has happened in the city, in spite of all the plans. I'm so tired of all the talk, it's nice to see something actually getting done.'

'Do you ever want to leave?' Lindsay said. She was quiet, her brow creased. Was she actually asking a question or was she trying to tell Heather something? Were Lindsay and Kevin thinking of leaving?

'I've stopped thinking about what we might do,' Heather said, choosing her words carefully. 'I don't want to have hope any more.'

Heather didn't want to worry Lindsay, but she was increasingly feeling trapped in the house. She loved the place when they first moved in, and there were so many happy memories, all those years when the children were growing up. Lately, though, it was something she couldn't escape, like a bad marriage in a country that had outlawed divorce. When she could think clearly enough to analyse her feelings, she did still love the house, the wooden floors, the remodelled kitchen, the cosy lounge heated by the woodfire and the garden she had put so much care into over the years. It was EQC she felt was the abusive spouse, trapping them there, not responding to their complaints, pretending everything was fine, the house had been repaired properly. When it hadn't!

'Everyone needs hope, Mum,' Lindsay said, putting her arm around Heather's shoulders.

'I'm not unhappy, love,' Heather said, only half convincing herself. 'I just feel like our choices about where we live are limited.'

'Well they are limited,' Lindsay said. 'Ours, too. We've talked about selling the house along with the claim. Letting someone else deal with it.'

'Where would you go?' Heather said, surprised that Kevin and Lindsay had talked about doing something that drastic.

'Don't worry, we're not going anywhere,' Lindsay said, smiling. 'We would lose money doing that, so we've decided to hang on.'

'I suppose that's all we can do,' Heather said.

They decided to spend the afternoon making a roast dinner for that evening. It would give both of them a chance to escape from the drudgery of trying to understand the insurance process and trying to figure out how to make progress on Neil and Heather's complaint with EQC. They agreed that insurance and earthquakes would not be mentioned, which at first made for long silences, but soon they started talking about the children's progress at school. Then it was time to pick them up from school, which Lindsay did while Heather peeled and chopped potatoes and kumara for roasting.

When Lindsay arrived home with the children, she took over in the kitchen and told Heather to go and play with the children. Olivia and Jack were putting together a jigsaw puzzle on the coffee table, one of jungle animals around a watering hole. Heather worked at being very bad at putting it together while Olivia and Jack told her about school. She remembered doing the same with Lindsay and Sonya when they were little, when Jason was just a baby and Heather had not yet gone back to work. That was in the house Heather was feeling so trapped in now. They had moved in just before Lindsay started school, when Heather was heavily pregnant with Sonya. She remembered trying to get the house organised while keeping track of a four-year-old and feeling awful. Heather was not one of those women who glowed during pregnancy. She just felt tired all the time, and after each baby she had experienced what was now recognised as post-natal depression. Each time, it had taken her a couple of years to pull herself out of that dark place, the pit with the steep, slippery edges.

Lately she felt that despair creeping in again, felt that she was slipping away, down into the dark. All those years ago it was the little things that would pull her back into feeling alive, things like playing with her children. Playing with her grandchildren had the same effect now, showing her what her priorities should be. What was important to them was the people who loved them, and Heather decided she would try every day to remind herself that it was the people she loved, and who loved her, who were important, not the house she lived in.

Dinner was a loud event, the children noisily telling the adults about school and their afternoon playing with Grandma. It was good to have that distraction, and the only mention made of the Prime Minister's comments was when Alice greeted her, giving her a big hug and whispering in her ear, 'The PM is a ginormous arse.' Heather squeezed her tight and sniffed back a tear.

After dinner, Lindsay, Kevin and Alice did the dishes while Heather and Neil got the children ready for bed. Then they had cups of tea in the kitchen, talking about nothing much, which was lovely for a change. Earthquakes and insurance, insurance and earthquakes, she'd had enough of both of them for several lifetimes, and it was nice to talk about how the children were doing at school and when the weather might start getting warmer now that the end of winter was near.

As they were saying goodbye, Heather turned to Lindsay and hugged her, holding her tight. 'Thanks very much,' she whispered. 'It's been a lot of fun.'

'We'll do it again soon,' Lindsay said, kissing her cheek. 'Take our minds off all this.'

Heather nodded, but said nothing more. She and Neil walked out to the road where Neil had parked his van. She started to cry and Neil reached for her arm, giving it a squeeze.

'We'll get through this,' he said.

She nodded and sniffed back her tears. It was nice of him to say, but she was far from convinced. She would find ways to stay away from the edge of that pit. She had to.

Shelter

September 2013

Charlotte got off the bus at the first stop in Redcliffs to give herself
a long walk home. She studied the shipping containers on the other
side of the road. Maersk, P&O, Maersk, Maersk Sealand and more
Maersk, the company's seven-pointed star logo repeated along the
road. The containers were stacked two high into ten columns,
twenty of them set up to stop rocks falling down the cliffs from
hitting any cars on the road below, or people on the footpath. It
made the road into Redcliffs narrow and cars had to slow down to
thirty kilometres per hour. The containers had been there for so
long now that Charlotte struggled to remember what was behind
them. There had been a cave, and Charlotte wondered if rockfall
had blocked off the mouth of it. Although she had lived all of her
life in Redcliffs, she could never remember going into the cave. It
had always been spoken of as being off limits, too dangerous to go
into. There had been houses near the cave, too, but the only one
Charlotte could remember was a yellow one, different in style from
the other houses in Redcliffs, a kind of North American desert look
to it. It was three stories high, but Charlotte couldn't remember any
of its neighbours. She had been going past that stretch of road ever
since she could remember, yet she couldn't remember what had
been there three years before. Funny how memory worked, it had to
be reinforced if it was going to stick. Charlotte wondered what else
she had forgotten.

She walked past the school with its empty grounds. She had
hung around in town, walking around the container mall and the
building demolitions before catching the bus home. She had spent
so long in town she had missed seeing the school pickup, all the
cars lined up on the road in front of the school, mums waiting for
the little kids as they got off the bus from the school they actually
went to. The cliffs behind the school had collapsed on the day of
the February quake and the massive piles of rocks were still there,
visible from the road. None of the school buildings had been hit by
the rocks falling, but there were more rocks coming down in the

June quake and so the school relocated to a school in Sumner. Kids now had to catch a bus from Redcliffs School out to Sumner. Charlotte felt sorry for them, she remembered walking to school as a little kid, it being a big deal being able to go with Sean once she was old enough to start. Then, when Sean went off to high school, Charlotte could walk by herself. Sure the little kids could walk to the pickup spot, but it wasn't the same thing as walking to school.

Charlotte decided to go the long way home and walk past the house they used to live in. It was where her family had been living when she was born, and she had been nine when they moved to the new place up the hill. Moving up the hill had been a mistake, the old house had been a happy place where her parents didn't argue. She wondered if they argued so much in the new house because of money. She remembered them talking about having a large mortgage, and it wasn't something that sounded like a good thing.

It would have been better for them to stay in the old house because it had already been demolished and rebuilt. Yes, it would have been awful to have your house so badly damaged that you couldn't live in it, but at least all that would be over with by now. Whenever she walked past the new old house, she wondered if the people living in it were happy, if they spoke nicely to one another, if the quakes were a distant memory. If she were the more obsessive type, she would figure out a way to see what they were like, make an excuse to walk by the house on a regular basis and catch glimpses of the happy, normal family of her imagination, one configured so closely like her own. Parents the same age, boy at university, girl four years younger still at high school.

This way home took her past Nanny's house. Charlotte thought about dropping in, but it would annoy her parents if she wasn't home by the time they arrived home. And if she went to Nanny's, she would find a reason to stay. And to stay a little longer. Then there would be a phone call and Nanny would have to say that, sorry, yes, she would send Charlotte home right away.

Charlotte had the weekend to look forward to, at least. She was going with her dad and her uncle Brent to collect firewood from a farm where one of the shelterbelts had been uprooted and blown over in a big storm a couple of weeks earlier. Thousands of homes had been without power and farms throughout the region had damaged irrigation equipment. It hadn't been too bad at Redcliffs, although it had been a windy night that Charlotte had trouble sleeping through. Brent and Dan's parents had a woodburner, so they would get as much wood as they could and store it up for the next winter. Chopping up trees into firewood and stacking wood into a trailer wasn't the most exciting thing Charlotte could be doing over the weekend, but it was a change, a chance to get out of the city. And spend some time with her dad, that was what she was looking forward to most of all.

The thing she liked about spending time with her dad was that there was no questioning, no prying into what she was doing. Not that she had anything to hide, she was pretty boring as far as teenagers went. But she didn't like being interrogated about her 'plans for the future'. She was sixteen, what was she supposed to say? She was going to do a degree that would get her into a career and give her a public profile and a way into politics and changing the world? There was a girl at school like that, India Cooper, but she wasn't someone Charlotte would be caught hanging around with. Her mother would love having India Cooper for a daughter, she would be able to pour all her frustration over the EQC assessment process they were going through into making sure her daughter would be able to change the world for the better.

That Saturday with her dad almost didn't happen. Charlotte got up early and got dressed in old clothes for a day she knew would involve a lot of dust and debris. She was in the kitchen spreading Marmite on her buttered toast when her mother came in and pointed out she should be spending the weekend studying for exams. They were over a month away! And, Charlotte pointed out, she had studied every night that week, she should be allowed some time off to do something different. Dan came through and won the argument for her, simply saying, 'C'mon you, Brent's meeting us there in half an hour.' Charlotte stacked her toast on the palm of her hand, grabbed her backpack and ran after her dad, who was in the garage starting the car.

'I was saying something,' Charlotte heard her mother calling after her. Charlotte could imagine the disgusted look on her face at being foiled once again.

'What was your mother saying?' her father asked as he backed down the driveway.

'Just that I need to do some studying later,' Charlotte said. She was too slow to think up a decent lie and when he stopped at the bottom of the driveway and didn't pull onto the street right away, she thought he was going to insist she go back inside and do as her mother wanted. But he was stopping to get out and hitch the trailer to the car's towbar. Charlotte let out her breath, relieved.

'I'm sure you're keeping up just fine,' Dan said as he drove down the hill. 'And it will probably do your mother good to have the house to herself for the day.'

That didn't make sense. 'She hates the place,' Charlotte said.

'No she doesn't,' her father said. 'She just hates the situation we're in. She's promised me she's just going to relax for the day, do some reading. That isn't related to the house.'

Charlotte said nothing. Clearly her father wasn't listening to her mother very closely, because Charlotte heard Rebecca say she hated the house pretty often and she didn't think a day trying to relax in the place she hated would be enough. Her mother needed a month, or maybe even a year. So it wouldn't be happening any time soon.

Soon they were on the Southern Motorway, heading out of the city and towards the mountains. The part of the motorway they were on was new, it was being built when the earthquakes started and its completion hadn't been slowed down by the quakes. Funny how the western side of town had so little damage compared to the east.

'Do you ever wish you'd stayed on your side of town?' Charlotte asked. Dan had grown up in Harewood, in the northwestern part of the city on flat land near the airport.

'Only because of the house,' Dan said, glancing at her. 'I like the hills, I like living where we live. That's why your mother and I decided to live there and not over this side of town.'

'You have that in common?'

'Yeah,' he said, nodding. 'We both love the hills.'

'You should start cycling again.' Before the quakes, it was possible to cycle from one end of the hills to the other along the Summit Road. Before her parents separated, it had been Dan's Saturday morning thing, to cycle up the hill to the Summit Road, then along the Summit Road and back down the hills and home. All up, it was around thirty kilometres of cycling and Dan did that every week.

'I could stand to lose a few kilos,' he said, keeping his eyes on the motorway.

'I didn't say that!' Charlotte protested. But yes, he did have a small potbelly he didn't have when Charlotte was little.

'But I could,' he said, looking at her and grinning.

'Suppose,' she said. 'You are old now.'

He laughed and they both fell silent again, watching the mountains drawing nearer. As they got closer to the place where they would meet Brent, Dan had Charlotte look up the location on his phone and tell him which way to go. Soon they were driving along roads bordered by farms, and the number of trees that had come down was staggering. Alongside one road, roots bound up with clumps of mud faced the fenceline, one after the other tipped over into the paddock by the force of the wind.

Brent was already working when Charlotte and Dan arrived at the fallen shelterbelt. Brent had earmuffs on and the chainsaw was chewing through a branch. His back was to them and they waited until he was finished with that branch. No point risking startled motion from a man operating a chainsaw, Dan said.

Brent spent the rest of the morning chopping up trees while Dan split the wood and Charlotte loaded it onto the trailers. Once the trailers were full, they went to Charlotte's grandparents' house to start unloading the wood and stacking it behind their garage.

They had dinner there and it was getting dark when Charlotte and Dan started the trip home. Charlotte ached all over and her arms were covered in sticky sap. She would need a hot shower when she got home, then maybe she could go spend the night at Nanny's, watch one of the old movies Nanny loved so much and fall asleep in front of the television. She asked her father.

'You've been spending too much time there lately,' he said. 'We'll watch a movie at home tonight and tomorrow we'll do something together.'

'But you said Mum could use some time home alone. You could go for a bike ride and I'll stay at Nanny's.'

'We'll spend some time together as a family,' he said, his voice firm. Charlotte kept pushing anyway.

'Sean's not coming home this weekend.' They were on the causeway crossing the estuary, nearly to the entrance to Redcliffs. Then they were past the shipping containers, sentinels protecting them from whatever hazard might come down off the cliffs above.

'We aren't talking about Sean.'

She said nothing. They turned down the road that led to their house and were soon pulling into the driveway. Charlotte opened her door and was about to step out when her father touched her arm.

'We're trying, Lottie,' he said. 'I'm sorry it's like this, but we don't know how to make it better, how to fix the house problem, but can we at least spend some quality time together tomorrow? Didn't we have a good day today?'

She pulled her arm away from him, stepped out of the car and slammed the door shut before running inside.

The Cracks are Showing

October 2013

Time was overtaking Marjorie, she knew that. She was going to bed early and getting up late, despite her best efforts to resist this worrying trend. The days were getting shorter for Marjorie even as spring was drawing out the light part of each day. She still managed to go for a walk each day, but wasn't able to get as far as she used to. Whereas a loop around the block was once well within her reach, she was now limited to walking down to the river and back, a short one kilometre walk that became more difficult each passing week.

The neighbourhood was changing, houses disappearing, leaving sections that stood empty for months before anything was done. Around the corner from Marjorie's house, an old weatherboard villa had disappeared, one that had been there ever since Marjorie had moved into the neighbourhood as a young wife and mother. It had been a beautiful villa, built in an era when as much attention was paid to detail as was paid to cost. It was now being replaced by a modern weatherboard and concrete block mix that was larger than the old villa had been, taking up much of the section. It was the way people built these days, making the most of their land, not concerning themselves too much with a garden. Marjorie would find it difficult to live in such a house, not because of the materials used, because she did think it could be made attractive and it was nice to see people using their imaginations and mixing building materials instead of going with just brick or just weather boards. No, it was the garden she would miss in such a place. She had always enjoyed having a vegetable garden, growing food for herself and her family, not being dependent on the bland, uniform offerings of the produce section at the supermarket. Even after the worst of the quakes, Marjorie had been able to feed herself from her garden.

The owner of the house being built seemed to have done well out of the insurance process. The new house would be modern and warm. No doubt the owners would have put some of their own money towards the build, they wouldn't have been able to get a larger house built otherwise, but they had done well. Not so for the woman next door to them, Joan Armstrong. She had lived in the house since the 1960s, raising her children there. Although a decade younger than Marjorie, Joan had been a widow for many more years than Marjorie had. And, unlike Marjorie, Joan missed her husband, even now, nearly three decades after his death.

Joan had moved out for her repairs for three months late in 2011. Now, over a year after she moved back in, she was seeing cracks appearing in her walls and she was having difficulty shutting and opening some doors and windows. Her oldest son had paid a foundation specialist to inspect the house and the specialist had found unrepaired damage to the foundations. Marjorie had heard of such things. Alice's grandparents on her mother's side had badly repaired foundations and were having difficulty getting Fletchers or EQC to do anything about it. But in Joan's case, the specialist had identified foundation damage that should, he said, have been repaired, but it didn't appear that any such effort had been made. Joan had been too trusting, Marjorie thought, and had never insisted on seeing the scope of works or having it reviewed by someone other than EQC or Fletchers. Joan's son was talking to EQC about what needed to be done, but it was going to take a long time. Alice's grandparents had discovered their dodgy repairs over a year ago and there hadn't yet been any action.

Marjorie had stopped buying houses, the market was getting too risky. There were two main problems that Marjorie could see. The first was that some houses had been poorly repaired, those like Joan's and that of Alice's grandparents, and often the poor standard of repairs was only discovered some months after the homeowner moved back in. The second problem was owners selling houses but pocketing the money that should have been spent on repairs. This was fine if the house was being sold as-is-where-is, and Marjorie had bought several such properties for very good prices. The problem was when there was an expectation that the house was being sold along with the payout that would allow repairs to be made. There were some cases where an EQC payout had been handed over to the new owner, who later found out that there had been more than one claim against the property and so more than one payout. The new owner thought they were buying a house along with a payout sufficient for repairs only to discover that there was more damage and not enough money to repair it. Buyers needed to be more vigilant these days, and Marjorie was no longer feeling energetic enough to make that effort.

It wasn't just the state of the real estate market that made Marjorie stop buying up properties. Andrew had worked hard at getting her insurance claims settled and although he hadn't been able to get as much as she wanted, they had done all right. Recently he had found two TC3 properties next door to one another and obtained the geotechnical engineering report from the vendor to see what kind of foundations would be required. The houses on the sections were beyond saving, both were very badly out of level from liquefaction during the February earthquake. But Marjorie could put two townhouses on each section, which would make the cost of the groundwork more economical. It looked promising, but Marjorie was hesitating. Andrew was looking tired. Usually full of energy, the last year had taken its toll on him. His hair was starting to grey at the temples, which was normal in a man his age, but what disturbed her was how pale and washed out he looked. He said it was his workload, but she suspected the work she had asked him to do on her insurance claims had taken too much out of him. Insurance companies elevated twisted logic to an art form, he said, and had little regard for the laws they were supposed to be operating under.

Marjorie was thinking that she should just let the TC3 properties go, for Andrew's sake. She was getting soft, she realised. Whereas a decade ago she would have told herself to go for the deal, more recently, she had been thinking about how she didn't want to spend her last years pushing her grandsons into working hard for her when they had already gone above and beyond what any reasonable grandmother could expect of them.

Alice had visited a few nights earlier, asking questions about the past, the family's history. Marjorie had discouraged her children from asking about their English relatives from the time they were young, the whole family knew it was an off-limits topic. But Alice hadn't grown up around the family and was curious. Marjorie talked, but just a little bit, she intended giving a list of names, nothing more. She found herself telling Alice about Edward, how he had signed up as soon as he turned eighteen and was so excited to be doing his part for his country. Andrew looked like him, Marjorie told Alice, the same build and colouring. When Marjorie was growing up, Edward could always make her laugh. She had missed him so much over the years. She also told Alice about her other siblings, Gwen, Charlie and Lizzie, and about how the house they grew up in had been bombed. It was a surprising release, to voice some of the thoughts that had haunted her since the earthquakes began.

'This was all a very long time ago,' Marjorie said. 'I find it difficult to talk about.'

Alice nodded. 'Losing so much of your family in one go can't have been easy.'

'Nothing about that war was easy,' Marjorie said. It was time for a change of subject. 'Are you feeling any better about your job?'

Alice was puzzled at the question and seemed to be thinking about how to answer it.

'I know it's not what I want to keep doing,' Alice finally said. 'I don't think I'm helping the rebuild at all, I'm not helping people get their claims settled fairly.'

Marjorie studied the girl, was touched by the concern etched on her young face. 'The rebuild has never been about settling claims fairly, Alice. It's about keeping costs down. Nowhere is that more true than at Southern Response, because the Government never wanted to bail out an insurance company.'

'That's why we're so careful, because it's taxpayers' money,' Alice said, shaking her head. 'But it takes such a long time to work out what a fair settlement is.'

'It also takes time to properly pull the wool over people's eyes and figure out how to make voters think they're being served well when all that's being served is politicians' own interests,' Marjorie said. 'All governments are like this.' Alice's view of the world was one where people looked out for each other. That wasn't the world Marjorie knew. No one had ever looked out for Marjorie, not until she married Walter. But that hadn't lasted long.

'But it shouldn't be like that,' Alice said, seeming much younger than she was.

'No, it shouldn't,' Marjorie said. 'But it is, and you can't change it. No one can.'

Obstacles

November 2013

In the months since their project manager's last visit, Lindsay and Kevin had prompted the insurance company for their geotech report, which they had received a few weeks later. It told them nothing. It was, it seemed, based on what their project manager had told the geotech company about how the house would be repaired. It seemed backward, surely the expert advice was supposed to be the basis for the repair solution, not the other way around?

A few days after the geotech report arrived, they received the new scope of works. Their issue with the previous scope of works was that it proposed just gluing the cracks in their foundation. There had been no explanation as to why the insurance company had changed their minds about lifting the house and replacing the foundation. The new scope of works recommended replacing about a third of the ring foundation, which, although an improvement, wasn't good enough. Kevin and Lindsay could see crumbling parts of the rest of the foundation and didn't see how the insurance company could say it was okay to replace one crumbling part of the foundation but not the other. They were considering how to voice their disagreement when the insurance company sent them an offer to cash settle.

Cash settling would let them repair their house the way they wanted to. Even better, they wouldn't have to rely on the PMO's project manager, who didn't seem terribly inclined to listen to them when they pointed out more damage. After all, he was the one who wrote the scope of works that replaced a third of the foundation but ignored the extent of damage to the rest of it.

'Did that guy come around?' Kevin asked when he arrived home. Lindsay was in the kitchen getting dinner ready, cutting vegetables into chunks. She slapped the knife she was using down on the bench, making a loud bang when the knife's metal handle hit the stainless steel benchtop. She turned to Kevin.

'No, and he's not answered his cell all afternoon,' she said. That was the second builder they had contacted to try to get some idea of how much it would cost to lift the house and replace the foundations. Lindsay and Kevin had decided they could save money by replacing the damaged walls and ceilings themselves, and that money could be spent on the foundations. But if they couldn't get someone to quote for the foundation work, they couldn't make a decision over whether or not they could stretch the cash settlement far enough. Accepting the cash settlement without having a good idea about how much the foundation repair would cost risked ending up in a position where they weren't able to afford fixing the house properly.

'Well if we can't get anywhere with builders, we might have to just let them go ahead with the repair,' Kevin said. He filled a glass of water from the tap and sipped at it, leaning up against the bench. 'There's an email from the insurance company, they say we've missed the deadline for making a decision.'

'What?' Lindsay said. 'We didn't have a deadline.'

'I didn't think we did either, but that's what they've said.'

Lindsay wiped her damp hands on a tea towel and marched through to the lounge where the laptop was set up, Kevin following through. She found the email detailing the offer. 'No deadline, no timeframe.'

Kevin just nodded, and Lindsay felt her anger rise at his calmness. This was serious, how could he just stand there?

'Did you say something when you talked to them on the phone?' Lindsay said.

'No, Lin, I didn't,' he said, and she heard the edge of anger in his voice. 'There was never anything about a deadline.'

'Well what are we going to do?' Lindsay swallowed back tears, her throat sharp from the effort. 'They can't just force us to make a decision without the information we need. Can they?'

Kevin shook his head. 'I don't know. But I think we should write and point out that there has been no deadline, and that we've been waiting a long time. We've been overcap two years, after all, they can't just say we've got six weeks to make such a major decision.'

'Do you want me to do that?' Lindsay said. She had already created a new email and was stabbing at the keyboard.

'Yes, I'll finish up dinner,' Kevin said.

They said nothing to the kids or Alice, but all three seemed to know there was something going on and were unusually quiet over dinner. Later, while Alice was getting the kids bathed and into bed, Lindsay and Kevin went through what Lindsay had written, asking the insurance company for more time and pointing out that they had been given no deadline.

Lindsay was exhausted when she dropped into bed that night, but she couldn't sleep. She lay staring up at the ceiling, listening to the sounds of the house: Kevin snoring softly beside her, the house creaking slightly in the wind, a train passing in the distance. The house was their home, it had been for nearly a decade, where she and Alice and Kevin had made a home together, where Olivia and Jack had lived all their lives. It needed to be fixed properly, and Lindsay wasn't convinced that their insurance company's strategy would achieve that. Then there was the question of where they would live while the house was being repaired, what would happen if the repair dragged on for too long and their accommodation allowance ran out. They couldn't afford to pay rent and a mortgage, and Lindsay had heard of people in that situation, parents of other kids at the school who were stressed out of their minds, not knowing when they would finally be able to go home.

They had talked a couple of years ago about actually leaving Christchurch. That had been in the middle of all the quakes when they were both worn out, not knowing what was going to happen with their house, not knowing if the quakes would ever stop. Since then, Lindsay had started to feel more settled. The city felt like home again, and Kevin hadn't said anything about leaving for over a year.

Lindsay loved the part of town they lived in. The hills were nearby, always within view, breaking up the sky that would otherwise stretch away into the Pacific Ocean. She had lived on the western side of the city when she and Andrew were married, when Alice was a baby and Andrew was still at university. She didn't like it, the hills were too far away, and it just seemed flat everywhere. Funny, he had stayed over that side of town, but she had gone back to where she grew up at the first opportunity she had.

If she imagined living anywhere else in Christchurch, it was closer to the hills. Her parents were closer to the hills, a block away from the river and a quick walk down to the park in the inner loop of the river. The river was lined with willows at the end of the park, and the view looked up into the valley that stretched up towards the summit of the Port Hills. It was a view Lindsay found comforting, like the looming hills were some sort of emotional anchor. She had grown up there, in the house her parents were still living in. They didn't want to stay there forever, but their retirement plans had been derailed by the quakes.

For too long, Lindsay had felt she was at the mercy of the quakes. They dictated the course of her life. She could plan on getting a good night's sleep so she could tackle a list of tasks the following day, but aftershocks in the night derailed that plan because once awake she had such a hard time getting back to sleep. Functioning on no sleep had never been fun for Lindsay. It was something she endured while her children were little, but she knew, then, it was a phase that would pass. There were fewer quakes now, but the insurance process had stepped in and taken their place. Life would be going in a particular direction, but then, without warning, there was an assessment to be carried out, paperwork to review, processes to attempt to make sense of, and she would have to stop whatever she was doing and focus on the house instead. The interruption to their lives showed no sign of ending any time soon.

The quakes weren't the first time Lindsay's life had been interrupted. She had certainly never intended to be a mother so young, but looking back she realised that having Alice had saved her, in a way, from a career she was unsuited for. She was never cut out to be a lawyer, and working through the insurance stuff the last couple of years had reminded her of what that world was like, the endless regulations and the convoluted thinking. Now she was pleased she hadn't gone down that path. Studying law was simply something her family had expected her to do, as she was the first to go to university. It was either that or medicine. Funny that when she had decided what she wanted to do, it was actually medicine, or closely related. But that, too, had been interrupted.

Once Alice started school, Lindsay worked as a receptionist at a doctor's surgery. She stayed there until shortly before she had Olivia, and they had asked her to go back. She did consider going back, she liked the work, the biological nature of it and the contact with patients. But then Jack came along, and Lindsay decided that once Jack started school, she would train in something medical, maybe nursing. In the end, she settled on radiography. It seemed like interesting work, with a lot of patient contact, but without the burden of responsibility for medical decisions that affected people's lives. The local polytech had a three-year radiography course that Lindsay was going to find out more about, but by the time Jack was getting ready to start school, there was so much uncertainty about the house and the earthquakes that she and Kevin decided to wait for another year. Then in 2013, their situation seemed even more complicated since Lindsay was tied up with helping her parents get through their botched repairs and everything else they were going through. She had been thinking lately that she should look at enrolling in 2014, that way she would be qualified and working by the start of 2017.

Now they had to make a decision about the house, and Lindsay couldn't even start to feel comfortable about the idea of the proposed repair going ahead. It wasn't right, but neither of them had the technical knowledge to argue the point with the insurance company. They needed an engineer of their own, or a lawyer, she wasn't sure which one. Maybe both? What she did know was that they didn't need her taking on studying while managing the kids, the house, Kevin's books and the insurance claim. She would postpone her course of study once again.

Delaying Tactics

December 2013

Following the High Court ruling in the Quake Outcasts case, the Government appealed the decision. The Court of Appeal overturned one part of the High Court's decision, that the creation of the red zone had been illegal. But it agreed with the High Court judge that the fifty percent offers to vacant land owners and uninsured property owners had been illegal. Although the Quake Outcasts had won their case with regard to the Government offer, the Government told them there would be no revised offers before the end of the year. Suspecting more delaying tactics would follow in the new year, the Quake Outcasts group decided to take the case to the Supreme Court in order to protect their hard-won legal victory.

Lindsay's parents felt like everything had ground to a halt and that 2014 would be another year without progress, just as 2013 had been. Lindsay was worried about them, especially about her mother, who would often cry at little things.

Alice had resigned from her job with Southern Response and would finish in a couple of weeks. She was going to work for Gerald, helping to run the office at Moorhouse Architectural. Not an ambitious job as far as Lindsay was concerned, but it was better than working for an insurance company, especially one whose reputation was shaping up to be nearly as bad as that of EQC. EQC had been plagued by claims of nepotistic hiring practices and staff running businesses on the side that benefited from their roles at the organisation. Alice's year and a half with Southern Response had changed her, she had withdrawn to some degree. When Alice told Lindsay she was resigning, Lindsay had tried to get her to talk about it, but all she would say was that it was hard going to work every day and hearing the other side.

'Do you think we're wrong to push?' Lindsay had asked. After their insurance company had pressured them for a decision, Lindsay and Kevin had decided to engage their own structural engineer to carry out an assessment of the house. The insurance company had come back to them acknowledging that there had been no deadline, but insisting that they make a decision early in the new year. The whole experience had left them feeling even more wary of the repair strategy, that the insurance company was trying to push them to make a decision quickly so they wouldn't notice something important.

'No,' Alice said, shaking her head vehemently. 'It's not that, it's how people at work talk about claimants. Like they expect too much, and I don't see it the same way. They're always saying we have to be careful because it's taxpayers' money, but the Government has said they would honour the contracts, that's all people want, for the Government to honour their contracts like they said they would.'

'I think that's what most people want,' Lindsay said. 'Not patch jobs.'

Alice was quiet for a moment. 'It's not too much to expect,' Alice said. 'I think there are too many patch jobs being scoped and I'm sick of keeping my mouth shut.'

Lindsay was relieved. She wondered at times if she and Kevin were missing something, that they were being greedy. But what Alice said was true, they were only asking for their contract to be honoured.

Alice offered to look after Olivia and Jack for a few days early in January so Lindsay and Kevin could get away. Lindsay didn't understand when Alice first offered and just stared at her, mystified. 'You know, without kids, so you don't have to worry about organising anyone but yourselves.'

'Oh,' was all Lindsay could say.

'Think about it,' Alice said.

Lindsay discussed it with Kevin.

'Great idea,' he said right away and suggested they take Lindsay's parents with them.

'That's not really getting away,' Lindsay said.

'No, but they need a break, your mum especially, and I don't think it's going to happen unless someone takes her by the hand and makes her have a break.'

Lindsay nodded. He was right about Heather, she was drowning in insurance matters. If it wasn't the repairs to the house occupying her mind, it was the red zoned section. It would be good for all of them to get away. But still, there was another problem. 'We have no money,' she pointed out. Although that wasn't strictly true, they were trying to save as much as they could for the structural engineering report they needed to have done.

'Tom has a place in Kaikoura he's said we can borrow,' Kevin said. Tom was the guy Kevin had been doing work for all year. He was a good guy. He wasn't taking the Fletcher's jobs, instead he had an arrangement with a building company that was working on commercial properties. It wasn't nearly as dodgy as some of the residential work, and Kevin was finding working for Tom better than trying to pick up work on his own.

'You have this all sorted out, don't you,' Lindsay said. He nodded. She thought about it for a moment. 'I'll ask them,' she said.

The next morning she dropped by Neil and Heather's after dropping the kids off at school. Heather's response, worryingly, had been that they couldn't go away because something might happen with the house.

'Nothing's going to happen with the house if you go away for a week, Mum,' Lindsay said. 'Nothing's happened all year, it's not going to happen, especially in the first week of the new year.' She should have asked her father, she realised, he would see the value of a week away and then he would get to deal with Heather's anxieties instead. But it was too late now, she had to push on through.

'A few days away might be nice,' Heather conceded. 'But I need to ask your father. I'll let you know tonight.'

Of course the answer was no. It was too late to ask her father now, and Heather insisted that Lindsay and Kevin needed time to themselves, they hadn't taken a holiday since before the quakes. Heather said they would have a break just staying at home, helping Alice out with the kids if she found them too much. It was an excuse, Lindsay knew, but she let it go, she was just too tired to argue.

Lindsay was nearly as worried about herself as she was about her mother. She found it hard to get out of bed each morning, to focus and get just the basics done. She was struggling to keep up with clothes washing, with the cooking and with vacuuming the house to keep on top of the plaster dust from the cracks in the walls and ceilings. If something didn't change soon, she wouldn't be able to get out of bed each morning, and she didn't know what would happen then. She didn't want to think about it.

Quake City

January 2014

Kevin's nieces were staying with them while his brother and sister-in-law were spending a long weekend up in Hanmer. The weekend was over and Kevin had gone off to work on Monday morning, leaving Lindsay and Alice to manage the four kids, Olivia and Jack, nine-year-old Katie and eleven-year-old Ruby. Katie and Ruby were missing their mum and dad, looking forward to seeing them later that day, and it was up to Lindsay and Alice to keep them entertained until then. Fortunately, Kevin's brother and his wife had left their minivan, borrowing Lindsay's car for the trip, so Lindsay and Alice were able to pile all the kids into one vehicle to get them around.

Orana Park, Alice had suggested, but Ruby and Katie wanted to see the city. Why? Although they lived only two hours south of Christchurch, they had heard so much about the devastation caused by the earthquakes that they wanted to see it all up close. Lindsay and Kevin were in the habit of escaping to his brother's place in Timaru whenever Christchurch became too much for them, and Katie and Ruby were curious about what they were escaping from.

'Okay,' Lindsay said. 'Let's go rubble necking!'

They all piled into the van and drove into the city, Alice pointing out buildings in different states of disassembly along the way. They parked on Cambridge Terrace, then walked down Hereford Street so the kids could see the little green Shands building, over a hundred years old, one side nearly fallen off it. Lindsay and Alice pointed out buildings they remembered, a bookshop both had liked, the Drexel's restaurant that did the best pancakes, the old KFC site, the chemist where Lindsay used to get her photos developed when she was a teenager.

The kids didn't seem to understand, even Olivia and Jack, who lived only a few kilometres away. But their parents and Alice had sheltered them from what was going on in the city. They had been in a couple of times, when significant buildings were being demolished. Both Olivia and Jack loved the diggers, it was all excitement and noise as far as they were concerned, they didn't understand that this had been where people shopped, where mums and dads and aunts and uncles had come to work. Where some of them had died while doing so. But that wasn't something she wanted to try explaining to them, all four of the kids were too young to have to think about not having a mum or a dad.

'You know how Stafford Street has all those shops on each side?' Alice asked Ruby and Katie. They were walking along High Street towards the Cashel Street intersection and everywhere there were gaps where buildings had been demolished, their rubble ground into fill for the basements.

Ruby and Katie nodded. Stafford Street was the main shopping street in Timaru, typical of the retail centres of New Zealand small towns.

'This used to be like Stafford Street,' Alice said. 'There were shops all along here, all the way up there.' She pointed into the distance, where the kinetic sculpture towered above the street, its orange disc divided into four wedges, always moving slowly, rotating, marking the intersection of High, Manchester and Lichfield Streets. 'Imagine if you went into Stafford Street and it wasn't there.'

Both girls looked like they were trying to picture what Alice was trying so hard to explain, but she could see it wasn't working. Over their heads, Lindsay gave Alice a shrug. Alice shrugged back, she wasn't going to try to explain further. When they were older, though, they would remember this and maybe understand. It was too much for little kids.

'Are these for a train?' Jack said, excited at the tram tracks. 'Can we wait for the next one?' He loved trains, loved it when there was a train going over the rail bridge. He liked to stand under the bridge and look up at the carriages going by. It kind of freaked Alice out to do that, but, she would tell herself, they've fixed the bridge, they've fixed the bridge, they've fixed the bridge, finding that by the time the last carriage passed, she was repeating that mantra in rhythm with the train passing overhead.

'No, it's for a tram,' Lindsay said, 'but they aren't running any more.'

Jack looked disappointed but brightened up when Alice pointed out that because there weren't any trams or trains they could walk along the tracks.

So they walked up the tramlines and crossed Colombo Street to reach the container mall, the brightly coloured shipping containers arranged to form the small shopping centre. All the kids thought it was pretty cool, although they were disappointed that there wasn't really anything they could buy or play with. That was okay, Lindsay said, because they could all have ice cream.

They found an ice cream caravan in the mall and ordered, then walked around, looking up at the remaining buildings and the containers. There were more people in the mall than Alice had expected, a mix of tourists (wearing backpacks and carrying cameras) and locals. Although the sky was blue and sunny, the day was cool, a slight wind blowing from the east.

'Can we go there?' Ruby said. She was pointing at a building that housed a museum display called Quake City. Alice had heard of it, but wasn't sure she really wanted to go inside. She had lived through the quakes, did she really need to see an exhibit telling her about it all over again?

Lindsay gazed at Alice, saying, 'We could do that. But you need to finish your ice creams first, so do that and put your rubbish in the bin.'

All four kids quickly munched their way through the last of their cones and dashed off to the rubbish bin.

'Do you think this is a good idea?' Alice said.

Lindsay thought about it. 'Their parents talk to them about the quakes pretty plainly,' she said. 'They know people died.'

'Yes, but do they know what that means?'

'I don't know. But we'll keep an eye on them, move them on quickly if anything's too much.'

The exhibition started with explanations of earthquakes, European and Maori, and then there was a pad where the kids could jump up and down to see how big an earthquake they could make. Poor Jack, at age seven, was really still too small to make as big a quake as he wanted.

Past that there was a theatre screening interviews with people who had been in the city during the February quake. These people, sitting against a pitch black background, were describing their experiences of the quakes. Alice sat down on one of the plastic chairs and the four kids slid into seats beside her, bookended by Lindsay. Lindsay shot her a glance, jerked her head to indicate they should move on. But Alice ignored her.

They watched for a few minutes, it was the end of one interview and Alice couldn't really get the gist of what that person's experience had been. The next subject was a man, a fireman. He was talking about someone trapped in a building. When Alice realised he was talking about someone who was dying, she started to slide along her seat, bumped her hip into Olivia and pushed the kids along the row.

'Time to move on,' she whispered, and Lindsay stood up to let the kids out. They rushed off to the next exhibit.

'Do you want to stay?' Lindsay said.

She shook her head. 'I'll come back another day.'

'If you want to stay, I'll take the kids home.'

Alice thought about it. 'Okay, but I'll go through the rest of it with you.'

Alice followed the kids through the rest of the exhibit. The kids lingered at the Lego rebuild of the city longer than Alice thought possible.

'Maybe CERA should hire these kids,' Lindsay said, smiling. 'The rebuild might actually get underway at last.'

Alice laughed. The rebuild had been a long time getting underway. She remembered the news at the start of 2013 saying that was the year the rebuild would be in full swing, and now it was the start of 2014, and again, people were saying the rebuild would get properly underway this year.

Once Lindsay left with the kids, Alice went back to the darkened theatre and sat in the back row. She watched the interviews all the way through as various people came in, watched a few minutes, then moved on. She recognised some of the people interviewed, some had appeared in newspapers around the anniversaries of the February quake or when inquests or Royal Commission hearings were being held. One man had been flying home to Christchurch from Auckland when the plane turned back. The control tower in Christchurch had been evacuated due to an earthquake, they were told. He was able to reach his sons, but his wife's cellphone went to voicemail. He saw on the news that a building had collapsed, the CTV building, where his wife worked. Alice thought about the helplessness of not being in Christchurch on the day of the quake, of not knowing, just watching from afar, news reports delivering tiny pieces of information, never enough to provide the full picture, but enough to paint a nightmare. She hadn't thought about that, of people from Christchurch who happened to be away on the day and had to watch. Everyone's experience was different. Was everyone changed as a result of the quake? Alice knew she had changed, although she hadn't decided yet whether it was a good change. Gerald would tell her it was up to her whether it was good or bad. Was that true?

A month after the February quake, Alice had spent an evening on YouTube watching news footage from the day of the quake. It was surreal, the alarms in the background, the wreckage she herself had walked through. It must have seemed surreal for viewers on the day: a city in New Zealand without water, without power, without a properly functioning cellular network. Fallen buildings, people dead, dying, crying, not knowing what to do.

Now, nearly three years later, watching the interviews, she wondered if she would forever be struggling to grasp what had happened in Christchurch. What must it be like for those who had lost people? For people whose injuries had permanent effects? She could walk away from Christchurch and forget it had ever happened, but those people would always wear the scars, in their hearts or on their bodies, and she felt that it would be wrong to ever forget.

The man whose wife was in the CTV building was offered a seat on an air ambulance going back to Christchurch. It had flown a sick child from Christchurch to Starship Hospital. There were no other flights down, all the commercial flights had been cancelled. Flying in to Christchurch, he could see the smoke in the city, the smoke Alice had smelled that day. He never saw his wife again, but he kept calling her cellphone, leaving messages so that if there was a chance she was still alive, she would hear his voice. He wanted her to hear his voice. It was unbearably sweet, and Alice sniffed back tears, wiped them from her eyes and cheeks.

Alice wondered about the child who had been flown up to Starship, how for its parents the day of the quake was much less about the quake, it was about their ill child. Were both on the flight with the child? Or just one? Was that one then in the position of worrying about the other parent, still in Christchurch? For them, the quake was just background noise, another complication in an already complicated day. So many stories, Alice was starting to realise, all different, all painful for different reasons, and she could never hear them all, bear them all. It was too much.

All Right?

February 2014

The office was quiet for the morning, the usual uncomfortable silence hanging between Alice and Suzanne. Gerald had hired Alice to take over the running of the office, guided by 'the old pros', as he called them. Together, Suzanne and Sylvia had been running Gerald's office for over a decade, and they had it running smoothly. The systems Alice was learning were well organised, it was easy to find what she needed to find and, unlike her time at Southern Response, she didn't feel compelled to reorganise things so they made sense. Alice enjoyed the work. There was a lot of contact with the workers and suppliers and it was interesting seeing people's dreams for their repaired homes coming together.

But she didn't enjoy working with Suzanne, who, for some reason Alice couldn't figure out, had taken a dislike to her. Alice had asked Sylvia what Suzanne's problem was, but Sylvia couldn't come up with anything concrete. 'She doesn't adapt to change well,' Sylvia finally said, but why she should take that out on Alice was mystifying, especially as from how Suzanne and Sylvia both talked, they both wanted to work less. Surely training up Alice quickly would let them achieve that goal sooner?

It wasn't that Suzanne was openly cruel or vindictive, it was that she was less than helpful. If Alice was working on something she hadn't done before, she had to pry every detail out of Suzanne, whereas if Alice was training someone, she would point out to them the pitfalls rather than waiting for them to fall in. Alice had a hard time reconciling the lovely grandmother Charlotte described and the formidable woman she shared an office with.

'It's about time,' Suzanne said, a firmness in her voice Alice was used to hearing directly only at herself. She glanced over to the meeting table in the centre of the room, wondering what it was that she had only just now accomplished to Suzanne's satisfaction. Suzanne was reading the newspaper. Alice stayed at her desk, sipping her coffee, watching Suzanne, whose mouth was set in a grim line, her eyes drawing together in a scowl.

'What?' Alice asked quietly, curious at what had perturbed Suzanne but unsure whether she really wished to engage in conversation about something unpleasant.

Suzanne looked up from the newspaper and across to Alice, her blue eyes gazing into Alice's. 'Police are looking into what charges they can press over the CTV building,' she said.

'That is about time,' Alice said, scooting her chair over to the table and then trying to read the newspaper article upside down. Suzanne spun the paper around so Alice could read it properly.

'If nothing can be done to hold someone in the engineering profession accountable for that building,' Suzanne said, 'then there's not really much point having a professional body setting standards, is there?'

Alice glanced up from the article. 'No, there isn't,' she said, looking back down. 'It says IPENZ hasn't yet determined whether or not there was a professional breach.' Alice turned the paper back around to face Suzanne. 'It's disgusting, really, that after three years, no decisions have been made.'

'You were doing an engineering degree, weren't you?' Suzanne said. Alice felt uncomfortable under her scrutiny.

Alice nodded.

'Why didn't you go back?'

Alice thought about the many reasons why she had decided to stop studying back in 2011. Even if she knew the definitive reason, the moment when she had decided she wasn't going back, would she tell Suzanne? 'It was hard keeping going with study after the February quake,' she finally said. 'The roads, the temporary lecture theatres, just everything taking so long.' It sounded weak, even to her.

'Hmmm,' Suzanne said. 'It is hard to start studying again once you've stopped.' Her tone was dismissive and Alice felt her own doubts about her decisions sweep over her. She flushed.

'That's not...' Alice said.

'It's exactly why I don't want to see Charlotte lose her momentum,' Suzanne pushed on. 'She did very well last year, should do just as well this year, as long as she stays motivated. People who take a year off between high school and university too often end up taking off another year, then a decade, then the whole of their lives.'

'I don't...' Alice started to say.

'She needs to work hard at her studies,' Suzanne said, apparently oblivious to Alice's protest. 'She has a good future ahead of her, she can be anything she wants.'

Alice couldn't remember Charlotte ever talking about having a year off. She did know Charlotte was having trouble settling in to her last year of high school. Sean had moved into a flat and Charlotte wasn't happy about being home alone, waiting for her parents to come home, then figuring out ways to avoid them when they were home. The insurance claim had not progressed and her parents couldn't get any information out of EQC as to when they could expect a decision of one sort or another. They had tried to get their insurance company involved as they were sure their house would be overcap, but the insurance company said they had to wait for EQC's decision. Did Suzanne know how unhappy Charlotte was? Was it worth trying to tell her? Probably not. One thing Alice had noticed about adults in the last couple of years was that they never took the problems of young people seriously. And Suzanne was no different. If anything, she was worse.

Suzanne went home at lunchtime, leaving Alice to run the office alone for the rest of the day. That was okay, there was plenty of work and Alice felt like she flew through it without Suzanne lurking in the background, judging her every move. Before long, it was five o'clock and time to go home.

Roadworks on the way home meant traffic was slow, leaving Alice to crawl along in second gear. She ended up behind a bus that was advertising the All Right? campaign. All Right? was a mental health awareness programme that had started around the second anniversary of the February quake. The three-year anniversary had been at the weekend and there were posters all over the city saying it was all right to grieve, to feel frustrated, to feel blue every now and then, to feel overwhelmed some days, or to feel pretty stoked. They were trying to cover the whole range of emotions people might experience while recovering from a disaster, to make people realise it was all normal. Alice had certainly felt all those things the buses, bus shelters and random posters were talking about. And she thought she was all right, but what Suzanne had said about not getting back on course with her university degree was bothering her.

Alice knew she wasn't going back to university. The engineering profession no longer appealed to her. It wasn't just the role engineers had played in the deaths in the city, it was also that some engineers seemed happy to recommend cheap repairs or dismiss damage as historic because they were getting so much business from the EQC and insurance companies. IPENZ was investigating one engineer working for EQC because numerous people had laid complaints about how he would show up for a brief inspection of a property and then dismiss damage as historic or claim the home was a leaky home, when the homeowners had clear evidence that the home had no weather tightness issues before the earthquakes. But that process was taking a long time, and Alice felt sorry for the people whose lives were on hold while IPENZ deliberated. Were those people All Right?

Lindsay and Kevin were having trouble finding a structural engineer to do an assessment of their house. They had told their insurance company they wanted to get an independent report done on the house, which the insurance company had agreed to, but any engineering firm they got in touch with had a waiting list months long. In the meantime, the insurance company kept putting pressure on them to give them the report. Surely the insurance company knew very well how hard it was to schedule an engineer's visit in Christchurch?

Between the pressure the insurance company was applying and the difficulty of finding an independent engineer, Alice was worried that Lindsay and Kevin wouldn't get a fair deal from their insurance policy, that the house wasn't going to be repaired properly. And if that was happening all over Christchurch, it would be a long time before the city would be all right once again.

If It Keeps On Raining

March 2014

Lindsay had been awake on and off through the night, aware of the vast volumes of rain falling on the city, listening to the steady patter on the driveway outside the bedroom window. The house she and Alice had lived in before moving in with Kevin had a steel roof, and Lindsay had loved listening to the rain falling on it, something she had missed in this house, with its heavy concrete tile roof. It was the only thing she didn't like about the house when they moved in. Now? There were the cracks and the dust, the sloping floors, the jammed windows, the back door that wouldn't stay shut unless it was locked. She still liked the house and looked forward to the day when it would be fixed, although that picture was getting harder and harder to hold firmly in her mind.

The rain had slowed by six-thirty when Lindsay got up to go to the toilet and put the jug on. She was sitting in the kitchen sipping at a coffee when Alice came through.

'The street's flooded,' Alice said.

'No way,' Lindsay said, standing up and putting her coffee on the table.

'Way,' Alice said. 'Come see.'

Alice's bedroom was on the front of the house facing the road and Lindsay went through to look out. It was true, the road was covered in water and there was even water up the start of their driveway. How far up the street did it go? Lindsay had grown up in this part of town and remembered the occasional high tide or heavy rain that caused the river to flood and creep up the streets, but never as far as this. She couldn't remember it ever going higher than the half dozen or so houses closest to the river. A car passing by was going too fast and sent a wave washing up driveways. That would not be appreciated closer to the river.

She made Kevin a coffee and took it through to him, gently nudged him awake.

'The street's flooded,' she told him, then repeated herself as he started to wake up.

'No way,' he said. He pulled himself up in bed and swallowed a mouthful of coffee. He stepped out of bed and pulled aside the curtains. 'Wow,' he said. 'I wonder how your parents are.'

Lindsay hadn't thought of that and immediately went back into the kitchen to call her parents. The river had broken its banks there, too, but it hadn't reached their house. Well that was something, at least. Over in Avondale, the Bennetts were fine, which was a relief. Lindsay's grandad was increasingly frail and her grandmother was finding it difficult looking after him. Although their street and a good part of the section were flooded, the house was not. One less thing to worry about for the day.

Kevin came through, dressed up warm. 'I'm going to drive around and have a look, check on your parents and grandparents.'

'Grandma and Grandad are okay,' Lindsay said, putting down the phone. 'Mum and Dad, too, but the water's pretty high. Hopefully it won't keep raining.'

'We'll check on all of them,' Kevin said. 'See for ourselves.'

Lindsay nodded. Lindsay's grandparents had a habit of minimising any difficulties they were having, it would be good to see that everything was okay with their own eyes.

Alice came through to the kitchen and said she would go, too, but Lindsay said no, she would go, Alice could stay home with the kids. It looked like Alice was going to protest, but then had second thoughts.

They took Kevin's work van, with Kevin driving. He backed slowly out onto the road and turned to go away from the river, towards Neil and Heather's house. Getting out onto the main road wasn't a big deal and the road to Neil and Heather's was clear. But as Heather had said, the river had broken its banks and the road around the corner was flooded.

Neil was outside the house and he, Lindsay and Kevin walked along the road to the bridge across the river. 'It's going down,' Neil said. The rushing waters were a thick ripple of brown. 'It was much higher two hours ago. We've been very lucky, but a lot of places downriver have had water through them.'

'Is it the quakes?' Kevin said. 'Is it because the land is lower? I thought this side of town was a bit higher rather than lower.'

'It is,' Neil said. 'This part of the river has flooded before, about ten years ago...'

'In the nineties,' Lindsay said. 'Well before the quakes. I remember some guy kayaking along the road.'

There was still muddy water pooling on the road running alongside the river. A car drove slowly along, pushing a small wave up over the kerb and onto the footpath.

Back in the house, Heather was vacuuming, furiously shoving the vacuum's head into the corner by the front door. It seemed strange that she would pick that rainy, windy day to attempt to get the entryway clean. Neil took his shoes off and left them on the doorstep, sheltered from the rain, and Kevin and Lindsay did the same, swapping worried glances.

'Your mother's not getting any better,' Kevin said as they were driving towards Lindsay's grandparents' house.

'Mmm hmmm,' was all Lindsay said. She didn't want to talk about a problem that seemed to have no solution, Heather wouldn't listen and none of the subtle tricks they had tried to use on her had worked.

They had discussed how Heather was coping before and had agreed to make a point of doing things as a family, giving Heather opportunities to relax and escape from the house and Christchurch, if possible. But it was getting harder to convince her to go more than a few kilometres from home, and a trip out of the city for an actual holiday was not a possibility. She wanted to stay near home, she would always say, in case someone needed to visit the house. Lindsay could understand feeling that way, there were times when she thought about not visiting someone or making an appointment, in case the insurance company wanted to schedule a visit. She had to keep telling herself the insurance company would be reasonable, they wouldn't expect her to drop everything at a moment's notice so they could come and have a look at the house. She had tried explaining this to Heather, but Heather insisted someone had to be at home all the time, or at least nearby, just in case.

'We have to try doing something, Lin,' Kevin said, sidestepping her evasion. 'We can't just let her fall apart, it's not good for her heart, and it's not good for your dad. He looks terrible.'

'I know that,' Lindsay said, nearly spitting out her words. He was right, Neil's clothes were starting to hang off him, and he had never been a big man. 'Dad knows that, Jase does, even Sonya knows that. But Mum won't listen and we can't make her, what? Relax?'

'And you're just happy letting whatever happens happen?' Kevin said. He wouldn't look at her, which was fair enough while driving, but he wasn't even glancing at her, he was just staring straight ahead, his fists tight on the steering wheel.

'Things will change when the baby's born,' Lindsay said. 'It will give her something to do, helping Carla.' Jason and Carla were expecting their first child in July, a little boy.

'That's a long time to wait, Lin. You're happy to just let it go until then?'

Lindsay didn't reply, it was a conversation that would go nowhere.

Lindsay's grandmother picked up the tension between them and once Kevin was helping Grandad check the garage and garden shed, she asked Lindsay what was going on.

'Insurance,' Lindsay said. 'We can't get an engineer to visit until May and the insurance company's putting pressure on us to go ahead with the repair.' It was true, but easier to discuss with her grandmother than whatever was going on in her mother's head. 'How's Grandad? He seems pretty good today.'

'Yes, today's a good day,' was all Grandma Bennett would say, even when Lindsay prompted her to say more. It seemed that no one in the family was willing to talk about the problems they were facing, everyone was just bottling it up.

That night on the late news, there were stories about the flooding in Christchurch, especially about an area north of the Avon River called the Flockton Basin. Residents said the area was much lower now than it had been before the earthquakes, which made it more prone to flooding. This flood was the sixth since the quakes had started where water had been through the houses. Residents were calling for the City Council to take action, to do something to stop them having to face yet another flood. The council, though, had no answer, and it looked like the Flockton Basin could only look forward to more flooding. And winter hadn't even started. If it kept raining like it had over the last day, the city was going to have serious problems.

Lindsay reached for the remote and switched off the news, to sharp looks from Kevin and Alice. 'Enough,' she said, getting up from the sofa. 'I've had enough of the misery being inflicted on this city by inept bureaucrats. I'm going to bed.'

From the bedroom, she heard the TV come back on, but then the volume dropped and all she could hear was a low drone. Yes, she knew that switching off the news didn't stop the suffering, but she needed a break from hearing about it.

Full Replacement, As When New

April 2014

In the 1990s, New Zealand insurance companies began selling a new type of insurance policy. For contents insurance, it was advertised as 'new for old'. If, say, your house caught fire, your contents would be replaced with new contents. So if you had a twenty-year-old three-seater sofa, it was replaced with a new three-seater sofa, not a secondhand one.

The house equivalent of this was 'full replacement'. You insured your house for a particular floor area, and if something happened to your house and it had to be rebuilt, the rebuilt house had to be to the same standard as it was when it was new. A twenty-year-old house would be replaced with a new house. If a house needed repairs under the insurance policy, it needed to be repaired to the 'as when new' standard, not patched.

At first, full replacement insurance was not available for older houses. But as insurance companies began to compete more and more fiercely for the New Zealand homeowner's money, sense finally left the country when one company started offering full replacement insurance on hundred-year-old villas. Other companies soon did the same.

This was the position Lindsay and Kevin found themselves in: owners of a sixty-year-old house with foundation damage and a full-replacement-as-when-new policy. But they were also on TC3 land, green-zoned but prone to liquefaction in future quakes, so the Government had introduced much tougher design standards for foundations. And tougher design standards are more expensive. A suspicious person would conclude that insurance companies began slashing scopes to not have to replace damaged foundations to that new, tougher standard. A house that had been scoped for complete foundation replacement, as their house had, would change to just replacing the cracked parts of the foundation.

Lindsay and Kevin were becoming suspicious people.

It had taken them a couple of months, but they had finally tracked down the name of a reputable structural engineer, who had carried out a preliminary assessment of their property. They forwarded a list of questions to John Rutherford, their project manager, but weeks later there hadn't been any answers. Instead Rutherford had decided to engage an engineering firm to carry out a full structural assessment. When Kevin asked why, Rutherford said that a proper assessment hadn't yet been done.

'I asked what the basis for the cash offer was if there hadn't been a proper assessment,' Kevin said, telling Lindsay about the phone call.

'What did he say?'

'Nothing. Just asked for a time to come around.' Answering questions, it seemed, was not Rutherford's forte.

'So when?'

'I didn't say, I said I'd have to sort out some time off work and I'd get back to him. I'm thinking Monday afternoon, knock off early, then take the kids out to McDonald's.'

'That works,' Lindsay said. 'Do something distracting afterwards. You know, there really shouldn't have been a cash offer if there wasn't a proper assessment. This feels like they're just trying to head our engineer off at the pass.'

'That it does,' Kevin said. 'But it'll be another three or four months before we get our full assessment, maybe it will take that long for their guys to finish their report.'

'Monday then,' Lindsay said. She leaned over and kissed him on the cheek. 'Thanks for taking time off, I don't want to be dealing with them by myself.'

'I haven't done it yet, I'll talk to Tom tomorrow, see what he says.'

And that was that. Kevin would talk to Tom on Wednesday, Tom would get back to Kevin and Kevin could then get back to John Rutherford.

Letting their insurance company know they were engaging their own structural engineering report had resulted in them being assigned a new claim manager. Whether that was a good thing or a bad thing they couldn't be sure. Maybe the complexities of their claim were being taken seriously? Or maybe the new claims manager was a big gun, hauled out for customers perceived as being especially difficult? Kevin preferred to assume the first, whereas Lindsay took the new claims manager's name as a bad sign: Malcolm Bitterman. 'It's like the guy was born to take out his frustrations on others,' Lindsay said.

'You're jumping to conclusions,' Kevin said. 'Let's just see how things play out.'

On Thursday morning, Lindsay received an email from Bitterman stating that they were obligated to provide the insurance company access to the property for investigations. The tone was almost threatening. She called Kevin to see if he had talked to Rutherford, which only wound him up. 'It's been a day and a half since he called,' Kevin said, exasperated.

'Yes, that's true,' Lindsay said. 'But we need to deal with this right away.'

'Okay, I'll do what I can from here,' Kevin said.

Over the next hour, Lindsay watched their inbox fill up with communications between Kevin and Bitterman. Lindsay watched anxiously, pacing the kitchen between emails, waiting for the next instalment in the dispute, hoping that Kevin could hold his temper, explain their position and at least get through to these people that Kevin and Lindsay had valid concerns. Bitterman had been told, he said, that a request for access had been made over a week ago and ignored. Kevin replied that the request had been made less than two days before, there was no delay and there was no attempt to deny the PMO access to the property. He needed, he pointed out, to arrange time off work to be on site for the visit and could not suggest any dates until he knew what days he could take off. Bitterman eventually apologised for being misinformed, but Lindsay felt her big-gun conclusion was proven correct. Bitterman had been assigned to their claim to make them do things the insurance company's way.

When Kevin arrived home that night, he said a date had been arrived at, two weeks from then. Lindsay tried to talk with him about Bitterman's emails, but he stopped her.

'I've had enough for one day, Lin,' he said. 'I just want to stop thinking about it, have dinner, play with the kids, whatever, anything but the house.'

She nodded her agreement, but really she wanted to talk about what had happened, if maybe they should talk to someone about getting a new project manager. Since Rutherford seemed unable to schedule appointments, why would they trust him to manage the repair of their house?

Donut City

May 2014

Alice was having dinner with some of her old Southern Response workmates at a bar made of shipping containers. The bar was in the suburb of Addington a few kilometres southwest of the city centre, where a number of central city businesses had moved while the central city was still cordoned off and businesses were trying to figure out ways to stay in business. Even now, three years after the February quake, businesses were struggling to get going in the centre of Christchurch, while in nearby suburbs businesses were thriving. Some people were calling Christchurch a donut city, nothing left in the centre.

There were eight of them at the table sharing pizza and chips. One of them, a guy called Scott, had never worked with SR, he just ended up hanging out with them because his mates from the web design company he worked at had not shown up. Of the others, only two still worked for SR.

Kylie whispered to Alice that Scott's story wasn't very believable and insisted he had just latched on to them because he was trying to pick up Alice. Alice told her that if the missing workmates story was a lie, it was because he was trying to pick up Kylie, not Alice.

'Come on,' Alice whispered in Kylie's ear, 'the only reason he's hanging out so close to me is because he's trying to talk to you.' This made Kylie blush. 'Watch,' Alice said, and excused herself to go to the toilet, pushing past Scott to get to the aisle. She glanced behind her and saw Scott move along the table to sit next to Kylie. Alice winked at her and turned to continue on her way to the outside. She needed air, not the toilets. The place was simply too crowded and noisy.

She stood outside and breathed in the cold air. It was raining and the air was damp, but Alice had always enjoyed the smell of rain. There was the occasional car going past and people walking along the footpaths, more people than she was used to seeing around the city. This was the western side of the city, which hadn't suffered the same degree of population loss that the east had. On a weekday night near Alice's home, there was so little traffic that she could pull out onto the main road without looking and not hit another car. If she were inclined to.

It had been a noisy week. Alice's great-grandfather had died over the weekend and the funeral had been a large family affair.

Grandma and Grandad Bennett had been living with Heather and Neil while their house was repaired, and being in a different house had revealed how confused Grandad was. One day he went missing, and Neil, Heather and Grandma Bennett had no idea where he was until the builders at the house called. Grandad had walked six kilometres and was exhausted, upset and confused because they wouldn't let him into his own home.

Heather and Grandma Bennett kept a closer eye on Grandad after that, but he still managed to escape a couple of times. Each time, Heather found him walking the road back to his home.

Grandad Bennett never got to live in his house again because early in May, he came down with a cold that quickly went to his chest and then developed into pneumonia.

Heather's sisters and their families had descended on Christchurch to see Grandad and say their goodbyes, so every night for the past week, Alice had arrived home from work to find she was sleeping on the sofa because there was someone in her room. That was fine, she was so worn out that she fell asleep quickly, and it was good to have a catch up each morning with whatever uncle or auntie or cousin wandered out of her room.

Alice had never lost someone she was close to, not that she could remember. Her grandfather's mother had died when she was seven, too young to really understand what death meant. Now her great-grandad was gone, a quiet, gentle man who found enjoyment in his garden and walking the dog along the river.

Her phone buzzed. It was Kylie asking if she was coming back.

Inside, Alice's seat had been taken as the others shuffled themselves around so she sat down across from Kylie and Scott, who were deep in conversation.

'Scott's telling me about how there are too many guys around town calling themselves project managers,' Kylie said. Scott's arm was around Kylie's shoulder and she was leaning heavily into him. How many beers had she had?

'A three week course doesn't make someone a project manager,' Scott said. 'Guys I work with study hard to qualify as project managers, go on courses at nights, and have study groups and they have to work so many hours in project management to get the right number of credits.'

'How long does that take?' Alice asked.

'As long as a year,' Scott said. 'And then they sit a four-hour exam. These guys working for the PMOs, they're not real project managers.'

Alice nodded. The project manager Lindsay and Kevin had been assigned showed no evidence of being able to coordinate the screeds of information people were collecting about their house, and he certainly didn't have the communication skills to sort out conflicts. If anything, he was simply making matters worse for them. He couldn't seem to listen, or maybe he just didn't want to. Alice had said to Kevin that they should ask for another project manager, but he had said no, the insurance company would just think they were trying to delay the claim and he was determined to be cooperative.

'You know we all work for Southern Response,' Alice said to Scott. Kylie shot her a look that said stop, while Scott glanced sharply at Kylie with a look of puzzled disappointment. Southern Response was in the news almost as much as EQC, and its reputation was nearly as bad. An accountant writing for a business and finance website had said that Southern Response was systemically undervaluing their claims, ripping people off. Alice wasn't sure that was true, but she wasn't sure it wasn't true, either.

'Really?' Scott said, his voice sharp and high.

'Not all of us,' Kylie said quickly.

'Okay, not all of us,' Alice said. 'Except Kylie and David, there.' She pointed down to the far end of the table. 'The rest of us have seen the light and left.'

'I'm looking to get out as well,' Kylie said. Was she? She hadn't said anything. Those who had left did seem happier and more relaxed than those still working for SR.

Scott excused himself from the table, saying he was going to get another beer.

Kylie leaned over the table and hissed at Alice. 'Why are you being such a cow?'

Alice paused. 'I'm sorry,' she said, trying to assemble her thoughts. She was confused and upset because of her great-grandad, but instead of dealing with it, she was taking it out on Kylie. 'Do you really want to leave SR?'

'Yes, I do,' Kylie said, and started to cry. Alice got up and pushed around the corner of the table to squeeze in beside Kylie. She put her arm around her, which only made Kylie cry harder. 'I hate it,' she said. 'The people are so miserable and I hate talking to them when I can't do anything to make it better for them. You're so lucky to be out.'

'Have you looked for something else?'

Kylie shook her head.

'If it's gotten that bad, maybe you should start. Ask around. Take a couple of days' leave and just go door-knocking with your CV, see what turns up.'

At that point, Scott returned. He put down his pint and sat down across from Kylie and Alice.

'What's up?' Scott asked, glancing between the two of them.

Kylie looked at Alice, a mischievous gleam in her eyes. 'I thought you weren't coming back,' she said, sniffling and wiping at her eyes.

'Ah...' Scott said, looking uncomfortable.

'I'm kidding,' Kylie said, kicking him under the table. 'I was just telling Alice how much I hate my job.'

Scott relaxed and swallowed a large gulp of beer. 'That's okay then,' he said, 'because it would be weird if...'

'Yeah, it would be weird,' Kylie said.

Driving home later on, Alice decided to go through the city for a few more minutes of quiet before going home. At the end of 2013, various authorities had said 2014 would be the year the rebuild took off. But it was May already, and the city was still as stalled as it had been a year before.

The central city streets were lit up, but not the way the bar and the main road through Addington had been, places that were open and full of people. Here in the middle of the city there were street lights and traffic lights, and equipment on building sites was lit up for safety, but there were too many empty blocks of land that were simply dark holes, gaps in the city, and the buildings that were there were dark and empty. She wondered what it looked like from above, if satellites passing over saw an obvious gap in the heart of the city, the empty donut hole.

Alice crawled along the city streets in second gear, tucked up in her warm car, insulated from the cool late-autumn air of the city. Why would people be out? It wasn't just that it was cold, it was that there was nothing to do past five o'clock when the container mall shut down, no pubs, no bars, no movie theatres. When would that change?

She was stopped at the lights near the police station. There was no traffic crossing in the other direction. Even the police station was empty and dark. It had been abandoned after the December 2011 earthquake and the police had moved into new buildings a few blocks away, near the hospital and Hagley Park. It had been announced recently that the old police station would be demolished, but there was no news about what would replace it. The only certainty was that it would be an empty plot of land for some time before a decision was made on its future. That was how Christchurch worked.

Across the river opposite the old police station was The Terrace. Before the quakes, there had been a strip of bars and restaurants. Their replacements were well underway and they were supposed to open at the end of 2014. But there had been bad news a few weeks ago, that the development had stalled. The developer said he wasn't in financial trouble, he was just trying to figure out how to make the best use of his money. Alice wasn't sure what to make of that, except that there wouldn't be anything to do in the city at night for at least another year. Alice was twenty-two now, no longer a teenager, as she had been when the quakes started. Would she look back on these years and see a hole in her life, something she had missed because of the quakes and the rebuild?

Her great-grandad's last memories of the house he had raised his children in was it being occupied by irritated builders who wouldn't let him in. His home had anchored him and his memories, and he had never expected to leave. Now he would never go back.

The city was like that for too many people, a series of memories no longer anchored in space. There was only the hole and it was getting harder to look ahead to the day when there would be something to keep people in Christchurch.

Resignation

June 2014

To Alice, the biggest tragedy of the whole earthquake sequence was the collapse of the CTV building. One hundred and fifteen people had died in a building that just pancaked, and although two years had passed since the Royal Commission findings, no one had been held accountable. The Royal Commission had shown up the failings in the design and construction of the building and in how it had been assessed following the September and December 2010 earthquakes. Actually holding someone responsible for those mistakes seemed to be impossible.

There was a code of ethics engineers were supposed to follow, it was something Alice had learned about in her year at university. Engineers were supposed to be accountable to a professional body, the Institute of Professional Engineers New Zealand. IPENZ did start an investigation into the engineer whose consultancy was responsible for the design of the CTV building, but had to drop the investigation when the engineer resigned from IPENZ. There was nothing further they could do to hold him accountable once he resigned. That there was clearly something seriously wrong with the engineering profession made Alice feel a little more settled over her decision not to go back to university.

Another thing that bothered Alice about the engineering profession was how much trouble Lindsay and Kevin had getting an independent engineering report on the house. Most engineering companies seemed to be doing insurance company work, which meant it had been difficult finding one who didn't have a conflict of interest, who could carry out an independent report on behalf of a homeowner. This was why it was taking so long for Kevin and Lindsay to get a full engineering report, the engineer they had engaged was so busy he wasn't able to do the full site visit until May, and then it would take up to six weeks before the report would be complete. That meant they would have it by July, but in the meantime, the insurance company had commissioned their own engineering report, which had been speedily arranged. That report agreed with the repair strategy their project manager, John Rutherford, had recommended, which was to replace the concrete ring foundation on the kitchen end of the house. That didn't seem right, though, because there were other parts of the foundation that were cracked and crumbling just as much as the part of the foundation the insurance company planned to replace. Why replace half the ring foundation while ignoring damage to the other half? It didn't make sense.

The same day Bitterman, the claims manager, sent Kevin and Lindsay the engineering report, he started applying pressure on them to sign a document that said the repair could go ahead without a building consent. He kept emailing them every couple of days asking when they would sign the form and send it back. Kevin objected to going ahead with the repair before they had their own engineering report, but Bitterman insisted the form needed to be signed.

'No way,' Lindsay said. 'No way at all that's happening.' She wanted to get a lawyer to make the insurance company stop applying pressure, but Kevin said no, they would wait for their own engineer's report and then the insurance company would listen. Alice didn't say anything, but she wasn't so sure the insurance company would listen, and what would Lindsay and Kevin do then?

In the end, they had no choice but to agree to the repair going ahead because Bitterman sent them a formal letter saying their claim might be declined if they didn't cooperate. Not that it would be declined, just that it might. Kevin signed the document but crossed out the part that said they agreed to the work going ahead without a building consent. 'If they're going to do this repair,' Kevin said, 'they're not going to lump us with responsibility for it by skipping the whole consent process.'

Within a few days of Kevin sending the form, Bitterman started sending people around to prepare documentation for the building consent. After the first visit, Kevin emailed Bitterman to ask why the consent was going ahead when their own engineering report hadn't yet been reviewed by the insurance company. Bitterman replied that getting a building consent was taking a long time and they needed to get the paperwork underway, but Kevin and Lindsay would have the chance to review the consent application before it was lodged with the City Council. That didn't answer the question about their own engineering report.

'The report's not far away,' Kevin said. 'Let's wait until we have that before spending any money on a lawyer. They're more expensive than bloody engineers.'

'Surely they won't get a building consent,' Lindsay said, 'when there's damage that the repair strategy doesn't cover.'

Alice hoped that was the case, that the consent wouldn't get approved, because if it did, it would put even more pressure on Kevin and Lindsay than she thought they could handle. Already conversations about insurance were strained, with clipped words, long silences and strident pacing. Kevin and Lindsay had never had big arguments, at least not around Alice, and it made her worry for them, and for the little kids.

Railroaded

July 2014

Heather and Neil were making no progress with EQC on their repairs. They had submitted their foundation specialist's report to EQC nearly a year ago, but when they contacted EQC after a couple of months to check on progress, EQC said their report wouldn't be actioned. No explanation, no nothing. After discussing what to do next, Neil called EQC to lodge an official complaint, but he was told to complain to Fletchers EQR, as they had actually carried out the repairs. But that complaint had gone nowhere, because the person they had investigating their complaint was the person who had managed their repairs. Of course they were going to say nothing was wrong!

Publicly EQC was reporting that eighty percent of claimants were satisfied with their repairs. At first, Heather struggled to get her head around how their repair could go so awfully wrong when EQC could get it right in most cases. Maybe she and Neil were being too fussy? It was a big job EQC had to manage, maybe they should consider themselves lucky to have been seen to so quickly. She tried to enjoy living in their repaired house, but then, while gardening, she would notice the cracks appearing in the foundation. She found herself reluctant to spend time in the garden, because seeing the state of the foundation just reminded her of the problems with the house that it seemed they could not solve.

That EQC was determined not to face the problems with their repair was abundantly clear, and it seemed Neil and Heather weren't the only claimants being ignored. At the end of 2013, *The Press* reported that EQC had been excluding customers from their customer satisfaction surveys if those customers had complained. Over 30,000 customers had been marked as 'do not survey', which made Heather angry, because that was a big chunk of people who weren't being asked how happy they were with their repairs. It looked like EQC had been fudging the statistics to make the repair programme look more successful than it actually was.

Heather and Neil weren't the only ones in the neighbourhood having problems with repairs. A house around the corner had been empty for the summer, nothing had taken place on the site for months. A young family had been living there and when Heather ran into the mother at the supermarket, she found out that their issue was that borer had been found in the framing and EQC wanted them to pay for new framing. But surely if it weren't for the earthquake damage, there would have been no need to replace the framing? After all, borer was common enough in the city's older houses and she had never heard of one falling down because of it.

Another house nearby had been lifted so that its foundations could be replaced. That had been in summer, the foundation work went ahead over a couple of months and then the house was lowered onto the new foundations. Heather had expected to see work proceeding and the house's family soon moving back in, but instead there was still temporary fencing around the property and no sign of any workers. A neighbour told Heather that the builders were finding it impossible to get the house level and after months of delays, the owners had filed in court against the insurance company and the builders. The owners had originally objected to the scope of works, as the cost of the house lift and subsequent works was pretty close to the cost of a rebuild. But the insurance company had railroaded them into going ahead with the repairs, and so they had given in, moved out and hoped for the best. At the point where the owners decided to file in court, the botched repair was well over the cost of a rebuild. It really would have been easier to just demolish the old house and rebuild, but instead even more money would go on lawyers and court. Those poor people.

Just knowing about a couple of cases of repairs gone so horribly wrong had resulted in Heather wondering what was going on for other houses in the neighbourhood that were being worked on. Were the owners happy with progress? Would their lives go back to normal once they had moved back in? Or would they have poor quality repairs to deal with, as Neil and Heather did? Walking around the neighbourhood was no longer relaxing, she just kept seeing repairs that, maybe, were going wrong, and wound up back at home feeling more stressed than she had when she decided to take the walk in the first place.

Heather also worried about what was going to happen with Kevin and Lindsay's house. They weren't happy with their proposed repair and had engaged an engineering report of their own. But their insurance company wasn't interested in their report and had simply dismissed it, then insisted the repairs go ahead. The process of applying for a building consent was underway.

The afternoon Lindsay had received that news, Heather had picked up the children from school. When Heather arrived at Lindsay's, Lindsay was crying. Heather put a movie on for the children in the lounge, shut the door and went through to the kitchen, where Lindsay was making cups of tea.

'I think you need to get a lawyer, love,' Heather said when Lindsay told her.

Lindsay nodded. 'Kevin says no, we're not there yet. I think he's thinking of the money, we've already spent so much on the report, we can't really afford a lawyer. He's hoping the consent won't be granted.'

'And what will you do if it is?' Heather asked. She had heard of this before, one of Neil's workers was preparing to move out of his house, trying to find a flat for him and his family to move into. They weren't happy with the proposed repair, but the City Council had granted a building consent, so he didn't see that he had any choice but to let the repair go ahead.

'I don't know,' Lindsay said. 'Maybe we'll just have to let them go ahead with it.'

'You have to fight it, love,' Heather said. 'After what your engineer said about the whole foundation being compromised, you can't let them just go ahead with it. You've said yourself the whole ring beam could just fall apart.'

Lindsay shrugged. 'But it might be the only way ahead. We can't keep going through all this.' She was quiet for a few moments. 'Bitterman just kept emailing him and emailing him and emailing him saying this form had to be signed. They said our claim could be declined.'

'Surely that's illegal!' Heather said.

'No, they didn't say they would decline our claim,' Lindsay said. 'Just that it could be declined. We couldn't take that chance, because then we would need a lawyer and would need to file in court and that could get expensive very quickly.'

In the end, Heather could only give Lindsay a hug and offer to make them dinner. She felt so helpless, she couldn't do anything to make the situation better for them.

Each morning, after Neil went to work, the emptiness of the house started to get to Heather. It was a cycle she didn't know how to break out of: she would make Neil's breakfast and lunch, have a brief chat with him while they drank their tea and Neil ate his porridge, kiss him goodbye and then, within half an hour of his car pulling down the driveway, she would be fighting back tears, feeling her mood slipping into blackness. She tried to keep herself busy, getting stuck into something that needed doing to avoid thinking about the house or the section, but it wasn't working. And walking around the neighbourhood was no longer an option.

Heather felt trapped in the house, trapped in the neighbourhood, unable to do anything to dispel that sense of confinement. She could see no time in the future when they would be able to choose where they lived and what type of property they would live in. She barely remembered what it was like to have those choices.

The only things that were helping Heather to pull herself together each day were picking up the children from school and the thought of her new grandson, Jason and Carla's baby that was due at the end of the month. She didn't want to be the type of grandmother her grandchildren dreaded being around, so each afternoon, she made the effort to seem happy, even if she didn't feel it. Most days she suspected she was coming across to the adults at the school as dippy, verging on hysterical. Being around the children helped and she went to bed each night, determined to have a better day the next day.

But the next morning, she would be fighting back the tears once again, trying to find a way to talk herself into thinking that there was a future, that the rest of their lives wouldn't be this post-quake hell. Where they were now felt like the end of the line.

The Bubble

August 2014

Charlotte had promised her mother she would spend the afternoon studying, and she had intended to keep that promise. Truly. After school, she had gone straight home, made herself a cup of hot chocolate and some Marmite and cheese on crackers, then settled down to work on her geography assessment. She had chosen geography for the afternoon because it was the one subject she was still marginally interested in. But she couldn't get into it and instead of forcing herself to concentrate, she did the prep for dinner. Once she had chopped vegetables and had chicken marinating in the fridge, she went for a drive.

Charlotte finally had her restricted licence, which meant she could drive by herself. Without her restricted licence, she had been stuck relying on public transport to get anywhere, which could be downright dodgy after the sun went down.

Perhaps out of guilt at neglecting their remaining child, her parents had helped her to buy a little bomb to run around in, an ancient Toyota Corolla that wasn't flash, but did the job, got her to and from school each day, to the supermarket and the shops, to wherever she wanted to go. But never to the mall, Charlotte shuddered at the thought of becoming one of those girls who hung out at the mall doing nothing. No, she preferred to drive around the city and see if anything had changed, then up around the suburbs, up the hills, practising using her gears properly, because Augustus – her little Toyota Corolla – had a manual transmission. Her mother had said she should get an automatic, but she couldn't afford something newer, even with their help. After all, she was supposed to 'focus on her studies' and an after school or weekend job was forbidden. That meant the only money she had to put towards the car was what she had earned waitressing over the summer. Her father said a manual was a good idea, that would mean Charlotte would be able to drive any car. He also said that naming the car was ridiculous, cars were meant to take people from place to place, they weren't friends or family members and shouldn't have names. But Augustus was her friend, a friend who helped her escape from her lonely home life.

Charlotte wasn't doing well at school, but she kept that to herself in case her parents pinned the blame on Augustus and took him away from her. When she was at school, she was finding it hard to pay attention to what she was being taught. It wasn't just one subject she was finding difficult, it was all of them. And this difficulty focussing was starting to worry her. It was keeping her awake at night, and even after she did manage to fall asleep, she would wake early and worry about what she had not yet managed to learn to her satisfaction.

Driving was when she felt free, like there was something new and exciting in her life, and driving around the city was always an adventure. Roadworks were everywhere, and a street she might be able to go down one day would be blocked off the next or reduced to one lane. The traffic patterns were the only thing that changed about the city, there seemed to be little in the way of demolition any more. And although 2014 was supposed to be the year the actual rebuild really took off, not much was happening. There wasn't much in the way of buildings going up, just empty land occasionally interrupted by a stray building.

People were getting frustrated about their homes. Well, more frustrated, people had started getting seriously frustrated as far back as 2012, after the quakes had stopped and the insurers no longer had the excuse of ongoing seismic activity to prevent repairs and rebuilds from going ahead. There had been an article in *The Press* a few days earlier about how much trouble people were having getting their insurance claims settled. The article was talking about trouble with private insurers, and although Charlotte's mother talked a lot about how much better their situation would be if only they could get overcap, it sounded like people who were overcap were having just as much trouble as those still stuck with EQC. Charlotte was starting to see her mother's desire to finally get overcap as a fantasy she was clinging to, something to make her life bearable. What would happen when that bubble burst? Charlotte needed to get through the school year and go on to university next year, preferably one that was away from Christchurch, because she didn't want to be around when her mother discovered that dealing with their private insurer was just as bad as trying to deal with EQC.

Charlotte drove into the city and parked her car in Manchester Street. She walked up New Regent Street, past all the Spanish mission-style buildings that lined the street, their alternating blue, green, yellow pastels a splash of colour in the overcast city. The street was built in the 1930s and was shut to traffic. A tram line ran the length of the street, part of a loop around the city that was intended for tourists, it wasn't part of the city's public transport system. Charlotte couldn't remember ever going on the tram, it simply wasn't something used regularly by the people of Christchurch.

New Regent Street had been reopened about a year earlier, following repairs to all the buildings. Well, almost all of them. There was a cluster at the northern end of the street that was still fenced off. The businesses that had opened were struggling to survive, there just weren't enough people finding their way to New Regent Street. It was a few blocks away from the shipping container mall and even if tourists did venture into the Square to see the remains of the Anglican Cathedral, there was nothing to indicate the existence of New Regent Street's set of shops just another block away.

But New Regent Street wasn't Charlotte's destination. She was headed for the Town Hall a couple of blocks away, on the banks of the river. There was a lot of tension between the City Council and the Government over how to use money allocated to the Performing Arts Precinct, the part of the central city set aside for a new Court Theatre, a music centre and space for the Christchurch Symphony Orchestra. It was all meant to be based around the repaired Town Hall. Gerry Brownlee, the Minister for Earthquake Recovery, favoured demolishing the old Town Hall and replacing it with a new one, but the City Council had decided to repair the old one. Something about architectural significance, whatever that meant.

For Charlotte, what the Town Hall meant was time spent with her family. When she was about seven or eight, her grandmother had taken the family to the Christchurch Symphony Orchestra every few months. The symphony had regular concerts that were fun for kids and more traditional concerts, which Charlotte found boring at the time, but now that she was older, she wondered what it would be like to go again.

Charlotte walked past the front of the Town Hall, staying close to the barriers that separated it from the road. Through the dark glass, she could see into the foyer, where the floor looked gritty, and she wondered if it was plaster dust or dirt blown in from the outside. There had been a rumour in 2011 that the basement of the Town Hall was seething with rats, one of many rumours of rat infestations that had spread about the cordoned-off city in the months after the big quake.

It was sad to see it so destitute, fenced off, with nothing happening. It was never a pretty building, just slabs of pebbled concrete reaching into the sky with the occasional stretch of unpatterned concrete to break the monotony of it, but Charlotte loved the soft red seats, having one all to herself, waiting for the lights to go down and the music to start. What she treasured the most about those concerts was the trip home, drifting off to sleep in the back seat, between Nanny and Sean, while her parents chatted away in front, talking about the bits of the concert they liked the best. They were happy then, her family in its cosy pre-quake bubble. But now, her family was as wrecked and dismal as the Town Hall.

There had been accusations from the City Council that the Government had seized control of the development of the Performing Arts Precinct in order to make the rebuild look good in an election year. Whatever the case, the relationship between the council and the Government wasn't good. Why couldn't people who were supposedly adults pull themselves together and make decisions? Because they were just arguing about it, nothing was being done, the city was not getting a Town Hall back, leaving the Christchurch Symphony Orchestra without a true home.

Charlotte's home was no longer a true home, thanks to EQC. There was, EQC said, about $300,000 worth of damage to their house, which, Charlotte thought, should put them overcap and with their private insurer. But apportionment didn't work that way. Her parents had filed claims for four quakes, and EQC divided the estimated cost by four quakes, to come up with $75,000 worth of damage per quake, as though each quake had done an equal amount of damage. That kept them undercap and EQC insisted the house would be repaired as part of the Canterbury Home Repair Programme. Her parents weren't happy about that, there were too many rumours of bad repairs.

They had photos of the house, inside and out, after each of the major quakes, and her father was putting together this information to ask EQC to reconsider how the damage was apportioned, because the photos clearly showed that it was the February and June 2011 quakes that had done the most damage. But that assumed that they would listen to reason, and Charlotte didn't think for a moment that would be the case. It was just another bubble that would soon burst.

Breathless

September 2014

It was late on a Wednesday night and Alice was drifting off to sleep when there was a tap on her door. She drew herself up from the pull of sleep and shielded her eyes as light from the hallway fell through the doorway. It was Kevin.

'Your grandad's up at the hospital with Heather,' he said. 'She's having trouble breathing.'

Alice sat up, wide awake. 'Her heart?'

'He says he doesn't think so, but the doctors want to be sure,' Kevin said. He swept his hand over the top of his head, pushing his hair back and forth, then rubbed his face and scratched at the side of his mouth. 'But I think he's worried, he wouldn't have called otherwise.'

'She's at public?' Alice said, putting her feet onto the floor. 'Are you going to go up?'

Kevin shook his head. 'We're too sick.' Lindsay had come down with a cold the previous week and Kevin had quickly followed. Both had fever and chills and were having trouble sleeping from coughing.

'I'll go,' Alice said. Kevin nodded and shut the door, leaving Alice to find clothes to change into.

Jason had called and was going to the hospital as well, he said he would drop by and pick up Alice. Sonya, who had moved to Dunedin at the start of the year, texted Alice asking her to let her know what was going on. 'Ask about her troponin levels,' her text said. 'It's a marker for heart attacks.' Alice texted back saying she would let her know as soon as she knew anything.

Jason parked by the river and the two of them walked towards the hospital. It was strange being in the city at that time of night, it was so empty, the streets bare of cars and traffic lights going through their signals, directed at no one. Red lights high up in the sky flashed from the different cranes dotted all over the city. A cold wind blew from the east and Alice zipped her jacket all the way up to her chin and tucked her hands into the pockets.

Jason talked to the receptionist, who directed them through the security doors. A nurse took them through to the ward, a big open space only loosely partitioned off for patients. Equipment beeped from all directions. Heather was in a bed on the far side of the room, propped up, wires sticking out of the top of her hospital gown. Neil sat beside her, holding her hand. She was taking in shallow breaths, almost coughing, and Alice could see that she was scared, trying to control her breathing, which seemed to just be making the coughing worse.

Jason leaned in to kiss her on the forehead, followed by Alice. Neil told them the doctor thought she might be having a panic attack but wanted to run some tests, just to be sure.

'I'm so embarrassed,' Heather muttered, looking away from them. She was pale and tiny, as though the giant hospital bed was swallowing her.

'Better safe than sorry, love,' Neil said.

Jason pulled up two chairs and lined them up alongside Neil's chair so they could all sit with Heather.

'These things happen, Mum,' Jason said. 'And it's happened more since the quakes.'

Alice wasn't sure whether he meant panic attacks – which was what she thought this was – or heart attacks. Both had been on the increase since the quakes started. There was something called broken heart syndrome, where stress caused part of the heart to freeze up. Before the earthquakes started, Christchurch Hospital saw only a couple of cases a year, but after the quakes there were so many instances of it that a research group was formed. They had about fifty patients, mostly women.

Heather's problem, it turned out, was not a panic attack, nor was it broken heart syndrome. It was a heart attack, plain and simple. It was about four in the morning when the doctor came and told them that Heather's blood tests were showing the biochemical markers they expected to see in a heart attack, and she would be admitted to the hospital. Neil wanted to stay, but was looking pale and strained, so Heather, Jason and Alice insisted he go home and get some sleep. Jason wanted to get home to Carla and the baby and said he would drop Neil off and leave Alice with the keys to Neil's car so she could go home if she needed to.

Alice stayed with her grandmother, worn out but unable to sleep while waiting for Heather to be taken up to the ward. Alice stayed until Heather had been settled, then went home.

It was six o'clock, and both Lindsay and Kevin were already up, looking like they had hardly slept.

At eight, Alice called Gerald to say she wouldn't be in to work that day, then went to pick up Neil. He said he had managed to get some sleep, but he didn't look like it, his thin hair was standing up at the back and he was still wearing the clothes he had been wearing when he left the hospital.

The doctor had already been by the time they arrived on the ward, and Heather was being prepped for an angiogram to see how blocked her arteries were. There were quick hellos and then Neil went with Heather for her test. Alice sat down on a chair beside the empty bed and stared out onto the busy ward, watching people go past. Nurses and doctors walked rapidly, efficiently, while patients meandered, their slippered feet making soft scuffing noises on the linoleum.

Before long, Neil and Heather were back, looking grim. Heather had blocked arteries and needed a bypass, probably a double. She would stay in hospital until the surgery, which would be in a week or two.

The morning of Heather's surgery, Alice, Neil and Kevin went to pick up Grandma Bennett so she could see Heather before the surgery. Since Heather's admission, only Kevin had recovered from his cold, while Jason and Carla had come down with it. Alice was still free of it, but she was tired, sleeping at the drop of a hat, and she suspected all the nights at the hospital after long days at work were going to catch up with her before too long.

The sick members of the family could only call Heather to have awkward pre-surgery conversations. Alice listened to Heather's side of a couple of these conversations, but it annoyed her. Heather always said that what would be would be, trying to keep her voice cheery and light. Her grandmother could die, this might be the last time Alice saw her, what was she supposed to say? And how could she say it without Heather saying, 'What will be will be'?

At the end of another phone call, Alice felt the right words falling together in her head, but they abandoned her as soon as she opened her mouth and all she said was 'I love you' and 'I'll see you later'. It didn't seem like enough, especially after Heather held on to her so tightly when she said goodbye. Outside the room, Alice burst into tears that she tried to cover up as Neil, Kevin and Grandma Bennett came out.

'Right,' Neil said, his voice strained. 'What do we do to get through the rest of this day?' It was a pointless question as they had already agreed it would be a movie day around at Neil and Heather's, with a family dinner at the end of the day.

The family was having dinner, the adults at the dining table and Olivia and Jack in the lounge. Baby Eddie was sleeping in his carry cot in Neil and Heather's bedroom. The only conversation was coming from the coffee table, the kids chattering away. The adults were too anxious from the afternoon's wait to talk and were just pushing their food around their plates, taking the occasional uninterested bite. The phone rang and Neil leapt up from the table to answer it.

It was the surgeon. Heather was fine, the surgery had gone well, her heart was strong and there was no reason she shouldn't recover completely. One or two family members could visit her in recovery in a couple of hours.

It was easier to finish dinner after the phone call, and it was decided that Neil and Alice would go up to see Heather, while Kevin would take Grandma Bennett home.

Alice waited outside the ward while Neil went through. She was unable to focus her thoughts and paced mindlessly until Neil came out and she went in.

It was a large, open room with beds and monitoring equipment in a semi-circle, like something from a sci-fi movie. There was a lot of space between each bed and no curtains. Obviously being able to get to patients quickly was more important than privacy.

Heather seemed to be unconscious, so Alice hesitated to approach. She was awake, a nurse reassured her, but still feeling the effects of the sedative. Heather had tubes up her nose and down her throat, taped to her face to keep them in place. Alice reached out and stroked her hand, which caused Heather to crack open her eyes.

'Hi Grandma,' Alice said, trying not to cry. 'It went well, really well.'

Heather mumbled something unintelligible. Was she panicking?

'This is normal,' the nurse told her. 'She'll be wide awake in a few hours and tomorrow we'll have her walking the ward.'

'Really?' Alice said.

'Yes, really,' the nurse reassured her. 'She'll be as good as new in no time.'

Alice kissed her grandmother on the forehead and said goodbye.

The physical aspects of the surgery had gone well, and from what the specialist had said, Heather had every chance of recovering quickly. But how would she go at handling stress? Although the hospital preferred bypass patients to be cared for at home following surgery, Neil had discussed with the social worker how the situation with the house had contributed to Heather's stress. She would stay at a convalescence hospital near home for the first weeks of her recovery and only go home once she felt she could face it.

Neil and Kevin were going to repaint the inside of the house and fix up any quality issues they found along the way. 'We'll still pursue EQC over the foundation problems,' Neil said, 'but Heather needs to feel like her home is her home once again, and not some suffocating weight.'

Alice had been with Neil when he discussed Heather's recovery with the social worker. A lot of people in Christchurch were going through this sort of thing, the social worker said. The quakes and the drawn-out insurance process were proving too much.

Hearts were being broken all over the city, crushed by the weight of the so-called recovery.

Pulling the Wool

October 2014

Marjorie's greatest strength had always been her ability to get the measure of people. When such things started being talked about more openly in the 1980s and 1990s, she heard it said that watching and weighing of people was a skill often cultivated by the children of alcoholics, looking for certainty in an unstable environment. That was true of her, and that skill had seldom failed her over the years. As her physical strength ebbed, though, she noticed that her ability to read people was also in decline.

Tony had dropped by on his way home from work. He had invoices Marjorie needed to settle for work done on her properties. She flicked through them, checking the amounts and the work done against her mental list.

'Haven't we paid this one already?' Marjorie said, passing one invoice back to him. She hadn't paid it yet, she knew. She peered up at him, waiting to see how he would respond. The look on his face reminded her of a day when he had wanted another piece of her caramel slice. He was eight or nine then, and already had a tendency to lie, something he had learned from his father, Stan. Tony was growing into a copy of Stan, and although there was enough of a difference of age that his attempts at bullying his older sister were ineffective, he took every opportunity to intimidate his younger cousins. Marjorie had tried to encourage Andrew to stand up to him, but Andrew was small for his age, trusting, and still believed every tale Tony spun.

That day Suzanne had been clear, no more sweets, but once she had gone back out into the yard, Tony had crept back into the kitchen, unaware that Marjorie could hear him from the lounge, his feet pattering over the old farmhouse's wooden floorboards. She went through to the kitchen quietly, avoiding the creaky floorboards, and in her most imposing voice asked him what he was doing. She needed her imposing voice as her grandchildren grew older, she was always a petite woman and soon they would tower over her.

'Mum said I could have another piece,' he said, snapping his hand away from the plate, his eyes wide and expectant.

'I'm sure she didn't,' Marjorie said.

Tony glared at her, the expression on his face brightening as he saw something behind her.

'Let the boy have what he wants,' a loud voice said. It was Stan.

Marjorie turned to face him. 'His mother said no,' Marjorie said.

'No, she didn't!' Tony said.

Marjorie sighed, exasperated. Of course Stan would let him get away with the lie. In Stan's eyes, his son was a prince who could do whatever he wanted. He was doing the boy no favours.

'Go on,' Stan said to Tony, who grabbed a piece of the caramel slice and shoved it greedily into his mouth to tear off a bite, smearing chocolate icing and crumbs across his face. He ran off outside while Stan turned to face Marjorie.

'You do not tell my son what he can and cannot have,' he said, his voice cold.

'The boy lied,' Marjorie said. 'It's getting to be a very bad habit.'

'My boy is not a liar,' he said, turning and walking out of the house.

Prevented from acting to curb the boy's bad habits, Marjorie had only been able to observe, so she knew when he was hiding something. Usually.

Recently, Tony had been presenting invoices for work on his own properties, getting her to pay by saying it was work on her properties. She was embarrassed to realise, going through her paperwork, that he had been doing it for some months without her noticing.

Grown up Tony collected himself and flicked his eyes over the invoice. 'You're thinking of the Russell Street invoice,' he said. 'I can understand your confusion, the work's been similar. We paid that a few months ago.'

She remembered. This invoice she was questioning was legitimate, she simply wanted to see how he reacted when challenged. Hopefully, catching him off guard would serve as a warning, get him to stop, because she didn't want to have to make an issue of this in the family, not at this stage in her life. Her world would be reshaped into one driven by his attempts to defend his greed, and she would be robbed of her hard-won peace.

'You're right, of course,' she said quickly. A smile of relief passed over Tony's face, then concern.

'Are you getting enough rest, Grandmother?' he said, passing the invoice back to her. 'Maybe this is all too much? Should I be doing more with the finances?'

She shook her head, keeping her eyes down, an old woman ashamed at how dim she had become. 'I'm managing,' she said. 'I just need some rest.'

He paused, hesitated to express his next thought. 'Have you given some thought to what we talked about a few weeks ago?'

She hadn't, she told him. She started to stand up from her chair and then dropped back into it, feigning a tired spell.

'Are you all right?' Tony said, leaping up from his seat.

'I'll be fine,' she said. 'I just need a lie down.' She slowly pushed herself up from her chair, forcing Tony to move out of her way. He took the hint and said his goodbyes, while helping Marjorie over to the sofa.

The sound of his footsteps faded and she heard the engine of his ute start up then fade as it moved off along the street. She pushed herself up into a sitting position and tucked the woollen blanket around her legs. She had been feeling cold recently, even though it was well into spring. Outside, her yellow magnolia was flowering. Suzanne had given it to her before the earthquakes and this year it was heavy with blooms the colour of lemon curd. Dozens of flowers were in different stages, from just opening up to dropping their heavy petals into the soil below.

It was no secret in the family that once Marjorie died, her property portfolio was to be sold off and the proceeds split among her children. Tony had expressed no expectation of receiving a specific inheritance, but he had offered to act as executor. He knew her holdings, he said, he would know how to get the most out of each one. That was true, he had been managing her properties for a long time and knew exactly what each one was worth. But then he would be in a position to conceal how much of her money he had spent repairing his own properties.

Then there was the house, the one she had built after Bill died and was still living in now. She intended to die in this house, her safe place. Here she had been able to shape her world into what she wanted, free of anyone else's expectations or influence. If allowed free rein, Tony would demolish the house in the interests of maximising the value of her estate, destroy her garden and develop the land, she had no doubt about that. That he thought she didn't recognise his intentions only reinforced her view of him as cunning but ultimately not smart enough to harness the power of that cunning.

Gerald and Sylvia would take good care of this house. And if it weren't for Tony's indiscretions, she would trust Gerald to act as her executor. He would follow her instructions and make sure that his sisters received good returns on her property investments. But if Gerald noticed any irregularities in what had been spent on repairing some of those properties, he would 'do the right thing'. No, Andrew would be her executor. She hadn't yet asked him, but he had never been able to say no to his grandmother. He would follow her instructions and, if he noticed Tony's indiscretions, he would keep it quiet once he realised Tony was the cause. Andrew could always be trusted to look after the family's interests. He would keep her secret.

Marjorie woke to the sound of the front door opening and Alice saying hello. She was carrying three plastic shopping bags. That was right, Alice had arranged to do Marjorie's shopping after work that day. Alice used her foot to push the door closed behind her, then walked through to the kitchen.

The sky was darkening, with the sun disappearing behind the mountains in the west. Marjorie got up and walked slowly to the kitchen, following Alice, trying to shake the sleep from herself in order to appear lively. Alice saw through her efforts and asked if she was all right.

'Just a long day,' Marjorie said, sitting down at the dining table, watching Alice unpack the shopping bags. 'Did you have enough?' She was sure the list she had given Alice would be, at most, two bags' worth. She had given Alice cash for the shop and she was sure it wasn't near enough to cover what the girl was starting to unpack.

'Just over,' Alice said. 'But don't worry about it, my treat.'

Alice had bought a cooked chicken, which she unwrapped and started pulling apart, putting the pieces onto a plate. There was also fruit, including a pineapple and tamarillos. Marjorie loved tamarillos, but it was too cold to grow them in Christchurch. It was a bit late in the season for them, Alice must have paid a fortune for these.

'I don't need all these things, Alice,' Marjorie said. 'Really, you shouldn't have done this, take some of it home.'

But Alice insisted. 'You need to eat, you need to keep your strength up.'

'How much strength do you think I need for the time I have left?' She had shocked the girl, for which she was immediately sorry. 'I'm sorry,' she said. 'I know you think I will live forever.'

'No, of course not,' Alice said, flustered. 'But...'

Death was difficult for the young. It was such a far-off prospect that when it intruded on their view of the world, they were shocked. Alice had been acutely aware of the fragile nature of life from following the Royal Commission into the earthquakes, but the freshness of that pain had faded for her, only to re-emerge following the death of her maternal great-grandfather and the recent near-loss of her grandmother. She had trouble coping with the idea of losing someone, and she had been fussing over Marjorie too much in the last few months.

'Could you at least aim for one hundred?' Alice said.

Marjorie pushed herself up from the dining table and went into the kitchen. 'I'll try,' she said. 'Would you like some chicken?' She pulled two dinner plates from the cupboard.

'Love some,' Alice said, happy. 'I'll get some lettuce.'

Alice put a salad together from the garden and from some of the food she had bought, making up two plates for dinner. She chopped the pineapple and dressed it with chopped mint and sugar. 'For dessert,' she said, covering it and putting it in the refrigerator.

They sat down to their dinner, and after they had discussed Alice's day, they began talking about the EQC situation. There had been articles in *The Press* questioning whether foundation repairs were being carried out properly. That this was an issue was no shock to Marjorie, she had never had any illusions about people's honesty and could see how the managed repairs situation presented some people with irresistible opportunities. It was human nature, after all, to seek one's own advantage.

'The Government's ignoring it,' Alice said. The Ministry responsible for building standards, MBIE, had brought out a set of repair guidelines that had reduced the standard to which properties were repaired. 'I think that's what's happened with Mum and Kevin's repair,' Alice said. 'The insurance company was going to replace the foundations, but then the MBIE guidance came along and the insurance company decided to use it as an excuse to just patch instead. It's ripping people off and no one in authority is going to put a stop to it.'

'But fixing everyone's foundations properly would be very expensive, you can understand why these companies are trying to find a way to save money,' Marjorie said, playing devil's advocate, a role she thoroughly enjoyed when Alice was the other party. The girl was a good mix of compassion and intelligence. No, not girl, young woman, Marjorie reminded herself. Alice was no longer the naive girl Andrew had reintroduced her to four years ago, she was figuring out how the world works and how to find her way in it.

'But if there's a contract that says the higher standard applies, why is the Government coming along and saying no, ignore the insurance contract, just use this standard instead?' Alice said, countering. 'It shouldn't be possible for a legal contract to be set aside like that just because the Government decides it's going to be too expensive.'

'That's true,' Marjorie said.

'And if the people speaking out are right, and this is another leaky homes crisis on the horizon, someone needs to stop it before it gets there,' Alice said.

Clearly she had been talking to Gerald on the topic. He had seen the leaky homes crisis coming in the 1990s, when the Government changed the Building Act to allow the building industry more freedom to regulate itself. The leaky homes that had resulted had cost the country over $10 billion in rework and caused untold stress to people unfortunate enough to find themselves the owners of these poorly-built homes.

'It has all the hallmarks of that,' Marjorie said. 'The building industry is allowed to regulate itself, as is the insurance industry. There's too much room for corruption when there's a lot of money to be made and an industry is allowed to do as it pleases. Business can't be trusted to do the right thing when there's no one keeping an eye on them.'

'I just hope someone does something about this soon,' Alice said, that naive girl there once again. 'People are worn out and should be able to move on.'

'That's also true,' Marjorie said, 'but it's not going to happen. That requires that someone steps up and does the right thing, and people don't do the right thing. They do the right thing for themselves, that works in their own interests. And nowhere is that more true than in politics. Politicians don't admit they're wrong, and they don't accept blame.'

'Not all people,' Alice said, annoyed. She got up and retrieved the pineapple from the refrigerator and served up two bowls. 'Eat up.'

Marjorie sighed, half-heartedly, but spooned a piece of the fruit into her mouth. It was good, but she was starting to feel full and picked slowly.

'No, perhaps not all people are like that,' Marjorie said, pushing on to the point she wanted to make. 'But there's not enough people determined to do the right thing to stop this EQC and insurance business from dragging on for many, many years. I'll be long gone and you'll still be learning more about what's gone wrong with the Christchurch rebuild.'

Alice sighed and all signs of the naive girl were gone as she dropped her spoon into her half-empty bowl. She looked defeated. Marjorie remembered that feeling, in the weeks after Walter's death, when she felt unable to go on. But she had gone on, pulled herself back together.

'I hate thinking that this could still be going on in a year's time, or ten years' time, that my family could still be caught up in it,' Alice said, 'when it's gone on long enough already. But I know you're right. There's no signs of anyone coming clean on this debacle, and the Opposition isn't asking the right questions.'

'So what can you do?' Marjorie said.

Alice looked confused. 'But you've just said nothing can be done, that there is no point,' she said.

'I didn't say that,' Marjorie said. 'I'm saying this is how the world is, greed and self-interest are its primary driving forces. Don't deceive yourself into thinking that can be changed, because you will spend the rest of your life beating your head against a wall hoping for change.'

'What do I do then?' Alice said.

'Be who you choose to be, Alice,' Marjorie said. 'Don't let this world choose that for you.'

All the Signs of Stress

November 2014

Lindsay got up and went to the toilet. She was bleeding but she wasn't in any pain, so she didn't take anything, just made herself a coffee and went back to bed to read. Kevin was still asleep and she left him to it. He had spent too many nights lately going over insurance, and he deserved a decent lie in.

It wasn't until a few minutes after she was back in bed that she felt the cramping start and she considered getting up and getting some painkiller. It was cold, though, and the bed was warm so she stayed where she was. Soon, though, the cramping was worse and she moved to get out of bed and get some painkiller but instead sucked in her breath and fell back onto the bed. It was bad. She tried again, but it was too bad to move. She nudged Kevin, gently, to wake him slowly, but he was out to it. Alice. Alice would be up, Lindsay had heard her wandering through the house earlier. She texted Alice.

Alice brought her a strip of pills and a glass of water, then sat down on the edge of the bed. 'Are you going to see the doctor?' she asked, her voice quiet as Lindsay gulped down the pills.

Lindsay nodded. 'I thought last month was bad,' she said. She pushed her hands into her belly, trying to dull the pain until the pills kicked in. She had been having painful periods since before winter, when she had started worrying more and more about her mother's anxiety, together with the pressure from the insurance company to proceed with the repairs. Since Heather's heart attack, Lindsay's symptoms had been worse, and she needed painkillers constantly for the first days of her period.

'I'll get the wheat bag,' Alice said, and Lindsay just lay there waiting, waiting for the pills to work, waiting for the microwave to beep, waiting for the wheat bag. Kevin stirred as Alice returned with the wheat bag, mumbled was everything okay. Alice left the room and soon Lindsay heard the jug starting to boil. She told Kevin she didn't think she'd be of much use today, because of the pain, and soon Alice returned with a coffee for Kevin.

'Just rest, babe,' Kevin said. 'Me and Ali can get it done.'

They had a trailer and were finally going to do something about the backyard. They had neglected it since the quakes. They had made some efforts in that first summer to help the plants recover from being submerged in liquefaction silt, but water restrictions meant they gave up. It was hot that summer, and Lindsay would forget to water the yard on their allotted days, and she didn't want to be watering on other days. That's what water restrictions were about, recognising that there wasn't much water and cutting back so everyone got their fair share.

Sometimes Lindsay wondered whether it was worth playing fair, when it was so obvious others didn't see things the same way.

Once Kevin had finished his coffee, he got up and pulled on his dirty work clothes from the laundry basket. 'I'll put a load on later,' he said. He made her another coffee and brought her some toast, then kissed her forehead and disappeared out into the yard.

The painkillers took over an hour to kick in, and when Lindsay could move comfortably, she got up and sat through in the kitchen, watching the activity in the backyard. Kevin and Alice were taking down two trees, with the help of Olivia and Jack, who had been given the task of filling up the trailer with the smaller branches that were coming off the trees.

The pain was better the next day, and after dropping the kids at school, Lindsay went home and made herself breakfast. She sat at the dining table and took in the view out back. The trees Kevin and Alice had taken out had opened up the backyard and the kitchen was warmer from all the sunlight coming through. Lindsay remembered everything she liked about the house and the section when they first moved in, their plans to modernise it and raise their children there. Enough dreaming about the years they had lost to the delay in settling their claim, she had invoicing to do. Kevin was picking up more work, so there was one less thing to stress about.

Their claims manager had told them the a couple of weeks earlier that the consent application had been lodged. It would be maybe six weeks before they heard one way or another whether consent was granted. Lindsay hoped not. Getting consent would energise the insurance company, motivate them to proceed with their half-baked repair. They weren't even clear what the repair entailed, John Rutherford still hadn't answered their questions or come back to them when they pointed out parts of the scope of works that didn't make sense. They should ask Bitterman for the consent application, but that would involve contact, and both Lindsay and Kevin detested contact with the man. Kevin, especially, would descend into some dark place for the rest of any day in which he had contact with Bitterman. Lindsay had never seen him like that, not even when his father had been dying.

Lindsay was working at the laptop in the lounge when Charlotte knocked on the window. Lindsay glanced at the clock on the computer, it was nearly one o'clock and time for lunch. She opened up the back door to say hello to Charlotte and invite her in. But Charlotte just stood there, uncertain. Her face was red from trying not to cry, but in spite of her efforts a single tear rolled down her cheek.

'Is Alice home?' she asked, wiping the tear away.

'No, sweetie, she's at work,' Lindsay said.

Charlotte struggled to find words. 'I just thought,' she said. 'It's lunchtime, maybe she would come home for lunch.'

'You could...' Lindsay started.

'I didn't want to go by her work, because I don't want Uncle Gerald to see me.' She started crying properly, sniffing back tears.

'What's happened?' Lindsay said, reaching out to pull the girl towards her and into the house. 'Come in, have some lunch.'

'I'm not hungry,' Charlotte said, wiping tears away. 'But thanks.'

'Well I am, so you might as well have something, too, while you tell me what's wrong,' Lindsay said. She put the jug on, pulled a loaf of bread from the pantry and started getting ingredients from the fridge. 'Coffee or tea?'

'Milo?' Charlotte asked.

'Milo it is,' Lindsay said. She started buttering bread while waiting for Charlotte to start talking.

Charlotte pulled two cups from the pantry. 'You?' she asked.

'Coffee,' Lindsay said.

By the time the jug had boiled and Charlotte had made the drinks, Lindsay had finished making two sandwiches, which she plated and put on the dining table. Both sat down and Lindsay started eating while Charlotte sipped at her Milo.

'I've really messed up my exams,' Charlotte said at last.

'You had one this morning?' Lindsay said.

Charlotte nodded.

'I remember how stressful exams were,' Lindsay said. 'There were times I thought I had done really badly, but ended up doing okay.'

Charlotte shook her head. 'No, I know I've done really badly.'

'Okay then,' Lindsay said. 'What about your other subjects?'

'Pretty much the same,' Charlotte said, her eyes down, focussed on her sandwich. She picked it up and took a half-hearted bite, chewed slowly.

'What do you want to do about it?' Lindsay remembered the pressure she had felt over doing well on exams, that her whole future hung on getting it right. She felt sorry for Charlotte. From what Alice said, her family were the high expectations type, and with the brother doing well at university, there must be enormous pressure on Charlotte to follow in his footsteps.

'Not tell my mum and dad,' Charlotte said.

'I get that,' Lindsay said. 'But you never know, they might understand.'

Charlotte shook her head and started crying. 'No, they won't,' she said. 'They'll be disappointed and upset and on top of all the house stuff...' She sniffed hard through her blocked nose.

Lindsay reached for her hand and squeezed it. 'It's okay,' she said. 'What are you supposed to be doing this afternoon?'

'Studying for another exam,' Charlotte said.

'Well how about doing that here for the afternoon, Alice will be home at four-thirty and you can talk to her.'

Charlotte nodded. 'That would be good.'

'You have your stuff with you? So you can study?'

Charlotte nodded again. She looked like she was five years old.

'You can work here in the sun, and I'll be through in the lounge. You can come with me when I pick up the kids. How's that sound?'

'Great,' Charlotte said, giving a brief smile.

They tidied up from lunch and Lindsay settled back in front of the laptop while Charlotte spread her study materials out on the dining table. The afternoon passed quickly and after picking up the kids, Olivia and Jack took Charlotte out into the backyard to show her their handiwork while Lindsay started preparing dinner.

From the lounge, there was an alert from an email arriving. It was from their claims manager and said that consent for their repairs had been granted. The next step, he said, was getting a builder on site to tender for the work and start discussing temporary accommodation.

Lindsay felt a headache starting in her temple, the kind of headache that often turned into a migraine for her. This was another thing Lindsay was experiencing far too often lately, since around the time her painful periods had started. She needed to go to the doctor, but kept putting it off. Too much to do, especially now that they had to figure out some way to stop this dodgy repair from going ahead.

Stress was taking its toll on Lindsay, she recognised that. She needed to do something to stop it from getting to some sort of crisis point, as it had with her mother. Charlotte, it seemed, had reached her own crisis point, with the stress at home affecting her studies. Lindsay wondered what the long-term effects would be on Olivia and Jack. She and Kevin tried to shelter the children from what was going on with the house, but were they doing an effective job of that? Or were their children hiding their problems, the same way Charlotte had, it seemed, been hiding her problems from her own parents?

Soon the edges of her vision started to blur so she topped up her painkiller. Maybe it would head off the full-on migraine. She hoped so, she needed her thoughts in order when she and Kevin talked about the house that night, especially if Kevin retreated into a black mood. If that happened, she would leave him alone to work it out, as trying to talk through it only seemed to put more pressure on him. There was enough stress from dealing with the insurance company, it wasn't good to be a source of stress to one another.

Looking Out For You

December 2014

Although it was officially summer, Alice had a winter cold. She was blocked up and her throat felt like there was something sharp stuck partway down. She kept waking herself coughing in the night, and in the morning when Olivia and Jack were chattering away in the kitchen, Lindsay brought Alice a lemon and honey drink and a paracetamol.

'You want me to let Gerald know?' Lindsay said.

'Yes, please,' Alice whispered. It hurt to speak too loudly. She dragged herself up into a half-sitting position and sipped at the drink, which took the edge off the soreness in her throat. She soon fell back asleep.

When she woke she was damp with sweat, but she wasn't sure if it was because the room was so hot or because she had a fever. She opened the bedroom windows. Although it was hot outside, the fresh air was welcome. She got back into bed but threw the duvet off, using only the sheet.

She checked her phone. It was 11:30 and the house was quiet. She got up and walked through to the kitchen, where Lindsay was sitting at the laptop working. All the windows were open and a slight breeze was coming in. 'You feeling better?' she asked while continuing to focus on the screen.

'Not really,' Alice said. She pulled out a chair and flopped into it.

Lindsay stood up and came over to her, used the back of her hand to feel her forehead. 'You're warm,' Lindsay said, 'but that might be the day.' Alice moved to get up and get the thermometer but Lindsay told her to stay there, she would get it.

'Up just a bit,' Lindsay said a couple of minutes later. 'You hungry?'

'Just a little.'

Lindsay heated up some soup and Alice ate a couple of spoons of it while Lindsay kept going with her work. Once she finished, they could watch some DVDs, she said.

'Not *Treme*,' Alice said. *Treme* was a drama set in New Orleans after Hurricane Katrina. Wrecked buildings, emergency repairs, temporary accommodation, depopulation, insurance issues. It was all too depressing, and that was just the first episode. Maybe once she felt better she would try again. Lindsay had asked why she wanted to watch it, she said she wanted to understand how a city moved on, wanted to see that was possible, because it didn't feel like Christchurch was moving on.

'*Person of Interest* then?'

Alice nodded. But she fell asleep only a few minutes into the episode.

When she woke up, the television was off and Lindsay was stretched out on the other sofa, reading something on the laptop.

'Whatchya reading?' Alice asked.

'News stuff,' Lindsay said. 'That engineer's been expelled from IPENZ. You know, the EQC one doing the cursory inspections, ruling damage historic. Heaps of people complained about him. Expelled for three years. Hardly seems enough, really. Negligent and incompetent.'

'Really?' Alice said. 'I figured IPENZ would let him wriggle out of it somehow.'

'Here, have a read,' she stood up from the sofa and passed the laptop over to Alice. 'I'll get you a drink.'

'A coffee, thanks,' Alice said and started reading.

Lindsay came back with two drinks, set one down on the coffee table near Alice and sat back down. 'It's a good start,' she said, 'sounds like they'll be having to redo a lot of assessments.'

'He can appeal,' Alice said. 'They won't do anything till they've tried that one.' She sat up properly and passed the laptop back to Lindsay before starting to sip her drink, which wasn't a coffee. Lindsay didn't think sick people should have caffeine, whereas Alice thought sick people should have whatever they wanted as compensation for being sick. It was an argument that had run for many years, one that Alice knew she would likely never win.

'Sounds like the guy was just doing everything to minimise the cost of repairs rather than actually get the job done right,' Lindsay said. 'Engineers have a code of ethics, don't they?'

'Sure do,' Alice said. 'Google IPENZ and ethics, should be easy enough to find.'

'Yup, found it,' Lindsay said. 'Talks about moral obligations, duties and integrity. And working for the benefit of society.'

Alice scoffed. 'Yeah, that's what it's supposed to be about. Not like that first guy you had around, the one who was clearly just signing off on the project manager's opinion.'

'You have a low opinion of engineers these days,' Lindsay said. 'Not all of them are bad.'

'Yeah, well, I haven't seen much in the last four years that gives me confidence in these so-called professionals,' Alice said. 'Engineers, project managers, lawyers, builders, all of them, will dispense with their ethics as soon as there's lots of money to be made.'

'Do you include Gerald in that?' Lindsay said.

'No, of course not,' Alice said. 'He tries to do the right thing. Or seems to.'

'Just seems? You don't sound too sure.'

'It's not that, it's just there's this real grey area in what's ethical and what isn't. You have to look after your customers, but you also have to look after your own business, and your workers. Gerald's very interested in looking after his workers properly.'

'That's a good thing,' Lindsay said. 'It motivates him to manage the workload well, look after the business's reputation.'

'Yeah, he's not after making a quick buck,' Alice said. Lindsay was always reserved about any mention of Andrew's side of the family, except when it came to Gerald and Sylvia. She seemed to have a lot of time for them both, which made Alice wonder why she hadn't made the effort to ensure Alice stayed in touch with them. 'So you think Gerald and Sylvia are pretty okay?'

Lindsay thought about it for a moment. 'I do,' she said. 'They're good people. They try to be anyway, very thoughtful.'

'But you wouldn't say that about Andrew, would you?'

Lindsay gazed at her.

'I'm not sure what I would say about Andrew, I don't think I ever really knew him,' Lindsay said at last. 'When we got married, I thought he was pretty cool, always good for a laugh, and he was smart.'

'Those are good things, right?'

'Usually,' Lindsay said. 'The problem was that after you were born, he didn't really change.'

Alice didn't understand. Of course a person would change after their child was born, it's a big deal. Alice had changed when Olivia was born, and Olivia wasn't even her own child. Even before that, when Lindsay was pregnant and the baby moved around so much Alice could see Lindsay's belly moving, Alice understood that a new baby was something wonderful. Your world would change.

'I'm not saying he didn't love you,' Lindsay said, her voice softer. 'But he was immature and didn't really understand that his life needed to change. He was only able to continue with university because we had his parents' support. That was a good thing they did for us, and I was grateful, but Andrew just went on with his life, like he wasn't married, didn't have a child and responsibilities. I was at home with you, and Andrew was either at lectures or out with his mates. I felt like we didn't matter.'

'And it just went downhill from there?'

'I suppose you could say that,' Lindsay said. She looked at her watch. 'Time to pick up the kiddies. I'll make sure they leave you alone. Given it's so hot, I think I'll take them to the beach, wear them out there, rather than let them loose on you.'

Alice laughed, which hurt her throat, then flopped back onto the sofa. She heard Lindsay's car back down the driveway and got up and poured out what was left of the sickly lemon and honey drink. She made herself a coffee and went back into the lounge. She was thinking about what Lindsay had said. It was the first time Lindsay had really said anything about her marriage to Andrew.

Some members of Andrew's family were definitely interested in making a profit, and people didn't seem to be high on their priority list. Alice had gone along to a family barbecue. Andrew and his cousin Tony had been talking about buying up damaged houses, using their industry contacts to get the repairs done cheaply and then selling them on. When Alice asked later if that was ethical or moral or whatever, Andrew explained the difference between insurance policy entitlements and repair quality. 'A repair can meet the Building Code,' he said, 'but not meet the insurance policy. So someone who settles with their insurance company might want to take the money and move on, especially if the repair cost is high on a low-value house.'

'But that's not right,' Alice said. 'If they're given the money for repairs, they should go on repairs.'

'That's not what an insurance contract is about,' Andrew said. 'They're given the money to get them back into an equivalent house, not necessarily that exact house. Insurance is about protecting their financial position, not about protecting the house itself. And the way insurance companies are settling now, people can do that, go and buy another place and sell the damaged place as it is.'

Alice nodded. It kind of made sense. Then again, not really. 'Insurance thinking and common sense don't really go together, do they?'

'Insurance is a legal contract, and it goes by the law,' Andrew said.

'Not by common sense,' Alice said.

'That's not what I said.'

'Okay, but the damaged place, it could be repaired for a lot less than the settlement?'

'In a lot of cases. As when new is a pretty high standard, that's what the insurance companies are paying out, it can be a lot higher than a repair that just gets the place back into a reasonable state.'

'But are they paying that out?' Alice said. 'My grandparents, my other grandparents, have a neighbour who was paid out for repairs, he had a scope and everything, but when he went to get a builder sorted, he couldn't afford to fix the house. Even if he stuck to the scope.' She didn't say anything about what Lindsay and Kevin were dealing with, it was none of Andrew's business.

Andrew nodded. 'That does happen,' he said. 'People don't do their homework.'

'But what if the insurance company didn't help him to do his homework?' Alice said.

'That's not their job,' Andrew said.

'But they'll say, I don't know, they say we're looking out for you, like in the ads. It doesn't seem to be very looking out for you if they force the homeowner to settle for less than they know it will take to fix the place.'

'Insurance is not a social service, Alice,' Andrew said. 'It's a business.'

'Then they shouldn't be allowed to advertise themselves as though they're benign and generous.'

'Maybe they shouldn't,' Andrew said. 'But I think that's a conversation you need to have with the Commerce Commission.'

Later, Lindsay came home with Olivia and Jack and a hot chicken. Lindsay pulled it apart and made a salad while Olivia and Jack sat in the lounge with Alice telling her about their day and how there had been so many people at the beach. Jack had decided he wanted to be a lifeguard when he grew up, looking out for the people swimming and surfing.

It wasn't long before Alice went to bed. She had opened up the windows earlier to cool the room down, but it was still too hot to get to sleep quickly. She lay in bed looking out the window. Cloud was piled high in the classic nor'west arch.

Alice's bedroom was on the front of the house, facing the street. She remembered one night when she was still in high school. She saw lights flashing outside. She pulled back the drapes and a white four-wheel-drive was moving slowly down the street, purple and yellow lights flashing. It looked like a security patrol and seemed odd, a little frightening even. What were they looking for? Soon another ute came into view, same make, same flashing lights. But that second ute had a sign on it saying 'House Follows'. The next vehicle was a truck carrying the promised house, a weatherboard affair in what might be cream, though it was hard to tell so late at night. On the side facing Alice was a single long window. It wasn't exactly an exciting house. The house truck was followed by another four-wheel-drive. Three vehicles, looking out for the house and for the neighbourhood it was passing through. Now, though, it seemed no one was really looking out for the city's houses.

Alternatives

January 2015

Alice was going on a tramp with Andrew, Charlotte and two of her half-brothers. It was a five-day tramp in the Lewis Pass a couple of hours away from Christchurch, and on the drive up there, the two boys talked about the big earthquake the week before. They wondered if they would feel aftershocks and were excited at the possibility. The quake had been a 6.0 in magnitude, on the western side of the South Island, under the mountains near Arthur's Pass. It had been felt throughout much of the South Island, and Alice had been in the kitchen having breakfast when she felt the house sway, the ground swelling up under her feet. She knew it was from further away than those in the Christchurch sequence and she pushed away thoughts of panic at the possibility of people being harmed. If it was remote, it wouldn't be a problem.

'We're too far north to feel any aftershocks,' Charlotte had told them. 'Of course if the Alpine Fault goes, we'd definitely feel that.' She explained to them the risk the Alpine Fault posed to the whole South Island, that it was expected to generate a magnitude eight quake sometime in the next fifty years.

Both Liam and Hugo were in their teens now, but only Liam was old enough to have any solid memories of the months following the September quake. They had spent most of 2011 and 2012 away from Christchurch and so the trauma of ongoing aftershocks was something they knew about but didn't feel. Even nearly four years on, Alice still felt her heart race at a big aftershock, that moment of fear over what could be about to happen.

They left Andrew's truck in the carpark and started along the track, getting into the rhythm of putting one foot in front of the other. The first day was easy, just four hours walking that was mostly flat until a final climb up towards the first hut.

Alice had been pleased to get away from the atmosphere at home and up into the mountains. On the drive up to the track, she hadn't been able to get her family's situation out of her mind. It was in her head, churning away, over and over, what had happened to Lindsay and Kevin in the past year and what they faced in the year to come. What the insurance company was doing was wrong, going ahead with a repair that ignored damage anyone could see, over the objections of the homeowner, the person paying for the insurance policy.

After Christmas, Kevin had taken Olivia and Jack down to Timaru to stay with their cousins for a couple of weeks. Both Lindsay and Kevin said they should be having fun during the holidays and hanging around their stressed parents was in no way fun. They were right, it wasn't fun at all, but Alice thought sending the kids away was a bad idea. It gave Lindsay and Kevin an excuse not to make an effort. Instead, they were just at home, doing their own thing, reading or playing games on a tablet or the laptop, barely talking because they couldn't figure out what to do next about the house. Having the kids at home would have forced them to put the house situation to the back of their minds, eventually.

An hour into the walk, she dropped back to where Andrew was bringing up the rear and let the others get ahead.

'Can I ask you some legal stuff?' she said. Although Alice had talked to Andrew about insurance company behaviour in general, she had never mentioned Lindsay and Kevin's situation to him. But he might be aware of what was going on if his parents had told him, Alice regularly talked to Gerald and Sylvia about how worried she was about what would happen with the repair of the Bowen house.

'About insurance?' he said. He smiled to encourage her. Andrew was one of those people who enjoyed their work and enjoyed talking about it outside of work.

'About Mum and Kevin,' she said.

She explained, as briefly as she could. Lindsay and Kevin weren't happy about the proposed repair, it seemed to ignore quite a bit of damage. What they were especially unhappy about was that the original scope of works had said the whole foundation needed replacing, but now they were only going to do part of it. But the insurance company was insisting on going ahead with the repair to the point where they had received a building consent.

'How has the insurance company responded to their engineering report?' Andrew said.

'With more reports from their own engineers restating their belief that their own strategy meets the policy,' Alice said. 'Mum and Kevin don't know whether to get their engineer to fire back or if that's just pouring more money down the drain.'

'If the insurance company isn't going to pay attention to the first engineer's report, there's no point,' Andrew said. 'It sounds like they need a lawyer.'

'But Kevin doesn't want that,' Alice said. 'I think he thinks it sends the wrong message, that they want to sue.'

'It does send a message,' Andrew said. 'It says that they're serious about getting their policy honoured.'

They were walking side by side along the track, and Alice looked across at him. 'He says there are plenty of other alternatives to try before getting a lawyer,' she said. Andrew restrained a laugh. 'But I'm not convinced that there's anything effective.'

'No, there's nothing really,' Andrew said. 'If you go to the ombudsman, you need to go through all the insurance company's processes...'

'... and get a letter of deadlock,' Alice smiled at him. 'I know, I looked at that, but it seems to take a long time. And there have been so many things done the wrong way that it's hard to know where to start.'

'You could see about getting their file,' Andrew said. 'From the insurance company.'

'Can you do that?'

'Make a request under the Privacy Act, they're entitled to the information, it is about them. They don't need a lawyer to do that.'

Andrew told her to get Lindsay and Kevin to write the insurance company's privacy officer requesting their whole file. It might take a bit of time, he said, but they should be able to get more information than they already had.

'I'll do that,' Alice said. She was relieved at having another possibility. Maybe Lindsay would let her help out with getting through whatever information they received. They would have to act quickly if the insurance company was determined to get the repair underway. The claims manager had already said they would meet in the new year to discuss temporary accommodation.

But having an alternative that Lindsay and Kevin would find acceptable relieved Alice of her worries about what was happening at home. She was finally able to relax and start enjoying the scenery, being in the sun in the mountains, the air fresh and warm. Soon they started the climb up to the first hut and the effort wiped the last vestiges of her worries from her mind. At the top of the climb, they reached a plateau that stretched out towards the first hut, the mountains and the clear blue sky behind it. This was the point of tramping, escaping civilisation, feeling the weight of it all falling away.

On the Move

February 2015

Alice started running following the September quake, when she moved home. Then she had found it difficult to sleep at night, always waking to aftershocks. Or, on quiet nights, she had trouble falling asleep until there was an aftershock. Running wore her out, making it easier to fall asleep.

Although she had grown up in the neighbourhood, she saw it in a different way after the September quake. The constants were the lines of the hills, the jutting points, the hill that looked like it had a nipple, the crag of Castle Rock, when it still looked like a castle. She wished she had paid more attention when she was a child, so she could compare, assemble some sort of history of Alice then, Alice now, and construct some sort of journey, rather than the random wanderings that had made up her life so far.

She needed to make decisions. No one was putting pressure on her, no one but herself. At first, after she left university, Lindsay had tried to talk to her about why she had decided to do so. But it always felt like Lindsay was trying to talk her into going back, so Alice discouraged those conversations. She did talk to Gerald and Sylvia about it, they didn't really seem to judge one way or the other, but she could only get so far, she wasn't sure herself why she had decided to leave university, it was more a feeling that staying was no longer possible. Now, four years later, she had worked in a café, in the insurance industry and for her grandfather's building company. After all that, the only thing she knew for certain was that going back to university and continuing with her engineering degree was not an option.

She had started running more often over the summer. She had found it hard to go more than once a week the last couple of years, working full time, feeling so overwhelmed by the circumstances Lindsay and Kevin found themselves in and looking around, seeing other people in the family going through similar things. But Charlotte had pestered her to make the time and lately they were running three nights a week and Sunday mornings.

It was Sunday morning and Charlotte met Alice at the house. Charlotte had her restricted licence and was enjoying the freedom of being able to drive herself anywhere she wanted to go. Charlotte wanted to run the City to Surf, the annual walking and running event that started in the city and finished at the beach, but since the quake it had started in the southwest of the city, at Pioneer Stadium and ended at Ferrymead. So not the City to Surf, more like the Spreydon to Ferrymead, which just didn't sound right to Alice. She was holding out for the return of the real thing, she told Charlotte, she would see it as normality finally returning to the city. Charlotte didn't feel as strongly about doing the 'right' City to Surf as Alice did, but she understood why Alice did and said yes, they would do the first real City to Surf together, and until then, they would just keep practising.

Alice wondered why they hadn't taken the start of the event back to the city centre. The city was open, after all, and there was a lot happening, new buildings going up all the time, it was looking great. She thought it might be because of the state of the eastern suburbs. The City to Surf drew publicity, and having people running through suburbs that were still in a woeful state following the quake would reveal the lie of how well the rebuild was going.

For the morning, Alice and Charlotte had decided to go up the Rapaki Track and back down the Huntsbury Track. It was about ten kilometres all up, but there was a café at the bottom of the hill that did a pretty good brunch.

They left Charlotte's car near the café, then started towards the road that led up to the track, their warmup. The day was going to be hot, and they were starting early to avoid overheating.

At the gate that marked the start of the track, Alice and Charlotte began jogging up the hill. The day warmed up quicker than expected and when they reached the saddle that looked down onto the Avoca Valley and the estuary, they stopped to take a drink. They sprinted to the top of the track, where there was a slight breeze.

On the run down, Alice told Charlotte she had decided not to go back to finish her engineering degree.

'Everyone expects me to,' Alice said, 'but you're not surprised. Why not?'

'I don't know,' Charlotte said. 'I just can't see you doing it.'

'Well what can you see me doing?' Alice said. 'Because I could use some help in that area.'

'Why? Aren't you going to stay with Gerald?'

'For now,' Alice said. 'But I need to figure out something else, I don't think I want to be filing paperwork and making phone calls forever.'

'Well what then?'

'I don't know,' Alice said. 'What are you going to do?'

'Hey I still have a year of high school to go,' Charlotte said. 'I don't need to make up my mind for another year.' Charlotte had failed her exams the previous year and was repeating Year 13. But she had switched schools and was feeling much better about the change.

'If you don't make up your mind, there's always accounting!' Alice said. Charlotte's parents were both accountants.

'No way!' Charlotte said and sprinted ahead of Alice.

Alice caught up to her.

'You know what I hate about now?' Charlotte said.

'What do you mean by now?'

'Now. This part of my life,' Charlotte said. 'I hate that I have to make a decision about what I'll be doing for the rest of my life.'

'Do you?' Alice said. 'I mean, what says we can't change?'

Charlotte thought about that for a moment. 'You'd have to go back to university, get another degree.'

'That's what they tell you at school, but most of the people I've been working with have never been near university,' Alice said. Her friends from uni, from that first year, had finished their degrees and quite a few of them still didn't have reliable jobs. So not only were they doing the type of office work that Alice was doing, they were also paying off student loans. Although not going back to university in 2011 had almost been an accident, something she had only half decided, it had turned out better for her, because she knew, without a doubt, that engineering was not for her, and she had discovered that while earning money, not while accumulating student debt.

'I don't think my parents would be too happy if I didn't go to university,' Charlotte said.

'Do you want to go?'

'I don't know,' Charlotte said. 'I don't want to do commerce. That's what Mum and Dad want me to do.'

'What do you want to do?' Alice said.

Charlotte shrugged uncertainly, but there was a glimmer in her eyes. She had something in mind. 'I'm really enjoying my writing courses.'

'No one makes a living writing,' Alice said, and cringed inwardly. It was something her mother would say.

'I'd mix it with something else,' Charlotte said. 'I'm thinking of doing a science degree, then I'd go to Otago, they have a science communication course. Maybe do science journalism.'

'Wow, you're really serious about this,' Alice said, surprised at how well-formed Charlotte's plans were.

It was time Alice started formulating her own plan.

Cash Settling

March 2015

The Canterbury Home Repair Programme run by Fletcher EQR and the private insurers' project management organisations were, in theory, supposed to make the recovery process easier for the region's homeowners. The idea was that the insurer, or EQC in the case of the CHRP, would manage everything, get the job done and get people back into their homes as soon as possible. But as the months and years passed, it was clear to Alice that this strategy had been put in place to contain costs for the insurers and EQC, not to make their customers' lives better.

In February, Lindsay and Kevin's insurance company had sent a builder to tender for the repairs to the house. During the site visit, Kevin pointed out damage that the builder didn't seem to be aware of. They had heard nothing more about temporary accommodation, a conversation Lindsay said it would be difficult to have, about how this insurance company was going to force them to move out of their house and carry out repairs they didn't agree with.

Alice had broached the idea of making a Privacy Act request to the insurance company for their file, and Lindsay and Kevin had both agreed to go ahead with that. Now it was simply a matter of waiting for the information, which the insurance company had twenty working days to supply.

In March 2015, one insurer started telling its customers they would be cash settled, that there was no longer the option to be put into their managed repair programme. This was especially upsetting for those who had recently been made overcap, just holding on to hope that their dealings with their private insurer would be better than those with the EQC. For those people, being told they would be cash settled after all that time fighting EQC to get their houses assessed properly was a bitter conclusion to the whole sorry saga.

'That wouldn't be too bad,' Lindsay said, when Alice told her about the cash settlement news. It was the end of the day and Lindsay and Alice were making dinner. 'After so long, at least a cash payment is a way out of whatever hell their insurance company is putting them through.'

'Yes, but will people be paid enough to repair their house properly?' Alice said. The guy across the road was in that position, as was one of Neil and Heather's neighbours.

'But how do you fight that?' Lindsay said. 'If the insurance company says they're going to repair, you can't really stop them, if they say they're going to cash settle... No, you can't fight these companies, they're going to do what they want.'

'You know there's a Facebook group for TC3 people?' Alice said. Lindsay had agreed to apply for their file, but it was clear that she didn't think it would do any good. Alice hated that Lindsay had given up. She needed to know that they weren't the only ones struggling with bullying insurers.

'What does that have to do with anything?' Lindsay said. She left the room to go through to the lounge, where Olivia and Jack were arguing over something. 'Hey!' Alice heard her say, then, 'Play nicely or I'll have to come back through here again.' Alice cringed as Lindsay strode back through to the kitchen. There were only soft voices from the lounge.

'That was a bit harsh,' Alice said, keeping her voice soft. 'Especially holding the knife.'

Lindsay sighed and gave a half-hearted laugh. She brushed a strand of hair away from her face with the back of her hand. 'I'll make it up to them, make a pudding,' she said. 'Or...' She glanced over at Alice.

'I'll make a self-saucing pudding,' Alice said. 'Chocolate or caramel?'

'Chocolate,' Lindsay said. She preferred Alice's caramel pudding but knew Olivia and Jack liked the chocolate version best. 'I'll go and get some ice cream to go with it.'

Alice put a frying pan onto the stove, started to heat it up and added some oil.

'What do you mean a Facebook group?' Lindsay said. She tipped the vegetables she had chopped into two pots, one for carrots and broccoli, the other for potatoes.

'A bunch of TC3 people post stuff to the group,' Alice said. 'It's a closed group, so people who aren't part of it can't read the posts.' She put the chunks of beef and the sliced onion into the hot oil and stirred, then walked over to the dining table where she had left her bag when she arrived home. On her phone, she searched for the group and showed Lindsay its landing page. They couldn't see anything but the cover image and a list of members.

'You can see everyone who's in the group,' Lindsay said.

'Yeah, but you have to be a member to view the posts,' Alice said. 'It could be useful. Over two thousand members, probably going through a lot of the same things as you guys.'

Lindsay shook her head. 'No, people would be able to see that I'm a member. Can you do it?'

Alice thought about it for a moment. 'No,' she said. 'I used to work on claims, there might be Southern Response people in the group whose claim I've worked on.'

'That would be a problem?' Lindsay said.

'I don't know,' Alice said. 'Could be. But you should join.'

Lindsay thought about it for a moment. 'No,' she said. 'The insurance company could find out we were in it. And that might just make things worse.'

That seemed wrong to Alice, that Lindsay should worry about the insurance company disapproving of them trying to understand what was going on with their claim. But she had pushed Lindsay far enough, so left it alone. She would wait and see what came of the Privacy Act request, and maybe that would help Lindsay and Kevin decide what to do next.

'If you were offered a cash settlement, would you take it?' Alice asked, changing the subject. She stirred the meat and onions, which were starting to brown up.

'I still want a managed repair,' Lindsay said. 'I think. I don't want the hassle of dealing with foundation repairs, not when we've paid – and are still paying – insurance to take care of things like this.' Lindsay often pointed out that they were still paying full-price on insurance as though the house were undamaged while getting truly awful customer service.

'But?' Alice said.

'I don't know. A cash settlement would mean this is all over with, at last, and we could get those muppets out of our lives.'

'But you couldn't fix the house,' Alice said. 'Not with what they're offering now, based on the current scope of works.'

Lindsay shook her head. 'No, we couldn't,' she said. 'Not without taking on a bigger mortgage. And who knows where that would end? If the land's really bad, this place could be a bottomless pit.'

Alice nodded. No doubt that thought had crossed the minds of the insurers, which was why they were suddenly so keen on cash settling people. The cost of foundation repairs on TC3 land were enormous, especially if there were problems with the water table, which was the case for a lot of properties in eastern Christchurch.

For Lindsay and Kevin's house, there seemed to be little point in pouring all that money into what would be, in the best of circumstances, a renovated state house. But it wasn't her house, and she could only help them get as much information as they could to make a good decision. If a good decision was at all possible given the corner their insurance company had forced them into.

The Excess

April 2015

Heather could hear a bellbird. The sky was brightening at the start of the day and there, in among the usual dawn chorus of blackbirds and thrushes, was a bellbird. For all the years they had lived in their house near the river, Heather could remember only a few occasions where she heard the rich, melodic song of the native bellbird. In the last year, though, she heard them regularly, along with the occasional squeak of a fantail. She wondered if it was the residential red zone further north. Most of the houses had been cleared from the red zoned land and nature was taking over. If native birds were doing well there, maybe they were spreading to the still-inhabited suburbs. Christchurch was changing, in ways good and bad. Everything was changing.

Heather stepped out of the bed, moving slowly to avoid disturbing Neil, who was snoring softly. She put on her walking clothes and headed outside. She walked towards the front of the section, following the sound of the bellbird, searching for it in the trees along the fenceline that faced onto the road. There in the kowhai tree, the slender olive green bird gave a call far louder than seemed possible for such a small bird.

It was cold and soon the mornings would be bitter. Heather had been walking each morning since the start of the year, part of her programme for taking care of herself, building up her fitness following her bypass as well as looking after her mental health. So far it was working, but Heather didn't like being outdoors in the cold, it would take real effort to get up each morning, especially once the days started getting shorter. But that problem was a few weeks away, Heather would deal with it when it arrived rather than worrying about it now. She was trying to focus on dealing with the problems at hand, rather than becoming mired in what could go wrong.

She headed along the river towards the hills. Her usual walk was a zigzag through the neighbourhood's streets, but it was getting too easy, and today she would add a bit of hill in. Her first hill goal was

getting over a slight rise without having to stop for breath, and
once she had achieved that, she would try some of the hill walks up
the valley, towards the Summit Road.

She had to pause once to catch her breath while going up the
hill. At the top, she stopped to look out down Port Hills Road
towards the Heathcote Valley. She and Neil had planned to spend
their retirement there, in a house built to their design, on the
section they still owned but could do nothing with. It was a dead
dream, Heather accepted that now, and she was starting to think
what they might do once it was all over, the issues with the house,
the problem of the section. Her mother was nearly ninety and in the
months since Heather's father had died, was looking it. Her house
was too big for her, and Neil and Heather had talked about having
her move in with them. Heather didn't like the idea, as having her
move in then out again, should re-repairs ever take place, would be
too stressful. But none of Heather's sisters seemed inclined to want
to take their mother in, and none of them was near enough to be of
help on a regular basis.

There had been good news a few weeks ago, which helped
Heather's mood enormously. The Supreme Court had decided in
favour of the Quake Outcasts, the group of red zone landowners
who had taken the Government to court over its fifty percent offers
on bare land. The half-price offers had not been lawfully made, the
court ruled, and the Government had been directed to reconsider
their decisions and make new offers. Although it wasn't over yet,
the end was in sight, Neil and Heather would finally receive an offer
on their red zoned section, one that would be more than half of the
2007 value. The Supreme Court had given the Government no
leeway for further excuses. It had taken such a long time, over
eighteen months since the High Court had first ruled against the
Government, but finally seeing a just decision gave Heather hope.

Their house re-repairs still weren't sorted, but there was
progress there, even though it didn't directly relate to their house.
The Ministry responsible for building standards had been asked to
survey houses where the owners had questioned the quality of
foundation repairs. The results had been disturbing. Of the fourteen
houses inspected, there was only one that actually met the required
standards. Another hundred houses would be inspected to see if the
survey findings were part of a wider problem. Once the results of
that survey were complete, Neil and Heather had decided they
would approach EQC once again.

Heather turned and walked back down the hill. She heard a
runner's footsteps coming up behind her and slowing down. It was

Alice, who stopped. Her hair was pulled back in a ponytail, but some curls had come loose and hung around her sweaty face. She leaned forward, resting her hands on her knees, gasping for breath.

'Gran,' she managed to gasp out.

'Good run?'

Alice nodded, gulping in breath. 'Really pushed myself.'

'Don't let me stop you,' Heather said.

'No, I've done enough, I'll walk with you.'

They headed back towards Neil and Heather's house.

'Got some stuff from the insurance company,' Alice said. 'They said it'll be a few more weeks before they can give us the full file.' Alice had helped Lindsay write a request to the insurance company for their file, and they had been waiting over a month for the information to start coming through.

'Anything useful?'

'All stuff we already have,' Alice said. 'But I was thinking, with the building consent, shouldn't Mum and Kevin have a copy of that?'

'Well, yes,' Heather said. 'The consent was applied for on their behalf. Don't they have it?'

'No,' Alice shook her head. 'The claims manager was supposed to let them see it before making the application but he never did. And things were so hectic then.' She paused.

Heather nodded. She had still been recovering from her surgery at the time. She hated that she had been such a burden, had so worried everyone in her family. She wouldn't let that happen again.

'Call the council,' Heather said. 'They shouldn't have any problem giving you a copy. Well, giving Lindsay one anyway.'

'Good idea,' Alice said. 'Did you hear EQC's started sending out excess invoices?'

'Yes, I did hear that,' Heather said. Late in 2014, EQC had announced it would start billing for repairs done under the CHRP. That struck people as strange, almost like an afterthought, as insurance companies usually expected an excess to be paid before work commenced. The EQC official line was that it was deliberate policy. It didn't make sense.

'You know the EQC excess is different from your standard insurance excess?' Alice said. 'It's a percentage of the repair value. So when you get your excess bill, you'll know how much they spent on repairs. No reason you can't ask them for a breakdown of costs.'

Heather stopped and turned to Alice. 'We could ask,' she said, choosing her words carefully. 'But we can't make them give us the information.'

'Yes, you can,' Alice said. 'Like we're doing with the insurance company, there's an Official Information Act that applies to government departments. So when your invoice comes in, you can Oh-Eye-A your scope of works...'

'... and that would give us a way forward with our complaint,' Heather finished. She was excited. For the first time in her life, she was anticipating the receipt of a bill.

Telegraph Road

May 2015

Long, straight roads run for tens of kilometres across the Canterbury Plains, and it was one of these roads that Charlotte and Alice were driving along at one hundred kilometres an hour. Grassy paddocks and evergreen windbreaks passed by at a blur, the road stretching off to the distant mountains. Freedom to Charlotte was driving these straight roads far away from her everyday life, and if she had enough money, she would just get in her car and drive, fill the tank once again and keep driving.

'It's the next intersection,' Alice said, glancing up from her phone. 'Another four kays.'

The road they were on was Telegraph Road and in September 2010, the Greendale fault had ripped across Telegraph Road and shunted the northern half of the road east and the southern half west. The shift had been half the width of the road, so the centreline from each side of the road ran into the road edge markings. Charlotte had been reading about the geology of the earthquake sequence for the writing class she was taking at her new high school and she wanted to see what the fault looked like nearly five years after the big quake. She had a GoPro attached to the dashboard to record the trip.

She slowed the car as they reached the next intersection. There was no one else on the road so they crept along, looking for signs of the big quake.

Charlotte pulled the car off the road and turned off the engine. She removed the GoPro from the dashboard and stepped out of the car. Alice followed. 'This must be it,' Charlotte said, panning the camera across the road ahead of her. There was a slight kink in the road, but what was more noticeable was the displacement of the irrigation ditch running along one side of the road.

'Seems to be,' Alice said, checking the spot they had stopped at against the information on her phone. 'You wouldn't know unless you were looking for it.'

Charlotte switched off the GoPro and pulled her phone from her pocket. They walked around, looking for further signs of the rupture, but there was only the irrigation ditch and the resurfacing that had been carried out to rejoin the broken road. Charlotte took some photos, just as reminders for when she was writing her blog post.

'You can understand why it's so hard for scientists to figure out what's going on in the landscape,' Charlotte said, turning to Alice. 'It's just four years since this, and there's barely any sign.'

Alice turned and walked back to the car, pulling her jacket tight about her. 'We need to get going,' she said, 'if we're going to get back in time.'

Charlotte followed and they drove back into the city, to Alice's house. They needed to be back in time to watch the demolition of the police station. Explosives had been set and the demolition was going to be streamed online. Alice's little brother wanted to go into the city to see the demolition, but authorities were recommending that people stay away, there could be flying debris.

They reached the Bowen house just in time. Everyone was in the lounge watching the live stream on the television. Charlotte and Alice fell into beanchairs in front of the roaring fire.

The police station was fifteen storeys high and had been stripped before the demolition, so the sky behind it was visible through the levels, bright as the sun dropped behind the mountains. There was a flash of light and the sound of an explosion, and white awnings that had been draped around the building's lower levels puffed out. Then... nothing. There was another bang and then suddenly the lower level crumpled and the building fell forward, smashing into the ground. Dust billowed away from the site. Jack and Kevin whooped, punching the air, while Lindsay rolled her eyes.

Charlotte knew the Bowens were having problems with their insurance company, but in spite of that, they seemed to be able to take a break and have fun with their children. Charlotte's parents, though, found it difficult to take a break. For four years, they had been consumed over the future of their house and getting out of the clutches of the EQC. When Charlotte had failed her exams at the end of the previous year, it finally became clear to them that something had to change. When she said she wanted to switch schools, they had agreed without argument.

The new school had made a difference, broken Charlotte out of the cycle of different shades of misery she had been stuck in. She had dropped economics and accounting, continued with maths, geography and science and taken up journalism and creative writing. She could finally see a future beyond living in a broken home with broken parents who couldn't agree on how to escape the mess they found themselves in. For one thing, Charlotte hoped she could leave home and board with her grandmother next year, which would be her first year at university.

Kevin and Lindsay went off to get fish and chips, leaving Charlotte and Alice with the little kids. Charlotte reviewed her footage of Telegraph Road, which Olivia and Jack wanted to see.

'Does something happen?' Jack said.

'No, nothing happens,' Charlotte said, 'but that's the point.'

Jack's face scrunched up. He was confused. Charlotte smiled, that was fair enough. She was trying to capture something that was barely there, something that was fading from the New Zealand consciousness.

Telegraph Road looked straight when you just drove along not paying attention. It was only when you slowed down and had a close look that you could see the kink in the road, the evidence that a large quake had broken the surface here. The road had been realigned, part of it replaced so that it appeared to run straight across the plains. That approach worked for a road, but the same strategy was being applied to the city. Christchurch's houses had been damaged by the earthquakes and the repair strategy was to patch them up to look good, to ignore the underlying damage.

The Government was doing too good a job realigning public perceptions of the rebuild. Outside of Christchurch, New Zealanders were forgetting about the earthquakes. There was very little in the media – television, radio, news websites – about people in Christchurch who were struggling to get their insurance claims settled. The local newspaper had regular stories about the challenges people were facing with getting EQC and insurance companies to deal with their claims properly, and there were more stories each month of repairs that had been badly carried out and had to be redone. But these were written off by authorities as anomalies, not the true picture of what was happening in the city.

One TV programme had regularly covered insurance and EQC issues, but it had just been cancelled. Campbell Live had been on TV five nights a week for a decade. It had been in the background of Charlotte's life ever since she could remember. Her parents always watched TV3 news and kept the television on TV3 to watch Campbell Live at seven o'clock. They thought Campbell Live had been cancelled because the presenter, John Campbell, spent so much time highlighting the difficulties people in Christchurch were having getting their claims sorted. Charlotte thought it had been cancelled because John Campbell was old, like her parents. The television station he was working for wanted to target people in their twenties and was clogging up the channel with reality shows, what they thought their target market wanted to see. No one Charlotte knew was interested in them, not Sean, not Alice or any of the kids at school.

On the fourth anniversary of the September quake, Campbell Live had filled a school hall with people who had unresolved claims. Since then, the only time Charlotte could remember the Christchurch situation being covered on the national news was on the anniversary of the February quake. That had just been politicians talking about how well the rebuild was going. That was the picture the rest of New Zealand was being fed, and it wasn't true.

Did the people of New Zealand want to know what was really going on in Christchurch? How people were being bullied into accepting insurance settlements that would leave them without enough money to fix their house properly? From what Alice said, that was what was going to happen to the Bowens. And unless Charlotte's parents could find someone at EQC who was going to take their claim seriously, it was going to happen to them, too.

Discovery

June 2015

Lindsay collected the envelope from the letterbox on her way out at lunchtime. It was from the insurance company and contained a USB stick and a brief cover letter. She resisted the urge to go back inside and review its contents, there were simply too many other things to do that day. Lindsay was having lunch with her grandmother, and then they would do Grandma Bennett's weekly shop. Then there were the kids to pick up from school, Kevin's billing to get finished, dinner to make. So many things to do, and starting to wade through the insurance company's files would have to wait.

That night, once the kids were off to bed, Lindsay finally started to examine the contents of the USB drive. What had arrived wasn't a neatly put together summary of their house, the damage to it and the process of determining how to repair it in a manner that met their insurer's obligation to them. It was a collection of files divided into two categories: files from their insurer and files from the insurer's PMO, both in roughly chronological order. Figuring out what was going on with their claim was going to be like untangling a ball of wool. She would have to leave it until the next day. But first, before going to bed, she would have a flick through the largest file.

It was over five hundred pages long, but it looked like the place to start. It was a record of all the PMO's communications, so included emails to Lindsay and Kevin, to contractors and to the insurance company. There was so much repeated material! Lindsay swore to always trim her own emails back to the bare minimum, no content nested to three, four, five, six levels.

At midnight, Kevin prompted her to stop for the day, to come to bed, but she was just starting to get her head around it all, so kept going.

Two hours later, her eyes were heavy and she was starting to have trouble following the threads of information, and not just because of the convoluted nature of the conversations. It was time to go to bed.

In the bedroom, she left the light off and changed into her pyjamas, trying not to wake Kevin. He needed to function the next day, but once she had taken the kids to school, she could crash if she needed to. She hoped not, though, she was noticing some inconsistencies between the dates she and Kevin were aware of things happening and when they had actually happened for the insurance company and the PMO.

The next morning, Alice offered to take the kids to school on her way to work, leaving Lindsay to start trawling through the information without needing to change out of her pyjamas. She could have taken the kids to school in her pyjamas, after all, she didn't really need to get out of the car. But no, she wouldn't let her life degenerate to that point. Pyjamas were home-time clothes only. That had been a difficult enough lesson to teach Olivia her first year of school without running the risk of provoking accusations of hypocrisy now that she was creeping up on those teenage years.

One interesting finding: the engineering report the insurance company had commissioned had been available several weeks before it had been passed on to Kevin and Lindsay. There were nearly a dozen emails over the course of the following month from a woman at the PMO asking their claims manager whether Kevin and Lindsay had responded and could she do anything to help speed up the process. Then one morning Bitterman finally emailed them the report. A couple of hours later, he emailed the woman at the PMO saying Kevin and Lindsay hadn't responded, that they were being uncommunicative. Lindsay wasn't sure whether to laugh or punch something. She couldn't wait to tell Kevin, but didn't want to burden him with all this stuff while he was trying to focus on work, so she called her mother instead.

'That's a bit off,' Heather said, and Lindsay was irritated that she didn't at least raise her voice. 'What will it mean for your claim?'

'It doesn't mean anything, really,' Lindsay said. 'But it does confirm what we suspected about him playing games.'

'At best, he was putting off doing something. Or maybe he forgot,' Heather said. 'And he's covering up his own mistake.'

'So he's not a jerk?' Lindsay said. Why was her mother trying to explain away this guy's behaviour?

'No, I'm not saying that,' Heather said, 'because clearly he is. But a deceptive game-playing claims manager is different from an incompetent one. You'll need to decide which one he is, because it will affect how you handle him.'

'When did you get so devious?' Lindsay said. She had never thought of her mother as a calculating person. If anything, she was too often willing to believe the best of people.

'Oh, darling,' Heather said. 'Since we were fletchered.'

Lindsay was silent for a moment. 'It's not fair that dealing with these people is making us turn into the type of people we've never wanted to be.'

'I think of it this way,' Heather said. 'We're the same people we were, we've just had to develop a few more skills to deal with the nasty people of this world.'

'I suppose.'

'You don't sound convinced,' Heather said. Lindsay heard the concern in her mother's voice.

'I don't think I'll know until this is all over, and right now, looking at this massive stream of incompetence and deception, I don't feel like it's ever going to be over.'

'I wish I could tell you when it will be finished,' Heather said. 'I wish I knew.'

'I know,' Lindsay said. 'Until then, I feel like I'm wading through a sewer.'

Two hours later, she hit gold. It was in the form of instructions to the geotechnical engineering company who had been engaged to carry out an investigation, which was then cancelled. The first set of instructions stated that their foundation was to be completely replaced. It wasn't a spectacular find, but it backed up the first scope of works Kevin and Lindsay had received. It showed that the repair strategy of lifting the house and replacing its foundation hadn't been something only briefly considered, as this was a full six months after the scope of works had been written.

The real piece of gold was the instructions Rutherford gave to the geotechnical engineer shortly before the offer of cash settlement had been made in 2013. Because Lindsay and Kevin had asked why the geotechnical investigation had been cancelled, Rutherford had instructed the engineer to complete the investigation, and part of his instructions included a new repair strategy, one Lindsay and Kevin hadn't seen before. It showed that parts of the foundation should be replaced along the eastern and western sides of the house. But when Rutherford submitted the building consent application to the City Council in 2014, he included diagrams showing that the foundation along the northern end of the house would be replaced. This 2014 strategy ignored several metres of crumbling foundation, including the part that Kevin had pointed out to the tendering builder earlier in the year.

If you combined the two repair strategies, the one submitted to the City Council and the one Rutherford had drawn up in 2013, nearly all the visible damage was covered and over three-quarters of the ring beam would be replaced. But Rutherford hadn't done that. Instead, he had submitted to the council a sub-standard repair strategy that completely ignored damage he had previously identified. The man was incompetent, and it was provable.

'What do we do about it?' Kevin said. Lindsay's happiness had been evident when Kevin arrived at home, but they agreed to postpone discussion of the files until after the children were in bed. Now, she, Kevin and Alice were gathered around the dining table, examining the files she had printed out during the day.

'Complain,' Alice said. She put the two repair strategy diagrams side-by-side. 'Point out the issues, ask for a new project manager and a review of your file.'

'What about Bitterman?' Lindsay said. 'We could say he's not acting in our interests, not the way he withholds information from us.'

'What information?' Kevin said. 'There's only one engineering report and the consent application he withheld from us. That we can prove.'

Lindsay started to object. She didn't want to deal with Bitterman any more.

'If he's effective,' Alice said, 'from the insurance company's point of view, then complaining about him and Rutherford runs the risk of making it seem you're not happy with any aspect of the claim.'

Kevin was nodding.

Reluctantly, Lindsay nodded her agreement. They were right, better the devil they knew. Lindsay would focus her efforts on drafting a complaint about Rutherford that they would then submit to someone higher up in the insurance company than Bitterman.

Lindsay lay awake that night, her mind racing. They could actually make progress, if they had a different project manager, if they could show Rutherford's assessment of their house had been substandard. She had hope, but she didn't want to let that hope grow. It had been nearly four years since their claim was passed over to their insurance company, and after all that time, hope was a dangerous thing.

Duty of Care

July 2015

It had taken a couple of weeks to sift through all the information from the privacy request and assemble the complaint, but Alice thought it had been worth it. It gave Lindsay and Kevin hope of a way forward other than agreeing to what their instincts told them was a substandard repair. Letting the insurance company going ahead with their planned patch job was, Alice could see, inviting disaster. There were too many reports of badly repaired houses and too little acknowledgement of the problem on the part of authorities and insurers to feel comfortable letting the repair go ahead.

Neil and Heather had received their excess bill, which indicated that the value of their repairs had been close to $80,000. That seemed outrageous for what appeared to be a cosmetic cover-up of their structural damage, so they put in an Official Information Request for their scope of works. If they were going to pay the $800 excess, they said in their request, they wanted to know exactly what they were paying for. By the end of August, Neil and Heather should have the information they had asked for.

Earlier in the year, the Ministry responsible for building standards had surveyed fourteen houses at the request of the homeowners. Thirteen of the houses had substandard foundation repairs, and that finding was concerning enough for the Ministry to carry out another survey, of a larger pool of houses. The houses included were those who had repairs carried out without a building consent and where the homeowner hadn't raised any concerns over the quality of repairs. The point was to get a feel for the overall quality of repairs in Canterbury, and put to rest rumours of widespread shoddy repairs.

A claimants group said the survey was a whitewash. Through the Official Information Act, the group had obtained information on how the houses were selected for the survey. EQC and insurers had put together a list of just over two thousand properties that fit the survey's criteria. EQC and insurers then chose three hundred of those properties to pass on to the Ministry for consideration. Of the three hundred, the Ministry selected about a hundred to survey. It looked like EQC and insurers had been able to hand pick what properties were surveyed, which could skew the survey results in their favour and, therefore, mask the true extent of repair quality issues.

Alice hoped the survey wasn't biased, because authorities finally acknowledging that there were issues with the quality of repairs would make her grandparents' lives easier. And she didn't like to think about building a future in a city where tens of thousands of houses harboured hidden earthquake damage. The problems would linger for years, if not decades, coming to light only when people sold their houses and prospective owners commissioned a building inspection. Or worse, when there was another big quake and insurers started declining claims on the basis of 'historic' damage from the 2010 earthquake sequence. No, repairs had to be done right now, not swept under the carpet and left to be someone else's problem. Her generation's problem.

The most troubling aspect of the so-called recovery in the past few months was the efforts being made by EQC to overturn IPENZ's findings against the EQC engineer who had been found negligent and incompetent at the end of 2014. The engineer was appealing the findings to what was called the Chartered Professional Engineers Council. CPEC, apparently, could overrule IPENZ's finding, and the EQC's chief executive had written to the CPEC chairman saying how difficult it would be for EQC if the findings of negligence and incompetence were allowed to stand. CPEC had been asked to 'correct the problems with the decisions' and to consider that the findings, if not overturned, had serious consequences for both EQC and insurance companies, which meant money. EQC was, in effect, asking CPEC to transfer the risk away from EQC and insurance companies to homeowners. EQC's cost-cutting mindset was forcing substandard repairs on the homeowners of Christchurch, and EQC was asking CPEC to let them do it.

Alice was stunned when, at the end of July, IPENZ's findings of negligence and incompetence against the EQC engineer were overturned. That decision said, in effect, that engineers had no duty of care towards anyone other than their client. An engineer's client could frame the brief in a way that sidestepped the engineering code of ethics and, in effect, left people like insurance company customers hanging out to dry.

CPEC's decision could still be appealed, if IPENZ decided to take the issue to the District Court. Hopefully they would, because if they didn't, it was the engineering equivalent of the medical profession discarding the Hippocratic Oath.

'What does this mean for us?' Lindsay asked as Alice tried to explain the implications of the decision. 'We aren't with EQC, so it shouldn't affect us, right?' Alice could hear the worry in her voice, the hope that was quickly fading. They had talked recently about getting their engineer to review the repair strategy in light of what they had uncovered about the work proposed. Cost was holding them back, and uncertainty about whether it would actually help them.

'It means you shouldn't rely on the engineering profession to help you,' Alice said. She felt drained, all her optimism about the city's future poured out, taking with it all her energy. She had no hope left to try and bolster up her mother. 'The insurer will just brief their engineers to get the answer they want, and then when you get another opinion, they'll just counter it and you'll have to spend more money. They have deeper pockets than you do, they can go on like that forever.'

'So our engineer's report is just wasted money, then, isn't it?'

'No, it's not,' Alice said, shaking her head. 'It tells you the state of the house and what needs to be done to repair it. It's black and white, he's taken into consideration the state of the house when it was new and proposed a repair to bring it back to that state, which is what your insurance policy says you're entitled to.'

'But we can't get there, we can't make them do what their policy says they're supposed to do. I'd be happy right now if they'd just put it back to how it was on the 3rd of September 2010, and we're not even close to that.'

'The only way is a lawyer,' Alice said. 'That's the only way to get your policy honoured now.'

Lindsay nodded slowly, colour draining from her face. She sat down on the sofa beside Alice. 'That could be thousands. Tens of thousands. We can't afford that.'

'But if it's the difference between a repair that renders your house worthless and locks you into, well, what Grandma and Grandad are having to go through, isn't it worth it?'

'I don't know,' Lindsay said, her words slow. She turned to look at Alice. 'Our only real hope now is that our complaint gets heard, isn't it?'

Alice nodded, reluctantly. She leaned into her mother and put her arm around her. There was nothing else she could do.

Part IV: Bleak City

Look on my works, ye Mighty, and despair!
— Percy Bysshe Shelley, Ozymandias

Laying the Blame

August 2015

Any lingering doubts Alice had over abandoning her engineering degree had evaporated when IPENZ decided not to appeal CPEC's decision in favour of the EQC engineer. IPENZ had folded its cards and walked away from the game, and minimising costs had won over doing what was right. What was the point of having a code of ethics if a client could brief an engineer in such a way that the duty of care an engineer had towards the public was reasoned away?

Why was no one standing up for Christchurch claimants? The EQC had lobbied CPEC to overturn IPENZ's decision so that the EQC wouldn't face a huge bill for having to revisit repairs. The opposition parties were nowhere to be seen, raising no questions over why the state-owned insurer was behaving the way it was. It seemed that legal action was the only way to get a claim sorted out fairly, which meant the fair settlement of a claim was out of reach for many people. It wasn't right.

Even legal action was a limited option. The District Court heard disputes under $200,000 in value, which left only the High Court for anyone arguing with an insurer over a patch job versus a proper repair. Unfortunately, taking a case to the High Court was very expensive.

Because legal action looked like the only way forward for Lindsay and Kevin, Alice had looked at the list of High Court cases related to insurance issues that was published every few months. There was a separate earthquake court, meant to fast track homeowners through the court system, but when Alice read through the list, she wondered what being on the slow track looked like, since so many of the cases listed had been filed over two years ago. Judicial decisions were available on a government website, but hardly any had been handed down relating to earthquake claims. Were claimants giving up? That was definitely a possibility, Alice could see how exhausting the whole process was for her family. Or were insurers settling? If they were settling out of court, that meant they were largely in the wrong, because if they were right, why wouldn't they let it get through the courts and set a precedent that would help them get all the other claims off their books? Alice was pretty sure the Bowens' insurer was in the wrong, but how far would they have to go to prove it? Alice would do everything she could to help them pull all that information together.

There were a lot of cases against Southern Response on the list, and Alice was happy she no longer worked there. Everyone she had worked with was gone now, and every single one of them was happier for it, including Kylie, who had decided to go to polytech and do a construction management course. That was a surprising twist, Kylie had been so miserable over the whole rebuild towards the end of her time with Southern Response that Alice had expected her to leave Christchurch, if not the country. But there had been good things about the job, Kylie said, and she was interested in the building process, and if anything, her time at Southern Response had taught her how it shouldn't be done.

Had Alice known about the coming earthquakes before starting university, she would have done law. She would be finished by now and able to help Lindsay and Kevin. But she wasn't psychic, and in reality, she would simply be a year ahead of Sean, who was mired in running errands for more experienced lawyers and would be for another four years at least. That was how the profession worked, Andrew had told her, newly graduated lawyers didn't become really useful until they had a good five years' experience under their belts. How depressing.

There had been good news for Neil and Heather when the Government finally made new offers on red zoned bare land. They were offering 100 percent of the 2007 value. It was enough for Neil and Heather to decide to take the offer and move on. There were still the house repairs to deal with, but being able to put the section behind them seemed to lift a weight off Heather's mind. They had waited so long for some resolution on their section, and it seemed the justice system had finally worked for someone in the city.

Neil and Heather had received their scope of works for their house, and although all the costs were blacked out, the scope had enough detail to help them make some progress with the EQC. Their foundation specialist's report detailed the work that had been carried out on the foundations and it didn't match what the scope of work said, so Neil called EQC and started pointing out the differences. The woman he spoke to had asked him to send in the information and they would have a look. Heather had taken that as another brush off, that once again no action would result. Neil insisted that the woman had been interested to hear that repairs on the scope hadn't been carried out.

The findings of the survey of foundation repairs were finally released in the middle of August, and although EQC and insurers had been able to hand pick the properties that were surveyed by the Ministry, the results were overwhelmingly bad. Clearly Neil and Heather weren't the only ones who had substandard repairs. Out of the 101 properties surveyed, a third of the repairs did not meet the required standard and would have to be redone. Even worse, three of the houses initially selected for the survey had been excluded because there had been no structural repairs, although the insurer had supplied documentation indicating that structural repairs had been carried out.

That sounded like fraud on the part of the contractors to Alice, but she was wondering lately if she was becoming paranoid from seeing what her family were going through with insurance companies and EQC. She ran the idea past Gerald.

'There could be a reasonable explanation for it,' Gerald said. 'But fraud seems the most likely.'

'What would be a reasonable explanation?' she said.

'Mix up with the paperwork,' Gerald said. 'You know what it's like, trying to keep track of everything going on.'

'Surely, though, if you're invoicing for work, you're going to make sure that work has actually been done,' Alice said. She would be mortified to send a bill for work that hadn't been carried out, and it would be queried right away by the customer. She pointed that out to Gerald.

'Yes, but the rebuild isn't a normal business environment,' he said. 'This Fletchers and EQC setup has cultivated secrecy in the name of commercial sensitivity, and there's probably some contractors who've tried their luck. Bound to be.'

'My grandparents were never allowed to see their scope,' Alice said. 'We've only recently seen a copy through the Official Information Act, and all the costs are blacked out.'

Gerald shook his head sadly. 'There's no need for that, not at this point when the work's been done. And there's no excuse for not telling customers exactly what work will be carried out, even if you do conceal the costs.'

'This is bad news for Christchurch, isn't it?' Alice said.

'Yes it is,' Gerald said. 'And you can guarantee that instead of figuring out how to put things right, EQC will be trying desperately to figure out how to shift the blame.'

EQC and the Earthquake Recovery Minister did quickly snap into damage control mode. EQC would be reviewing thousands of structural underfloor repairs, the Minister said on the six o'clock news that night. Kevin predicted that blame would be laid at the feet of builders. 'It's the bad scopes and the tight-arsed budgets that've led to this,' he said, stabbing his finger towards the television. 'Not to mention everyone and his dog clipping the ticket instead of keeping track of what's going on.'

The next morning there was a follow-up article on *The Press* website in which the Minister said the Government would be going after the cowboy builders. That made Kevin laugh, and Alice could see he was trying not to be smug too early in the morning. 'Just let it out,' she told him. 'You might hurt yourself if you don't.'

Kevin was right, Gerald told her at work that day, it wasn't the fault of builders at all. 'Yes, people should speak up if they're being asked to do substandard work,' he said. 'But the current climate hasn't made it easy for them. If they don't keep in good with the big players, there's no work for them.'

In the days that followed, the finger-pointing continued. At a media conference, the chief of Fletcher Construction, the parent company of Fletcher EQR, said that the builders responsible for the substandard repairs would be asked to fix them at their own cost. If having the builder back on site wasn't acceptable to the homeowner or if the builder had gone back to Ireland, then Fletchers would foot the bill. The Ireland comment unleashed the fury of Irish people living in New Zealand and even rated a mention in the Irish Times.

Builders were speaking up, but were doing so anonymously through the pages of the Christchurch Press. Workers who pointed out bad workmanship or warned homeowners that damage was being missed without the protection of anonymity had found that work dried up.

A drop in building quality was a known problem following natural disasters around the world. EQC had stated, after the first earthquake, that they recognised the potential for this problem and that getting Fletcher EQR to run the Canterbury Home Repair Programme would prevent it. What they had put in place was a regime that encouraged corner cutting and sloppy scoping and discouraged any builders who tried to do the job right. No, the builders weren't to blame.

Risk Transfer

September 2015

It had been five years since the first earthquake, and Lindsay could barely remember what their lives had been like before then. She remembered the months after the September quake clearly, the exhilaration over the city having dodged the bullet of The Big One because the quake occurred in the middle of the night. There hadn't been crowds of people in the city to be killed or injured by the unreinforced masonry buildings that had been shaken apart by the force of the quake. They were lucky, she remembered people saying, herself included. That sense of blessedness had been crushed on the day of the February quake and still, four and a half years on, people were trying to make sense of what had happened to their city. Only now it wasn't just the natural disaster they were trying to make sense of. There was also the bureaucratic disaster.

Just before the five-year anniversary of the September quake, the Government announced that the timeframe for making earthquake-prone buildings safe would be halved. It was good news, the legislation the Government was working on had initially allowed building owners fifteen years to make buildings safe, but now it would be seven-and-a-half years. The tightening of this requirement to make buildings safe was largely the result of the efforts of the only survivor of the Number 3 Sumner bus.

In the February quake, a building had collapsed onto the bus as it drove along Colombo Street, killing eight of the nine people on board. When the legislation was announced and the timeframe was stated as fifteen years, the lone survivor lobbied for a shorter timeframe. The risk to life of buildings with unattached parapets, chimneys and gables was simply too great to allow such a long timeframe, she argued.

A parapet had fallen onto the Number 3 bus because the parapet was not attached to the building. It was known before the February quake that the building had been damaged in the earlier earthquakes, and the survivor pointed out that it wasn't the earthquake that had killed the others on the bus, but the building and the fact that its parapet hadn't been made safe. It was, she said, a failing on the part of the building owner, for not making the building safe, and on the part of the City Council for not ensuring the building was made safe or, at the very least, fenced off.

She had made an interesting argument about the transfer of risk. As far as unreinforced masonry buildings were concerned, not enacting legislation requiring them to be fixed transferred the risk from the owner, who would need to spend money to upgrade a building, to the public. The most direct risk was to lives, those lost and those damaged. Indirect costs were in the form of taxes people paid to fund the public health system. Her own recovery from the building collapse had so far cost the public over $100,000. There had been several thousand injured in the quake, and who knew what the cost of that was, not just in terms of public money, but also in the effects on their lives and those of their family and friends. The risk had, indeed, been transferred from a handful of building owners onto the people of Christchurch.

Lindsay remembered going into the city after the September quake, resuming normal life by going to the places that had survived September, she and Kevin doing their part to keep businesses going. They had taken their lives in their hands, she realised. All the buildings she was in the habit of visiting in the old city were unreinforced masonry, the kind that had killed forty people in the February quake, and all the places she used to walk around were near unreinforced masonry buildings. Had that quake occurred while Lindsay and Kevin were in the city, Olivia and Jack could be orphans, raised by Lindsay's parents, or by Alice.

A risk Lindsay was no longer willing to take was with her mental health, and she had recently caved in and started taking an antidepressant. She had gone to her doctor about her painful periods earlier in the year, and he sent her for a pelvic scan, which showed nothing to worry about. When she went back to the doctor to follow up, he told her having more pain wasn't unusual as menopause neared. Menopause! She certainly hadn't been thinking about menopause before the quakes started. He prescribed stronger painkillers and asked her about stress, which resulted in her bursting into tears and telling him all about the house and the insurance. She was so embarrassed. He had given her a prescription for an antidepressant that she had no intention of taking, but when she told Kevin about the conversation, he had gone quiet.

'You think I need an antidepressant?' she said, offended.

He stared off into the corner of the bedroom, past her. 'There are times when you're not yourself lately,' he said. 'You're too emotional...'

'Why? Because I'm angry about the house? Because you're just as angry as I am and I don't see you describing yourself as "too emotional".'

'No, not just angry, Lin,' Kevin said. He looked tired, too tired to argue, and she could see this was something he had been thinking about for some time. 'You remember all those months when we saw your mother falling apart...'

'So I'm falling apart now?'

'No, you're not there yet,' he said. 'But I can see the start of it.'

Lindsay turned and stalked out of the bedroom, hearing Kevin give a long sigh. He didn't follow, and she stayed up late that night, waiting until she could hear him snoring before she finally went to bed.

They said nothing about the conversation the next morning, but throughout that day, she thought about what he had said. He was right. Her moods had been all over the place during winter, and possibly longer. When they had uncovered their project manager's incompetence, Lindsay had tried not to have hope. But hope had taken root, tucked away in a secret part of her heart. When the insurance company hadn't acknowledged the substance of their complaint and left Rutherford assigned to their claim, that hope had splintered, stabbing her to the heart. The only thing they had to hang on to was the insurance company's request that they point out the flaws in the scope of works. Kevin had since done exactly that, going through the scope and highlighting every single thing he could spot that was wrong. His report on the scope of works had gone to ten pages, and although he had sent it on to the insurance company weeks ago, they were still waiting to hear something. Anything. The wait had been messing too much with Lindsay's head, she realised. She needed to fill the prescription and start taking better care of her mental health. Staying away from insurance paperwork might be a good idea.

That had been two months ago, and the first thing she had noticed about the antidepressant was that she slept better. Too well, at times, when she would nap in the afternoon after texting her mother to pick up the kids from school. She needed that sleep, she told herself, and she wouldn't be on the drug forever.

Lindsay's moods were more even lately, and she was starting to feel like her old self again. This was good, she wanted her old self making the major decisions she and Kevin faced, rather than her emotional self, second- and third-guessing all their decisions, overwhelmed by what-ifs and all the risks that would be heaped on them if their insurance company got its way.

The financial risk of the rebuild was being transferred from EQC and insurers to the homeowners of Christchurch. Lindsay could see that happening in their own lives.

The riskiest thing that could happen to Lindsay and Kevin was letting the repairs go ahead based on the current patch-it-up scope and then the repairs going badly as more and more damage was discovered. If the repairs ran on long enough, Lindsay and Kevin's temporary accommodation allowance would run out, leaving them paying mortgage and rent while waiting to move back in. Even if the managed repair went well, Lindsay and Kevin would need to keep a very close eye on every step of the process, which would be as exhausting, if not more so, than the last five years. That was transferring the risk onto their children, who needed their parents' attention. Olivia would be a teenager and at high school in another three years. Lindsay had missed out on too much with all her children because of having to deal with the insurance issues.

Most insurance companies were cash settling rather than managing repairs. Although Lindsay and Kevin's insurance company had made them a cash offer in 2013, it hadn't been enough to repair the house. And when Lindsay and Kevin hired their own engineer, the insurance company has taken that cash offer off the table, insisting they would get a managed repair. But now it seemed all the insurance companies wanted claims off their books and cash settling was the trend. Managing repairs was proving too expensive when homeowners insisted they be done properly, and cash settling was a way of transferring the risk of unknowns back to the homeowner.

If there was an offer, would they take it? The offer, especially based on the current scope, wouldn't give them enough money to fix the house properly.

The EQC and insurance companies had been paid money to take on the risk of a natural disaster, yet their efforts weren't going into meeting their obligations. Instead, they were furiously shovelling the risk back on to the people of Christchurch.

To the Grave

October 2015

Suzanne had thought she would feel relief once Marjorie was gone, but instead her mother's death had emptied everything from her heart and filled it with grief. She struggled to understand this, it had always been a contentious relationship, fraught with conflicting emotions for Suzanne. Her efforts to please her mother had never met with her love, or even the merest sign of approval.

It had happened quickly. Yes, Marjorie had been growing more and more frail, shrinking into an even tinier woman than she had been for all her adult life. At ninety-four years of age, it was obvious she wouldn't be around much longer. But it had still been a shock to find her asleep in her favourite chair, eyes closed, facing out towards the stream. Well, asleep was what Suzanne had thought at first.

Andrew had been appointed Marjorie's executor, which had provoked some mumbling from Suzanne's younger sisters at the funeral, and from Tony, Suzanne's son. No doubt there would be some arguments over Marjorie's estate, but Suzanne didn't care. They were arguing about things and things didn't matter, not when someone who had been there Suzanne's entire life was now gone. Strangely, though, Marjorie's will had been clear that it should be Suzanne who went through her personal effects and determined who they should go to. She had been entrusted with something deeply personal, and that trust was very unlike her mother.

Suzanne had never thought of herself as a bad daughter. She was never rebellious when she was young, even though she had been young in the sixties, when rebelliousness was all the rage. As she grew older, she did her best to look after her mother, especially once her father had died. But it was never enough, nothing she had done ever gained Marjorie's approval.

In the years since the quakes started, Marjorie had changed, almost softened, but it had been towards Andrew's daughter, Alice. Suzanne had been jealous, she realised that now, and had judged the girl harshly as a result. Suzanne was her mother's daughter after all, judging and weighing people, determining whether or not they deserved a role in her life. How could it be that a girl who had nothing to do with the Moorhouses for so long could gain Marjorie's attention when Suzanne, who had been attentive and dutiful for so many years, could not?

She found a photo in her mother's belongings, tucked into the back of an old book. It was of a girl and a young soldier and the back of the photo said 'Kathy and Walter, October 1940'. They looked happy. The girl looked like Alice. She must have been Marjorie's sister or cousin.

The family knew little of Marjorie's background. The only family member she had ever mentioned by name was her brother Edward, who had died in the war when he was only nineteen years old. All the others had died in the Blitz, but Suzanne knew no names. Marjorie's views of the world had been shaped by the war, that was clear, even if Suzanne was never party to the details. Marjorie had always refused to vote, saying governments only served themselves, as evidenced by the way they sent young men off to war, killing them outright or sending them home so damaged they would have been better off dead. They couldn't make her vote and be part of their game, choosing one side over the other.

It had seemed to be the loss of her brother that had grieved her the most, even in light of the loss of the rest of her family. Yet here was this other young soldier with someone who was clearly related, the first glimpse Suzanne ever had of someone on Marjorie's side of the family.

She went to see Gerald at his office and showed him the photo.

'She does look like Alice,' he agreed, smiling. 'Such a lovely girl, I wonder who she was.' He turned the photo over and read the inscription. 'It's Mother,' he said.

'What?'

'The girl is Mother. Mother was Marjorie Kathleen. She must've been known by her middle name at some stage.'

'So who was Walter? I thought she said her brother was Edward.'

He shook his head. 'I don't know. You know more than I do if you know her brother's name.'

'You knew her middle name,' Suzanne pointed out. 'I can't believe I've never known that.'

The door opened and Alice said hello, came in and sat down in front of her computer. Gerald passed the photo to her.

'This is Mother as a girl,' Gerald said. Suzanne and Gerald peered intently at Alice to see if she would notice the resemblance.

'Looks like Charlotte,' Alice said and passed the photo back to Gerald.

'Suppose it does, too,' Gerald said, examining the photo once again. 'We think she looks like you.'

Alice put her hand out and Gerald handed the photo back. 'Suppose so,' she said. 'Charlotte and I get asked if we're sisters.'

'Look at the inscription,' Suzanne said, and explained about Marjorie's middle name.

'Who's Walter?' Alice asked.

'Her brother, we think,' Gerald said.

'No, that was Edward,' Alice said. 'She talked about how much she missed him.'

Suzanne felt that twinge of jealousy once again, that Marjorie had discussed these things with Alice. But she pushed that feeling to the back of her mind, her curiosity winning over her jealousy. 'Is there any way we can find out for certain?'

Alice turned to her computer, brought up a webpage and typed in a search. 'A friend of Mum's has done some family history. Apparently a lot of British birth records are available online for free. What was her maiden name?'

'Reeves,' Suzanne and Gerald said at the same time. They only knew that because there was a Reeves Road in the neighbourhood they had grown up in.

Both of them stood behind Alice, watching what she was doing. She entered a search for Marjorie for births over the space of two years. There weren't many results, and they each listed the mother's maiden name. 'From that we can search for her brothers and sisters,' Alice said. She changed the search and the results showed five children: Marjorie, the oldest, then Edward, Gwendoline, Charles and Elizabeth.

'No Walter,' Suzanne said. 'So who was Walter?'

'No idea,' Alice said, shaking her head.

Gerald was studying the photo and looked for a moment like something had occurred to him. He glanced over at Suzanne.

'What?' Suzanne asked.

'Nothing,' he said. He passed the photo back to Suzanne. 'You keep it,' he said. 'She wanted you to have it.'

He was right. Marjorie had been specific about who should go through her belongings. 'But why wouldn't she tell us if she was going to leave this behind for us?'

'Of course she never told us, that would be revealing a weakness,' Gerald said.

It made sense. 'But why leave the photo?'

He thought for a moment before answering. 'Because she couldn't bear to destroy it.'

It made no sense. She studied the photo once again and glanced up at Alice, who looked as happy as this young girl had been so many decades ago. That was what Marjorie had seen in Alice, a reflection of her former self, of someone she had left behind.

She asked Alice to email her the address for the website they were looking at, maybe she could find out more about Marjorie, about her parents or even her grandparents.

At home, Suzanne placed the photo up against her bedside lamp. She wanted to have it close. Marjorie had kept it all those years, and Marjorie had specified in her will that it was Suzanne who should go through her personal effects.

That night Suzanne couldn't get to sleep from turning over in her mind all the questions she had about her mother's family. She turned on the light and examined the photo again.

In the lounge she turned on her computer and visited the website Alice had sent her the address for. This time, she searched only for her mother, under her maiden name, from her date of birth right up until the end of the war. Listed were her birth, as expected, and two marriages. Two. The first was in the second quarter of 1940, to Walter Finlay. Finlay was Gerald's middle name. Suzanne had always wondered where it came from, and now she knew. The photo was from a few months after her mother had married Walter Finlay, who must have died in the war. Marjorie had kept the photo for all these years because she had loved him and couldn't bear to let him go.

The webpage was still open, listing Marjorie's birth and her two marriages. Suzanne had always thought her parents were married in 1942, but the website said 1943, in the second quarter. Suzanne herself was born in September 1943, the end of the third quarter. Fancy that, all those years Marjorie and Bill had celebrated the wrong anniversary, saying they had been married a year longer to avoid admitting to a wartime indiscretion. Suzanne laughed, and then stopped short.

She searched but could find no deaths for a Walter Finlay that made sense, given what she knew. It seemed the free database didn't list deaths in combat, so she googled for lists of British soldiers who died in combat. There was a war graves website, and she entered her search terms.

There were only a handful of results, so she quickly found what she was looking for. Walter Finlay, age 23, husband of Kathy, died on the 16th of February 1943, seven months before Suzanne was born. Had Marjorie ever told Bill? She had married him under her maiden name, so possibly not. But there was no way of knowing now, and it no longer mattered.

Suzanne felt relief. Her mother's attitude had never been about her, it had been about what she had lost and couldn't bear living without.

Options

November 2015

Neil and Heather had finally received the payout for their red zoned section in October. A month later, Heather still wondered if she was going to wake up from this cruel dream and realise they still owned a piece of land they could do nothing with. The first few mornings, she checked their bank account while making cups of tea, admiring the substantial jump in their balance and wondering what they could do with it. On the fifth day, she resisted the temptation, to keep doing so would be obsessive and she needed to keep an eye on her tendency to obsessive thinking.

There was so much to obsess about in Christchurch, that had been clear when Heather and Lindsay went to a public meeting about the quality of repairs. The meeting had been held in the temporary cardboard cathedral and was packed. It was good for both of them to see that others were affected by the same issues they were experiencing, it wasn't just their family being especially unlucky. Lindsay said afterwards that she felt less alone seeing all those people in the cathedral.

The Government was ignoring the shoddy repairs fiasco, and the Opposition seemed unable, or unwilling, to really dig into the issues that the foundation repairs survey had raised. A petition had been launched calling for a Royal Commission into earthquake repairs, something the Government insisted there was no need for. But a full third of the surveyed repairs failing was serious, anyone with a brain could see that. Instead, the Government was saying it wasn't many houses and all could be fixed up for under $1000 each.

That was rubbish. Going by the shoddy repairs to their own house and what had been proposed for Lindsay and Kevin's house, it was likely that issues with foundation repairs were because the work hadn't been scoped properly. If the scope of works was wrong, that was the fault of EQC and Fletchers, not the builder, and it should be up to EQC to carry the cost of re-repairs.

There had also been a court action filed by a group of one hundred EQC claimants. They claimed EQC wasn't meeting its legal obligations to homeowners and wanted the court to make declarations regarding the standard repairs needed to meet. Other issues the group wanted the court to decide were whether EQC was cash settling claims in a manner that left homeowners with enough money to carry out repairs and whether homeowners should be expected to pay for upgrades to electrical wiring and other wear and tear exposed because earthquake repairs were being carried out.

Heather knew the group was in for a long wait before its members finally had options, the way Neil and Heather did now. After all, the Quake Outcasts group action Neil and Heather had benefited from had first been heard in the High Court in 2013, and that had only recently been resolved.

Neil and Heather had agreed they wouldn't discuss options until the new year, to let them enjoy a holiday without the worry of the section hanging over them. Heather intended to stick to that promise. It held for two weeks, and it was Neil who broke it, bringing home a copy of the real estate book along with the shopping after work one day.

Heather didn't want to be interested. 'We can't afford anything in here,' she said, 'not without selling this place, and while the repairs aren't sorted...'

'We could,' Neil said, 'if we rented it out.'

'Only if the bank says yes,' Heather said.

'If I sold the business, the bank would say yes,' Neil said. 'They'd even say yes if we just rented this place out, on the strength of our history with them, and given the business is doing so well.' That had been one thing that hadn't gone wrong due to the earthquakes. The city's rough roads were hard on vehicles and mechanics all over the city never had to worry about a decline in customers, once their workshops were up and running following the quake. He could put the business on the market and see what interest there was.

'You've talked to them?' Heather didn't know whether she should be upset that he had gone behind her back, but she realised it was better this way. If the bank had said no, she would never know and wouldn't be disappointed and upset. She had spent too much time being upset over the past five years.

It was time to retire, Neil said. He was past retirement age, and she had turned 65 a few months earlier.

'We have two options, love,' Neil said. 'Sell the business and use the money from it and the section to buy something new, which might take as long as a year, or rent this place out and use the section money for the deposit on something. Then, when the business sells, pay off a big chunk of the new mortgage.'

'What do you want to do?' she asked. Her head was swimming. They had options, two of them, whereas just two months ago they had none. She had spent the last couple of weeks, since the money had been deposited, thinking they needed to wait for the repairs to the house to be sorted. But no, Neil said, they could think about moving on now.

The repairs of the repairs would take a long time, Heather knew that. An appointment had been made for someone from EQC's Remedial Repairs Team to come and inspect the repairs. It was nice to have progress, at last, but an appointment was no guarantee that they would be listened to, and Kevin was going to be there during the appointment to be their third pair of eyes. But that seemed like less of an issue now, because they had options. Two of them.

'Let's start looking,' she said. 'See about selling the business, and start looking.'

They decided to go out to dinner to celebrate. It had been a beautiful day, the temperature had been up around twenty-five degrees and they decided to walk to The Tannery, the Victorian-style shopping arcade on the banks of the Heathcote River. The way there was along the river through the suburb of Hillsborough, then through industrial Woolston.

As they were walking along the river, Heather thought about where they might move to. Her instinct was to stay here, close to family, but there was no way of knowing where Lindsay and Kevin would end up as long as their house was in insurance limbo. They had finally received word from their insurance company that they had been assigned a new project manager, who was going to work through all the issues with their scope of works. It promised progress in the new year, Heather thought, but Lindsay was far from convinced. As many in Christchurch had found in the last five years, insurance company promises usually came with hooks.

Jason and Carla were expecting another baby, due in April. Their Addington townhouse wasn't big enough for little Eddie and another baby, so they had bought a house in Hoon Hay, a suburb near the river but further west, and were moving in at the weekend.

'I don't want to buy anything built before the quakes,' Heather said. 'If we can swing it.'

She could see Neil nodding out of the corner of her eye as they walked along. 'I agree. Far too risky. Maybe something further out in one of the newer areas, like Rolleston or Lincoln,' he said, glancing sidelong at Heather to gauge her reaction.

'It's far from family,' she said. Where they were now was so handy, less than five minutes from Lindsay and Kevin and only ten from her mother and from Jason and his family. But travelling further to visit family would be a small price to pay for the peace of mind of knowing that they had bought a structurally sound property.

'It's close enough to Jase and Carla,' Neil said. 'And maybe we should see about having your mum with us. That place is too big for her.'

'You've thought this all through, haven't you?' Heather said, surprised.

'I have,' Neil said. 'I really think it would be good for us to have a fresh start somewhere else. Not too far away, because we need to be near the kids, but far enough to give us room to recover.'

'I love the idea,' Heather said. She hooked her arm through Neil's and kissed him on the cheek. 'And I love you.'

Sticks and Stones

December 2015

It was nearly the end of the year and looking back Lindsay didn't feel like they were any further ahead than they had been twelve months ago. Although their insurance company had assigned them a new project manager, they hadn't acknowledged the previous one's incompetence and seemed determined to stick with the same repair strategy, of just patching the foundations. Lindsay had been angry at how the insurance company had phrased the news of their new project manager, 'In the interests of moving this claim forward, we have assigned it to a new project manager.' Who knew what the new guy would be like?

Lindsay had stopped thinking about where else they might choose to live or about doing something new and different with their lives. Even her decades-old habit of doing something different in the house to cure her restlessness was constrained by the fact that she was restricted to moving furniture. There could be no renovations, there was no point in painting the lounge or the bedroom or looking at options for making changes in the kitchen. No point in doing anything.

Lindsay wanted to talk about leaving Christchurch, but Kevin said there wasn't any point to discussing it until they knew how badly off they would end up financially. Lindsay didn't want Olivia and Jack growing up in a half-finished city, where repaired houses needing to be re-repaired was considered normal. Going into the city was a lesson in contrasts, all the busy construction work going on in private developments south of the Square versus empty sections where nothing was happening north of the Square.

There was too much arguing going on between the people who were meant to be running the rebuild of the city. In the last week, Gerry Brownlee had called Treasury 'dopey' over a report Treasury published that said most of the Government's anchor projects were in trouble. Lindsay couldn't understand why a Government minister, someone trusted with authority, didn't seem able to take responsibility for issues. He could, however, be consistently relied on to call any critic a name.

Between their own insurance problems, what was going on with the houses around them and the governmental squabbling, Lindsay was sick of the whole place, and she didn't want her children growing up in a poorly-functioning city whose so-called leaders showed less maturity than your average new entrant.

School holidays were coming up and the kids only had two weeks left of school. Lindsay and Kevin wanted to do something holiday-like with them over the summer, not just have Alice look after them while Kevin worked and Lindsay did insurance paperwork. No, that was going to be shelved for at least three weeks, they were going to ignore their email so they could have an actual break. They had decided on camping near Arthur's Pass and were going to head up on Boxing Day, after the madness of Christmas was over.

That was the plan, anyway. All Lindsay had to get through was the next two weeks, but she wasn't sure she would be able to accomplish that because it was only Saturday morning and already Olivia and Jack had been arguing most of the morning. Lindsay hadn't even been able to finish making pancakes yet, so getting through the next two weeks without having some sort of explosion was seeming less and less likely. Maybe Kevin and Lindsay should go camping in separate places, one child each, that might be the only way she would get any peace and quiet, any real escape from the pressures of living in the city.

Lindsay could hear them in the lounge, back and forth, trading names. She stepped away from the bowl she was mixing pancakes in and brushed a loose strand of hair away from her eyes. She walked around the corner into the lounge where Olivia was sitting on the sofa with a book held to her chest. Jack was leaning against the edge of the sofa trying to see into Olivia's book, but she was holding him at arm's length.

'You're so stupid, Jack,' Olivia said. 'You're a poopyhead.'

'Olivia,' Lindsay said. 'Don't talk to your brother like that.'

Olivia dropped her arm and Jack stepped away from her.

'But he keeps bugging me with his stupid questions,' Olivia said. 'Make him leave me alone.'

'I get that,' Lindsay said, 'and I'll deal with that in a moment, but you shouldn't be calling your brother names.'

'Yeah, it's not nice,' Jack said.

'Jack,' Lindsay said. He had been about to say something else but shut his mouth tight. 'Have you made your bed?' She knew he wouldn't have made his bed yet. He shook his head and scampered off to his bedroom. Lindsay turned her attention back to Olivia.

'It's not like I hit him,' Olivia said.

'No, I know you didn't hit him,' Lindsay said. 'But it's not nice to call people names.'

'But he's being stupid,' Olivia insisted. She crossed her arms over her chest and turned away from Lindsay.

'Look at me,' Lindsay said. She reached out and touched Olivia's shoulder. Olivia shrugged her away. She kept her voice firm. 'Olivia, I want you to listen to me. When you call your brother bad names, you're not telling people anything about Jack, you're telling people something about you.'

Olivia turned to look at her, a puzzled look on her face. 'What do you mean?'

'Let's say I'm mad at your dad and I call him a poopyhead,' Lindsay said. Olivia giggled. 'Does that mean he's a poopyhead or does that mean I'm in a bad mood?'

'It means you're in a bad mood,' Olivia said.

'Is it right for me to call him a name because I'm in a bad mood?'

'No...'

'Would it be fair to say it's kind of mean of me to take my bad mood out on him?'

Olivia thought about that, scrunching up her face and about to speak, then changing her mind. Finally she nodded.

'So me calling your dad a bad name just says I'm being mean, doesn't it?'

'I guess so. But what if you're mad at him because he's being annoying?'

'I would ask him nicely to stop being annoying,' Lindsay said, rifling through her recent memories to make sure she was dealing with annoyances in that way. Olivia had a sharp memory and would bring up any instances of hypocrisy, and Lindsay and Kevin had been arguing over insurance issues too often.

'What if he didn't stop?'

'I would go to a different room and do something else,' Lindsay said. This wasn't working, Olivia was just going to come up with a series of actions that would skip right over the point Lindsay was trying to make. 'But that's not the point. The things we say about people, the way we talk about things, say more about us than they do about the people and things we're talking about. So I want you to practise, in the next few days, talking about things in a nice way. Can you do that for me?'

Olivia nodded. 'Even Jack?'

'Especially Jack,' Lindsay said. 'If he's annoying you, how about asking what he would like to do, and maybe you'll want to do it too. Don't just tell him to go away, think of something you'd like to do with him.'

'But I just want to read my book and he keeps asking what I'm reading,' Olivia said. She was getting agitated again, a whine creeping into her voice.

'He wants to know what you're reading so read it out to him,' Lindsay said. 'Would it hurt you to do that?'

'No?' Olivia said.

'So go back to reading your book and when Jack comes back in here in a few minutes, how about reading out loud so he can listen to the story?'

Olivia nodded and sat back down on the sofa. Lindsay went back into the kitchen and started heating up the pan for the pancakes. When the butter had melted and she was pouring the first pancake, she could hear Olivia reading her book to Jack. Maybe there could be a peaceful end to the year after all.

The Special Settlement

January 2016

The place was rotting. The air was full of the smell of damp and decay, vines and ferns climbing over bushes and trees, up towards the sun, out along any surface that supported growth. Everywhere Alice looked, things were growing up, over and around other things, vines strangling trees, smaller trees embracing larger trees, foliage everywhere celebrating the abundant water.

Alice was on Stewart Island with Charlotte. The others who were meant to go on the tramp had bailed out at the last minute, but Alice and Charlotte decided to go anyway, both had been looking forward to getting out of Christchurch, to getting into clean air and experiencing something different from the dry, dusty summer that was eventuating in the city on the edge of the Canterbury Plains.

Alice and Charlotte had come over on the ferry from Bluff the previous day and spent the night at a backpackers. After Stewart Island, they would go home the long way, via Queenstown, the Haast Pass and the lake where Charlotte's parents were staying with their friends. Andrew and Michelle wouldn't be there this year, they weren't on speaking terms with Charlotte's parents, which was part of the reason why the tramping plans had fallen apart, leaving only Alice and Charlotte.

Since Marjorie's death, arguments over her estate had split the family into factions. Gerald and Sylvia were in the process of moving into Marjorie's house and deciding what to do with their own. Marjorie's younger daughters objected to Gerald having the house, both had expected it to be part of the larger estate, sold off, with the proceeds split among Marjorie's four children. Suzanne neither objected nor agreed, she was too overwhelmed by the loss of her mother, which seemed odd to Alice as there had never been any signs of a warm relationship between them. The whole family was too complicated for Alice, she was just happy Charlotte and Sean were still talking to her, given that their mother was firmly in the sell-the-house faction, and so not speaking to Andrew.

Although doing his best not to take sides in the family argument, Sean wasn't able to get time off work for the tramp. The other disappointment had been Alice's friend Emma and her boyfriend Dave. Emma had been living in Melbourne since June 2011, but now she and Dave had moved back to Christchurch. They were staying around the corner from Alice with Emma's parents in their rebuilt house, and Alice liked having her old school friend nearby once again. But then Emma announced she was pregnant and was suffering from morning sickness bad enough to make Alice think twice about ever having children. Going on the ferry across Foveaux Strait, much less on the tramp, was not an option. Alice had suggested they fly across, but Emma said she wasn't keeping much food down at all, so would be unlikely to have enough energy for a three-day tramp. Alice tried to be happy about Emma's pregnancy, but it was too strange, such a grown-up thing to be doing, and she had been surprised when Emma said it was planned. She almost asked why they hadn't waited until after Stewart Island, but she knew that was a childish thing to ask, something thought by someone who really hadn't moved on to the adult stage of their life.

Alice had felt desperate to be away from Christchurch and home. The week before Christmas came the news that the City Council had finally reached a settlement with their insurers. Instead of the full value of the claims on various buildings and infrastructure, the council was getting sixty-eight cents on the dollar. 'That's with a team of lawyers,' Kevin said, 'and millions to fight them with. I don't see what chance we stand of getting even a fraction of what it will take to fix this place.'

Lindsay and Kevin had then agreed to put discussions about insurance on hold for the holidays, until mid-January when Kevin would go back to work. But the tension hung in the air, as though something was rotting under the floorboards. If Charlotte had decided not to go on the tramp, Alice would have gone by herself, just to get away.

The start of the track was marked by a sculpture of giant chain links. One brown link formed an arch that walkers passed under. Alice was familiar with the legend of Maui, how the South Island was the canoe Maui fished from, bringing up the fish of the North Island. But she wasn't aware of the role Stewart Island played, that it served as the anchor stone for Maui's canoe. The chain sculpture at the start of the Rakiura Track was matched, so the sign said, by another chain sculpture in Bluff, where the anchor stone connected to the canoe. They were all connected, everyone in the North Island,

the South Island and Stewart Island, they were all people with
stories, lows and highs, people dependent on one another, even if
they felt strong and self-sufficient or weak and isolated.

That first part of the track was straightforward: a gentle walk
along the coast, then a downhill bit to a late lunch on a golden
beach that stretched away to the north. Later, the track branched
off the main track, to the hut they would stay at for the night.
There was a steep downhill section near the hut, and Alice
wondered how they would go the next morning, having to do this
climb out of the bay back to the main track, where they faced a
series of steady upward climbs for at least half of the day.

There were already half a dozen other trampers at the hut when
they arrived, but it slept twenty-four, so they had plenty of choice
in bunks. Charlotte set up her burner to boil water for hot drinks,
while Alice set up their beds. Soon they were sipping coffee while
admiring the surroundings and chatting to the other trampers.

An American couple in their fifties was interested to hear they
were from Christchurch, they asked about how the rebuild had
gone. Past tense. Alice was going to make the point that the rebuild
was still only partway done, but Charlotte got there first, telling
them about how her parents were fighting to get EQC to
acknowledge all the damage to the house and pass them on to their
private insurer. Their insurer didn't want to know about the house
until the EQC had passed them on, so they had engaged an
independent engineer, but EQC didn't want to acknowledge the
damage detailed in that report. Charlotte's parents had hired a
lawyer to argue their case and drive home the specific points in
their engineering report in order to get them overcap.

'So the process hasn't really started for your family?' the man
said, amazed.

'No, not yet, because once they go overcap, they still have to go
through the whole assessment and scoping process with their
insurer,' Charlotte said. 'There's no way of knowing if the insurer
will take on board what they have in their engineer's report.'

'But if that report puts them over the top,' the man said, 'then
the insurance company should accept it.'

'Maybe, but not always,' Charlotte said.

'How long's it been?' the man asked.

'Five years since the first quake,' Charlotte said. 'Five years this
coming February since the seriously damaging one.'

The man shook his head and his wife clucked sympathetically.
'Insurance companies,' she muttered, shaking her head in unison
with her husband.

More trampers filtered in, shaking off their boots and leaving them outside to dry off before picking a bunk and moving through to the common room, which was heated by a woodfire. Before long, jugs and pots of water were boiling on top of the woodfire and on camp burners of different types. Alice and Charlotte had packets of freeze-dried food to rehydrate and soon they were filling their bellies with curried lamb that had a slight sponge-like texture.

A poster in the hut told the story of a special settlement at Port William, an attempt by the provincial government of the 1860s and 1870s to make back some of the money it had spent on the purchase of Stewart Island. They attempted to draw Scottish settlers and Alice could see that the climate of Stewart Island might roughly equal that described by the Scottish people she had known. The idea had been to start settlement at Port William, the site of the hut she was currently standing in. Settlement would spread towards Patterson Inlet, a thousand families seeking to make a better future for themselves in this place, which would be called Rakiura Town. But it never happened. The provincial government could only attract five families of Shetland Islanders, who arrived in 1873 and ended up rattling around in barracks intended for 150 people. The promises made about opportunities to make a living and the development of the island had been empty promises, and the damp of the place led to despair among the settlers, who had all left the island by the end of 1874. The poster said the government of the day blamed the failure of the settlement on the immigrants, who were said to be too lazy. But had prospects for life on the island been misrepresented? It seemed unbearably sad, to cross the world in search of a better life only to find yourself lied to, the benefits of the place oversold.

The only trace left of the Shetland Islanders, Alice read, was the flowers and trees they had planted. Outside the sun was going down, and Alice sat on a picnic bench under a eucalyptus tree where a kaka was singing melodiously, like a slide whistle filled with water. Was the eucalyptus one of those planted by the settlers? Possibly, or the offspring of those planted nearly 150 years earlier. She wondered if they'd had the opportunity to sit outside on a summer night and listen to the singing of a kaka or if they had simply been too overwhelmed by the despair of the situation they found themselves in. She hoped they had enjoyed it, seen some of the beauty of this place, even if for only a moment.

The next morning, Charlotte was up first and got the water boiling for breakfast, and they quickly packed up and headed up the steps to return to the main track. That day's track would take them across the island to the North Arm of Patterson Inlet, meaning there would be no coastal views until the end of the day. The track was muddier than it had been the along the coast, and the dark mud oozed across the tops of their boots and up their gaiters. 'It's like Whittaker's dark chocolate, the Ghana one, the seventy-something percent,' Charlotte said.

'I don't think Whittaker's would like you saying that,' Alice said. 'Comparing their chocolate to mud.'

'But it's beautiful,' Charlotte said, 'so dark and rich and delicious looking.'

'It's mud,' Alice said. 'I'm sure you won't see it the same way when you're scraping it off your laces.'

'You sound like my mum,' Charlotte said. 'So factual, such an accountant. I'm trying to be whimsical here.'

Alice shrugged, as much as she could with her pack strapped to her back. 'Do you think it's like an orgy of foliage in here? It's all just growing everywhere, all over each other, anything goes.'

Charlotte gave her a strange look. 'Now that's just disturbing,' she said. 'Are you sure you got enough sleep?'

'You wanted whimsical,' Alice said.

'Yeah, but that's just plain perverse.'

'Did you read about the special settlement?' Alice asked.

'Yeah,' Charlotte said. 'Pretty sad, really. They come all that way to find what they were promised wasn't anywhere to be seen.'

They were starting up another hill, which put a temporary end to conversation. Alice found herself thinking about the Shetland Islanders. The blame for the settlement's failure had been laid at the feet of the settlers, that lazy lot, which was why the provincial government tried again to attract settlers in 1875. Because, of course, it couldn't be the government's fault for overstating the island's prospects. The second attempt also failed.

Alice wondered if there was a Brownlee in that government, dismissing any complaints from the Shetland Islanders as the utterings of carpers and moaners. Government has such power, Alice thought as she forced her feet onto the next steps, pushing her way up the hill. Do the powerful ever take responsibility for the consequences of their decisions? Traditionally, it seemed as though the election cycle was meant to hold governments accountable. If they made too many mistakes, they would be voted out. But these days, it seemed governments had too much control over their public image, were able to paint a portrait of success, while underneath the spin was a layer of something rotting, coming apart. What did it take to make people notice? And what about businesses that kept on pouring money into advertising? Did your average person ever think to look at what lies beyond the advertising, or did it take something bad happening to them personally to open their eyes? The way it was looking lately, the Government and the insurance companies would walk away from badly repaired and inadequately repaired homes the same way the provincial government had walked away from Port William's Shetland Islanders.

They were going downhill again, and Alice commented on the lack of bird life. They had seen a few tomtits, cute little birds with their sleek black caps and creamy yellow breasts. They could hear grey warblers in the canopy, but really, there was far less bird life making itself known than she had expected.

'People ruin everything,' Charlotte said. 'Bringing all the predators here, eating up all the birds. We shouldn't be allowed to go anywhere, we just mess everything up.'

'We do seem very good at that,' Alice said.

'You know,' Charlotte said, 'it seems that governments have always sucked. I mean, that special settlement, it's just like Christchurch. The Government said it was going to be one way, like today they say there's no problems with repairs, no problem with underscoping, and they refuse to consider the evidence.'

'They blame the people for having the wrong attitude.'

'Right,' Charlotte said. 'For not seeing the world the way they want them to see it.'

'For not buying the spin.'

'Yeah, that's it. PR is the name of the game, but not everyone wants to play the game. Hey look,' Charlotte said, looking down at the track. 'It's Whittaker's 50 percent cocoa on this part of the track.'

It was a theoretical game to Alice and Charlotte at that point in time. Neither of them owned houses or rented, but in the future, how would they approach investing in property? They would need places to live in and both could see the value of the argument a lot of adults made that rent was just paying off someone else's mortgage. But they had seen how owning a house could switch from being a source of security to being a nightmare.

As they drew near the next hut a couple of hours after lunch, Alice wished they had another hut to go to, then another, and that they could stay here always, away from the stress of life in Christchurch, get out of the game.

Spin

February 2016

Charlotte was going to board with her grandmother for her first year at university and Alice was staying with them for the weekend, helping Charlotte to move her things in.

Sunday was Valentine's Day. It was hot and an easy decision to go to the beach after lunch. They drove out to Sumner, which was so packed with people and cars that they had to park a kilometre from the beach. They walked towards the beach, stopping at an ice cream stand to buy a cone each. At Cave Rock, Charlotte stopped.

'Have you ever been in there?' Charlotte said. The huge rock on the foreshore was named for the cave that ran through it. There were also steps up the side of the rock, which a man was climbing up, a small boy on his back.

'Not for a long time,' Alice said. 'Before the quakes.'

'You want to? I remember going through as a little kid, but I'd like to see what it's like now. I remember it being enormous, but looking at it, I think that's just because I was little.' At only five feet two inches tall, Charlotte was still little, although Alice didn't say that.

'Finish our cones first?'

They stood across from the rock, watching people disappearing into the mouth of the cave. When they finished their cones, they dropped their serviettes into the nearest rubbish bin and were about to walk down onto the beach when Alice heard the rumble. She had only a moment to think that it couldn't be right when she felt the earth surging beneath her feet and heard buildings being shaken, the sound of concrete, bricks and glass clashing. That sound again. Alice wasn't sure whether to crouch down, and she and Charlotte shot each other anxious looks, unsure what to do. The people around them were the same, some crouching down but most looking panicked, not knowing where to go or what to do.

The quake passed and the sound of it was replaced by shouting, crying and swearing. People pulled out phones and started trying to make phone calls and send text messages. Five, Alice was thinking, that was a five, we don't have fives any more, just threes. She pulled her phone out of her pocket and tried to send a text to Lindsay, but her hands were shaking too much and she couldn't see clearly enough to read what she was typing. She blinked away tears. She would give it a moment.

'Look!' Charlotte pointed towards the ocean, turning and raising her phone. In the distance, brown dust was billowing out from the cliffs. A dozen people turned to watch, holding up their phones to take photos and videos. Alice felt her heart racing, the panic welling up in her throat. People died in cliff collapses, and it was a hot summer day, there could be people there, walking the tracks, on the beaches below or swimming in the water. No, this couldn't be happening again, it had been nearly four years since the last big quake, how could this be happening again?

'Are you okay?' Charlotte asked. She was glancing between her phone and Alice, tapping out a message to someone, probably her grandmother. The sky about the seaside suburb was full of dust, drifting away from the cliffs like a brown fog.

Alice nodded. 'I'm fine,' she said. 'Just that feeling, it reminded me of the twenty-second, walking home and there was a five something.'

Charlotte put her arm around Alice's shoulders and squeezed. 'Let's go home, I'll check on Nanny, then we'll go to your place.'

They started walking back to where they had left the car. The traffic out of Sumner was backed up, people leaving the beach behind to go home and check on family and friends, to see how much mess they had to clean up this time. Once Alice and Charlotte pulled into the stream of traffic, it took them half an hour to get to Suzanne's house instead of the usual five minutes.

'I'm fine,' Suzanne reassured them, giving them both hugs. 'I've lost two cups and a wine glass, that's all.'

'No damage?' Charlotte said.

'Nothing I can see,' Suzanne said. 'And there's certainly nothing to suggest I'll be falling into EQC's clutches any time soon.'

The three of them walked through, checking all the surfaces to confirm that the house had indeed held up. Alice and Charlotte decided to head back to Alice's house to see how it had survived the quake.

Lindsay and Kevin were sitting on the steps when they pulled up the driveway, each sipping at a glass of wine. 'We have bad news,' Kevin said, lifting his glass of wine in a mocking toast. 'The house hasn't come off its foundations.'

'We were just saying that it would put to bed the whole issue of whether or not the foundation should be replaced,' Lindsay said. She swallowed back the last of the wine in her glass and reached behind her for the wine bottle, poured herself another glass.

Alice laughed. 'You'd just have to make another claim and go through the whole business again,' she said. 'Livvy and Jack would be in high school by the time it got sorted.'

'Yes, I suppose we should be relieved nothing's been made worse,' Kevin said.

Kevin went inside and brought out another bottle of wine, along with two wine glasses. 'You're eighteen?' he said to Charlotte. He winked at Alice.

'Nearly nineteen!' Charlotte said, indignant.

They all crammed together on the verandah, enjoying the sun and the wine while keeping up with the news websites. Information started to flow in, pictures of the cliff collapses and stories of near misses. A group of lifeguard trainees had to swim for their lives to avoid chunks of rock falling onto the beach and into the water, and cyclists going along the Sumner-to-Redcliffs road heard rocks hitting the shipping containers that protected the road from rockfall. In the city, there didn't seem to be much damage, although buildings and shopping malls were evacuated and checked. There was liquefaction in the northeast once again. Surely that must be depressing to deal with after going through the whole repair or rebuild process. If people weren't still waiting on EQC or their insurer.

'If I hear a single mention of kia kaha Christchurch, I will scream,' Lindsay said.

'Then best stay away from Facebook,' Alice said. There were a few mentions of the worn out platitude in the comments on news items she was scrolling through.

'You know,' Lindsay said. 'It really is just another earthquake.'

They all turned to look at her, but no one said anything. Clearly they had missed a train of thinking she had been following for some time.

'I mean for anyone who's had to battle EQC or the insurance companies, this is just another earthquake, it's impersonal and it's nothing compared to what EQC and the insurance companies have put us through while the Government has just sat back and let it happen. I found the earthquakes stressful, but I didn't need antidepressants to get through them. The insurance company, though, the stress of that is ten times if not a hundred times greater than all the earthquakes put together. No one is strong enough to withstand that. Telling people to stay strong just doesn't cut it any more.'

'For people like us,' Kevin said, 'the insurance stuff has gone on twice as long as the main earthquake sequence. About eighteen months versus, what?' He counted through the number of months since they had been made overcap and passed on to their insurer. '2012, okay, that was a write-off, there were still quakes and geotech stuff needing to be done, but 2013, 2014, 2015, that's thirty-six months, twice as long as the quake sequence.'

It was so long ago, but Alice still remembered the day of the February quake clearly, finding Andrew and the two of them walking along the river, across from the PGC building. A quake about the same size as today's quake had hit, and on the beach out at Sumner, she had felt that same panic, that of not knowing whether to crouch down or run, of turning in circles and hearing the sounds of buildings being shaken, concrete grinding, glass clattering. The adrenalin surge had been the same, leaving her shaking, her heart racing, having to just stand still for a minute and sort herself out.

Earlier, on the way back to Alice's house, Alice and Charlotte had stopped across from Redcliffs School, which the Government was trying to close down. The families were fighting back, they said there was no risk of rockfall. The Government said it wasn't the rockfall risk, it was the risk of disruption, which seemed to Alice a silly argument as in a big quake, every school was disrupted, whether they were under cliffs or on the flat.

'I can't see anything new,' Charlotte said. There were no signs of fresh slips, nothing to suggest that the cliffs had crumbled further. 'I wonder if today will make a difference to it closing.'

'Those for closing it will spin it as proof it needs to be closed, those against will spin it their way,' Alice said.

Lately everything was about spin. CERA had announced that the region's mental health statistics were improving, showing how much Christchurch was recovering. Yet a few days later, the police were saying they were responding to far too many suicide attempts. Who could be trusted? The ones looking out for the people, Alice concluded, and that wasn't CERA, especially once it became known that CERA had spent $2.5 million on public relations in the past year. That money would buy a lot of spin.

The next lot of spin came when insurers released their quarterly rebuild and repair stats. Insurers had, it was claimed, completed over 5000 rebuilds and repairs in 2015. But that included cash settlements where no actual building work had taken place. Then someone questioned those figures, pointing out that the figures accompanying the Insurance Council's press release showed that was the number of rebuilds and repairs completed in total, over the whole five years since the quakes started. It was all about how the figures were spun.

Then there was the EQC staff morale survey. *The Press* reported that only a quarter of EQC staff believed the organisation was delivering on its mandate. But the EQC chief executive hit back, saying that a high proportion of staff believed in the organisation's mission. That was true, according to the survey, but only a quarter of them believed they were actually achieving it.

In the week after what became known as the Valentine's Day quake, Alice couldn't decide whether she wanted to stick around for the anniversary of the 22nd of February quake or get away, up into the mountains for one last tramp during the warm summer weather. The thing that finally decided her against staying was news about another earthquake, one in Taiwan. It had happened at the start of February and there had been a couple of building collapses that immediately made Alice think the buildings had been poorly built. Then, just a few days before the quake anniversary, Alice read a news story that said the developers of one of the buildings had been charged with negligent homicide. Within days of the building collapse, the developers had been charged, but here in Christchurch, it had been five years and no one had been made accountable for the CTV collapse, despite well-documented shortcomings and faults.

A few months earlier, Alice had read about the Prime Minister being congratulated by overseas businessmen because the rebuild of Christchurch had been so well managed. They were talking like it was already complete! It was only the spin job that was complete. No, the quake anniversary would be something she would bypass this year, the programme would be all spin about the progress of the rebuild.

Unseen Damage

March 2016

Lindsay and Kevin were trying not to like their new project manager, but he seemed to listen to their concerns, and they weren't used to that. His name was Callum and he had come to Christchurch for the rebuild from the North Island. He had visited at the start of February, to have a look at the place for himself, he said, and Kevin had taken him around the house, pointing out all the obvious issues with the foundation. Kevin said Callum had been non-committal, but he had paid attention.

Kevin had gleaned one piece of information from Callum on that visit, that John Rutherford was no longer working for the PMO. They were downsizing, Callum had said, now that the rebuild work was coming to an end. 'But there was something there,' Kevin said. 'In how he said it.'

'I don't care why,' Lindsay said. 'I'm just happy Rutherford's no longer assigned to our house.'

'I don't know,' Kevin said. 'I'm choosing to think our complaint had something to do with it.'

Lindsay left it. They had both felt so powerless in the last three years that she could understand why he felt the need to believe that their complaint had been taken seriously.

Now Callum was visiting once again. He had a structural engineer and a geotechnical engineer with him and after brief introductions, they got down to business. Lindsay and Kevin waited nervously, pacing up and down the driveway while Callum walked the engineers around. They spent a long time poking and prodding at the stretch of foundation that Rutherford had left out of his scope of works.

'Is this from Valentine's Day?' one of them asked.

'No,' Callum said. 'It was like this when I first visited and that was late January? Early February. Before the quake, in any case. Mr Bowen,' he said, turning towards Kevin, 'how long has this part of the ring beam been like this?'

Kevin stepped towards them, but Lindsay stayed back. She didn't want to appear too eager, didn't want to let them see how much she hoped they would finally get this right. 'Since February 2011,' Kevin said, shrugging casually. But from behind him, Lindsay could see the tension in his shoulders and neck.

Callum nodded, and Kevin stepped back towards Lindsay. Lindsay glanced at him to try to figure out what he was thinking, but his facial expression gave nothing away.

It wasn't until Callum and the engineers left that Kevin finally said something. 'Do you think that all this time, they haven't known that damage was there?'

'Rutherford knew. You pointed it out to him and the builder, didn't you?' Lindsay said.

'Yes,' Kevin said. 'But I'd pointed it out to Rutherford before and he'd ignored it, maybe he discouraged the builder from putting it into the tender.'

'Well they've seen it now, we just have to wait and see what happens. Again. So nothing changes.'

'No, Lin,' Kevin said, smiling. He put his arm around her shoulders, squeezing, and kissed the side of her head. 'This is really good. The first geotech report was done by someone working from the data and Rutherford's diagrams, they hadn't seen the foundation for themselves. They can't not acknowledge this.'

Lindsay shrugged. 'Maybe. Maybe not. We'll see.'

Kevin went back to work and although Lindsay had planned to catch up on housework, she couldn't stop thinking about what Kevin had said. Maybe this mess they had found themselves in for the last couple of years was just one lazy project manager who couldn't be bothered documenting the damage properly. She started up the laptop and started going through files, looking for photographs that documented the damage to the foundation. She couldn't find any in the insurance company's files, although she did find photos of other parts of the foundation, the parts they did plan to repair.

What Lindsay did find, though, was photos of the insurance company's newly discovered damage in their EQC file. Although they didn't have issues with EQC, Lindsay had asked for a copy of their file when she had first made her Privacy Act request to the insurance company. The EQC photos were from five years ago, so they had proof that the damage had been there all along. It probably didn't mean anything as far as how their claim would progress, but it was good to be vindicated at last.

She showed Kevin and Alice that night, after the children had gone to bed.

'So that's it?' Alice said. 'All along the PMO's not been looking at the foundation properly, reporting back to the insurance company that it's not as damaged as it is?'

'Seems like it,' Lindsay said.

'But what about the structural engineering report they had done in 2014?' Alice said. 'Surely the engineer doing that was looking at the whole foundation, not just at where Rutherford was pointing?'

'He was young,' Lindsay said. 'Maybe he was intimidated.'

'There's no out clause for feeling intimidated in the engineering code of ethics,' Alice said sarcastically.

Kevin got out his bottle of whiskey and poured each of them a couple of fingers. 'Today needs celebrating,' he said.

'We're not there yet,' Lindsay said, shutting down the laptop and putting it away. She sat down on the sofa beside Kevin and sipped the drink. 'So how do we use it?'

'I don't think you do,' Alice said. 'Wait and see what the insurance company has to say and go from there. But if they're going to stick to their repair strategy, it might be time for a lawyer.'

Lindsay threw Alice a look, she should know better than to bring up the L word in front of Kevin. To Lindsay's surprise, though, Kevin didn't object outright.

'I still don't like the idea of bringing in a lawyer,' Kevin said. 'At this point, we seem to have a good project manager at last...'

'You don't know that,' Lindsay said. 'Not for sure.'

'When those engineers asked today about it being new damage, he could've just gone along with it,' Kevin pointed out. 'But he didn't. No, he's good. But what I was saying, if the insurance company refuses to deal with us properly at this point, there's nothing more we can do. We'll need a lawyer.'

The following week, an email arrived from their claims manager asking for their patience as the issues brought up by this new damage were worked through. The foundation probably couldn't be repaired, he said, which made Lindsay whoop with joy. She called Kevin right away and told him the news.

'New damage,' he said tightly. 'Did you see that?'

'Yes,' Lindsay said, 'but at this point I don't care, they've acknowledged the damage, they have to do something about it now.'

'True,' he said, and his voice was lighter. He said they should go out to dinner that night, celebrate.

Should she have hope? She didn't want to. When they complained to the insurance company about Rutherford, she had hope then and had been badly disappointed. The insurance company revisiting the scope of works was, on the surface, a big step forward, but it wasn't enough. Their mistakes hadn't been accompanied by an apology or a promise to get their claim sorted and let them move on with their lives. Their mistakes hadn't even been properly acknowledged.

For the next few days, Lindsay wrestled with her desire to hope. She was starting to get twisted up over it, feeling positive, that their claim would soon make progress, then pulled back into the pit of despair that said this was their life and always would be. What finally stopped her from obsessing was the early birth of Jason and Carla's second child.

Carla's blood pressure was going up and so she was induced three weeks early. A day of anxiety was erased when the little girl was finally delivered, and shortly after seven o'clock that night, Lindsay held her new niece for the first time. She was tiny, smaller than any of Lindsay's babies had been, and looked fierce and angry over being forced into the world early. Lindsay couldn't blame her.

'She's beautiful,' Lindsay said. She thought about the future that stretched out before this little girl, the type of person she might grow into and the city she would be growing up in.

It was dark, so Jason walked Lindsay out to the carpark.

'This happened quickly,' Lindsay said. 'Too quickly, I haven't bought you guys anything yet.'

'Don't worry about it,' Jason said. 'Caught us a bit off guard as well.'

'What happened?'

'Too much stress,' Jason said, and she noticed how tired he was looking. It wasn't just from the sudden delivery of his daughter. He told her that the house they had moved into at the end of last year needed second-time repairs. EQC had been in touch because it was part of the group of houses that needed to be rechecked following the fallout from the shoddy repairs survey. Its foundation repairs had been done without a building consent, and a couple of weeks ago, they received the report. The work done was cosmetic only, and the foundation repairs listed on the scope of works hadn't been completed. 'So we get to go through everything Mum and Dad are going through,' he said.

Lindsay was trying not to cry when she arrived home and Kevin teased her about going all soft over the new baby. She broke into sobs and told him about Jason and Carla's house. Even once their own claim was finally settled, her family would still be going through the same nightmare.

That seemed to be Christchurch's future, for more and more damage to come to light. But what about the unseen damage, what the pressure was doing to people's lives? Would the recovery ever truly be over?

Mixed Feelings

April 2016

Gerald and Sylvia had moved into Marjorie's house. It felt incongruous to be living in his mother's house, to be its elderly owner, an old man walking around the land he had played on as a young boy. It would take some time to get used to.

Gerald felt he was beginning to understand his mother at last. Suzanne had told him about their mother's first husband and that she suspected Walter Finlay had been her biological father. He agreed. In the photo of Walter, Gerald could see a resemblance between Walter and Suzanne's daughter Rebecca in the shape of their eyes. He wasn't certain just from the photo, but it made sense in light of what Suzanne discovered in the records. Marjorie had loved Walter, it seemed, and his loss had damaged her in ways that had never mended. Gerald wished he had understood that while she was alive.

Suzanne had done more research into Marjorie's family history and discovered that although her parents died during the war, three of her siblings had survived. Her youngest sister had died in the 1980s. Marjorie had outlived them all by nearly three decades. Another interesting find was that her mother's name was Annie, which made Suzanne and Gerald laugh. Marjorie used to get so annoyed with Gerald when he would shorten 'Suzanne' to 'Annie'. Clearly she didn't appreciate the reminder.

'But she named me,' Suzanne said.

'No, Dad named you,' Gerald said. 'After his sister who died in the influenza epidemic. Mother had no say in the matter.'

'I never knew that,' Suzanne said, drifting away into her own memories.

Suzanne was different since their mother's death. She had been freed from something. She missed Marjorie, more than she had ever expected, she'd said once. But she did feel free of Marjorie's expectations and judgements, of the constant sense of having missed the mark. She missed the little things, she said, the cream horns and the gingernuts, and the enjoyment Marjorie got from a tree or bush in bloom. 'She said once I looked like her mother, that I got my hair from her. Maybe I reminded her too much of her past, of her mother and Walter.'

Gerald knew the power of memory, how something that happened long ago could suddenly fill a person's mind, as though the intervening decades had never occurred. Maybe Suzanne had done that for Marjorie, dredging up feelings and memories she found too painful to entertain.

He remembered once being at his mother's house when a plane went over. This was an unusual occurrence as the airport was on the other side of the city, but a company was running tours, flying an old DC3 over the city. Marjorie was in the kitchen pouring ingredients into the cake mixer when they heard the sound of the plane flying overhead. She froze, her shoulders tensed, and because what she was doing had been interrupted, she smashed an egg on the edge of the mixing bowl rather than cracking it into the mix. She became flustered, trying to pick the chips of eggshell out of the mix, which only resulted in her tipping the bowl over and spilling the mix onto the bench and floor. Gerald couldn't remember ever seeing her flustered before.

Gerald reassured her it was all right and helped her with the mess. It was the sound of the plane, she said, and he understood. She had lived through the Blitz and the sound of the DC3 flying over had brought it back to her.

It had been that way for Gerald with the Valentine's Day quake. It had been so long since there had been a big quake that the memory of them had faded. But when he heard that approaching roar and felt the shaking start, he froze and that same fear he had in the February 2011 quake washed over him, making his gut churn. He didn't think that reaction would ever leave him.

There continued to be aftershocks, even now, over two months later. They were just threes and fours, but for a city that had been through eighteen months of regular aftershocks followed by three years of EQC- and insurance-related stress, it was too much for many.

The region's mental health services had been stretched too far, and the District Health Board was fighting to get the Government to take their concerns seriously. In 2015, there had been newspaper articles about a dysfunctional relationship between the DHB and the Ministry of Health. The population was stressed and had grown as workers moved into the region for the rebuild. Yet funding hadn't kept up. The District Health Board had gone as far as making a complaint against a Ministry of Health official who claimed he hadn't been told the emergency department was under pressure, in spite of having been copied into emails discussing the crisis. After the complaint was dismissed, three senior doctors spoke out and said the Ministry was being wilfully blind over the issue.

It seemed like the Ministry of Health had a vendetta against Christchurch, that it was holding a grudge because of the earthquakes, withholding extra funding that international experts said would be needed for mental health services in a region recovering from a natural disaster. But that couldn't be right, Gerald thought. Surely even bureaucrats would have compassion for a region that had experienced what Canterbury had gone through?

It wasn't just the DHB warning of mental health issues. The police said there had been an alarming increase in callouts for attempted suicides. Local doctors were seeing an increase in depression and anxiety and said there needed to be more funding to cover the rising need.

But no one seemed to be listening and just before the five-year anniversary of the February quake, there had been news stories about cuts to mental health funding. But on the anniversary of the quake, the Prime Minister insisted the funding cut was a myth, implying that everyone trying to highlight the problem was simply misreading the numbers. Any increase in demand for mental health services was the result of the Valentine's Day quake, he said.

More money was finally added to the mental health budget at the start of March, for the Valentine's Day quake, of course. It felt to Gerald like the Valentine's Day quake was being used as a way for the Government to do something about the problem the DHB had been trying to tell them about for months without having to admit to being wrong.

Gerald was grateful that his family were, by and large, recovering well. He worried the most about his niece Rebecca, Suzanne's daughter. She and Dan had filed in court against the EQC and their insurance company, and it was sad that they had to go to those lengths to get the damage to their house recognised. But the fight to get overcap had cost her and Dan their relationship with their daughter because Charlotte had moved out to board with her grandmother. Charlotte wanted to focus on doing well during her first year at university, and she couldn't do that while living with her parents. He hoped one day Charlotte would understand and would be able to mend her relationship with her parents.

Although it was well into autumn, the days were still warm. Gerald and Sylvia were holding their first family gathering at the house, a throwback to the gatherings Marjorie held each year. Andrew and Liam, Andrew's oldest son, had taken charge of the barbecue, and the smell of charring meat drifted across the yard to where Gerald was walking along the stream. It was a beautiful place, this city. He sat down in the wooden garden seat his mother had loved to sit in on a summer's day and looked back towards the house.

The house and yard were noisy with the Moorhouse grandchildren. Soon there would be another one. Their daughter Laurel and her husband had moved back from Sydney, and Laurel was expecting a little girl in the spring. Laurel and Joe had bought the house Gerald and Sylvia had lived in since the earthquakes. It wasn't their forever home, but it was a start, a house they knew was structurally sound and would hold its value, which couldn't be said with certainty for much of the city's housing stock.

Gerald was pleased to have both his children living in the same city once again, but he was saddened at the thought of the city his grandchildren were growing up in. The ugly reality of the rebuild would continue to unfold, and Gerald didn't like what it said about human nature.

He could see Alice, with Charlotte, chatting to Laurel, who Alice had never met before. Gerald actually hoped Alice would leave Christchurch. Moorhouse Architectural was now being run by a manager, and Gerald no longer had any day-to-day input, but Alice was still there and she did seem to enjoy the work. But she was becoming worn out from the stress of what her family was going through, and Gerald was worried about her.

The Government's failure to acknowledge the magnitude of the shoddy repairs situation was distressing to Gerald. It meant that buying a house would be a risky business for many years to come. Official figures were that EQC had 5500 houses that required further repairs and another 2300 that needed unconsented foundation repairs reviewed. Through the grapevine, Gerald had heard they were getting over one hundred requests for reviews each week. He couldn't imagine the pressure it was putting on the people whose houses were affected, who faced going through the whole assessment, negotiation and repair process once again.

A joint statement had been issued just that week as the result of a group of claimants taking EQC to court. The EQC and the claimant group had reached agreement on a number of points of law regarding the standard of repairs. What had happened throughout Canterbury was that houses were being repaired to a pre-earthquake standard rather than to the higher standard specified in the insurance contract. The situation had resulted in numerous arguments between homeowners and the organisations that they were paying to insure their homes. Contractors engaged by the insurance industry had been telling homeowners that what they could expect was that their houses would be brought back to pre-earthquake condition, and any homeowners who pointed out the as-when-new terms of the EQC Act or their insurance policy were labelled difficult customers with unrealistic expectations. But their expectations weren't unrealistic, they were based on a legally binding contract.

The joint statement was hailed by the claimants' group as a landmark decision, one that meant many of the claims EQC had handled would need to be revisited because the wrong standard had been applied. The EQC immediately turned around and said the joint statement proved they had been working to the as-when-new standard all along, despite the fact that there were numerous examples of EQC documentation that said homes would be repaired to their pre-earthquake condition. The joint statement *was* a major victory for claimants, but it was apparent that the EQC was going to fight them each and every step along the way. Gerald wondered how hard the District Health Board would have to fight for the mental health funding necessary to help all those poor people recover from their treatment at the hands of the EQC.

Gerald had wished, for a time, that Andrew would get more involved in helping claimants. He had done such work for his grandmother, but, Gerald knew, it wasn't the type of work he enjoyed. Then Gerald watched a news story in which one lawyer talked about burnout. This man had done a lot of work for Christchurch claimants, but reached the point where he could no longer function. It almost broke him, he said. No, it was best for Andrew to focus on his family.

Liam had finished school at the end of the previous year and was working as an apprentice for Moorhouse Architectural, under a builder Gerald had considerable respect for. Gerald saw in the boy a growing love of putting things together that he recognised from his own youth. He had considered keeping one foot in the business to help train Liam, but in the end he realised it was time to finish up. He would be seventy later in the year and had already put off retirement for too long.

Building was a good career choice. The fallout from the shoddy repairs crisis was going to be bigger than the leaky homes crisis of the early 2000s. That had cost the country $10 billion, this creaky homes crisis would cost much more. Gerald hoped that this time, the industry could learn from the mistakes it kept on making and recognise that cutting corners always cost more in the long run.

'You're deep in thought,' Laurel said, startling him. She fell heavily onto the seat beside him and pressed her shoulder up against his.

'Enjoying having everyone together,' he said, bumping her shoulder back.

'I can't believe how grown up Charlotte is,' Laurel said. 'She was barely past my knees when I went to Sydney, and now look at her, she's all the way up to here.' She indicated a point just below her shoulders.

They both laughed. 'Yes, she's tiny,' Gerald said. 'But don't underestimate her, she's as strong-willed as Mother. What do you think of Alice?'

'I like her,' Laurel said. 'I'm surprised how much she and Charlotte are alike, given they're second cousins rather than cousins. They hang around a lot, so maybe it's just that familiarity thing.'

Gerald nodded. 'No, they are quite alike. I think it's because they're both like Mother.'

'That's a terrible thing to say,' Laurel said, and Gerald laughed with her. Suzanne had told Laurel her secret, and in the months since she and Joe had moved back, Gerald had talked to Laurel about feeling like he was only now starting to understand his mother.

'I mean in their own ways,' Gerald said. 'They have her strength of character...'

'You don't have to explain, Dad,' Laurel said. 'I get it.'

'Get what?'

'You miss your mum.' She put her arm through his and snuggled in close.

'I do,' he said. 'I really do.'

The Joint Statement

May 2016

In November 2015, a group of claimants called the Anthony Harper Action Group had filed a claim against EQC seeking clarification of how EQC was interpreting its underlying legislation. In April 2016, the two groups were able to reach an agreement. They released a joint statement and court proceedings were stopped.

The Anthony Harper group hailed the joint statement as a landmark. At last, they said, it was clear that houses were to be repaired to the as-when-new standard, not to a pre-earthquake standard. The EQC said they had been doing this all along, flying in the face of the reality experienced by thousands of Christchurch homeowners. There were numerous examples of EQC newsletters and media statements referring to the pre-earthquake condition homes would be repaired to.

Both parties were saying different things. Alice knew who she believed.

Gerry Brownlee, the Minister for Earthquake Recovery who had oversight of the EQC, was out of the country when the announcement was made. He was also the Minister of Defence and it seemed he preferred being in Iraq to staying in New Zealand and answering questions about the EQC. Ian Simpson, the chief executive of the EQC, was also, apparently, nowhere to be found and let some Acting Chief Executive speak for him on the six o'clock news.

'Does he actually believe what he's saying?' Lindsay said.

'Does it matter?' Alice said. 'The statement is clear, the standard is as-when-new, and we can use that in getting Grandma and Grandad's repair sorted. Jase and Carla's too. And think about it, if this truly was vindication for the EQC's position, wouldn't Brownlee and Simpson be crowing from the rooftops about it?'

Once the Minister was back in New Zealand and asked about the joint statement in Parliament, he said that the information claimants wanted had been on the EQC website all along. Why, then, did so many people find it necessary to file in court when, really, all they needed to do was go to Google? It seemed the Minister thought that eighteen months of earthquakes had rendered the people of Canterbury stupid.

A group called Canterbury Claimants would be holding a public meeting for people who were having issues with the EQC. One speaker was the chair of the Anthony Harper group action, another was the lawyer who headed it up. Other speakers were names Alice recognised, people who had been speaking out in the media in the years since the earthquakes, warning that there was a serious problem with the quality of repairs. Alice and Lindsay decided to go together. There would be information that could help Neil and Heather decide how to proceed with their complaint.

The night of the meeting was windy and cold and the streets around the cardboard cathedral were packed with cars. Alice and Lindsay parked a couple of blocks away. By the time they reached the cathedral, it was nearly full.

They found a couple of seats at the back and squeezed past an elderly couple. The woman smiled tiredly, her frizzy grey hair springing haphazardly from a bun coming loose at the back of her head. Her husband was white-haired and frail, his shoulder slumped. He was crumpling into himself.

At first, Alice found the size of the crowd reassuring. There were so many people in the same position as her grandparents and her aunt and uncle, people who were fighting against the EQC. But then, about half an hour into the talk, she was becoming angry. The way EQC had handled the joint statement worked politically, one speaker said. No one had to admit they were wrong. Really? That was the primary concern here? Not repairing people's houses the way the law said they should? The wind had started gusting outside and sounded like it was beating against the roof of the cathedral, trying to tear it apart. Inside, Alice was full of churning anger and she could barely sit still. She had picked up a copy of the joint statement when she arrived at the cathedral and now she found herself twisting the sheet of paper into a tight spiral.

On the way home, Alice and Lindsay talked about the implications of what they had learned.

'The EQC's going to fight people all the way, aren't they?' Alice said.

'Yes, they are,' Lindsay said. She was driving, keeping her eyes straight ahead as they drove home through the empty streets.

'So there's nothing we can really do for Grandma and Grandad? Or Jase and Carla?' Alice felt her anger draining away, being displaced by weariness and disgust.

'We can help them with the proving it part,' Lindsay said, her voice grim. She was gripping the steering wheel with both hands, as though trying to crush it. 'They said get everything from EQC, we'll help them to do that, then we can ask for a review.'

Alice felt energised by her mother's determination. 'And maybe that will just do the trick. Stick together, show how determined we all are.'

It was difficult for Alice to get to sleep that night. The wind had picked up once again and kept knocking tree branches against the side of the house. She kept thinking about the city and the promises made about its future in the months after the February quake. People were worn out then, but they knew the quakes had to end eventually. Then there was the 2011 Share an Idea campaign that asked people what they wanted for their rebuilt city. Thousands of people had responded and generated tonnes of ideas. The campaign gave them hope for a brighter city one day, one rebuilt to take advantage of the unique opportunity all the devastation presented. A smart rebuild would make something good out of the bad. But now, five years later, Share an Idea seemed to be dead. If it wasn't dead, it was well and truly buried, although no one knew where. It was like someone packed all the ideas away into a box and stored it in a warehouse somewhere. It was probably in the same warehouse the Ark of the Covenant ended up in at the end of *Raiders of the Lost Ark*.

Alice thought about all those people in the cardboard cathedral, and about all of those people who weren't there, the ones too tired to attend or too tired to pay attention to the news and to know that there was a way to fight the EQC. Then there were those who died without having their claims settled.

One day over the summer, Alice and Charlotte had gone for a walk along the estuary shoreline. They ended up talking to an old lady who was working in her garden, deadheading roses. The house was concrete block and her husband had built it fifty years earlier. She loved living by the sea, she said, and she had wonderful views of the estuary.

'Did you have much damage?' Alice asked. 'Did you have to move out for repairs?' Her eyes were drawn to cracking between the concrete blocks behind where the woman was standing. The cracking zig-zagged across the wall diagonally.

'Just some cracking,' the woman said. 'Some men came and said I only had cosmetic damage and paid me out.'

Alice and Charlotte exchanged glances. Charlotte had seen the cracking in the wall, too.

'I don't know if that's true,' the woman continued with a glint in her eye. 'But my family can sort it all out once I'm gone.'

'That wasn't cosmetic damage, was it?' Charlotte said, as they were walking away.

'No, but I think she knows that,' Alice said.

'What kind of a jerk do you have to be to try to rip off an old lady like that?' Charlotte said.

Alice had no answer for her then, but after the public meeting she had attended that evening, she understood better how the deception had been achieved. Thousands of people in Christchurch had been short-changed by the EQC, the organisation set up to provide New Zealanders with the economic protections necessary to recover quickly from natural disasters. And thousands of people had let it happen because it wasn't happening to them or, worse, because they stood to profit from the deception.

The most disturbing point made during the evening had been made by two speakers, and that was the fact that land damage issues had been left until last. Many repair and rebuild decisions had been made quickly, thoughtlessly, in order to achieve repairs as cheaply as possible. Yet some parts of the city were lower than they had been before the earthquakes and more prone to flooding, especially around the rivers, the estuary and the coast. The land was still settling, which was apparent from the cracks still appearing in the Bowens' driveway. But foundation decisions were being made assuming that the land was settled, stable. Lindsay and Kevin were still living in a damaged house five and a half years after the first quake and it seemed awful to Alice to contemplate that, in fact, they might be the lucky ones. There was one thing worse that not yet being repaired, and that was having the wrong repair.

Winners and Losers

June 2016

Charlotte had survived her first series of university exams, although she wasn't confident that she had passed. She would never feel truly confident about an exam again, after the disasters that resulted in her repeating Year 13. But she had worked hard and felt confident in how much she understood. How well that would translate into her exam results was beyond her control now. It was time to relax and enjoy the break.

She was in Wanaka for the week with Andrew and Michelle's family. Alice had taken a week off work to come along, and everyone but Charlotte was spending long days up on the skifield. Charlotte wasn't a skier, she didn't like being snow-cold, but she didn't mind it up in the mountains, breathing in the clean air and going for runs along the lake.

At Andrew and Michelle's holiday home, Charlotte had claimed a sofa in the sun where she spent each afternoon reading for her next semester. The family teased her about being too studious, that she should just relax and have fun, but what she was learning about was fun. She loved learning about how the planet worked and being able to look out the window across a lake carved by glaciers. Thousands of years earlier, the land Charlotte was looking at had been locked up in hundreds of metres of ice. Glaciers had carved the horn of Mount Aspiring on the other side of the lake and scoured the lake itself so deep that it reached below sea level.

Before the earthquakes started, Charlotte remembered someone visiting from Australia calling New Zealand 'the Shaky Isles'. Up until that point, she had done the usual earthquake drills at school without really thinking about it, but the name Shaky Isles had prompted her to ask her mother whether it was actually true. Her mother told her about how New Zealand had a lot of earthquakes, but hadn't had many since Charlotte was born. There was a big quake early in Wellington's settlement, then the Murchison and Napier quakes in the 1930s. There was a big fault running through the South Island, her mother explained, and one running through Wellington. Those were the Big Ones that people were expecting.

Her mother told her about a spate of earthquakes Christchurch felt in the 1990s, before Charlotte was born. There was a magnitude six earthquake in Arthur's Pass and its aftershocks had been felt in Christchurch on and off for months. Her mother had been in the city for one of those quakes, in a tall building that had swayed. Charlotte found it hard to believe, then, that buildings would move. They just seemed too solid. Now, though, Charlotte had seen the way seismic waves moved through the earth, making it roll. The earth's power was incredible, and terrifying. But smart people developing and following sound engineering principles could reduce the threat to lives.

Earthquakes weren't something to be feared, Charlotte had decided, but something to be respected. That was why buildings needed to be built properly, or not built in places where the ground wasn't stable. Preparation needed to be taken seriously.

Some people didn't get it, though. Sometimes Charlotte wondered if people liked being afraid. One problem was that people found science confusing. Seeing how the quakes were reported in the media annoyed Charlotte, and she was thinking about what she would do once she finished her science degree. She didn't want to be a journalist, but maybe something to do with communicating science. The university in Dunedin had a science communication programme and maybe Charlotte could end up making documentaries. That would be very cool.

But she had a long way to go, she was only six months into her three-year degree, and she didn't want to blow it, so she spent as much time as she could learning about her subjects and telling her cousins about it.

One night after the family came back from skiing, they went to a Mexican restaurant in the town. They had ordered corn chips and dips for starters, which everyone was quickly working their way through. Charlotte was trying to explain glaciers to Andrew and Michelle's youngest, Mattie, who didn't understand how ice could cut rocks.

'But it's just sitting here in my glass,' Mattie said. 'It's not cutting the glass and I can hold it, it won't cut me.'

'No because you need a lot of it, so the weight of it is so enormous that it moves,' Charlotte said.

'Why does it move?' Alice said. She was sitting across from Charlotte and Mattie, laughing at Charlotte's efforts to teach.

'Because of gravity,' Charlotte said. She shot her filthiest look at Alice. Mattie nodded, but looked confused. She was only ten. 'And because it's so heavy,' Charlotte pressed on, 'and because it's moving, it cuts what's underneath it.'

The waitress cleared the table and started bringing their mains. Charlotte started eating her burrito when she saw that Alice was upset.

'What is it?' Charlotte asked.

Alice shook her head, but Charlotte persisted. 'Those guys over there,' Alice said.

Charlotte glanced over to where Alice gestured. Another large group had come in around the time they were ordering their meals. This group was mostly men, rather than a family, in their twenties and early thirties, and quite a few of them looked sunburned from skiing.

'They've been talking about Christchurch,' Alice said. 'How well they've done from the rebuild.'

'Yeah?' Charlotte said, turning to look again. She quickly turned back. 'Ignore it, they're just jerks.'

Alice shrugged, but looked sad. She started half-heartedly cutting into her enchilada, then chewed slowly at a small piece. At the other table, one of the skiers stood up, lifting his half-empty beer mug into the air. 'Thanks, Christchurch,' he said, and his mates cheered.

Back at the house, Charlotte and Alice poured a couple of glasses of white wine and talked about the diners at the other table. They were sitting in Charlotte's favourite study spot with the lights out. There was a smattering of lights from the town, but the lake stretched away into the darkness. The sky was clear and full of stars. They went outside and stared up at the Milky Way arcing over the dark mountains.

'I know some people have done very well out of the rebuild,' Alice said. 'But they don't have to be such jerks about it.'

'I suppose it depends on whether they did well from doing a good job or did well from screwing people over,' Charlotte said.

'What type did those guys seem to you?'

'More the screwing over type, really.'

Alice nodded. 'It makes me wonder what I would do if I ran into the builders who messed up my grandparents house, or the ones who didn't do the work they should've on my aunt and uncle's house. Or what if I ran into Mum and Kevin's idiot project manager or their claim manager? Am I going to go around for the rest of my life running into people I'd want to punch in the face if I knew who they were and what they'd done to people?'

'You can't go around punching people,' Charlotte said. 'But I get it. I'd love to punch the EQC for what they've done to my parents, but I'd be standing in a very long queue.'

'Some people will never recover from the rebuild,' Alice said, 'and that bothers me.'

'Yeah, me too.'

They were both silent, watching the sky.

'Winners and losers,' Charlotte said.

'What?'

'You know, early on in the piece, someone, some politician said there would be winners and losers out of the rebuild,' Charlotte said.

'That was about the red zone offers,' Alice said.

'That was it. Anyway, it was true,' Charlotte said. 'Some people have done well, some haven't. Winners and losers. But quite a few of the winners are the real losers. For what they've done to people and not realising the harm they've done.'

'To the real losers, then,' Alice said, raising her glass and then swallowing back the last of her wine. 'May they suffer pain and distress at the realisation of the role they've played in what's going on.'

Charlotte nodded and sipped at her wine. It would never happen. Losers seldom realised the harm they did. They only thought of themselves.

What Lies Beneath

July 2016

Alice was sure the insurance company was playing games with Lindsay and Kevin. Although they had finally acknowledged that the foundation needed to be replaced, the structural engineering report they had commissioned was sloppy. The biggest issue was that because of land height changes since the earthquakes, the house was now in a flood management zone, which needed to be taken into account in determining the height of the replacement foundation. Kevin had emailed their claims manager to let him know of the mistake, but they had heard nothing back. It had been a month.

In her reading about insurance claims, Alice came across the idea of delaying, denying and defending claims. Insurance companies held their own insurance against events, and once they received the proceeds of this reinsurance, they would invest it and pay claims out of that pool of money. The basic idea of delaying, denying and defending claims was that insurers would maximise their profits by keeping as much of that money as they could for as long as they could, earning interest on the money they should be paying to claimants. Taking a long time to process a claim would wear claimants down and make it likely that they would take offers for far less than the true value of their claim. If they could find grounds to do so, they would deny the claim, or at least part of it. And if the policyholder kept pushing back, the insurer would push back even harder. The only way for a policyholder to get their claim honoured in the delay, deny, defend system was to take the insurer to court, and the insurer would then defend the claim vigorously.

The principle that underpinned the effectiveness of delaying, denying and defending claims was that the policyholder would become tired the longer the claim dragged on. The insurance industry, naturally, denied that this was their approach to settling claims.

It was what was going on with Lindsay and Kevin. What looked like progress was just another step the insurer was taking to draw out the claim and wear them down. And it was working.

Alice explained this theory to Lindsay one morning, after Kevin had left for work.

'So we're just going to keep going in circles?' Lindsay said, and Alice immediately regretted bringing it up. Lindsay looked like she might start crying.

'I think so,' Alice said.

Lindsay nodded. 'I think Kev knows this. He hasn't said much the last couple of weeks, but he's been very quiet. We can't afford to go to court, Alice.'

There had recently been a story in *The Press* about the cost to homeowners of taking their insurance company to court. The cost to file proceedings in the High Court was $1300, and a trial costed $3200 a day. Then there was the cost of lawyers and expert reports, and by the end of it all, a homeowner could expect to spend around $100,000 with no guarantee of a good outcome.

Alice had been thinking about this, and she could only see one way to make it easier for Lindsay and Kevin. 'Would you like me to ask Andrew to have a look at your claim?'

'No, absolutely not,' Lindsay said, irritably. She stood up and stalked out of the kitchen. Alice heard her in the bathroom, blowing her nose. She came back through in a minute, saying she was sorry. Her eyes were red.

'No, I shouldn't have suggested it,' Alice said. She was surprised at the strength of Lindsay's response and wanted to ask more, but she held back.

'Andrew has always taken the easy road,' Lindsay said. 'The one that makes him look good.'

'Law's not easy,' Alice said. It wasn't fair of Lindsay to take her frustrations out on Andrew.

'No, I don't mean that. He's a smart guy, no doubt about that, but he's only motivated to do what helps him be seen as the great guy, the fun guy, the super smart guy.'

That was pretty harsh. But was it true? Whenever Alice had talked to Andrew about insurance issues, he treated it like a game, one side against another, and didn't express concern for how people were being treated. Alice had attributed that to the detachment a lawyer needed to cultivate in dealing with legal issues.

The last time Alice had seen Andrew was in Wanaka in June. She had talked to him about going back to university and studying law, something she had been thinking about for months. People were suffering from injustice all over the city, and Alice hated how helpless she felt. She had been able to help her family by writing information requests for them and going through paperwork with them, but that wasn't enough.

Andrew was pleased to hear her say she wanted to study law. He was proud of her for seeing the opportunity, and he said post-quake litigation in Christchurch was going to go on for at least a decade, maybe more. Being a lawyer would secure her financial future.

'I think I know what you mean,' Alice said to Lindsay. Andrew took pride in having the big holiday home, in being seen around town with his big, happy family and in closing a big contract.

'When we separated, I was determined to never get in the way of him seeing you,' Lindsay said. 'So I organised your trips up to Auckland while he was there and didn't complain when he said he had to cancel. I just kept rescheduling. Then when he moved back here, I thought it would be different, but again, it was me doing the planning.' She paused, then took a deep breath. 'There was one weekend, he had a work thing in the morning, a golf game, and he was going to pick you up and take you to Willowbank for the afternoon. But he never showed up. You were so upset.'

Alice remembered that, waiting with her lunch packed into her tiny backpack along with half a loaf of bread for all the birds at Willowbank. She had cried while trying to eat her sandwiches at lunchtime, and afterwards Lindsay had walked her down to the river where they fed the local ducks, Alice being serious about it, 'pitching the chunks of bread near the birds' heads, while Lindsay tried to land chunks on their backs.

'I remember that,' she said. 'You kept getting bread on the ducks' backs by accident.' She raised an eyebrow, which made Lindsay laugh.

'After that, I decided to just wait and see when he got in touch.'

'And he never did,' Alice said.

Lindsay shook her head. 'You know, there was one time, when he was still in Auckland and I said to him that he needed to make time for you. He got really nasty with me and said it wasn't like he was a deadbeat dad. Like as long as the Inland Revenue wasn't coming after him for not paying child support he was an okay dad.'

'So I won't talk to Andrew about your claim, then,' Alice grinned.

'No. I'm sure you could push him to do it, but I don't want that. Life is complicated enough.'

'But you do need a lawyer,' Alice said. 'Maybe it won't get as far as court, but I think you need someone to show them you mean business.'

Lindsay sighed. 'I know you're right, I'll talk to Kev about it tonight.'

'Tell him your file's in good order, that will save some money because the lawyer won't need to do that for you.'

Lindsay looked at her suspiciously. 'Have you been researching this?'

'Maybe,' Alice said.

Another thing Alice had been researching was the statute of limitations. People had six years after an event to take legal action on that event, but as far as the earthquake sequence was concerned, the event that started the statute of limitations running wasn't clear. It was only a few weeks away from the six-year anniversary of the first earthquake and that could mean that people whose claims weren't yet settled would no longer be able to take court action against the EQC or their insurer, if the September earthquake was taken to be the initiating event.

Although the Insurance Council had publicly announced that its member companies wouldn't use the statute of limitations to deny a claim before 2017, that wasn't legal advice. EQC said the statute of limitations would start running from the time the claim was settled, but that also was not to be regarded as legal advice.

The EQC and the Insurance Council were basically saying, yes, there's this piece of legislation that means you can't sue us, but trust us, we won't use it.

Trust was thin on the ground.

There were thousands of unsettled insurance claims, and thousands of houses going through repeat repairs. If the statute of limitations running out meant people could no longer sue the EQC and insurance companies, then those unfortunate people would lose any power they had in what was already a battle heavily weighted in the insurer's favour.

Alice's concern was that Lindsay and Kevin's insurance company was using delaying tactics to get Lindsay and Kevin past the point at which they could take them to court to get their claim settled. If that happened, they would have no choice but to take whatever the insurance company was prepared to offer, which wouldn't be anywhere near enough to get the house fixed.

After the February earthquake, there was a lot of talk about rebuilding a resilient city by building back smarter. Part of building back smarter was repairing houses and building new ones so that they would recover well from future earthquakes and other natural hazards. Where the land had dropped, foundations should be built back higher, to reduce the risk of flooding. Where the ground was prone to liquefaction, foundations should be built back deeper, to reduce the risk of damage from shaking and liquefaction in future quakes. But half a decade on, foundations were being patched and the land underneath them was being ignored.

People had died in the February quake because of bureaucratic short-cutting, and now that same short-cutting mentality was being applied across the city. Alice had been excited about the possibility of living in the smarter city and building her future here. Now what excited her was the thought of getting out.

Love This Place

August 2016

The morning was warm for winter and there were no threatening clouds in the sky. It was a beautiful day and, now that the end of winter was near, there would be many more of them. After walking the children to school, Lindsay walked down to the river, then followed it towards the hills. There was a track that went from the road through a patch of native trees, nothing spectacular, just scrubby, dry bushes. Lindsay remembered following that track one morning in 2011, after walking Olivia to school and Jack to kindy. It had been one of those terrible mornings following a sleepless night interrupted by aftershocks, back when she still wanted to flee the city any time there was a flurry of quakes. The day was cool, it must have been late winter, or even early spring. Five years ago now. It was difficult to accept that it had been so long ago, but the evidence was there in the growth of her children and in the grey hairs appearing in Kevin's temples and her own hairline.

Their claim was still not settled, but they were further ahead and there were days when Lindsay could see the end of the road. The project manager would visit with a tradesman of one sort or another, working on different aspects of the scope of works, taking tiny steps forward. There were days, though, when Lindsay felt they were on a downward spiral, not really getting anywhere at all. Were their concerns finally being taking seriously or were they being worn down? Did it matter any more?

Lindsay and Kevin had met with a lawyer and their paperwork was in good order. All those late nights Lindsay and Alice had put in the year before had paid off. But they still had to make a decision. All they wanted was an offer that would let them move on with their lives.

Any offer made would likely be a ripoff, not enough to fix the house properly, but it might be enough for them to move on and start to recover from the financial hit. They could focus on their children and their lives together and make the most of Alice's last months at home.

For the longest time, moving on, for Lindsay, had meant getting away from Christchurch, but she accepted now that it was okay to stay. Whether it was in their repaired house or in a different place no longer mattered, they would find a way to make their settlement work, even if that meant her working full-time until retirement once the children were grown. Her dream of studying to become a radiographer was dead. They simply couldn't afford it. But her family was what mattered.

Most in her family were staying in Christchurch, and Kevin had steady work. Now that so many homeowners were taking cash settlements to carry out the work themselves, good tradesmen were finding it easier to pick up work. It helped that the extent of shoddy repairs was becoming more widely known, at least in Christchurch, but there was still no sign of the magnitude of the problem being acknowledged in Wellington.

The bush ended and Lindsay was on the part of the track that ran behind about a dozen houses whose backyards met the riverbank. Before the quakes, there had been ducks and geese along this part of the river, not the usual mallard and grey ducks, but more like farmyard animals. Olivia and Jack had loved going there to feed them. Those birds were gone now, they had disappeared following the February quake. Still, five years later, there wasn't as much bird life along the river as there had been pre-quake.

Lindsay continued walking along the track, avoiding the muddy patches where water pooled, and soon the track opened out onto a cul de sac where the road ran alongside the river. She could cross the bridge and head home or continue along the river for a longer walk home. She decided to continue along the river.

Further along, there was a culvert. Five years ago, in the middle of all the earthquake chaos and before the chaos of the rebuild got underway, someone had scratched into the culvert's concrete the words 'LOVE THIS PLACE'. At the time, it had made Lindsay cry, because she did love this place, although she wanted to run away from it and its constant earthquakes. The words had reminded her of how she felt about the city's hills and the rivers. It had nearly been spring then, as it was now, and there was the wild weather to look forward to, sudden rain showers and blustery winds, followed by warm, sunny days that promised new growth and ducklings, all the signs of life renewing itself.

Five years later, she loved it still.

On Good Ground

September 2016

Alice and Heather were in the kitchen of Neil and Heather's new house. There were boxes everywhere, and Alice was unwrapping crockery and handing it to Heather, who was finding the right place in the cupboards for plates, bowls, cups and glasses. Neil was down the hallway helping Grandma Bennett get her bedroom sorted out. Alice heard Neil teasing her about being pushy and her teasing him back about getting a move on.

It was Friday night and after work, Alice had driven out to Lincoln, the small town on the Canterbury Plains where Neil and Heather had decided to spend their retirement years. The house they were moving into wasn't the house in the valley that they had pictured for their retirement, but it was away from the city and, more importantly, it was 'on good ground', as their pre-purchase report said. If the Alpine Fault did go, their new place stood a good chance of surviving. They had actually considered that, they thought that not to do so would be inviting disaster, almost saying to the plate boundary, 'Kick here'. There was still risk, they weren't fooling themselves that it wouldn't happen to them again, but at least out on the plains, the risk was lower than had they stayed on the soft soils of the parts of the city they loved the most.

The six-year anniversary of the September quake was a couple of days away. Alice was staying with her grandparents for the weekend, helping them unpack and get settled, and they had agreed they would stay away from the news. Although Alice felt like she had been a bystander in the whole process, it frustrated her how outside of the city the rebuild was hailed as a great success, and there would be so much of that over the weekend. Yet how could it be a success? People had gone through so much pain, and were still going through it. Then there was the fact that the central city showed plenty of evidence of the rebuild's failings, including the blocks of bare land where the Government's long-promised anchor projects were meant to be, their expected completion dates stretching out towards the third decade of the twenty-first century.

The city was thriving in some respects, but it was in spite of the efforts of the rebuild authorities, not because of it.

Alice had read an article on an insurance industry website about how to increase levels of insurance in less developed parts of the world. It was vital for economic success, the article said. She felt sorry for people in those places, how they would be encouraged to invest their hard-earned money, take on more debt than they might otherwise be inclined to because of this idea that their investment would be protected by insurance. But then, when that insurance needed to be claimed on, the process was likely to be just as painful and time-consuming as it had been for the people of Christchurch. The only sense in which Christchurch's rebuild could be seen as a success was as a test bed for the insurance companies, who had been able to try out different strategies for minimising their exposure to a major disaster with little fear of the consequences in one of the most deregulated insurance markets in the western world.

The article painted a world in which success was measured by how much insurance people had, that insurance was a mark of affluence, because having insurance was what first-world countries do. There was something very wrong with that thinking and Alice had spent too long feeling helpless in the face of it, too long postponing her own life. How could someone stay sane in that world?

Alice had talked to Gerald about this a few months earlier. He listened without saying much and when she had finished trying, badly, to explain how she felt, he poured them both a whiskey.

'What's important to you, Alice?' he said. 'No, I don't want you to tell me, I want you to go away and think about what's truly important to you. Once you've figured that out, make that your focus, the anchor point around which you make all decisions. Think about this as your anchor project.'

She nodded and sipped her whiskey. 'What's important to you?' she had asked.

'It doesn't matter what's important to me,' he said. 'We're talking about you. But think about this, too: If you make a decision and it takes you in a particular direction, that doesn't mean you have to go in that direction forever. You can always make another decision. The only truly bad decision is the one you make and then work against. But if you figure out what's important to you and anchor yourself to that, that is bedrock for whatever decisions you make.'

Alice had spent a lot of time thinking about what he had said. He was right, there didn't have to be just one thing she chose to do, but what she needed to decide was what was important to her and take that first step towards building her life around it. There was one thing she knew for certain: If the next big disaster happened in her lifetime, she didn't want to feel as helpless and overwhelmed as she had for the last five years.

She was going to leave Christchurch, but not forever. She needed to be away for a few years, and studying law at the university in Dunedin was a way to recover and build on what she already knew about the law. There might not be another big disaster in New Zealand in Alice's lifetime, but there were always people exploiting other people and there was a need for lawyers who cared about people and seeing that the right thing was done for them.

Alice wanted to be able to help people, because it was people who were the most important thing in her world, and that was the ground on which she would build a good life.

Afterword

I'm really sorry for you all, but it is an unjust world, and virtue is triumphant only in theatrical performances.
— *W.S. Gilbert, The Mikado*

It is often said that disasters bring out the best in people. That was certainly true in Christchurch, with the Civil Defence response, the Farmy Army, the Student Volunteer Army and the many other people and organisations who pitched in to help in the immediate aftermath of Christchurch's largest earthquakes. As time wore on and as the recovery dragged, however, another truth about disasters started to emerge: that they bring out the worst in people, holding a mirror to a place's underbelly, bringing to light any systemic failures, greed and corruption that were already there. The disaster amplifies these things, giving them the space to thrive.

There have been winners and losers.

Those who have done best are undoubtedly those who worked out a way to exploit their fellow man, to recognise the opportunities the systems put in place presented and to make the most of them. Invariably these are people who are willing to put aside their conscience for their own gain. People who believe in karma believe that willingness to do wrong will come back on the corrupt one day, whereas those who believe in no such thing can take small comfort in the fact that the insides of those people's heads is probably not an attractive place. How do such people sleep at night? caring people might ask. The awful, uncomfortable answer is that they sleep just fine, because they don't care about the harm they do. They are not like us, they see other people as resources, simply a means to an end.

Those who have kept their heads above water throughout the recovery are probably those who accepted that the bureaucracy existed and wasn't going to become more efficient. These people found ways to keep out of its way, people who opted out of the Canterbury Home Repair Programme and managed their own repairs, people who had little damage and so were paid out, people who had the financial and mental resources to fight a shoddy assessment and escape the clutches of the EQC or their insurer's Project Management Organisation.

Those who have done poorly are those who have not been able to escape the bureaucracy, who are now finding their repaired houses are worth less than they were before the quakes started or who are still waiting for repairs to their failed repairs.

But by far the ones who have fared worst are those seeking help from the bureaucracy, trusting in EQC and the insurers to do the right thing. For some, pre-quake issues such as the ravages of old age, poverty and mental health problems have been exacerbated by the quakes and by the bureaucratic nightmare that followed. Health authorities are struggling to get the region's mental health problems acknowledged, for any increase in funding that would truly help these people depends on admitting that the problem exists.

In 2015, Prime Minister John Key visited Lloyd's of London and was congratulated on how well-managed the earthquake recovery was. Around the same time, the chairman of Southern Response, the Government entity set up to manage failed insurer AMI's earthquake claims, was appointed as chair of the Government entity that would replace the Canterbury Earthquake Recovery Authority when its founding legislation expired in 2016. This was in spite of the fact that, next to EQC, Southern Response is the most heavily criticised rebuild entity, one that was taken to court in 2015 in a group action alleging misrepresentation of policy entitlements, delays in claims handling and the systematic misrepresentation of the true costs of repairs and rebuilds. Whether that action will get any traction in the courts remains to be seen.

The leaders, the businessmen and the legislators have earnestly worked at their desire to not let this enormous disaster adversely affect the country's bottom line. They have wrapped it all up and moved on, patting themselves on the back and lining themselves up for well-paid directorships. They pay no heed, except in speeches, to the Maori proverb that underpins the lives of so many of us:

He aha te mea nui o te ao
What is the most important thing in the world?
He tangata, he tangata, he tangata
It is the people, it is the people, it is the people

Before 2010, ask anyone what part of New Zealand would have the unwanted honour of hosting New Zealand's next big natural disaster and the answer would not have been Christchurch. Common answers would have been Wellington (quake), the West Coast of the South Island (quake) or Auckland (volcano). These disasters are still to come, and they will be larger in both human and dollar terms than Christchurch. What will happen next is that the Christchurch model for disaster recovery will be deployed and the bureaucratic disaster that has unfolded here will unfold there, all over again.

What of the people?
What of the people?
What of the people?

Made in the USA
Charleston, SC
05 August 2016